THE MEMOIRS OF

HELEN OF TROY

THE MEMOIRS OF

HELEN OF TROY

A NOVEL

AMANDA ELYOT

CROWN PUBLISHERS · NEW YORK

Published in the United States by Crown Publishers, an imprint of the Crown
Publishing Group, a division of Random House, Inc., New York.
www.crownpublishing.com

CROWN is a trademark and the Crown colophon is a registered trademark of
Random House, Inc.

Library of Congress Cataloging-in-Publication Data
Elyot, Amanda.
The memoirs of Helen of Troy : a novel / Amanda Elyot.
1. Helen of Troy (Greek mythology)—Fiction.   2. Troy (Extinct city)—Fiction.
3. Greeks—Turkey—Fiction.   4. Mythology, Greek—Fiction.
5. Trojan War—Fiction.   I. Title.
PS3603.A77458M46   2005
813'.6—dc22   2005003653

ISBN 0-307-20998-9

Printed in the United States of America

Design by Fearn Cutler de Vicq

10 9 8 7 6 5 4 3 2 1

FIRST EDITION

For my mother, Leda

In ancient Greece, the poet was known as a Rhapsode—
one who stitches together fragments of song, sometimes of
diverse origins, in order to compose an original story.

THE MEMOIRS OF

HELEN OF TROY

❦ PROLOGOS ❧

Autobiography
From the Greek:
Auto, as in *self*
Bios, as in *mode of life*
Graph, as in *write*

hus, contained within these pages, is the story of my life, as I write it. As I have lived it. It is said that beauty is fading, but memories are lasting. With me, I confess it is the reverse. Although I am blessed with perpetual beauty, my remembrances are on occasion as fluid as the Aegean Sea—and like the sea, they are storm-tossed as well as sparkling: one moment turbulent, another placid. Many have asked me to recount the stories of my past: my childhood, my three marriages, and my ten children—of which only you remain alive, Hermione, and I can no longer even be sure of that. We never did permit ourselves to truly know each other. It is perhaps too much to hope that a reading of my memoirs will make you suddenly love me—but perhaps they will help you begin to understand me. You are far from the only one to hold me solely accountable for years of bloodshed and heartache. But I can no longer abide fabricated versions of my own life handed down as fact or truth by others who were not there or who have their own ends to achieve by painting me in unflattering colors. You have heard many tales from others, Hermione, but have never received them from me. It is finally time to clear my besmirched name, if only for my daughter to learn the real story of my life. Do not expect my memories and recollections to be unbiased, however, nor sanitized for your exceedingly tender sensibilities.

After all is said and done, we are what people consider us to be. To begin with, you know that I am not truly Helen of Troy. That is what I am called now, for it is how I am known. I am—I was—Helen of Sparta. I was born and raised in the very palace where you, too, entered into this world, above the fertile valley in the shadow of Mount Taygetos. Open your spirit, Hermione, to the story of how I won my heart's every desire, only to pay the greatest price for it that woman ever forfeited. It's the story of how I became Helen of Troy.

*The greatest glory of a woman
is to be least talked about by men.*

PERICLES (FIFTH CENTURY B.C.E.)

I learned that I was different when I was a very small girl: when the golden curls, which barely reached my shoulders at the time, began to turn the color of burnished vermeil. Your grandmother Leda, whom you never knew, told me that I was a child of Zeus. Since I thought my father's name was Tyndareus, her words upset me. Seeing my pink cheeks marred by tears of confusion, my mother handed me a mirror of polished bronze and asked me to study my reflection. "Do you look like me?" she asked.

I nodded, noting in my own skin the exquisite fairness of her complexion, and her hair the same shade as mine that tumbled like flowing honey past the hollow of her back.

"And do you resemble my husband Tyndareus?" she said to me.

I looked in the mirror and then looked again. For several minutes I remember expecting the mirror to show me my father's face, but Tyndareus was olive complected where I was not, his nose like the beak of a falcon where my own was straight and fine-boned, and his cheekbones were hollow and slack where, even then, beneath a child's rosy plumpness, mine were high and prominent.

"It's time for me to tell you everything," my mother said, and without another word, she clasped my hand and led me along the corridor of the gynaeceum, the women's quarters of the palace that overlooked a pretty courtyard inlaid with colored tile. I remember running my little finger along the polychrome frescoes that were painted on the courtyard walls, tracing the crests of the cerulean waves that depicted tales of Spartan sea voyages to Cyprus, Ithaca, and Crete, places whose names I'd heard, but which were no more than exotic sounds to me at the time. Even rendered in artists' colors, the Great Sea held an allure that I could not then explain. As a child, my favorite part of the painted waves was the spray that tipped each one; I was certain it was real enough to evaporate like soap bubbles on my fingertip. My mother told me that Aphrodite, our goddess of love and beauty, was born of the seafoam. She was the most beautiful goddess in the world, Leda said, and one of the oldest—as old as Zeus, although men had forgotten that, preferring to honor the newer, warrior goddesses— sexless Athena and Artemis the chaste. I had seen only five summers then, but on that day, my mother told me that I was old enough to learn the story of Aphrodite's extraordinary conception.

"Long ago," my mother began, "there was a tremendous battle in the heavens. Zeus's father, Kronos, who was the son of earth and sky, quarreled with his own father, Uranus; with a sharpened flint, Kronos destroyed his father's fertile manhood, severing it from Uranus's body and flinging it into the sea below. As it plunged into the hungry waves, the winedark water boiled up into a white froth—seafoam— from which emerged the goddess Cypris, who we call Aphrodite; she was accompanied by Eros—Lust—and Himeros—Desire."

"I don't understand," I said to her, focusing I suppose on the grotesque act of dismemberment and wondering how someone so beautiful could end up being born through such a disgusting exploit.

"Love and Beauty, Lust and Desire are almost as old as the world," my mother answered. They were part of an old religion, she said, long before Zeus became king of the gods. "Come, I'll show you."

Her decision seemed a sudden one. My mother had always consid- ered me too young to initiate into the mysteries of the old ways, when men and women alike saw wisdom in plants, divinity in trees and streams. That was before they devised gods in their own image and as- signed each one a separate sphere of influence, diminishing the power of the earth goddess with the invention of each new deity.

I'm remembering now that she wouldn't let go of my hand, even when I whined that her nails were digging into the soft pink flesh of my palms. "I'm sorry," she said, and gripped me tighter. She was walk- ing too fast for me, and I had to take two steps to every one of hers to keep up with her. I was practically skipping. Past the palace gate, we descended the terraced hills to the valley below, then traversed the entire length of the grassy plain that lay just beyond a small structure of sundried brick and hardened clay, a dun-colored farmhouse situated at the farthest edge of the city.

I'd wanted to slow our pace so I could pick a sprig or two of wild columbine to wear in my hair. "Are we in a hurry?" I asked my mother. She stopped for a moment and turned to me, still gripping my hand. She studied my face as though she wanted to weave my image into one of her tapestries to hang forever behind her deep green eyes.

"No, I suppose we're not," she said, and slowed our trot to a more leisurely walk. At the far end of the plain was a grove of trees.

"Where are we going?" I asked her.

"The altar," she said.

"But we already passed the altar," I insisted, turning and pointing back toward the palace. We sacrificed animals there on holidays and festivals, to bless a birth or honor a death, or to ask the gods for better weather. I always covered my eyes when Tyndareus or the priests slit the beasts' throats. Their blood, smelling of metal, issuing from the still-pulsing veins, would flow in a crimson stream onto the stones of the pergamos where we gathered to witness the ritual. It always made my stomach rise up to meet my throat. I never got used to it. Even today, I need to look away and hold my breath to avoid the sight and stench of hot entrails freshly spilt.

I'm remembering now that during the sacrifices, our mother made my older sister Clytemnestra hold my hand so I wouldn't run away and disgrace the family. And Clytemnestra would snicker beneath her veil and laugh at me for my folly, for my squeamishness. "Spartan women don't cringe at the sight of a little blood," she said. After that, when I shielded my eyes from the sacrifices, I turned them on Clytemnestra's face instead. As the life of a goat or lamb or calf was ended with a single sweep of the knife, my sister's expression grew oddly serene, although her eyes would shine like those of a woman in love. Clytemnestra liked blood. Clytemnestra . . . who always wore red from the time she was only ten summers old. . . .

"A different altar," my mother said. "Here, in the grove." I never knew there was any other. She led me from the sunlit plain into the cool blue-greenness between the poplars. I whined that my legs were tired and that I couldn't see anything except trees and asked if we could go home; but she begged a few more minutes of my patience, bringing me deeper into the grove until we came upon the ruins of a temple, at the center of which was a stone as high as I was tall. "This is the altar I spoke of," my mother said. "And there," she added, pointing at one of the taller trees, "was where we worshipped the Goddess. Her mask hung like an effigy from that tree. There, see? The one where the mother bird is building her nest. Birds are sacred to the Goddess."

I must have looked at her in utter confusion because we didn't worship just one unnamed goddess. In fact, there were so many gods that I couldn't remember all of their names. We offered tributes to Demeter at sowing time to ensure a bountiful harvest, and we brought her its gifts at reaping time to thank her. We poured libations to Dionysus at the advent of the grape harvest, made sacrifices to Zeus and Poseidon and Athena for victory in battle and safe passage on the high seas, to Artemis for a bountiful hunt, and even to Aphrodite to grant us success in affairs of the heart, but I'd not heard of "the Goddess."

"She is the center of the old religion," my mother explained impatiently, having fully expected her five-year-old daughter to comprehend this complicated theology. "I told you that Aphrodite was old, but the Goddess is even older. She has many names; in nearby Mycenae, for example, she is called Potnia—but she is the same being, the giver and sustainer of life. In the days of my mother, Eurythemis, and in *her* mother's, and in her mother's before *her*, stretching back for longer than any living man or woman can remember, there was a festival sacred to the Goddess that was held every spring in this grove. Only the *women* of Laconia were permitted to participate. The men knew enough then to keep away, respecting our celebration. There was music and there was dancing and there was wine."

My mother told me that my grandmother and all the women of her line were priestesses devoted to the Goddess just as she was, although Tyndareus had tried to put an end to the old ways a few years ago by destroying the temple, telling my mother that we would worship only the new gods from then on and that there was no room for the Goddess in Sparta.

I didn't see what difference it made *which* gods people worshipped as long as believing in different ones didn't make them fight the way I would hear my mother argue with Tyndareus. "And it's so pretty here," I said, dropping my voice to a whisper. My words disappeared in the rustling of leaves. The grove was deliciously fragrant, though I couldn't identify the aroma. Not pine, not lemon, not olive. The breeze bore the scent like a gift to my nostrils.

My mother placed her right hand on the altar. I reached up and did the same. I'm amazed that I can still recall how cool the stone felt against my skin. She described the sacred relic—a woman's torso sculpted from the wood of one of the pear trees near the grove—that once rested on a pedestal near the altar before an eternal flame. Snakes—another symbol of the Goddess's power—were brought to the grove on festival days, borne by temple attendants skilled at handling them. Coiling and uncoiling in their wicker baskets, the serpents represented her energy: powerful, unpredictable, and at times fatal.

"Every year," my mother began, "a woman was chosen to represent the Goddess at our festival. By tradition it would be the queen, who was also the chief priestess of the Goddess's temple. But after I married Tyndareus, he forbade me to enact her role, so another woman was selected every year to take my place." I remember how my mother's voice seemed to alter as she recalled her own past. Her words floated like musical notes on the air. Her eyes, too, were not focused on me, but were directed inward.

I interrupted her. "Why do you always call father *Tyndareus* and not *Father* when you speak of him to me?"

"I'm telling you why," my mother said, looking directly at me for the first time since she had begun her narrative. "There had been a terrible drought. The crops were dying and there wasn't enough to harvest. People were rationing food, and many of them believed the Goddess was angry because we had begun to worship the new gods as well. They were sure she was offended that I, their queen, had forsaken her by substituting other women in my stead at her annual rites. As a mob of citizens seeking both answers and revenge, their collective voices rising as one to a fevered pitch, they laid at my feet the blame for the Goddess's displeasure—which had brought drought to the people of Laconia. I had no choice but to submit my body once more or fall prey to the wrath of a hungry rabble unable to feed their children.

"Sacred to the Goddess is the image of the bird, and each year at the climax of the festival, her high priestess would be ceremonially mated with her bird-consort. I prepared to accept him, anointing my limbs with perfumed oil so that my body glistened as though I myself had stepped from the sea. My attendants oiled my hair until it shone like molten bronze, and they perfumed my throat and breasts with attar of roses. We drugged my husband's wine so that he would fall asleep in his cups, and by torchlight I made my way to the sacred grove and entered the temple.

"The women played their flutes and tambourines and, possessed by her spirit, danced ecstatically around the altar after they had removed my flowing ceremonial robes and laid me upon it. They poured libations, then handed me the sacred goblet of wine mixed with the juice of poppies brought from the Hittite kingdom. I drained it in one draught, the warm liquid searing my throat."

I found my mother's story both beautiful and terrifying. "And then what happened?" I asked, my question a breathless whisper. As many times as she had represented the Goddess in the mating ritual, nothing could have prepared her for what occurred next, she replied. For it was Zeus himself, disguised in the body of a great white swan, who took her upon the altar. Leda remembered lying naked on the plinth surrounded by the feverishly dancing acolytes of the Goddess, when they were startled by the sound of beating wings. Down through the branches of the swaying poplars swooped a swan so massive that his wingspan obliterated most of the light from the burning torches. The women ducked to avoid being knocked to the ground, but my mother bravely accepted her fate and mated with the great bird.

It was said that Zeus had looked down from Mount Olympus on the rites below and was so enamored of Leda's incomparable loveliness that he could not bear for her to yield her body to a mere facsimile of divinity. She must be his, and so she became. Spent and exhausted from their passionate coupling, Leda collapsed on the altar, awakening from a trancelike slumber to discover the great swan flown, the only evidence of his presence a long white feather—the same feather, Hermione, with which I now write this memoir on Egyptian papyrus. My mother kept the sacred talisman hidden in her jewel chest. I found it after her death and have treasured it ever since. I even took it with me to Troy, carefully stored among my jewels.

In time, my mother told me, she knew she was with child, and when I was born she considered attempting to convince Tyndareus that I was his daughter. But it was clear to both of them that even in my infancy, there was no resemblance. "You have your father's neck," she would say wistfully when I carried myself like a proper Spartan princess, spine as straight as a birch and as supple as a willow, head held high atop a long and graceful throat.

Forgive me, my daughter, for my temporary digressions. My memories intrude on me as I write, sometimes tumbling upon one another like water over the rocks in a stream, sometimes weaving together like the warp and weft of a tapestry.

We regarded the ruined temple, my mother and I, our right hands still resting on the cool plinth of the altar. "The day you were born and Tyndareus first looked at your perfect face and tiny form, he knew you were none of his blood. He is not a clever man, Helen, but he is not a stupid one either. Immediately, he ordered that the temple in the sacred grove be razed and no symbols of the Goddess permitted to remain. Not only that, but those who insisted on continuing to worship her would be punished. 'I humored you, Leda,' he told me, 'but you have taken advantage of my tolerant nature.' He told me that the only reason he would not order that you be taken to Mount Taygetos and left there to die, was that he feared the people's wrath when they learned that their beloved queen's tiny daughter had been abandoned on a mountaintop. I believe Tyndareus feared the wrath of your true father, but as a king he dared not confess it, for such an admission might connote weakness."

I shivered to think of what might have been my fate. No wonder Tyndareus had never smiled kindly upon me. I always thought *I* had been guilty of some transgression that had made him cross. His withholding of affection punished both wife and child. I remember now how often I heard my mother weep in the silence of her rooms when she believed there was no one to witness her tears. One day, long before she brought me to the sacred grove, when I must have been no older than three summers, I broke away from my nurse to visit my mother at her loom. I supposed I missed her. Her bare foot was propped up on a special foot support, and her chiton was pulled up above her knees so that she could twist the loose wool around her leg before spinning it. A basket holding the finished yarn rested beside her chair. A thick strand of red wool dangled loosely from her fingers while Leda sat trancelike, her gazed fixed on her spindle as though she would impale her heart upon its point. A single tear ran down her cheek, and I followed its course until it dropped onto her lap and made a tiny stain.

As *"Mitera!"* escaped my lips, my nurse caught up to me, grabbing me by the hand at the exact moment my mother turned to look at me. Her exquisite face wore a mask of ceaseless sorrow, or so it seemed, with her downcast eyes and her generous mouth turned down as if to stifle a sob. And as I tried to break free of my nurse's grasp and run to comfort her—oh, how I wanted to lay my head in her soft warm lap—I was tugged back, taken from her sight, and trotted down the corridor to the room we called the nursery.

I now remember many other times, when perhaps I was even younger, that I would hear Tyndareus's voice raised in anger against my mother, calling her to account for her suspected infidelity in the sacred grove. Her own voice would answer in a soft, placating tone that would, as their quarrel escalated, be replaced with one of enmity, and finally by one of supplication. Each time she would ask Tyndareus to be pleased that Zeus saw fit to favor their household with his progeny and that the kingdom of Sparta would indeed be blessed by my presence.

His reply would invariably be the same, and it was not until that day when my mother brought me to the sacred grove and revealed the truth of my paternity that I understood what he meant when he would tell Leda, "The child's beauty may be a blessing to her future husband, but every day I am reminded by it that she is no daughter of mine, and such a blessing becomes a *curse* on the House of Tyndareus." The words *faithless whore,* which of course I didn't understand the meaning of at the time, struck my mother across the face like a slap, and *that* much even a child of three can comprehend. Stung by her husband's insults, she would retreat to the comfort and solace of her loom, no longer permitted to be a priestess, no longer wanted as a wife.

Tyndareus refused to forgive my mother for her infidelity. And the sky goddess, Hera—my *true* father's wife—as jealous as any mortal woman, never pardoned Zeus for the indiscretion of becoming my father. But in this I was not unique. Zeus was notoriously profligate with his seed, for which Hera appeared to spend mortal lifetimes punishing him. Invariably, if one of Zeus's demimortal offspring was faced with calamity, Hera employed all her wiles in order to prevent her husband's intervention. So Zeus made but one appearance in my life and that was to create it. Trumpeting his animal lust for my mother, he descended to earth, soaring heavenward after he had slaked his passions.

Although Zeus never revisited me, other immortals of Mount Olympus saw fit to call at various times throughout my life. When I felt the shadow of their protection or the sting of their spite, I knew they were beside me. And as my body began to show the first signs of womanhood, I came to realize that my passions have been inherited honestly. My unabashed cravings for the blazing consummation that only two bodies can know—yes, Hermione, that was passed to me by immortal Zeus.

On the afternoon following my visit to the sacred grove, while my nurse was napping, I went looking for my mother to ask her a question. I think I must have wanted to know something more about the Goddess, what she looked like, I suppose. I remembered that Leda had mentioned the mask that the women used to hang from the tree by the temple. Was she beautiful, I wanted to know. Fearful to behold? My mother was not at her loom. The spindle had been thrust like a dagger into a hank of bloodred wool that rested in an osier basket beside her stool.

I don't know why, but I remember feeling that something was wrong. And I knew, deep inside, that I had to return to the sacred grove. There was no guard at the palace gate then. Tyndareus never feared intruders. The plain was broader than I remembered it. Crossing it alone seemed to take so much longer. I had to shield my eyes from the sun to keep from squinting, and I tripped and stumbled on a rock, tumbling facedown into the dry grass. It scratched my cheeks, as though I were giving a dutiful kiss to Tyndareus through the prickles of his beard. When I reached the poplars, I tried to remember which path we had taken the day before to get to the little temple, then chose the one that looked most worn. The wind sang a sad song through the trees, which sighed their response and inclined their bodies in ac- knowledgment of the music. I came upon the ruins, but saw no sign of my mother. *"Mitera!"* I called, and when I received a reply, I looked up to seek its source. In the same instant that I realized that what I had heard was my own echoing voice, I glimpsed my mother's sandal floating above my head.

A gasp broke unbidden from my lips as my eyes trailed the slender length of her body, past her long slim legs, her narrow waist, the breasts that gave me suck when the wet nurse refused to give her nip- ples to Leda's bastard child, to the soft gray veil that formed a silken noose around her swanlike neck.

Tyndareus acquiesced to the wishes of the people of Laconia and gave the queen a proper state burial, but it was a subdued ritual without the usual feasting and celebration. There were no funeral games. Because I was the one who had found my mother's body, I was carefully watched during the proceedings, lest I do something foolish, though I can't imagine why they were so worried. I wasn't thinking about following her to the underworld and couldn't have succeeded had I tried. Even Clytemnestra tiptoed around me for a full moon cycle before resuming her usual sisterly torment.

I was crushed by my mother's death; the trauma of discovering her corpse and the heartrending grief over losing the only parent I had known overwhelmed me. Clytemnestra's reaction betrayed a very different emotion. She knew she had never been our mother's favorite. Many times, I saw my sister steel herself against shedding a single tear in Leda's memory. Clytemnestra would clench and unclench her fists until the impression of her nails left half-moon lacerations in her palms. Where I felt incalculable sorrow and loss at Leda's passing, Clytemnestra found triumph. My perfection no longer made me anyone's golden child. "*Mitera* is dead and Zeus is too important and too busy on Mount Olympus to concern himself with you. You have no parents. But I have my *patera,* and he likes me best!" It was a churlish remark, but as I would soon realize, an accurate one. I *was* parentless—and nearly friendless as well—and between the two of us, Clytemnestra wielded more authority than ever before. This newly won power visibly delighted her, while of course it sickened me.

I thought my mother should have games, because I knew that it was proper and that without them she was not accorded all the honors of her station; but I was far too young to do anything about it. A week or so after her body was laid in the ancestral crypt, I ran the length of the plain near the grove and back to the palace and pretended that I was competing in the virgins' footrace at the Hera's Festival games and that there were other runners at my side. In Leda's name I beat them all and was crowned with the olive wreath and allotted a share of the sacrificial cow.

Hermione, it still pierces my heart that I never came to know my own mother until after she was gone. I have never stopped regretting it. Just as I began to learn who she really was—how much more than merely the woman who gave me life—she took her own away. To me, Leda was beautiful but distant, a sad figure who kept her sorrows and her secrets to herself until that day before she ended her unhappy life. This much I guessed, simply from overhearing my parents' quarrels: The earth, like a woman's body, is the giver of life; but nature can also be capricious—unpredictable—and men desire that which they can control and fear that which they do not understand.

My mother's unhappy marriage to Tyndareus had its genesis in something larger than both of them. The Greek chieftains such as Tyndareus, men of bronze, no longer wished to accept that the earth goddess alone was responsible for the miracles of creation. Like any mortal woman, they argued, she could be fickle and untamable. True, she yielded up her bounty to the skilled tiller of the soil, but she also caused droughts and floods, fire and famine. She was the great creator and sustainer of life, but also the great destroyer of it. For men to acknowledge her power was to concede their own. Once, there had been procreation celebrations in which the acolytes of the Goddess would enact mating rituals. That was back in the days when kings were inferior to queens in a culture that honored the mysteries of the life-giving female. Then came the invader kings from the north and everything began to change. Compromises were made to encompass elements of Goddess worship into the new religion in order for the ways of the Olympian sky gods and their mortal creators to gain acceptance. Throughout all Achaea it became the custom for an invader king to demand to marry a priestess of the Goddess in order for his reign to be secure. Such was the course of events with Tyndareus and my mother Leda.

As the high priestess of the Goddess, my mother acknowledged a power greater than that wielded by her husband, lord and king, who was himself capable of giving birth to nothing. Yet Tyndareus could not allow any challenge to his supremacy, especially one led by his queen. He despaired of appearing a weak ruler, controlled not just by his wife, but also by her ties to an ancient religion that had little use for the contribution of men unless it was in the service of mother earth. Tyndareus believed that capitulation, or even acquiescence to the power of the Goddess and her followers, left his throne ripe for usurpation and his body for certain death.

As I grew into womanhood, I learned from my own experiences that men would seek to tame a woman's body and spirit to their needs as they would look to control the earth, sea, and sky. I eventually came to mistrust *both* the old and the new ways. I resolved instead to follow the instincts of my body and the promptings of my heart. Looking back, I realize that this folly was just as silly—and as dangerous—as the dictates of the man-made Olympian gods or the female-worshipping precepts of the Goddess.

Clytemnestra, too, had little use for religion. My older sister worshipped power and all that it might bring her. Although she at first resented the comparison of her dusky prettiness to my golden perfection, Clytemnestra eventually learned to cultivate the power she could wield in being considered the daughter of darkness. Her eyes were a much deeper shade than mine, more like obsidian than nut brown. Her hair cascaded to her waist and, especially when it was oiled, gleamed like polished ebony. Clytemnestra always reveled in the dramatic. And her moods were dark, even when she was a girl. How else could she, the most ordinary of Leda's children, distinguish herself from me, her younger sister, destined by the Fates never to age once I reached my full bloom?

Clytemnestra and I despised each other for many, many years. When I began to fully understand her, it was already too late. How could I love her as deeply as I might have wanted to, or felt it was my duty to, when she saw my beauty as her curse and sought to blame me for every ill that ever befell her?

Many times when I was younger, as a form of self-protection from a lascivious gaze or a jealous taunt, I tended toward aloofness, learning to guard myself except when passion served my turn. Now I smile to write this, but there would come a time when passion *often* served my turn. Clytemnestra most certainly, and most of my playfellows, cruelly ostracized me from their games and kept me from meeting their brothers or any boys for whom they had conceived a fondness. My nurse encouraged me to join the other girls, thinking that I was developing an unnecessary shyness, but she was blind as a bard to their behavior. My elder sister, who was old enough to know precisely what she was doing, never missed an opportunity for devilment at my expense. When we were supposed to observe the solemnity of a funeral rite, for example, she would pinch me through my robes, hoping to give me a bruise as big and dark as a ripe plum. Or she would convince me to wrestle with her on the stone pergamos where she could easily best me because of her size. She would grab my hair until I shrieked in pain. When a clump came out in her hand, she'd claim that it was all part of our sport.

We Spartans placed great emphasis on the perfection of the physical form. Boys and girls were equally encouraged to excel in competition at various sporting endeavors. I would watch the girls or boys wrestle one another—often naked, as was our custom, to discourage prudish sensibilities about the beauties of the body.

I still remember the day when I was finally asked to join a game with Clytemnestra and her friends, joyful beyond measure that they were finally accepting me into their circle. One girl would be blindfolded with a linen rag and she had to remain sightless until she touched one of her playmates, who aimed to lead her on a merry chase with their singing and laughing voices. I was too trusting, just glad that my older sister had found it in her heart to include me. Clytie lured me straight into a bush of nettles, hoping that the stings would mar my flawless skin. I distinctly recall that I refused to give up the chase, despite the searing pain. For one thing, I wanted to win. For another, I didn't want my older sister to ostracize me anymore, and I was so sure that if I could prove that I wasn't afraid to follow her, she would have to play with me from now on.

Gamely, I broke through all the brambles to reach the other side, tagging Clytemnestra, who felt robbed when she saw that I had emerged unscathed and unscarred.

I was not the only sibling Clytemnestra resented. My twin half brothers, Castor and Polydeuces, were extraordinary young men with a nearly unparalleled taste for adventure. Polydeuces was the greatest boxer in all of Greece. I wish you had seen him, Hermione. He defeated every opponent who ever challenged him. And Castor had such skill with horses. Once I saw him tame a black Mycenaean stallion that all but breathed fire from his nostrils. With one caress tenderly ministered to the angry steed's rear fetlock, Castor rendered him as gentle as a newborn calf.

∼∼∼

And so, from my fifth summer, when I made my awful discovery, I grew to womanhood without a mother to nurture and guide me. I might just as well have been an orphan, as the anger that Tyndareus had visited upon my mother for her faithlessness was transferred to her golden child. He was Clytemnestra's father in every way, but never mine, showing not even a pretense of paternal affection. It was Clytemnestra, his natural daughter, who grew up in his image: pragmatic, hard, and unforgiving.

Though she had five summers on me, Clytemnestra and I were schooled side by side in dance and needle arts, in music and drawing, in the arts of the application of cosmetics, and in the arrangement of flora. My sister seemed to relish it, reveling in my failures. Despite my physical perfection, when it came time for the practical application of our lessons, my tiny fingers were clumsy where hers—owing to the greater dexterity of age—were nimble; my valiant efforts to master the practical arts as skillfully as she did always fell far short of the mark. Throughout our lives, Clytemnestra had few opportunities to prove herself my superior, and she made the most of every one of them.

We kept pets then, rabbits and small birds. Once I tried to teach a philomel to repeat a melody that a blind poet had sung to us one evening after supper. I must have been about seven years old then. The bird had a beautiful voice, which I taught myself to mimic, but I could not train it to learn the poet's ode. Clytemnestra could not decide which of us was vainer—the nightingale, for soundly failing under my musical tutelage, or me, for believing it would freely sing at my bidding. She threatened to strangle the bird if I didn't leave off instructing it. So I gave up, quite sure that she would be true to her word.

Despite years of ill treatment at her unchecked hands, there have been times throughout my life when I must concede a begrudging admiration for my older sister. The fierceness she showed in her maturity was, on occasion, laudable in her youth. I remember the autumn after my mother died—Clytemnestra was ten summers old—it was before the festival of Dionysus, and Tyndareus reminded us that a sacrifice was required of the royal family in order to ensure a good harvest and stave off Demeter's anger at once again losing her precious daughter Persephone to the dark embrace of Hades. Instead of taking a goat or lamb from the stables, he asked my sister to forfeit her pet rabbit Artemis, named for the gentle creature's not-so-gentle rampages in my stepfather's garden. My sister refused. It was the one time I can ever recall Tyndareus exacting a punishment where Clytemnestra was concerned. He threatened to take a birch rod to her himself if she insisted on denying his request and shaming the royal household. Clytemnestra, who barely reached the old man's waist, told him that she would willingly accept the penalty and stubbornly stood her ground. In front of the servants, Tyndareus swore like a sea raider and raised his hand to his favorite child, who took off for the garden shed and threw her small, defiant body over that of her cherished pet.

The king could not allow a ten-year-old girl, no matter how beloved, to publicly embarrass him. He followed her, his purple and blue robes trailing behind him like the angry wake left in the path of the sea god Poseidon. Wrestling his own small daughter, who struggled fiercely to protect her rabbit, Tyndareus finally succeeded in prying her hands from its thick white fur, all the while scolding Clytemnestra for her defiance of the wishes of the gods. How she screamed—yes, she did yell out "murder"—when Tyndareus removed his own knife from its sheath and, holding Artemis by her lop ears, slit the poor beast's throat, its hot blood spraying Clytemnestra's snow-white chiton.

Despite her frequent torments, that day I loved Clytemnestra. Loved her desperately. I wrapped my arms around her waist and together we wept. Yet, even in that unusual moment when I felt so close to my sister, we were markedly different. My tears were in sorrow, while hers were mostly in anger. Perhaps it was after that incident that Clytemnestra was determined to wear red. The color of warm blood. So it wouldn't show, perhaps. My sister scorned her father ever after. I don't believe that she anticipated that Tyndareus would master, rather than indulge, her. That day, she lost respect for him for another reason: In her eyes, physically fighting her for the rabbit was a sign of weakness. I read it in the determined set of her jaw and in the cold onyx darkness of her eyes. Tyndareus disgusted her. He had failed her. How I wished that she had allowed herself to turn to me then so we could share our disappointment, but the rabbit incident illustrated one of the most fundamental differences between us. Needing someone else made me happy. For Clytemnestra, needing someone else made her vulnerable. And that terrified her.

THREE

I had one girlhood friend. Polyxo, the youngest daughter of a local farmer, was the only one who didn't exclude me from play. Until we met, I preferred to remain alone rather than insinuate myself where I was clearly unwelcome. And for choosing isolation, I became the target of further derision.

We used to play a jumping game that was very popular in Laconia. It was the fashion for girls to wear short tunics then, and we would remove our sandals and see how many times we could jump and hit our buttocks with our heels. It's not nearly as easy as it sounds. The boys would gather to watch us, of course, and sometimes they would jeer or shout words of encouragement. *Thigh-flashers,* they called us. I became quite adept at the game, but little Polyxo, with her short, stubby legs, was somehow the champion of us all. On the playing field and in the wrestling pit, Clytemnestra was the undisputed queen, and no one could outrun her either. So it gave me a secret pleasure to see Clytemnestra bested in something, and Polyxo's frequent victories in the jumping game permitted her the confidence to approach her ring-leader's outcast younger sister.

We made a quite a pair: chubby Polyxo with her coarse black hair and olive skin that turned nut brown in the sun; and me, slender and golden bronze, with my ivory complexion that I was constantly re-minded to shield from the direct glare of Helios. My willful disobedi-ence resulted in a profusion of freckles across the bridge of my nose, which my nurse would then try to scrub off with lemon juice.

From the time I was about six or seven summers old until my fourteenth year, Polyxo and I were more like sisters than Clytemnestra and I could ever dream of becoming. Such is often the case between girlhood friends, I suppose. With Polyxo I could share my most coveted secrets, knowledge I would never trust in the hands of my older sister.

Between the comfort of Polyxo's presence and the danger of Clytemnestra's was my first cousin Penelope. Actually, she and I were not blood at all, unless you accept the fiction that Tyndareus was my father. His brother Icarius was Penelope's father. When they were younger, the brothers quarreled over the kingdom of Sparta. Tyndareus, in marrying my mother, emerged the victor. When Icarius eventually died, Penelope came to live with us in the palace. She was always an old soul, I remember. You have something of her gravity, Hermione. Where I always needed to be active, Penelope could sit for hours at her loom without uttering a word, completely intent on her weaving. Although she was between my age and Clytemnestra's, Penelope acted as though she had no time for girlhood games, nor, to her credit, did she ever appear interested in any of Clytemnestra's wily schemes. I remember her wit was lively, once engaged, but she did not actively seek mirth or merriment. The simplicity of the Spartan lifestyle suited her well, and it was expected that she would eventually make a good marriage, since she exhibited all the domestic virtues of a proper young lady with none of Clytemnestra's temper or my extraordinary looks—things that might tempt suitors to think twice before making an offer, despite our noble birth.

When I was a bit older, I used to enjoy watching Penelope while she worked at her loom. As she separated the colors, it reminded me so much of the way my mother's fingers had plied the lengths of thread that one day I asked Penelope if she had ever heard about the Goddess. "I'm busy now," she answered. "Why don't you come back and tell me all about her another time?"

Polyxo and I tugged on each other's hands to pull ourselves to our feet, and I apologized to Penelope for disturbing her. We left her room on tiptoe so we would make less noise, and when we got to the courtyard, Polyxo said, "I want to hear about the Goddess. My mother has mentioned her, but my father says she's wasting her time with the old ways and that she must grow accustomed to worshipping all the sky gods now."

"Can you keep a secret?" I asked Polyxo. She nodded and squeezed my hand. I brought her to the sacred grove and showed her the ruins of the little temple, trying to remember everything my mother had told me, pointing out where the relic once stood and where the never-ending fire had been kindled, only to be smothered for all eternity by Tyndareus. "Now that my mother is gone, he no longer needs to concern himself about the old religion and the followers of the Goddess," I sighed. We raced each other back to the palace, for I had yet another secret to reveal.

In one corner of my sleeping room stood a large wooden chest with a bronze hasp. I lifted the heavy cover and pointed to the colorful garments that lay inside, folded with reverential care. "These were hers," I whispered, "for ceremonies." I had never seen my mother wearing the accoutrements of a priestess; but her wishes had been, upon her death, that I should receive the chest and all its contents.

"Can we look at them better?" Polyxo wanted to know.

My fingers trembled as I lifted the first garment from the chest. It was a long, tiered skirt in the old Cretan style, bib-fronted and stiffened with horsehair, quite unlike any of our simple, flowing habiliments. It bore a colorful pattern, intricately applied, of vines and wildflowers. I felt the tremendous urge to try it on. Naturally, it was far too long and dragged behind me. I had to walk gingerly to avoid trampling the hem. Polyxo had taken another garment from the chest and was admiring it, though with an expression of extreme puzzlement. "What do you think this one is?" she asked me.

"I think you have it upside down," I told her. It was a short-sleeved bodice that cinched the waist tightly and completely exposed the bosom. I tugged my shift out from under the big tiered skirt, lifted it over my head, and allowed Polyxo to help me don the alluring top. It pushed together my then-budding breasts, creating the illusion of cleavage, although it would take a few more years before I would be able to turn heads. Still, I was somewhat intrigued by the result.

"You're quite a sight!" Polyxo exclaimed. She lifted a box, not much larger than a reliquary, out of the wooden chest and tentatively removed its pretty cover, inlaid with red marble taken from the quarries at nearby Mount Taygetos. "Look! No, Helen, smell!"

It was my mother's cosmetics box, filled with powdered colors, fragrant unguents, and strong-smelling herbal salves. Polyxo held a small bronze mirror in front of my face as though she were my handmaiden and encouraged me to experiment with the newly discovered treasure. I dabbed my cheeks and lips with cochineal and rimmed my eyes with cobalt. Content with the results, I rose and danced around the room as I imagined the acolytes had done while my mother waited naked on the altar for the arrival of her lover. "Do you think I look like a priestess?" I giggled, very pleased with myself. Poor Polyxo looked paralyzed, her face stricken with fear. "What's the matter?" I asked her, and she spun me around to face the doorway.

Tyndareus stood there, looking like Zeus himself about to hurl one of his mighty thunderbolts. "One whore in this house was enough!" he said. "Now remove those clothes immediately, and never let me hear that you have worn them again!"

"The Goddess was here before you were," I spat, finding my courage within my mother's priestly robes. "The Great Mother was the creator and sustainer of all," I added for good measure, straining to recall Leda's words. I knew that Tyndareus didn't like to be challenged. And besides, as my child's mind peevishly reasoned, he shouldn't be skulking about the gynaeceum, king or no king!

"The first woman on earth was called the *kalon kakon,*" the king said, nearly choking on the words. *"Kalon kakon,"* he repeated. *"The beautiful evil.* You were given to us by Zeus as a punishment!"

He turned on his heels and left us alone. Although we were both left trembling, Polyxo's tremors were born of fear, where mine were born of ire.

"How dare he," I fumed under my breath. "And what *had* brought him to the women's quarters in the first place?" I didn't need to wait long for my answer. A flash of carmine passing between the pillars of the portico told me everything I needed to know.

That night, the chest was removed from my room. I didn't see it again for several years.

~~

In my eleventh summer, a great announcement was made from the center of the pergamos. Clytemnestra would be married to Tantalus, King of Pisa. It should come as no surprise that I rejoiced almost as much as

the bride-to-be. My nemesis would be leaving Laconia, which was reason enough for me to celebrate. When she told me that Pisa was far
from home, my smile must have broadened even more. Here in Sparta I
would no longer be within reach of her jealous temper. Perhaps Tyndareus would cease to be so disapproving of me as well. It was nearly
too much to hope for.

I followed Clytemnestra about as she prepared for her wedding festival issuing orders imperiously as if she was already the Pisan queen.
She even chose which animals would be burned on the altar for the
ritual sacrifice. I went down to the palace stores with her and watched
her select the wine for the libations and those that would be consumed at the feasting tables. From the olives to the figs to the flowers
I would wear in my hair, my sister controlled every decision down to
the minutest detail. I began to wonder about the groom. Would she
control Tantalus, too? I found my tongue and took a rare opportunity to taunt her. "Didn't you hear the bard's song last night?" I said,
smug with the knowledge of what I was about to say. "The word for
wife is *damar*—the tamed one—and Tantalus will tame you, just as
Castor breaks wild horses!"

She grabbed a broom and tried to beat me with it, but I was too fast
for her. She broke a wine jug and blamed me for that, too. But as it
grew nearer to her wedding day, I noticed a change in her demeanor.
Clytemnestra's often strident cadences, to my astonishment, softened
to the melodic coo of a dove. Tantalus had come to stay with us during
the final week of preparations; and every evening in the Great Hall,
after the feasting had ended, while the servants cleared the remnants
of the meal, my sister would settle herself at her betrothed's feet and
favor him with a smile that would melt the winter snows on the summit of Mount Taygetos. I was fascinated by the metamorphosis. Was
this the effect of love?

The bard picked up his lyre and began to sing of Medea's love for
Jason, how the barbarian priestess was even moved to kill her own
brother and father for love of the Grecian prince. I looked from
Clytemnestra to Tantalus to Tyndareus and the Dioscuri and wondered
if the bard's choice had been wise. But Tyndareus was asleep in his
great carved throne, watched over by emblems of the lion and griffin,

Sparta's royal guardians. My half brothers were busy arm wrestling and didn't even hear the bard insert their names among Jason's brave Argonauts, even though the great adventure to capture the Golden Fleece took place several years before my brothers were born!

The bride-to-be and her groom were gazing at each other as if there was no one else in the feasting hall. Tantalus would reach out to brush an errant lock of hair from Clytemnestra's face, and she would bring his palm to her lips and give it a gentle, lingering kiss. I found myself unable to take my eyes from them. The way they would incline their bodies toward each other and exchange smiles filled with secrets only they could share, heated the feasting hall better than the coals in the pit at the center of the room. Perhaps this was the presence of Eros and Himeros—Lust and Desire—that my mother had spoken of six summers earlier. And if it was, I could barely wait to become a bride myself.

There were games, and for the first time, Clytemnestra didn't try to trip me or tie a knot in the lace of my sandal so it would chafe the skin on my calf. Of course that's because the contests were held in her honor, and therefore, she didn't participate in them. For the first time, too, I was victorious in every footrace. Polyxo grabbed me about the waist at the finish line and gave me a hug, even though we'd run shoulder to shoulder all afternoon. Flushed and glowing from my athletic triumphs, I presented myself to the king and lowered my head so he could place the wreath of laurel on my golden curls. Some of the Spartan women reached out to stroke my hair, for they believed its color was divinely bestowed and to touch it would bring them good luck. I always thought that was a silly wives' tale, but I was so happy that this time I didn't flinch from their attention.

I had yet to catch my breath after the final race, but there was nothing I could do about that. Tyndareus crowned me with the verdant circlet and smiled. I had won his approval—finally! I looked through eyes misted over with tears at the bridal couple and noticed that Tantalus was regarding me with favor; his approving gaze was one I had seen him reserve only for my sister, and it made my cheeks flush even redder. Clytemnestra was watching her betrothed watch me. A dark cloud eclipsed her sunny disposition. "Put on something proper!" she commanded, pointing imperiously at my short tunic, underneath which I was completely nude, as was the custom in athletic competitions. "You look like a flute girl!"

Shamed, I slunk off to the palace, tossing the laurel wreath into the dust.

The following day, the *proaulia,* or second day of the wedding festivities, I followed my sister to the temples to make the requisite offering to the gods. The Goddess was never mentioned; it was the sky gods or Olympians whom we were now expected to worship. A procession of girls and young women, our heads crowned with flowers, sang and danced barefoot along the rugged path to the temple of Artemis where Clytemnestra refused to permit the priestess to slaughter a kid, insisting on making the deadly incision herself. The stately sixteen-year-old bride, heavily ornamented in gold jewelry and clad in shades of fire, had come a long way from the little girl who tried so fiercely to protect her pet rabbit. My sister also placed a lock of her hair upon the altar and a bronze ring thickly plated with gold as the *zemia* or payment believed to ease the transition from virginity to womanhood. I felt a tinge of sadness on Clytemnestra's behalf, because it was traditional for the mother of the bride to help her daughter prepare for her wedding and to enjoy a place of honor at the ritual sacrifices. As our nostrils were seared by the smoke from the burning kid, I wondered what Leda might have made of our pilgrims' progress to several shrines, offering at each one a separate tribute. The virgin goddess Artemis received her due, and then we proceeded to the shrine of Aphrodite, where a basket of bloodred pomegranates was offered as a *proteleia* to the goddess of love to ensure a fruitful womb. Honors would also be accorded to the goddess Demeter, who in the Olympian pantheon provided the link between a woman's agricultural sphere, her social life, and her fertility. How crowded it must be on Mount Olympus! I mused, thinking that men had spent so much time inventing all these goddesses to do the work of one, who once oversaw all creation.

That night there was more feasting, hosted of course by Tyndareus. The groom's father was no longer alive, and we raised our cups and poured a libation in his memory. There were roast meats so succulent they took your breath away, and figs and dates and sticky sesame cakes mixed with honey, which Clytemnestra, after four cups of strong Ithacan wine, giggled were an aphrodisiac.

On the *gamos,* the final day of the nuptial celebration, Clytemnestra permitted me the honor of attending her in the bride's ritual bath. I drew the water from the Eurotas River and carried it to her room in a special vase called a *loutrophoros.* As she sank deep into the tile tub, I poured the river water over her head, then dipped a silver ewer in the warm bath water and allowed it to trickle slowly over her silken hair and skin. She looked like a naiad, a water nymph, with her tendrils of dark hair clinging to the curves of her breasts. My beauty is legendary, but the bards never did give my sister her due. She was a handsome young woman who turned many a head; and when I saw her in love, I realized how truly beautiful she could be when her eyes shone with desire instead of anger and the usually fierce set of her jaw softened into an almost gentle solicitousness. In those quiet moments while I bathed and dried Clytemnestra and then readied her to meet her groom by anointing her body with oils and dressing and scenting her hair, I took time to reflect upon our already complex and thorny relationship. I thought about how my sister's departure from Sparta would benefit her in a way I hadn't previously considered: Only outside my presence would people accept and admire my sister for who she was, not find her lacking because they were comparing her to me.

Clytemnestra had chosen a garnet-red chiton and a himation with a golden border embroidered with ivy for eternal love and lions for strength and courage. The himation had tiny bronze weights stitched into the rolled hem so that it would drape properly. I used a brooch decorated with a russet-colored Laconian porphyry stone to fasten it to her chiton. We draped the himation so that her left shoulder would remain bare.

I swept my sister's thick dark hair away from her forehead and coiled it into elaborate ringlets, placing a *stephane* of burnished gold on her head. The diadem complemented her golden owl-shaped earrings and the embossed cuffs, a wedding gift from Tantalus, which she wore on each wrist.

Once Clytemnestra was prepared for the final bridal procession, I quickly donned a white chiton, securing it with subtle gold pins at the shoulders and belting it twice about the breasts and waist. I placed a simple gold circlet in my hair, and when my sister wasn't looking, I dipped my fingers into the pot of crushed pomegranate seeds and stained my cheeks and lips. I stole a glance in her mirror and was pleased with the results. Apart from the sheerest tinge of pomegranate, I had done nothing at all to call attention to myself. I had forsworn all jewelry and wore an undecorated garment that would be considered perfectly proper attire for any eleven-year-old maiden. And besides, today was Clytemnestra's biggest day. All eyes were supposed to be on the bride.

Many years later, I was telling this story to Paris Alexandros. He laughed and said to me, "You really expected no one to be looking at you? One might as well have tried to eclipse the sun!"

❧ FOUR ❧

lytemnestra is blessed, I thought as I walked with her and Tyndareus in a procession from the gynaeceum to the home of her new groom. As Tantalus actually dwelt on the Ligurian Sea, in the wedding ritual his home would be represented by the far wing of the palace used by the guests of the royal household. *She loves her husband and will be delighted to share his bed and bear his children.* Such was not always the case, I knew. Women did not choose their own husbands; they were chosen for them by their *kyrios,* which for both Clytemnestra and me was Tyndareus, the king being her father and my male guardian. I supposed that he would do his best to ensure *her* happiness, as she was his natural child; but I despaired to think what manner of husband Tyndareus would eventually choose for *me.* First came the pledge, the *engue,* where the *kyrios* would hand over the bride to the groom and publicly state that it was for the express purpose of "plowing legitimate children"—yes, those were the words, as though his daughter's body were a fertile plain. Then came the *ekdosis,* or transfer of the bride to the groom, where she would leave the *oikos* or household of her birth and join his. My sister looked as though she was very much anticipating the plowing part.

Clytemnestra is blessed, I continued to think as the women of the town threw flowers at her feet, *that she loves Tantalus—for the way he gazes at her or makes her laugh—as much as Tyndareus loves him for his trading prospects in the Adriatic.*

After a few more steps, I began to feel a pain, a bit like a stitch that comes from running, except that it wasn't in my side; the sharpness settled just below my stomach. Suddenly I halted and cried out when it felt as though I had been stabbed in my womb. I clutched my belly and gasped to see blood trickling down my legs, staining my white robe crimson. My head swam a little, mostly I think because I had not yet eaten—(there would be a final feast after the groom had accepted his new bride into his "home," and I had been saving room for all the courses). But I recall being overcome with a queasiness and fatigue, which, coupled with another stab of pain, caused me to sink to my knees. Someone cried out, "The princess has fallen!" and a moment or so later, the procession halted.

Clytemnestra turned around to see me doubled over in the road, my knees clutched to my stomach. She disengaged her arm from Tyndareus and approached me. "Get up," she demanded, and I complied, embarrassed now that all eyes, even those of the common people, were fixed upon me. I smoothed the creases from my chiton and brushed away the dirt, but there was no disguising the bloodstains. Clytie's eyes blazed like a brazier. "I knew you would somehow find a way to spoil it," she hissed. "Even today, you must be the center of attention!"

Shame burned my cheeks. My sister was right; I had indeed managed to ruin the most important day of her life. I had most assuredly been an embarrassment to the royal family and had suffered the humiliation of making the transition to womanhood in front of everyone in Sparta. Of course, that's not what I thought was the matter at the time. I remember feeling angry that boys were pointing their fingers, girls were giggling, men tried to hide their blushes, and women laughed outright at my misfortune, since I was sure I was dying from some kind of deadly internal illness.

Tyndareus joined his daughter, and Clytemnestra appealed to him to get rid of the distraction. Once again, both of us were weeping, but my tears were born of shame while hers were, as always, of anger. "Go home, Helen," Tyndareus demanded. "Go back to the gynaeceum and stay there." I was being banished. He wouldn't even allow me to remain in the procession, blending my voice with the other women who sang the traditional songs to the bridal couple. I would not be welcome at the final feast and would not join the well-wishers who would bid the pair a last farewell from Sparta. As Tyndareus scanned the faces of the onlookers, he spotted Polyxo's open countenance. "You there!

You're Helen's friend. Take her back to her room and see that she does not leave it for the rest of the day." I saw him toss her something—a small coin or trinket—as though he would purchase her loyalty.

I clutched my skirts to my body as we made our way back to the palace. "Don't be ashamed," Polyxo said, uncurling my hand from the wrinkled linen. "It's natural. You should never stop up your ears or blind your eyes when your body is sending you a message." We reached the gynaeceum and I realized that Polyxo and I would be alone for the rest of the day. My nurse was attending the wedding festival, of course, and Tyndareus would not think to punish her by sending her back to care for me.

The water from Clytemnestra's ritual bath remained in the tub. I unbound my chiton and slipped it over my head. Polyxo retrieved the bloodied garment from the tile floor and placed her hand on my arm to stop me from climbing into the bath. "What are you doing?" I asked her. "Stop it, I want to wash."

"Not here," she insisted, tossing me the chiton. "*This* time, *you* come with *me*." I dressed again in the stained garment and Polyxo combed my hair. "Act proud," she said.

The town was empty. Everyone was either observing the festivities or participating in them. No one saw two young girls, one slim and fair, the other plump and dark, heading to the outlying fields. Eurodyia, Polyxo's mother, welcomed us into their humble farmhouse and gently inquired if my belly and back still ached as though I had done a day's work in the fields. As I had never experienced such toil, I didn't know how to reply. She laughed at my honest confusion and prepared an herbal posset for me to drink that would relieve the pain, showing me how she made the concoction so I could duplicate the recipe every month when the pains came.

"Every month?" I gasped. Eurodyia laughed at me again. "I'm sorry." I blushed. "My nurse isn't comfortable speaking about bodily acts, and I have no mother to teach me these things." Eurodyia's smile fell immediately, the creases along either side of her mouth turning earthward. She looked over at her daughter and then took me in her arms and held me. Even though I was too big a girl to be rocked as one would soothe a baby, Eurodyia did so. And I wept. I could not remember the last time I'd felt the loving contact of another being. My nurse, who was a servant of Tyndareus, was ill at ease in the role of a nurturer and thus kept her distance. My mother had been gone for years by then, but even so, I still couldn't recall her embrace.

"Shall I wash this for you?" Eurodyia asked me, fingering the linen of my chiton.

"I'll do it," Polyxo volunteered. "May we go to the river?"

Eurodyia assented. I drained the contents of my posset—already I was beginning to feel its restorative effects—and Polyxo and I bid her good-bye. But before we reached the banks of the Eurotas, Polyxo and I called upon some of her friends, girls who had previously been accustomed to avoiding my company. "They really are kind," Polyxo assured me, although I was not entirely convinced. "I think you will be surprised."

There were six of us all told, until we visited an elderly midwife named Adraste, known to Eurodyia, though not known well. Adraste had been a priestess of the old religion and knew the ways of the Goddess, but she feared retribution from Tyndareus if she continued to lead women in worship. "Your mother would have been joyful that you chose to celebrate your passing into womanhood by following the transition rites," she told me. "You have done well," she added, addressing Polyxo. Adraste retrieved an enormous willow basket from a hiding place under the floor, and after placing a length of white cloth and several peaches into the basket, slipped it over her arm and led us down to the river.

Beside the Eurotas, Adraste handed dried gourds and tambourines to the other young girls and taught them a simple song. The lyric praised the Goddess for creating and sustaining all life, then honored me (my name was inserted) as one of her daughters for reaching the day where I, too, had become capable of creating and sustaining life. As the girls sang, Adraste ground the peach pits with a marble mortar and pestle until the texture was a fine paste. She offered the bowl to Polyxo while she unpinned my chiton, letting the garment fall like a soft cloud about my bare feet. Polyxo applied the paste in a slow, swirling motion to my limbs, breasts, belly, and inner thighs. She was sloughing away my child's skin, Adraste explained, removing the dry, dead layer that was no longer necessary to nurture and protect my body. Then I would step into the current to cleanse and purify myself, washing away the body of a child and emerging a woman, with a virgin layer of new skin. The blood that flowed from my womb would commingle with the current, to honor the constant flow of creation, adding the fluid of my life-giving loins to the life-giving river.

My chiton was offered up to the river, too, and when I emerged from the Eurotas with nothing to cover my nakedness, Adraste took the clean white cloth from her basket and wrapped me in it. I was enveloped in the scent of eucalyptus. She offered me a pomegranate—one filched from Clytemnestra's bridal offering to Aphrodite, she acknowledged gleefully—and bade me peel it. I was mortified when some of the ruby-colored seeds burst in my fingers and stained my new garment, but Adraste assured me that was supposed to happen. The crimson-spotted cloth was symbolic of my new fertility. I offered the seeds to the other girls, who each partook of a dozen or so, to pray for their own fecundity. There were so many seeds, and I was making a dreadful mess of my new white shift. Several inches of fabric had turned a rich shade of violet. Adraste laughed. "It means you'll be *very* fruitful," she said. "And I don't doubt the signs for an instant," she added, appraising my beauty.

～～

The following morning I rose and dressed early so that I could bid Clytemnestra good-bye before she and Tantalus rode down to the harbor. Her body was stiff and unresponsive to my farewell embrace. Evidently, she still resented my inadvertent diversion of the previous morning. Not for a single moment was she willing to soften, although she knew as well as I that it might be several seasons before we saw each other again.

A year seemed to fly as swiftly as Bellerophon on his winged horse. Only once did we receive news of my sister and Tantalus. They were both well and happy, and she had just learned that she was with child. I tried to imagine Clytemnestra with a babe at her breast and could not summon a clear picture. Perhaps if she was as contented as she claimed, she might be a loving mother as well. I had my doubts of it, though.

By my thirteenth summer, I was already developing into a fine young woman, slim-hipped, long-legged, full-bosomed. My red-gold hair nearly reached my waist. I became fond of wearing it unbound, letting it swirl around my shoulders and down my back like a shower of molten bronze. Ever since I had discovered my mother hanging by her own veil, I had refused to wear one; although it flouted our custom and angered Tyndareus that I was displaying myself, causing excitement among the men and spreading envy among the women. My twin half brothers took it upon themselves to watch over me. I think they feared that my own curiosity would be more of a danger than the lusts of strange men. I idolized my older brothers—they had four winters on me—and spent as much time with them as they would allow. Having seen seventeen summers, Polydeuces and Castor had become strapping young men who turned many a Spartan girl's head and broke several hearts, so it had been rumored, during their numerous cattle raids in Messenia and Arcadia.

I would follow them down by the reeds along the banks of the Eurotas or up to the plains above the city where Castor allowed me to ride his horses once he'd broken them. We would race through a carpet of wildflowers: me—bareback on one of his snow-white stallions—and Castor, barefoot, with his shining black hair streaming in the wind, his bronzed chest glistening with moisture. Although he occasionally suffered from spasms that would cause his breathing to seize up, he insisted on running full-out every time, and I remember him being as fleet of foot as the massive beasts he tamed.

I would sit on a rock under the open sky and watch Polydeuces engage his mirror image as a sparring partner. In their sporting with each other, he sometimes drew blood. I would gasp and run to attend Castor, and the twins would exchange glances in their secret unspoken language that only the two of them would ever understand and laugh at me for worrying like a wife. There were slight differences between the boys if you knew them well. Castor's health was sometimes fragile, but he never allowed it to deter him from living every day to the extreme. Polydeuces had a touch of divinity about him. His smooth skin never bruised no matter how hard a blow he received. What they shared was a restless nature and a luminous joy for life's adventures—the more foolhardy and daring, the better. I possessed the same impetuosity but was starved of the opportunities to express it. My brothers' gender afforded them a freedom that would be denied to me forever, and while I could not have adored them more, I admit that I was envious that they could leave the boredom of Laconia at will.

~~~

One dry summer afternoon will be forever etched on my memory. In a way, it changed the course of my life. I had climbed an olive tree to gain a better view of my brothers' wrestling match, pleased as only a younger sister can be that they had invited me to judge their sport. I had just settled myself on one of the branches when I spied a messenger breathlessly running toward us, waving his arms as though he were fleeing a great calamity. "Clytemnestra has returned home!" he informed us. "The king has asked me to summon you immediately."

I leapt from my perch into Castor's arms, and we raced back to the palace. Of course, the twins arrived long before I did.

A great commotion had our servants scurrying for cover. The cacophony of angry voices led me to the Great Hall, where Tyndareus sat on his throne. His hair looked like it had not seen a comb since yesterday; his impressive headdress was askew. Clytemnestra had prostrated herself like a supplicant at her father's feet. Her body, which had been so lovely and voluptuous not two summers ago, had wasted away. She was too thin now, almost frail, and when she raised her face to Tyndareus, her pallor was that of a woman in deep mourning: eyes hollow and sunken, skin blotchy and pale. Her dark hair, neither dressed nor ornamented, hung wildly down her narrow back. Even her garments were unkempt and appeared to be torn and ragged. I placed my hand over my mouth to stifle a gasp. What had happened to my once-proud older sister?

The Dioscuri flanked Tyndareus, a twin on either side of the carved throne. Standing above the hysterically weeping Clytemnestra was an imposing bearded figure, mottled with freckles and richly clad in a lapis-colored tunic and a cloak with an intricately embroidered golden border. He wore bronze gauntlets and greaves as though he were dressed for battle. His russet-colored hair formed a lion's mane about his shoulders and was held in place with a heavy gold circlet.

I asked one of the serving women who he was. "Agamemnon, High King of Mycenae," she whispered, then scuttled off like a beetle lest she be caught conversing with the princess.

I wanted to approach my sister. If ever a woman looked in need of comfort, it was Clytemnestra. In that instant I forgave her maltreatment of me on her wedding day and darted past a guard, throwing myself on my knees at her side. "Clytie," I whispered, and she looked up and threw her arms around my neck. Her sobs commenced anew, and I rocked her as if she were a newborn babe, stroking her hair, gently smoothing the errant strands off her face. I remember being shocked to see bruises and scratches on her bare arms, but I had not the opportunity to question her about their origin.

"Helen, this is no place for you!" Tyndareus thundered. His outburst caught the attention of the High King, who turned to look at me. His eyes, cold and gray as the blade of a knife, cut mine down with one stroke.

"The beauteous Helen," he sneered softly. The tone of his voice sent a shiver of fear coursing through my body. Tyndareus ordered me to leave the Great Hall, and I made a grand show of doing so, only to return on tiptoe almost immediately, hiding behind an extremely large and unsuspecting guard.

What my prying eyes saw terrified me far more than Agamemnon's look had done. The High King told Tyndareus that Tantalus had conspired with the sea raiders and was thus a traitor to all Achaea. Agamemnon had therefore sailed to Pisa and had brutally murdered him. But that was not all. Agamemnon had also slaughtered Clytemnestra's infant son right before her eyes and was now claiming her as his bride, being a spoil of war. He had returned Clytemnestra to her homeland in order to convince Tyndareus to bless the new union. My sister tore her hair and beat her breast, keening like a woman in mourning—as indeed she was—for her butchered husband and child. She pleaded with her father to send the High King away, dismissing him as the barbarian he had shown himself to be, promising Tyndareus that she would do anything he wished—marry someone else of his choosing or become a priestess in the temple of whichever god or goddess he saw fit—if only he would spare her from going to Mycenae with Agamemnon. I wondered what Tyndareus would do. Clytemnestra had always been his favorite. I could see from his deeply rutted brow that he was in an intolerable predicament.

Agamemnon argued that in the past, he and Tyndareus had favored each other, thereby setting a precedent for diplomatic relations between Mycenae and Sparta. He had helped Tyndareus wrest the Spartan throne from his brother Hippocoön, and Tyndareus had aided Agamemnon in recapturing the High Kingship of Mycenae from his uncle Thyestes. Much remained to be gained from an association between the two kingdoms, he reminded Tyndareus, his assured voice and commanding presence overriding Clytemnestra's passionate protestations.

I was stunned, yet sadly unsurprised, that Tyndareus chose to rule against his own daughter, his favorite child. For the sake of an advantageous political alliance, he sacrificed his firstborn to a brutal baby killer and ravager of women, a man lacking in both conscience and soul, and brimming with the overweening hubris that would impel him to stop at nothing to gain whatever he coveted. Although Agamemnon had demanded a full wedding celebration, Tyndareus begrudged his daughter a final request: that the ceremonies be held without undue fanfare, despite the High King's status. Still, as I prepared Clytemnestra's ritual bridal bath once more and cut a lock of her hair to leave as a votive tribute to Artemis—a relic of the bride's former life—my sister remarked bitterly that the same rites were also undertaken at funerals. I remembered how happy Clytemnestra had been when she was preparing for her nuptials to Tantalus, and now I bathed, oiled, and perfumed a woman who was but a shadow of the other bride. Her entire demeanor was doleful, like a calf that knew it was bound for imminent slaughter. Holding a mirror before her as I dressed her hair, my sister looked past her own reflection to speak to me. "I wish to all the gods that you never suffer my fate. Learn from me, Helen."

Two days later, she would journey to Mycenae a most reluctant queen.

FIVE

As a younger child, I disliked spending so much time alone because it had not been my choice. But as I neared the bloom of womanhood, I learned to embrace solitude. I took to running every morning in the foothills above the plain, allowing my fair skin to become kissed by the sun. When I tired of my own company, I would invite Polyxo to join me, although she had become increasingly busy, now that she was old enough to contribute to the running of her family's farm. Soon, she would be eligible to marry, and I would see her even less. Polyxo knew that there was a vast difference between her station and mine. As we inched closer to adulthood, the only way I, as the remaining princess of Sparta, might be able to enjoy the continued companionship of my trusted favorite playmate would be to employ her as one of my serving women. But this practical option was unthinkable for both of us.

There would not be many more mornings when we would race each other across the plain and through the hillside, so each one became an occasion. We would bring a basket of pears and apples and cold slices of lamb, along with a small pitcher of wine, to a designated spot overlooking the sea, where we would leave it in the shade while we ran through the hills with the plentiful hares, deer, and wild boars for company. Then we would return, breathless and dripping with sweat, to devour our repast as we gazed out at the harbor watching for ships. Unfortunately, it was an unexciting tapestry, lacking all detail, as we rarely saw anything adrift on the sparkling swells.

I had just passed my fourteenth birthday. All Sparta had joined their princess in the celebration, pouring libations to my health and bringing offerings to the altar of Artemis to guard my virginity, while they left tributes to Demeter to grant me fecundity. I was of prime marriageable age. In fact, most Achaean girls were nuptialized soon after their twelfth birthdays, as their *kyrioi* could pretty much guarantee their virginity at that age. It was only a matter of time before Polyxo's father would formally announce her betrothal to a rather stalwart and earnest young man from Rhodes named Tlepolemus. The way my bosom friend admired her intended reminded me of the looks that had been exchanged between Clytemnestra and Tantalus during their wedding festivities. I wondered when my time would come and hoped that I would be able to rejoice in Tyndareus's selection of a husband.

"Have you ever watched his thighs when he runs?" Polyxo asked me. We were climbing toward our customary vantage point. Owing to the unusual heat we had been suffering for the past several days, our basket of provisions felt heavier than usual. Polyxo and I took turns carrying it into the mountains. "Helen, you're not listening to me. *Tlepolemus.* Doesn't he have the most beautiful legs?" I glanced at her and detected a blush spreading across her broad moonface. Polyxo began to laugh and nearly stumbled on a loose stone. I extended my arm so she could regain her balance, but she stopped to catch her breath instead. "Do you realize that every time I start to talk about Tlepolemus, you stop listening to me? Don't you care about my happiness?"

"Don't whine," I snapped. "Of course I do." I admit that I was probably behaving very peevishly then. She was my only friend, and her increasing obligations to her farm and family had already begun to curtail our time together. Once she was wed to Tlepolemus, she would most likely live on Rhodes, and I feared that I would only see her at festivals when she came back to visit her mother. Naturally, I wanted to see her married happily, but with the selfishness of an adolescent girl, my thoughts were on how losing Polyxo might affect *me.* I took the basket from her hands and settled it in a crevice between two rocks. "Let's stop," I said. "I don't feel like running today."

"What *do* you feel like doing? We could eat our meal and then go down to the river and pick wild oleander for our hair. You always like that," Polyxo said helpfully.

I sat down on one of the rocks. Its flinty roughness tickled and warmed my bottom. More and more I had begun to favor the short tunic popular with Spartan girls, particularly for running, when the longer chiton impeded my movement. The shorter garment showed the legs to great advantage and I was proud of mine. And Clytemnestra was no longer around to scold me for resembling a flute girl.

The Great Sea was the color of lapis from the Krokeai quarries. "Polyxo, do you see that?" She had seated herself on the other rock, and I tugged at her hem. I shielded my eyes from the sun and pointed toward the sea. A distant form silhouetted against the sky had broken the monotony of blue on blue. "There's a boat out there. With a black sail." She spied it, too, and we wondered at its business.

"Probably a trader coming to see the king," Polyxo guessed.

"Perhaps it's sea raiders!" Where Polyxo, like my cousin Penelope, always exhibited great pragmatism, I had inherited my siblings' tendency to high drama. Bored to distraction by the Spartan way of life, I looked for adventure anywhere I might find it, if only in my fertile imagination. I plucked a royal-blue veronica blossom, then another, with my bare toes and returned my gaze to the sea. The ship was no longer in view. The sun was not yet at its zenith. I proposed that we enjoy a brief run, then return to the basket for our meal and an afternoon nap. Feet flying, calves taut, running into the wind, we kicked dust into each other's faces on the rocky terrain, our usual friendly competition more competitive than friendly that day.

I had forgotten to mix the wine with water before we ventured on our journey. I tipped the oinochoe toward my throat and swallowed a long, refreshing draught, which—owing to my exhausted state after running full tilt for well over an hour, my dehydration, and my empty stomach—had an immediate effect. I lazily reached for an oat cake to chase the spirits, then ate another, and a third, before falling asleep.

I awakened with a start. Polyxo was tugging at my tunic and regarding me anxiously. The afternoon light had begun to wane. "We should be getting back," she told me. "We're usually home by now. Your nurse will worry about you, and my mother will have started preparing the evening meal."

She stood and offered me her hand, pulling me to my feet. My head swam from the change in equilibrium. Of course, I was *also* unused to undiluted wine! "I think I had a dream just now," I told her. "I was wearing the most beautiful silk chiton. It was pale rose-pink, the color of dawn. And a beautiful young man was feeding me figs." I knew these were a symbol of fertility and supposedly an aphrodisiac.

"You're drunk!" Polyxo giggled.

Her laugh was infectious and I caught the germ. "You think so?!"

"Steady now," she said, and gave me her arm. "A fine princess you are in this condition. We should stop at my house on our way back so we can sober you up. My mother will know what to do."

"Perhaps I can offer some assistance." The man approaching us had a voice as smooth and gentle as a summer breeze. His companion, who carried a large sack slung across his back, struggled to catch up. "My partner, Pirithous," the man said, shrugging off his friend's obvious shortness of breath. I remember noticing right away that even when he wasn't smiling, the lines about the man's mouth curved upward. His sorrel-colored tunic of light wool did nothing to distinguish his rank. His himation, too, was unremarkable and unembroidered.

Travelers? Traders? I wondered what they were doing wandering in the foothills of Taygetos.

"Princess Helen of Sparta, I presume?" the russet-clad man asked me. I nodded. "I thought as much," he replied. "But I don't like to make mistakes." With a quick jerk of his head, he motioned to Pirithous, and before I could utter a word, much less a cry for help, I was whisked off my feet as though I were lighter than a whisper and was imprisoned in the great sack. Polyxo found her tongue and began to scream that I had been kidnapped, which, apparently, was just what the men had expected—and in fact hoped—she would do. But even with my body on someone's back, the men reached the valley more swiftly than Polyxo's short legs could bear her. Her hoarse cries grew ever fainter until they disappeared on the wind.

The ride I took next did much to make me regret the wine I had consumed so freely, for the men did not release me from the sack, but tossed me up to the saddle where I was secured in front of one of the horsemen. Barely able to breathe, and willing myself to keep the contents of my stomach from being eliminated through my mouth, heart pounding to the rhythm of the hoofbeats, I struggled to relax and accept my fate until such time as I could attempt to free myself. They would have to remove my impromptu cocoon eventually, although I did imagine—but refused to believe—that they would leave me inside the sack to suffocate. Even in my upended and confused state, I did not think that my abductors' motive was murder. I remember wondering what would happen if I tried to make myself go to sleep, pretending the wild gallop of the horse was just the rocking motion of an overzealous nurse. After I slowed my breathing and accepted my current helplessness, I was able to discern a faint scent of brine, which grew stronger as we rode on. We were headed for the coast.

I heard the splash-crash of waves against the rocks and the call of hungry sea birds. The riders halted their mounts. I was handed down from one to the other like a sack of apples. The bag was untied and slipped down my body where it lay like a puddle of wine at my feet, and with wobbling legs I sought to gain my balance. The man who was not Pirithous offered me his hand with the grace of a prince, and I stepped out of my coarse confinement. "Don't worry about your land legs," he said. "You'll not be needing them for a while."

Just offshore was the ship I had seen from the top of the hill, a fifty-oared pentekonter. The rowers, who gazed at me as though they had just seen a vision of Aphrodite herself, sat poised at the oarlocks, ready for the command to proceed. The vessel's great prow resembled a massive bull rising out of the water, ready to charge its enemies. "I apologize, Princess, that the *Minotaur* is not outfitted for a woman's comfort, but I assure you that you will be treated in a manner befitting your station when you arrive in Athens," said the man who was not Pirithous. He held fast to my hand as we waded out to the ship, handed me up to his friend, who had boarded first, then stepped onto the *Minotaur* behind me. The anchor stones were raised and brought aboard, and in one great fluid motion we pushed away from the beachhead. The enormous square black sail was raised and grew big bellied from the south wind.

One of the seamen gave a shout and pointed ahead. "Dolphins!" he cried. I followed the line of his arm out to the Great Sea. As if Poseidon himself had summoned them, we were receiving a playful escort on either side of the hull, the dolphins racing and dancing and diving into the splashing waves. Our journey would be a favorable one.

My heart was racing. I confess that there was a part of me that was excited to be leaving the Laconian shores. The rest of me was terrified. The name of the vessel and the shape of its prow had provided me with two excellent clues as to the identity of my abductor, as had the destination he had named; but he had thus far neglected to introduce himself, although he clearly knew who *I* was.

"I am Theseus, king of Athens," he said finally, once the oarsmen had taken us several leagues from the coastline.

"I have heard the bards sing many songs of your daring adventures. You are a legend in your own lifetime," I said, watching the smile creases in his face.

"As legendary as your beauty," he replied.

"They will sing of *us* now," I said, unsure of whether I liked the idea or not. Theseus was a modern-day hero, it was true, but he was equally renowned for his amorous liaisons and multiple marriages. As Heracles was heralded by the bards for his extraordinary feats of strength, Theseus of Athens was celebrated for his seductive prowess. If the songs were true, he had married the Amazon queen Antiope—or her sister Hippolyta, depending on which bard you listened to—who loved him so much she sided with him in a war against her own people and took a fatal arrow through the heart for it. He had seduced the trusting Ariadne, daughter of King Minos of Crete; she willingly revealed the secret of the labyrinth that enabled him to kill the monstrous Minotaur, then willingly gave him her body and soul, only to be abandoned on a rocky promontory in the middle of the sea while Theseus returned to Crete to fetch her younger sister Phaedra for his bride. "Seduction and abduction very nearly rhyme, too," I added. "You make the bards' task easy."

Theseus stood behind me to steady my balance. I had never before set foot on a ship, and riding the waves was like balancing on a gimbal, a game I used to play as a girl. I remember thinking at the time how ironic it was that my abductor's physical proximity made me confident of my safety, rather than despairing of it. "Perhaps," he said, "I should have thought twice about kidnapping a Spartan princess. I had forgotten that Laconian women are known for their smart tongues. In Athens, a silent woman is considered a virtuous one."

"Then it's well for you—Theseus the Pirate—that we are not yet *in*

Athens." He laughed and said he had better things to do than trade barbs with a twelve-year-old girl. "Twelve?" I repeated. "Where did you hear I was only twelve?"

"The same bards, I suppose! It appears they are prone to hyperbole."

"Then you really didn't abandon one woman and then go off and marry her sister?"

"They got that part right." Theseus winced at the memory. "It was the stupidest thing I ever did—and I have been guilty of many rash acts in my lifetime." He touched my chin with his forefinger and tipped my face toward his. I lost my balance and fell against the bulwark. Theseus helped me to my feet and stepped back to get a fuller look at my person. If I recall correctly, it was the first time he had done so, and I smile to remember that he appeared to be quite taken with the vision before him. "How old *are* you then?"

"Just after the last new moon, we poured libations in honor of the arrival of my fourteenth year." I felt my cheeks grow warm, knowing what I was about to tell him next. "They made quite a celebration of my much anticipated fertility. They sang many odes to the sky gods— I forget which ones, you have invented far too many—in praise of it." Quickly, I wove the threads of the tapestry together. "You haven't abducted me to marry me, have you? You needn't have gone to all the trouble. You might have entered the palace through the front gate, and I am sure King Tyndareus would have heard your petition—providing you offered a suitably magnanimous bride-price." I stifled a snicker at Tyndareus's overweening greed. The king was rumored—(although no one spoke directly of such things to a girl-child)—not to be wanting for wealth, yet one would never know it to tour his kingdom. Our palace was much nicer and more spacious than any other dwelling in the city, but it was the Spartan ethos to give short shrift to any forms of luxury and adornment—of the home, of the person, and of the mind—in clear preference to a simplicity bordering on asceticism and denial. I hated it, and although I would have wished it could have been under more gracious circumstances, I was glad to see the Laconian shores recede from view.

I realized that Theseus had not answered my question, so I repeated it. "Did you kidnap me to marry me?" As I mentioned earlier, it was common practice for invaders to obtain their wives through capture.

"Would it disappoint you if I didn't? Or shock you, given my history?"

I swallowed a gulp of salt-sea air. "It would . . . shock me . . . given your history," I echoed numbly.

"Not that marrying the most beautiful girl in the world would be a mistake, mind you, but after one extremely happy marriage and one thoroughly miserable one, I have no interest in taking another wife. My first wife, Antiope—not her sister—brought me untold content-ment and gave me a son who, for all my exploits, was my most remark-able achievement." Theseus then told me how his second wife, Phaedra, had developed an unrequited passion for her handsome step-son Hippolytus, which brought the household to the brink of disaster. Never again, he said, after Phaedra took her own unhappy life, would he seek another bride.

"Then what am I doing being tossed to and fro by the pitching sea like a child's plaything?"

Theseus did not give me a direct answer. I should have expected as much from a man who was not a Laconian. When we arrived on the shores of Attica, he said, it would not take more than the chariot ride from the port to the Athenian acropolis for me to appreciate his city's magnificence. From the way he expressed it to me at the time, Theseus had spent so much to build up and fortify the Attic kingdom that he had taken to sea raiding in order to restore his sorely depleted cof-fers. It was how he had earned the sobriquet "Theseus the Pirate." He never had any intention of making me his queen. His strategy had been to abduct the most beautiful girl in the world—how fortunate for him that she happened to be the unmarried princess of a power-ful kingdom—and hold her for ransom. Tyndareus, knowing how valuable my unsurpassed looks were on the marriage market, would fear my violation at the hands of the notorious seducer and would im-mediately offer Theseus a large reward for my safe return.

The great pirate excused Pirithous from the tiller, resuming the stewardship of the *Minotaur,* and I was left on my own. Pirithous wasn't much of a companion or a conversationalist. The most I could learn from this taciturn Athenian was that he had agreed to accompany Theseus on his venture to Sparta if, in exchange, Theseus would agree to help Pirithous obtain Demeter's daughter Persephone from the dark recesses of Hades' underworld where she was his seasonal bride. I covered my mouth so as not to laugh at his folly. "You Athenian men seem to take extravagant fancies to the daughters of Zeus," I remarked, and poor Pirithous, his eyes fixed upon my bosom, became too tongue-tied to respond.

The seas began to roil and turn gray, and though the *Minotaur* was light and fast, each time the craft hit a downswell, I was assaulted with sea spume until my cheeks began to sting. I regarded the yellow-white froth and tried to recall every detail of my mother's story about the conception of Aphrodite in order to distract my mind from the state of my stomach. I began to feel a bit like I was on a very long and arduous ride, unable to stop my horse or dismount from his back. We undulated through the wild waters through the night with no coastline yet to appear on the horizon. Finally, I sank to my feet and fell asleep by the bulwark. Soon, I came to enjoy the sensual rise and fall upon the waves, the salty tang of the air, and the indescribable sense of freedom that comes from looking in all directions and seeing nothing but sea and sky, dressed in variegated shades of blue and gray. The sailors did not share my exuberance, although it amused them. Their life was hard, their task both arduous and monotonous, but I was a child with a sparkling new plaything, the enjoyment of which made me all but forget, for the duration of the voyage, the circumstances under which I had come to be standing on the *Minotaur*'s deck.

Shortly after dawn, we spied land, although the waters were very harsh, buffeting the ship from side to side. The oarsmen groaned and strained to keep the craft on course.

"Where are we?" I asked Theseus.

"The tip of Attica. Cape Sounion," he replied, pointing toward the nearing promontory.

"Why does the water here look so dark?"

"My own foolishness."

I gazed at the firm set of his jaw silhouetted against the clear sky, his eyes blinking back what I guessed were tears. The wind rearranged his thick dark hair, which was threaded with the occasional strand of silver. Theseus looked down at me and before his gaze returned to the indigo sea, I could see him deciding whether or not he wanted to tell me the story just behind his lips.

"When I set out for Crete under my usual black sail, my old father Aegeus, then the king of Athens, feared that I would be defeated by their monstrous Minotaur and never come home. I promised to send Aegeus a signal that all was well as I rounded Cape Sounion, accepting his gift of a white sail to hoist on my return voyage as a sign of my success; but if I had perished on my errand, my ship would return under the black sail. In the excitement of victory and in my haste to leave Crete, I forgot to change the sail. Upon sighting the black sail, my father, who stood on that promontory anxiously awaiting news of me, thus believed the worst. In despair, he threw himself from the cliff into the churning sea. That is why the waters are so uncommonly dark here." Theseus was silent for several moments. "He plummeted like a great white bird, his robes borne by the wind."

"You saw him die then?" I placed my hand gently on his forearm.

He nodded. "These waters are now called the Aegean Sea, in his memory. In mourning for him, I have sailed ever since under a black sail."

"My mother took her own life," I said. "We are kindred spirits."

fter rounding the rugged cape, the seas became calmer. The oarsmen's task grew easier, aided by a steady wind at their broad backs. We were headed for the mouth of a wide harbor toward a town so congested with structures that there was not a patch of green in view. "Is this Athens?" I asked Theseus.

"*That* is." He placed his hand on my shoulder and pointed off into the distance where a large citadel sat majestically atop a hill overlooking numerous other structures built into the terraced rise, like a king with so many supplicants at his feet. *"This,"* Theseus said, indicating our immediate destination, "is Piraeus. The port." He issued a number of commands to the sailors as we neared the shoreline, while I made my way to the bow to gain a closer look. Gulls circling overhead, diving and swooping into the cerulean waves for their morning meal, issued throaty caws while the high-pitched calls of fishmongers on the docks threatened to drown out nature's song. Our Spartan port of Gythium was an unprepossessing outpost compared to Piraeus. Never before had I seen so many people: sturdy Dorians like the people of Laconia, dark and stocky like Polyxo; Ionians from farther north, taller and more elegant of form and feature; many slaves, some of whom had skin the color of newly turned earth, and others who were the color of wheat, calling to one another in tongues I had never heard. Traders and merchants in colorful garments hawked everything from figs to ivory.

"You are laughing at me," I said to Theseus. The scents of sea and salt permeated his sunkissed skin.

"I had wondered what might stop the motion of your Laconian tongue."

When I was about to unleash it on him again—although I hoped, from the prominence of his smile lines, that he was teasing me the way my brothers often did—the Athenian king changed his tune.

"I have seen so much of the world," he sighed, "that I have forgotten what it is like to be capable of wonder. You have reminded me, Helen. And for that I thank you."

I remember thinking in that instant that he had rarely addressed me by name during our voyage. Perhaps there was a tinge of hubris within me that made me not want him to think of me as stolen booty, just another in a long line of pirated female captives. I wanted him to remember that I was Helen.

At the shore, Theseus and Pirithous bid each other farewell, and I was taken by chariot through the crowded streets of Piraeus. Now that I was on dry land, the throngs of people were even more overwhelming than they had appeared from the harbor. It astonished me to see them so clustered together that they were compelled to wait for others to move first before they could continue on their way. Our charioteer had to threaten to employ his whip before foot traffic would begrudge him a path for his horses. People scattered like insects into darkened doorways cut into the sides of the brick and mud buildings. I wanted to stop my ears from all the noise, to hold my nose from all the odors—variously pleasant and repulsive, depending on which street we traversed. I remember not wishing to embarrass either myself or my abductor-host, so I think I held my breath instead—or tried to—until we passed through Piraeus, emerging in more docile and verdant surroundings. The roads between Piraeus and Athens were more familiar terrain to me for their sparser development. We passed olive groves and simple dwellings similar to those I had known close to home. The inhabitants must have enjoyed the best of two worlds, I mused, deriving benefit from the comparative quietude of the countryside as well as the excitement of two bustling cities.

The hubbub of Piraeus had not fully prepared me to appreciate the glory that was Athens. Stately cypresses, like giants' green spears, shaded grand avenues that snaked up the hillside to the magnificently fortified acropolis. Dwellings with freshly whitewashed facades had multiple levels with residents living above one another like birds in a dovecote. Children played games in the streets instead of in the fields, chasing barking dogs that chased their own tails. It was impossible not to gape at my new surroundings; I had never seen the like of it in Sparta. Theseus took great pride in showing me an incline where many stone benches were nestled into the hill in concentric semicircles that faced an altar, so that the entire city could attend festivals. The Athenian temples and shrines were significantly grander than their Spartan counterparts, too; but by far the most impressive was the Temple of Athena, the city's patron goddess, that looked out over the sparkling Aegean with a vista unparalleled and unrivaled by any other.

We reached the acropolis at the summit of the hill and entered the palace grounds through a massive stone gate, guarded by armored sentries who raised their spears to us in greeting. Such fortification was alien to my Spartan sensibilities as well. The largest wooden door I had ever seen opened onto a sunlit courtyard rimmed with a portico of columns painted red as oxblood. At the far end of the pergamos, a shallow staircase of polished stone led to another defended entry. As soon as we descended from the chariot, I realized how dwarfed I felt by my new surroundings.

The second portal was parted for us and Theseus escorted me through it, leading the way to the palace itself. Slack-jawed, I marveled at the walls; every available surface was painted with repeating floral geometric patterns that bordered vast murals depicting hunting scenes or sea voyages. One series of frescoes showed a handsome, muscled young man, stripped to the waist, first grasping a giant snorting bull by the horns, then using the horns to cantilever himself onto its madly undulating back. I had heard of such athletic contests being held at the palace of Knossos in Crete, the kingdom of the bull, prior to the ritual slaughtering of the animal in a fertility rite.

"Yes, that's me," Theseus said proudly, if somewhat wistfully. "In my youth. Jumping the bull, that's called. I was the greatest champion they had ever seen."

"It looks like you could have very easily been ripped to pieces," I remarked with a shudder.

Theseus's smile creases deepen. "But that's half the fun! All my life I have courted adventure—and her sister, danger."

We passed another mural that clearly depicted the happy courtship of Theseus and the Amazon Antiope, besporting themselves with bows and arrows.

"Will you take me hunting?" I asked the king.

He shook his head. "It's not appropriate for young women to comport themselves like men."

"But . . . ?" I tugged at his arm and spun him around to face the mural. "Besides, I've hunted with my brothers from time to time."

"Your value will be even greater to Tyndareus if you are returned to him fit to become a queen," Theseus said. "True, I have often been unconventional." He turned an almost-wistful gaze upon the figure of Antiope poised to unleash a lethal dart from her bow. "I married a woman who was my equal in every way, including strength, and she was my greatest love. But there are few men like myself, and you will more than likely not be wed to any of them. I kidnapped a girl; I intend to ransom a woman—in every way but one."

I looked down to avoid blushing; not because his words shocked my virgin sensibilities but because I did not want him to see how quick my blood was to rise at his implication. I pretended to study the elaborately tiled floor, swirling with red and purple anemones, bordered by sea monsters, fearsome dragons of the deep, undulating their scaly opalescent forms through the cresting waves.

An elderly woman, elegantly attired, though short and slightly stooped, approached us with an ambling gait. She reached up to inspect Theseus's face by taking it between her gnarled hands and looking deeply into his eyes as though she would divine everything behind them. "Welcome home, son," she said, breaking into a smile. The woman then kissed me on either cheek. She smelled of oil of clove. "Welcome, Helen, to Athens." There was no need for me to wonder at her evident knowledge of my identity.

"My mother, Aethra," Theseus said. "She will see to it that you are well provided for while you remain in Attica." He excused himself, explaining that he had business to attend to and would see me at dinner. After embracing his mother once more, he disappeared into the recesses of the palace.

"Come," Aethra said. Her slow perambulation permitted me a closer inspection of my temporary home. No expense had been spared in the furnishings. Slaves busily polished chests and couches ornamented with gold and silver and inlaid with ivory from the East. I removed my sandals and followed Aethra up another staircase, enjoying the sensation of the cool, smooth stone against my feet. There were many rooms on the upper level, most of which were made private by the drawing of a curtain across the portal, but we halted in front of a sturdy wooden door. Aethra took a key from her girdle and opened it. "You will stay here," she told me, shooing me into the room as though she were a mother bird tending her young. "I hope it is to your liking." She issued a throaty command and two sturdily built serving women appeared. A second command sent them running for water to fill my bath.

I confess that it was difficult to remember that I was a captive. This room was more than twice the size of my quarters in the gynaeceum back in Sparta. It was airy, too, being windowed on two sides, with one vista looking out toward the azure waters of the Aegean and the other at a dense olive grove. The bed was so wondrous I couldn't wait to lie upon it, so I hurled myself onto the coverlet, a fleece as white as swansdown. It was the grandest bed I had ever seen; carved olivewood, with serpents that wound their bodies around each of the four posts, and dressed with the finest spun linens in aqueous shades, from turquoise to teal.

Aethra stood at the center of the room, enjoying my evident delight, waiting patiently for me to discover for myself the room's opulent appointments. A curved table shaped like a bean displayed pots of unguents and cosmetics. I ran over for a closer inspection and discovered a hand mirror—not of bronze as I was accustomed to in Sparta, but of silver. What a difference! Where one's image was blurred in the baser metal surface, the silver backing presented a reflection as clear as that found in an icy mountain stream. I could not help gazing at myself. So this is what I truly looked like! Aethra chuckled. "Yes, Helen, you are indeed as beauteous as they say." Gently, she removed the mirror from my hand, replacing it facedown on the table. "But we shall have to rename you Narcissus if you fall in love with yourself!"

The servants knocked to gain entry and set to work in one corner of the room, filling the tile bathing tub with warm water. Aethra lifted the cover from a large linen chest inlaid with ivy leaves fashioned in gold and removed several folded linen towels bordered with detailed handwork. Even the softest Spartan linens were coarse to the touch by comparison.

She dismissed the slaves after they had accomplished their task; I was surprised. I did not anticipate that the aged mother of the king of Athens would own the hands that bathed me. "I am sure you will be glad to remove your traveling clothes," she said to me, and unfastened the brooches that pinned my tunic at the shoulders. I suddenly became very embarrassed by my mean appearance; garments of the most finely woven linen in Sparta encrusted with salt from the continuous sea spray, my sandals in dusty disrepair, and my hair, clumped in masses of sticky tendrils that more closely resembled the serpentine locks of Medusa than silken tresses.

I stepped out of the tunic and stood before Aethra in all my nakedness. "Sweet Goddess," she breathed hoarsely, "my son is either the cleverest man in all Achaea or the most foolish that ever walked upon her fertile earth."

She held out her hand to help me into the tub. The servants had scented the water with oil of mint; sprigs of the herb floated on the surface. I immersed myself to the neck and inhaled their crisp, clean aroma. How good it felt to be able to cleanse myself! At that moment, if Aethra were to say that Theseus had ordered me not to leave the bath until I was ransomed by Tyndareus, I would have been perfectly content to obey his will. "This will refresh and invigorate you," she said, scooping some of the warm water into a pitcher. She gently doused my head and shoulders and scrubbed my back and limbs with a sea sponge soaked in grape-seed oil.

Aethra cupped my head in her strong hands and massaged water mixed with oil of lemon into my scalp. "You invoked the Goddess," I whispered, drowning in sensation. "Did you practice the old ways? Did you know my mother, Leda?"

"I was a priestess of the Goddess," Aethra replied. "But even my son believes in the Olympians. Men who feel compelled to jealously guard their own power fear the more powerful mysteries of woman. Even here in Athens, the Mother of All, she who used to protect our city, has been supplanted by the motherless daughter of Zeus."

And how preposterous, I remarked to Aethra, that the most powerful female of the new sky gods was not born of another female's body, for it was commonly believed that Athena, goddess of wisdom, sprang fully formed from the head of Zeus.

"It reflects man's ambivalence toward us," Aethra added, "that the wisest deity is a woman, but that no woman was needed to create her." She leaned over me, enveloping me in her clove scent, and rested her lips gently on my forehead. "I did not know your mother, though I knew *of* her. She was a much respected priestess of the old ways and fought bravely to see them continue."

It surprised me that Aethra had not heard that my mother had taken her own life. "If I had not been conceived through the festival rites, Tyndareus would not have found reason to continue to shame her for infidelity and she would not have hanged herself," I said miserably.

"It was your mother's destiny to follow in her mother's footsteps, and in hers before her as a priestess of the Goddess," Aethra soothed, "just as it was her destiny to give up her body to the ritual in order to please the Goddess and save her people from the devastation wrought by the drought."

I dared to disagree with her. "My mother *chose* to sacrifice her loins to the lust of the bird-consort. Just as she chose to respect the wishes of her husband by substituting another woman in her stead all those other years, she chose to defy Tyndareus the season I was conceived. Our actions have consequences, and it is difficult sometimes for us to accept responsibility for them." Even then, although I could articulate my beliefs, I did not feel at ease coming to terms with them. Perhaps it was easier, as most people did, to place one's entire life within the dexterous hands of the three Fates.

Aethra bade me step out of the bathing tub and wrapped me in a warm cloth scented with lavender. Suddenly I felt very drowsy. She helped me into the magnificent bed and gently pulled the fleece over my naked form. "Rest for a while," she murmured. "I will return before the evening meal to help you dress."

Hypnos, god of sleep, visited me almost immediately. When I awoke from the deepest slumber I can ever remember, Aethra was standing by the bedside. "Hurry," she said, "it is nearly time to eat."

Here in Athens I thought I had seen every luxury imaginable until Aethra threw open the doors of an olivewood cabinet carved to match the bedposts. She must have understood the dramatic impact of her gesture, for each shelf displayed a stack of folded textiles in all the shades of Iris's rainbow, from delicate rose to deep indigo and every hue in-between. She selected a length of cloth the color of smoky topaz, which she said matched the color of my eyes. I thought the subtle shade was quite sophisticated and was secretly pleased that it would make me appear older than my years. I exhaled audibly as Aethra draped the fabric over my body. "Why, what's the matter, child?" she asked me, thinking I had gasped in pain.

I had never felt anything so smooth, so soft against my bare skin. The fabric of the sepia-colored chiton felt like a fluid caress to every part of my body, from my shoulders to my ankles. "What *is* this?" I marveled.

"Silk. From the East." I had to laugh when Aethra added that talented little insects that lived in mulberry trees spun the filament. She may as well have told me that Aphrodite herself had woven it. Aethra encircled my waist with a golden girdle and, complimenting me on their daintiness, laced my feet into matching sandals. Then she dressed my hair by plaiting the lengths that framed my face, leaving the rest to remain loose and flowing. She wound the braids into an elaborate style at the back of my head and secured them with pins of tortoise shell tipped in gold. My headdress was a delicate gilded fillet. From an ebony chest overflowing with jewelry, Aethra selected a necklace and matching ear dangles of woven gold; she affixed them and admired her handiwork, then determined that two gilt cuff bracelets should dress my bare arms. As light as the filmy silk felt against my body, when I rose to walk I felt as armored soldiers must, weighted down by metal accoutrements.

We descended the marble steps to the main level of the palace and crossed a colonnaded courtyard that led to the dining hall. A large brazier recessed into the floor in the center of the room provided enough warmth to ward off the evening breezes wafting up from the Aegean. Theseus was already at the table, reclining on a couch, as was the custom for men. On either side of him were two straight-backed chairs: one for myself and one for his mother. Even with only three of us in the grand hall, the king of Athens was apparently still observing propriety. I would have liked to recline at the table just once, although I was sure that women enjoyed better digestion for having to sit up while they ate.

"You have gilded the lily, Mother," Theseus said to Aethra. He waved dismissively at all the gold I was wearing. "Helen of Sparta needs no ornamentation to enhance her beauty."

"I think it's wonderful," I said boldly, perfectly aware that attired and adorned as I was, I no longer resembled a little girl. I had not the feelings of a child, nor the desires of one, and was glad of Aethra's efforts.

I had never seen such a feast for only three people. I was surprised that the slaves served us roasted lamb. In Sparta, we only consumed meat during festivals and when honored guests were being entertained. There was no such thing in my experience as an honored female guest. After the meal, we were brought a dish of honeyed figs; and Aethra, claiming that her hip had been ailing her all day, requested her son's permission to leave us. We wished her a pleasant night's repose and watched her retreat from the hall. I felt sorry that she had exerted herself to bathe and assist me. "It doesn't seem proper that the mother of the king of Athens should act as my handmaiden," I told Theseus. "Surely there is a servant whom you trust to attend me just as well."

"A mere slave cannot educate you," he replied. "There is no one better than my mother to guide you on the path to womanhood. She is wise and of royal blood. And she has a stake in ensuring that your virginity is safely guarded. She knows well that you will fetch the highest ransom when you are the most desirable in marriage in every way."

"And what if Tyndareus refuses to play your game?" I asked Theseus, refilling my wine goblet. "He is not known for being a spendthrift, and it is no secret that he cares little for me. What if he decides to ignore your demands and leaves me here in Athens to languish indefinitely? Or what if he chooses instead to amass an army and wage war upon Athens for the crime of abducting the princess of Sparta?"

Theseus's smile lines crinkled even deeper as he laughed loud and long. "That, lovely Helen, will never happen. I have seen many summers and have taken more than one princess in my day. You may be the most beautiful woman in the world, and even the most desirable, but men do not go to war over a woman. King Minos never declared war upon me for abducting Ariadne—even after I *abandoned* her—and he was a powerful ruler with many strong allies. No one waged war on Jason for eloping with Medea, and Europa's abduction also went unavenged. So did the kidnapping of the Troyan King Priam's sister

Hesione many years ago." Theseus drained his wine in a single draught and refilled both our cups again. "Throughout all Achaea, and even in the East, it is one of the most common—and vastly accepted—ways for men to find a bride. Of course, when I brought you here from Sparta, my ambition was not to wed you, but to sell you back to Tyndareus. He will not spend more than I ask in ransom to outfit and armor countless ships and men and risk their lives for the sake of a pretty face—even for the sake of the most beautiful one in the world." He laughed again at my foolish question. "Men do not go to war over an abducted woman," he repeated.

The wine emboldened me to challenge the opinion of the great ruler of Athens on political strategy and diplomacy. "All right, then, tell me what *does* impel them to make war?"

"You mean apart from pride and honor?" he replied dryly.

I nodded. "Spoken like a Laconian! Already it is *I* who am having an influence on *you*!"

Theseus seemed as interested in schooling me as I was in learning. "Power. Profit. Land and all the riches that lie upon it and within it. Trade routes. If a ruler controls the trade routes, he can tax other traders for traversing them and also retain the finest goods for himself and his people. Old King Priam of Troy is a perfect example. The waters of the Hellespont are so treacherous and the winds so often unfavorable that traders are forced to put into port there for several months; they must pay Priam for the privilege, in addition to forfeiting a toll in order to travel through his domain, whether by land or sea. Your sister's husband, Agamemnon, has yearned to end this practice since he became High King of Mycenae, yet it is no secret among the Achaean chieftains that he seeks to gain control of these routes himself. Not only that, but the mountains of Anatolia, where Troy is located, are rich in minerals, especially copper, which is used to make bronze weapons and utensils. Men, Helen, like to control things, to master them, although"—he chuckled—"the one thing they have never yet been fully able to control is a woman." Theseus gazed at me and smiled. "Particularly those with a Laconian tongue!"

"We Spartan women are proud of our blunt speaking, sire. We must be known for something, and as we lack the lavish amenities available to your Athenian women, our wit must be our export!"

～

And as the weeks went by, so it went every evening in Athens. We ate meat each night, accompanied by olives and dates and the freshest fruits and vegetables, all washed down with generous amounts of the finest wine. We often entertained, and I was becoming a talented hostess, conversant in many subjects, as well as an accomplished dancer and musician. Theseus, himself a gifted lyre player, was pleased that in all things I proved a quick study.

On the evenings when we dined alone, after the meal, Theseus and I would sit in the solitude of the Great Hall and talk for hours, until the coals in the brazier became flickering embers, and on some nights until the embers turned to ash and the rosy appearance of Eos heralded the sunrise.

At Theseus's elbow I learned about the ways of the world beyond Sparta—beyond Athens, even—and came to understand much about the arts of politics and kingship. Should it ever happen that I would be widowed, I would know more than how to run a household, play the flute, or employ the little feminine tricks practiced by fine Athenian ladies—(like holding a ball of amber in my hands to keep them cool and prevent my palms from sweating). I would know how to use my power wisely. I feared raising the subject, for I thought he might discontinue my education, but one night I summoned the courage to remark upon Theseus's unusual willingness to speak to a mere girl about topics that were deemed the province of men.

"You are talking to one who married an Amazon queen," he reminded me. "There are some men who can admire a woman for her unconventional qualities. Any ninny can see your beauty, Helen, but few will see *past* it."

"And you are indeed one who sees everything," I murmured.

"Beyond your obvious physical attributes," Theseus said, "I admire your spirit. Your curiosity, your pluck—and your *mind*—which, with the proper nurturing, will blossom into a flower as exquisite as your beauty of form and face. And," he added, more to himself than for my benefit, "perhaps just as dangerous."

At that moment, I believe I experienced what it was to realize that one is in love.

B e careful, my son," I overheard Aethra warn Theseus one evening after supper. "She possesses a feminine wisdom that is beyond her tender years. There is a *knowing* within her that even she may not fully comprehend. It would be prudent to effect her ransom as soon as possible—before she realizes her own power and learns how to wield it."

Three months had passed since I came to Athens. Aethra had recently taken to sleeping on a cot in my room and barring the door before I retired for the night. For the first time since my arrival in Attica, I truly felt like a captive.

My admiration for Theseus increased with each passing day. He was not a man to crow about his achievements, but if he had accomplished even half the exploits for which he was renowned, he was indeed a remarkable man. He had slain tyrants, dived to the bottom of the sea to retrieve treasure tossed there by King Minos of Crete (perhaps that was how some people came to believe that Theseus's true father was Poseidon, lord of the deep) and was credited with inventing the official rules of wrestling. Of course, Theseus had also broken several loyal hearts in his lifetime, but I discovered that he was not indifferent to the pain his behavior had left in its wake, nor had he ever been exempt from great sorrows. Thus I found it within me to seek to understand him, rather than being quick to condemn. This benevolent king had seen his father needlessly die, had lost his one great love, Antiope, to Thanatos, god of death; and their son Hippolytus had perished in a fatal chariot accident. As Theseus continued to take me into his confidence, my sympathies for him grew. Many evenings, I needed to summon all my self-restraint not to reach out and caress his arm or enfold him in mine, or even to climb onto his lap and settle into his strong embrace. Surely my secret must have been written all over my face. Aethra, I know, watched me very carefully.

I'll never forget her satisfied expression when she announced a messenger from Sparta. My stomach fluttered anxiously while he was received as an honored guest; according to custom, he ate and drank with us before being permitted to disclose his news. The young man was surprised that Theseus permitted two women to be privy to his message. Aethra, however, looked as though she already knew it. If she had not purchased his intelligence outright upon his arrival, she had divined it. It was the first reply we had received since Theseus had sent a messenger to Tyndareus with his ransom demand.

"The sons of Tyndareus, Castor and Polydeuces, bearing one hundred talents of gold, are on their way to Athens to demand the release of their sister, Helen of Sparta," the messenger said, staring at my bare shoulder as he uttered my name. He stammered the rest of his communication.

Aethra raised her hands and uttered a brief prayer. Theseus at first seemed pleased; a hundred talents was an enormous sum. A royal ransom, indeed. Yet he became withdrawn, even morose, almost immediately. My behavior was the rudest of all. Despite being elegantly attired in a hyacinth-blue silk chiton, my hair elaborately curled with a metal wand heated in a brazier, I betrayed my girlhood by bolting from the dining hall. I ran up the marble stairs, threw open the door to my chamber, and flung myself on the bed, sobbing into the fleece coverlet.

I should have been delighted at the prospect of being reunited with my brothers, the dearest of my kin. Certainly, I looked forward to seeing them, and I had thought of them often over the past quarter of a year. But I was no longer the child who had been taken from Sparta. Theseus had fulfilled his promise—to have abducted a mere girl, but to see her returned a woman. *In every way but one,* he had added then. Those words were etched on my memory.

When Aethra finally entered my room, she believed I was fast asleep. I waited until I heard the irregular wheeze that signified her departure for the land of Hypnos, then tiptoed to my dressing table and anointed myself with perfume, dabbing the sweet honeysuckle fragrance on each wrist, behind my ears, and between my breasts. I stained my lips with color and smudged my eyes with kohl. With a silent prayer to Aphrodite to guide me in my mission, I unbolted the wooden door, closed it softly behind me, and quiet as a cat, made my way to Theseus's chamber.

His door was open just enough to light my path to his bed. The glow from the full moon illuminated the planes of his handsome face, making the few strands of gray in his thick dark hair resemble shimmering silver filaments.

It was my only chance. The Dioscuri might arrive as early as tomorrow. Apparently, Theseus did not sleep soundly, for he woke with a start when he sensed my presence at his bedside. I touched my finger to his lips. "I am like a master craftsman who has been given the finest tools," I whispered, "but I don't know how to use them. Teach me, Theseus. Please. Teach me." He began to protest but I stopped his mouth with a gentle kiss. "You are as celebrated in the art of seduction as I am renowned for my beauty. We are well matched." If I had followed in my mother's footsteps as a priestess of the Goddess, I would have chosen Theseus of Athens—adventurer, lover, ruler—as my bird-consort for the ceremonial rites.

Theseus rose from his bed and stood beside me. With a practiced hand he unlaced my girdle and unpinned the brooch that fastened my chiton to my right shoulder. He took my face in his hands, kissed me deeply, then ran his fingers through my thick mass of gold-red hair, which he spread in tendrils like the rays of the sun. His caresses explored my neck and shoulders, and in a single fluid motion he slipped the filmy garment down the length of my body. He extended his hand and I stepped out of the puddle of blue silk like Aphrodite rising from the Cytherean sea. "My god, you are exquisite," he murmured, appraising my nakedness.

He drew me toward him, the heat of our bodies palpable, and kissed me again, letting his tongue explore my own. Where Theseus led, I willingly followed. He gently ran his tongue over the outline of my lips, along the ridge of my teeth, then sent it dancing once more with mine. My body was on fire. Eros and Himeros had made me their captive, and the only thing I sought beyond the glories of remaining their prisoner was the even greater ecstasy of release. Like a woman possessed, I pulled Theseus onto the bed with me, opening myself to him. "Please," I whispered hungrily, "I want . . . now."

His eyes sparkled with amusement as well as desire. "You asked me to teach you. And your first lesson in the arts of seduction and love-making is never to rush. Ecstasy prolonged is the sweetest agony. Trust me." He gently nestled me among the soft coverlets and urged me to allow myself to enjoy each individual sensation. His lips and fingers flickered over my face and body, teasing my eyelids, lips, throat, breasts, belly, and even in the tender crook of my arms and behind my knees. Not a single part of my body was left unworshipped by his caresses. His mouth returned to the sensitive skin of my inner thighs, and with the prolonging he had promised, Theseus began to honor my sex with the slow, deliberate stroking of his tongue.

"My god," I whispered. Never could there have been a better tutor.

"The way for a man to truly please a woman in bed is to begin by taking everything one-tenth as slowly as he wants to go. We are always too eager."

"Who taught you that?"

"A wise woman told me so. It's the most valuable thing a son can know." He took me with his tongue until I felt as though waves were crashing over me and I was being borne aloft to Elysium. I was breathless. Theseus aligned his body with mine and took me in his arms. My tears of pleasure bedewed his cheeks as he held me.

"Now, teach me what to do with *my* mouth," I said, and he needed no further urging to instruct me in how to pleasure him. I suppose my greatest surprise was learning how much power a woman has when she takes a man between her fingers and lips, bringing him to the brink of ecstasy and then permitting him his passionate release.

"Make me a woman, Theseus. Completely." My voice sounded throaty and unfamiliar to my own ears.

"It will be my greatest pleasure," he murmured, and slid a silken cushion underneath me before covering the length of my body with his. All reason had flown out the window on the beating wings of a moonlit breeze. Neither of us gave a thought to how the loss of my maidenhead might affect my marriage prospects.

Love and Beauty, Lust and Desire are almost as old as the world. The memory of my mother's words enveloped me like Theseus's strong arms. My lover entered me gently, covering my mouth with kisses when I gasped at the first experience of that extraordinary commingling of pleasure and pain. With another kiss, Theseus assured me that the initial sting would never again interrupt my enjoyment of the most glorious gift known to man. Our tongues danced as our bodies coupled. I wound my arms around his neck, drawing him closer, deeper, matching my rhythms to his until we approached rapture like two wild horses racing head-to-head and collapsed in each other's arms, releasing our ecstatic cries into the still night air.

"I hope the servants sleep more soundly than you do!" I whispered after a moment or two, gazing into Theseus's shining eyes.

He rolled onto his back and raised his right arm to welcome me into his embrace. Eagerly, I nestled beside him, enjoying the warmth of his lean, powerful body. I traced the smooth planes of his chest with the tip of my finger, and he brought my hand to his lips and kissed each fingertip, placing a final kiss in the hollow of my palm. "Such pretty hands," he murmured, enfolding me in his arms and entwining his fingers with mine. "My sweet, sweet little Helen." He held me close while we both began to drift toward a bittersweet sleep.

"I will always love you," I whispered to him as a single salty tear fell from my eye and landed upon his breast.

⁓⁓⁓

The gentle light of Eos woke me. I was still sheltered in the warmth of Theseus's body, his arm lazily draped across my bare breasts. "Good morning," he murmured in my ear.

I rolled over and kissed his soft lips. "Thank you."

"Are you mad? Thank *you*." Theseus hugged me closer. I could have remained in that embrace forever, but I realized that I had to return to my room to bathe and dress for the new day. I redonned the blue silk chiton, fastened the girdle, and ran my fingers through my tangled hair with limited success in taming it. After a reluctant good-bye, I left Theseus's chamber for my own, only to discover that the door had been barred. Aethra must have awakened during my absence and wanted to ensure that we would discuss it upon my eventual return.

Shame had ultimately been my mother's murderer; after her death, I vowed never to admit it into my life. With head held high, I took a breath and rapped gently on the heavy wooden door. Aethra opened it and turned her woeful gaze on me. Her expression was full of the disapproval I had overheard her express to Theseus. There was no mistaking her comprehension of where I had passed the night.

"If it puts your mind at ease, you can believe that it was my destiny to share your son's bed," I told Aethra. Nothing would rob me of the joys I had experienced, nor attempt to diminish the memory as anything less than blissful. Aethra was in a religious tangle. To admit that it was in fact my choice to visit Theseus was to acknowledge the limited role of fate in one's life. "I wish to bathe," I said, and summoned the servants to fetch the water. Aethra helped me disrobe, clucking her disapproving tongue like an annoying mother hen. She had been prescient in acknowledging that through my sexual awakening I would discover the vastness of my own power. Already, only a few hours a woman, I began to feel its strength and to wield it like a flaming sword.

As I relaxed in my bath and mused upon my changed state, an alarm sounded, indicating an imminent danger. Theseus pounded on my door, ordering Aethra and me to dress and prepare ourselves for a journey. All was confusion as we hastily packed my textiles, cosmetics, and jewels into two large chests. I descended the stairs to find Theseus issuing abrupt commands to the palace guard. "What's happening?" I asked him. So soon had my happiness turned to despair.

"This was not what we had arranged," he growled, but upon seeing my anguished expression, relented and took me into his confidence. "The Dioscuri have brought more than the one hundred talents of gold we had agreed upon as your ransom. They have brought a small regiment and are spoiling for a fight. You and my mother must leave the acropolis for safer ground. I have summoned a chariot to bring you to Aphidnae."

"But where . . . ?"

"It's on the outskirts of the city, but well within Attica's borders. You will be protected there."

These were not the brothers I knew. Never would I believe that Castor and Polydeuces would break a treaty. I refused to accept

Theseus's explanation of events. "No! What if I decline to leave you? What if you tell my brothers that I am happy here in Athens and no longer wish to go home?" But well I knew, despite the passion we had shared only hours earlier, that I was not destined—or chosen—to be Theseus's bride. If I could not permanently remain in Attica, at least I could do everything in my power to protect his life and his throne.

"You must go," Theseus insisted. "This is no time for heroics."

"Let me speak to them. My brothers are adventurers, like you; they are not warriors by nature. If they disdain a sister's pleas, then I will go to Aphidnae with Aethra. For my sake, welcome them as you would any honored guests."

Reluctantly he agreed, although the chariot, filled with my possessions, was kept at the ready. I watched as Theseus greeted the twins, who did indeed behave as though they were spoiling for a fight. As guests, however, their role, as well as their host's, was sacred, and they could not instigate trouble or it would have been a tremendous breach of hospitality. Later that day, a lavish dinner was prepared and libations poured in their honor. Theseus sent Aethra to bring me down to the Great Hall so that my brothers could see that I had been well cared for. I entered the columned room, resplendent in a snow-white chiton twice girdled about my waist and breasts, with a simple gold circlet in my hair. I could not have appeared sweeter or more virginal to them. When they questioned me about my treatment at the hands of my abductor, I assured them, with gentle voice and modest demeanor, that Theseus could not have been kinder or more courtly and that his own mother had been my constant companion and chaperone. Every word I uttered was the truth. Polydeuces remained tight-lipped. Clearly, and to my immense dismay, he would have preferred to find me looking starved and ravaged so he could throw the first punch.

The Dioscuri had another surprise for Theseus. Oh, they had indeed brought the one hundred gold talents and had begrudgingly parted with them, but they had also located a young exile named Menestheus, son of Peteus, and had escorted him to Athens under their protection in the hope that he would challenge Theseus for the right to sit on the Athenian throne. This was their revenge for my abduction.

I grew tearful and defensive; Theseus became vitriolic, and it was all he could do to observe the proprieties of hospitality. He ordered me to depart immediately for Aphidnae. He would finish his business with Menestheus and the Spartan princes after I was safely in the countryside.

I had lost everything. It was ridiculous for me to imagine that I could continue to protect Theseus, the only man with whom I had ever known love. My adored brothers had betrayed me for their own ends. I had no way of knowing whether Tyndareus had sanctioned their attempt to topple Theseus's reign by delivering the would-be usurper Menestheus from exile. Perhaps this was yet another of their adventures, which in my girlish imagination I had once believed were glorious achievements of derring-do, not bloodthirsty conspiracies.

I asked only one favor of the men: that I be permitted a private moment with Theseus to bid him farewell. We stepped outside onto the pergamos. The evening was cool and breezy, our final parting infused with the scent of jasmine in the air. Suddenly, he no longer looked boyish. The smile creases, always evident even in his darkest moments, had disappeared from his face. Sobbing uncontrollably, I wrapped my arms around him, staining his tunic with my hot tears. Several moments passed before I could summon words to my trembling lips. "Be well," was all I could muster.

Theseus held me close and tenderly stroked my hair. "I will," he assured me. "And so will you. One day, sweet Helen, you will find someone who loves you as much as you love them."

"And may the gods be with you then," added Aethra, emerging from the shadows.

heseus had instructed us to wait at Aphidnae until word arrived that it was safe to depart for Sparta. Word from *whom,* I had no idea. But I knew, somehow, that he and I would never see each other again. I remained inconsolable for weeks, cooped up in a remote and rugged outpost with Aethra, deprived of the ability to bathe daily, except in the chilly waters of a nearby mountain stream, or to properly dress and adorn myself as had become my custom in Athens. This was no better than life in Laconia, although at least Theseus and I were not separated by the waters of the Aegean. However, I knew that his life was in danger while my brothers and Menestheus sought to dislodge him from the Athenian throne. The magnificent Theseus would not go down without a fight.

My new host, Aphidnus, was a kindly man, ill-disposed to asserting his authority over us. Unheeded by sky god believers, Aethra recommended her Goddess worship. I felt like the philomel I had once kept as a pet: neither fully caged nor truly free. Like Niobe, I was all tears, incapable of controlling my emotions. I gained weight, although I ate little. And naturally, I suspected it was all due to my heartrending separation from Theseus and my hasty departure from Athens. "Did my brothers come to take me home or to conquer Athens?" I asked Aphidnus. "I don't intend to malign your hospitality, but I am more than resigned to my fate and am as ready to leave for Sparta as I was a month ago, yet they remain in the city." The old man shrugged for lack of an answer.

Another new moon passed and we heard no word of either Theseus or the Dioscuri. I was given a loom, but I had no interest in weaving. Aethra expressed her concern that neither my mind nor my body were being suitably employed in useful occupations. I took long walks in the rugged hillside until my feet bled. I rarely spoke, except when addressed. I craved extravagances such as sesame seeds mixed with honey, which were of course unavailable to the remote Aphidnaeans, and when none were forthcoming, I behaved like a spoiled child.

My monthly courses had ceased, which I attributed to my anxiety about Theseus's safety, the fear that my brothers would never come for me, and that I would end up spending the remainder of my days in isolated Aphidnae. To coax the menstrual blood from my recalcitrant body, Aethra applied warm lambskins to my abdomen. When her efforts proved unsuccessful, she redoubled them through the *hodos*—a foul practice intended to lure the womb back to its proper place. I was made to inhale repugnant odors while a pleasantly scented concoction of aromatic herbs was applied between my legs. This, too, induced nothing but nausea.

Unable to sleep regularly or comfortably, I took to walking the uneven ramparts of the citadel that served as my temporary home. I looked south toward Athens and wept for love of Theseus. One night, Aethra joined me. She tugged on my woolen cloak to gain my attention and urged me to sit beside her. "You are carrying his child," she said, and proceeded to explain that many of the symptoms of what I believed was lovesickness were equally attributable to the early signs of pregnancy.

"If my brothers discover this, they will kill all of us," I warned. "They are not the men I knew them to be when I was a girl. We must return to Sparta before I grow too big." But how could a message be sent to the Dioscuri to hurry to Aphidnae without arousing suspicion? We resolved to wait two more weeks and if they had not come for me by then, we would have to ask Aphidnus to dispatch a runner to Athens with word that I was unwell and then hope for the best.

The twins arrived at the end of my third month in Aphidnae. I was relieved to learn from their lips that Theseus lived. He was demoralized, but otherwise unharmed. Castor and Polydeuces had left him and Menestheus to battle it out for the Athenian throne. I thanked the gods that my belly was not yet swollen enough to betray my secret. Yet there was another who could. I insisted that Aethra return to Sparta with us as my handmaid.

My brothers hastily assured me that Aethra would not quit my side; they were taking her as a captive, to be my slave. Though this angered me, I understood the diplomatic reasons for their actions, for Theseus had schooled me well. The debasement of the Athenian king's own mother was a double punishment and served a dual purpose: It continued to oblige the weakened Theseus to Sparta as he would want his mother to be well treated, and it reinforced Spartan superiority to have taken their enemy's mother—the highest-ranking female Athenian—into bondage.

Our journey was to be prolonged once again, however. Rather than head to the seacoast off the Euboean Strait, we traveled south instead. In repentance for waging war on Theseus, my brothers desired to be cleansed through the initiation rites of the Eleusinian Mysteries, an ancient cult centered in the coastal city of Eleusis. Aethra and I were not privy to the rituals enacted at each station on the way to Eleusis. My brothers refused to speak to me of the ceremonies, which were related in some way to the annual abduction and return of the goddess Persephone and to the worship of Dionysus, god of wine and revelry. Another new moon came and went before we set sail for Sparta.

I was not as intrepid a sailor as I had been aboard the *Minotaur*. Every dip and swell of the sea sent me running for the bulwark. So ill was I, so green with nausea, that I feared expelling my unborn child through extended regurgitation. I swaddled myself in a great cloak to disguise my burgeoning form from the prying eyes of those who could not wait to step over their threshold and tell their mothers, wives, and children that they had seen the beauteous Helen and that she was not the sylph of whom the bards sang.

Aethra gazed longingly at the rocky coast off Troezen, her homeland. There she had given birth to Theseus. Did she, too, know somehow that she would never see him again? I believe I felt her loss as keenly as she did.

And still, we were less than halfway home. Polydeuces teased me mercilessly for being such a dreadful sailor, but I was in no humor to entertain his jests. Even if I had been well, he and Castor had lost my trust, and they would need to do much to regain it.

Finally, we sighted Gythium, and soon we had beached the boat and waded ashore. I declined any offer of assistance, fearing that another jest might be made about my weight. Having survived the sea voyage, my next test of endurance was the horseback ride to the Spartan palace. With a bit of effort, I mounted Castor's milk-white steed and rode in front of him. Clearly, my brother had greatly missed his favorite stallion and kept urging him on to an ever wilder pace. I had never before feared galloping with him at such speed—had adored it, in fact—so there was little I could say that would convince him to slow down without giving him cause for suspicion. Finally, I pleaded a general weariness, and he begrudged me a canter.

By the time I stumbled into the tiled courtyard outside the gynaeceum, entered my room, and collapsed upon my bed, I had been away for nearly seven full moons.

~~~

Tyndareus let me alone so that I could get a full night's rest, but the following morning, I was summoned to the Great Hall. I wrapped myself in a cloak and pleaded illness from the arduous journey, but I could not escape my stepfather's anger. He thoroughly castigated me for bringing shame to the House of Tyndareus and for costing him a hundred talents of gold—nearly emptying his treasury, he raged. Fire blazed in his eyes when he demanded that I earn it back. It was time to see me married.

"She is quite a handful," Aethra said to him, boldly introducing herself. "And despite her beauty would make a groom a miserable man. She is still a willful child and should first learn how to be an obedient woman before she can become a pliant wife." Tyndareus took the bait. He could not have agreed more with Aethra's generously offered wisdom. "A half year of solitude and repentance for causing such an uproar within the Spartan kingdom would not be insufficient," Aethra added. "Deny her the privilege of appearing at your feasts and festivals. I will see to it myself that she is forbidden to enjoy the company of her friends and denied the adoring gaze of the public." I feared that one more word would plant a suspicious seed in Tyndareus's mind, but he proved as bendable to her will as they would have me be to that of my stepfather and of an eventual husband. Tyndareus was happy not to have me grace his rooms. As I grew older and lovelier, there was less and less that could be said, even by the most fatuous of flatterers, about any familial resemblance we bore to each other.

When we returned to the gynaeceum, I knelt and kissed the hem of Aethra's cloak. Certainly there had been many moments when I wished I could strangle her with my girdle, but there was no denying her cleverness and quick wit. And, lacking a mother's tenderness and guidance, I relied upon her to be Leda's surrogate as well as my confidante, tutor, nurse, and eventual midwife. She was a prickly woman who did not like to be crossed—something I often did—but I had to love her as the mother of Theseus and the granddam of the babe I carried within me.

Before my enforced confinement began, I did receive Polyxo, who was positively enormous with child, having married her sweetheart Tlepolemus shortly after I had been abducted. Since we had been together that afternoon, it was all the convincing her father needed to see her married promptly, lest she fall victim to marauders, as though pirates abducted only unwed virgins.

Little moonfaced Polyxo, who had resembled an ovoid *prior* to her pregnancy, was even more spherical now. I teased her about it, and she warned me, "Just wait until it happens to you. You won't be so quick to laugh!" For the first part of our visit, Polyxo tut-tutted about how unhappy she was that I had missed her wedding and what an extravagance it was for her family, but that her father had received a bride-price of a dozen goats and a newborn calf, which pleased him greatly. After that, she did little but talk of being pregnant: how swollen her ankles had become, how her fingers resembled stuffed dates, how she felt like a giant storage amphora, how she craved unusual foodstuffs that poor Tlepolemus was at pains to deliver, sending him all the way to Rhodes to suit her fancies. I listened intently, absorbing everything she said, particularly about the changes in her body, all the while pretending to wear a patient smile as though I was simply being polite, having not the least care in my head about the woes of an expectant woman. I spoke little, allowing Polyxo to give free rein to her tongue. Finally, she said, "But we never heard news of you while you were in Athens! Tell me, tell me everything that happened."

Polyxo had been my dearest girlhood friend, and although less than a year had passed since we had last seen each other, that girlhood had become little more than pretty memories for both of us. I could entertain her with tales about the cosmopolitan delights of Athens but could speak no further. I could tell her that I had learned to dance and play the flute and apply cosmetics, that I had discovered the luxuries of perfumes from the East and fabrics that caressed the skin like a lover's kiss, but I could not tell her that I had known the lover's kiss itself. And most assuredly, I could not let slip even the merest hint that I commiserated with her bodily condition. I also knew that by the time Polyxo was delivered of her child, I would have grown too large to pay her a visit. I hoped that she would forgive me for not being able to call upon her then, explaining that Tyndareus had imprisoned me within the walls of the gynaeceum for the next half year.

I forced my tongue to lie, made myself appear frivolous, and identified Aethra as Theseus's mother, yes, but also as my slave, kidnapped by Castor and Polydeuces in retaliation for my abduction.

~~~

Aethra and I had a few months in which to formulate a plan. As I grew ever larger and neared my time, I threw tantrums, some genuine, some fabricated, all designed to send the servants scurrying from my presence. They became grateful to Aethra for assuming the martyr's mantle and resigning herself to accepting responsibility for all my daily needs. After I passed my eighth month of pregnancy, during which my fifteenth birthday went all but unnoticed, I sent Aethra to petition Tyndareus. She confessed that she could no longer handle me on her own. "I am only a common house slave. Helen needs the firm hand and stern guidance of a married woman and a family member," she insisted. "We must send for Clytemnestra."

Tyndareus acquiesced easily, glad of any opportunity to see his favorite child again. My rejoicing was as immense as my fear. Clytemnestra and I had little use for each other. Yet we were blood, thicker than water or wine. I knew, however, that I was taking the greatest gamble of my life.

Three weeks after she had been sent for, my sister arrived. Her appearance astonished me as much as mine shocked her. Clytemnestra's body was even larger than mine, although her eyes and cheeks were as sunken and hollow, her pallor as sallow as it had been the last time I had seen her—the day she pleaded with Tyndareus to spare her from Agamemnon's bed.

I hoisted myself from my chair and waddled over to embrace her gently. "If I had known, I would never have summoned you from childbed," I murmured.

My sister immediately burst into tears. "There is no child," she wept. "She was born dead. A shriveled little thing. Perhaps I cursed my own body when I found out I was carrying Agamemnon's child. I could bear to nurture the seed of the House of Atreus, I thought, if I bore us a girl. The gods heard my pleas and accepted my libations, but they saw fit to mock me by killing my girl inside me." I stroked my sister's hair and tried to soothe her. "I even had a name for her," Clytemnestra sobbed. "Iphigenia. The mother of a strong race." She released herself from my embrace and bared her breasts as if to indicate their uselessness as appendages. "See! I am heavy with milk but have no daughter to suckle."

"Does Agamemnon know you lost your baby?"

Clytemnestra shook her head. "Three full moons after we returned to Mycenae, he left in the company of his brother Menelaus for a raiding party; I have not seen him since. When he departed, I told him that I might be with child, although I already knew that one had been growing within my womb for two months."

I explained my purpose in summoning her and told her that I had willingly gone to Theseus's bed. Aethra glumly concurred that I spoke the truth. "I had hoped never to be ransomed," I admitted, and extolled the virtues not only of my lover, but also of the delights of his palace and of Athens itself.

Clytemnestra nodded her head. "Mycenae is even wealthier than Athens," she told me, "and I was just as quick to acclimate myself to its riches, although not to its king. Agamemnon is as terrible as he is magnificent. I do not love him, I cannot love him, nor will I ever bend to his will, although I pretend to do so." She added that despite Agamemnon's initial lust for her, their marriage had been nothing more than an advantageous political alliance. The High King shamed her daily by making eyes at her own serving women, even fornicating with them if the opportunity arose. It was clear that the palace at Mycenae was home to an intensely mutual enmity.

I did not expect her to feel any love for the monster who had murdered her husband and infant son before her eyes. And now, my proud and beautiful sister had lost another child. Still, I would not become like her, already hollow and bitter before she reached her twentieth summer.

"If you are so miserable in his bed and household, why not take a lover?" I suggested boldly. "Particularly since Agamemnon's attentions are so easily distracted by the female form."

"*You* can do that. The laws are different here in Sparta." True, if a husband was weakly made and incapable of getting strong sons—the future of Sparta's martial dominance—then his wife was permitted to seek out a man who might prove a more potent sire.

"I have tasted love and will settle for nothing less when I am married," I averred.

My sister laughed for the first time since her arrival. "Bold words, my child, bold words! As if you had the ability to choose whom to wed. Aethra, I thought you had taught this simpleton the ways of the world!" Her taunt made me reconsider the decision I had taken. Many times a day I questioned my sanity, but I had no choice. Princess Helen of Sparta could not bear a child outside of marriage.

Clytemnestra, because she could never bear to see me happier than she, began to regale me with a list of the luxuries she had become accustomed to in Mycenae. Through the kingdom's extensive commerce, she was able to enjoy elaborate textiles, terra-cotta vases, oils, beads, trinkets attractive for nothing except their frivolity, precious metals, and grains. "The Mycenaean king is venerated almost as a god," my sister told me. "The people call my husband Zeus Agamemnon— the very resolute Zeus—for he will have his way in all things, and woe to any who try to block his way."

"That certainly appears to be true in his choice of bedfellows," I said. Clytemnestra glowered at me. If she had been in possession of one of the silver-handled daggers she had bragged about, she would have lodged it between my breasts. I began to understand how she might have been able to come to terms with being Agamemnon's wife. If the

High King was treated almost as a demigod, that would have elevated the status of his queen as well; if not as high as *his* exalted stature, it was still greater than the ordinary Achaean chieftain's queen, thus putting her closer to *my* demimortality. In Clytemnestra's mind, she would finally be able to compete with me on more even ground. Our rivalry had begun when I was born. I foresaw no finale to it.

~~

In her usual unobtrusive manner, Aethra began to assemble everything we would need in preparation for the birth of my child: plenty of warm water for the birth itself, cool water for sipping and for soothing compresses, clean linen for bandages and for swaddling, soft sea sponges and carded virgin wool to stanch bleeding, fresh olive oil to be warmed when the time came, salt, honey, and barley water. If barley water was not to be had, we needed a supply of fenugreek or mallow juice to cleanse the newborn. A sharp sterile knife would be necessary to cut the umbilical cord, and a soft pillow would be required on which to rest the infant. We sent for cuttings from the pink flowering Cretan dittany plant, which, once extracted and mixed into a posset with water, would aid me in expelling the afterbirth. I would need plenty of things to smell in case I fainted during the delivery. To that end, Aethra laid by a store of pennyroyal as well as apples, quince, melons, lemons, and cucumbers. I jested that if I didn't lose consciousness, the three of us could enjoy a refreshing dessert.

My sister's heavy postpartum appearance was a surprise element that made good sense to use to advantage. Tyndareus believed, as did the servants, that Clytemnestra was about to give birth any day. He cosseted her as though she were the infant herself, taking great pains not to upset her delicate condition, for she might be carrying the future High King of Mycenae. My sister did nothing to undeceive him. In fact, she played her role to the hilt, indulging in histrionic emotional displays. "She was such a loving sister to make so lengthy a journey in her condition, all to take a selfish little brat in hand." I wish I had been able to enjoy her performances. I listened to the descriptions of Clytemnestra's dramatics from Aethra, as I was still not allowed to leave the gynaeceum to consort with anyone, including Tyndareus. I could not have gone far, even if I *had* been permitted to appear in public. My body had grown so large, I felt like there were two Helens. My breasts, already full due to nature's gifts, had become pendulous and painful. When I walked, I waddled as though I were wading through the muddiest waters of the Eurotas, yet I felt as dry as a desert plain. I could stomach no food, and if I drank too much water, no matter how much I craved it, I could not keep it down. I was convinced that I wouldn't be able to stand another hour of such bodily torment and couldn't wait to expel the baby.

I feared what might happen if we didn't propitiate Eileithyia, goddess of childbirth, although I could not very well expose my visage to the Spartan people, let alone the residents of the palace. So, under cover of darkness one night, cloaked like bandits, our heads and faces shielded with woolen shawls, Clytemnestra, Aethra, and I sneaked out of the palace to her temple and left offerings of pomegranates and cucumber on her altar.

Only one element remained and we needed to figure out how to obtain it without arousing suspicion, as we had been maintaining the fiction that the pregnant Clytemnestra had come to Sparta with her own Mycenaean nurse. Babies were commonly delivered by midwives who traveled with a purpose-built birthing stool, the employment of which greatly eased parturition. Aethra owned no birthing stool. If we found a Spartan midwife and requested the loan of her equipment, she would undoubtedly ask questions that we could ill afford to answer. We could trust no one. Old Adraste, who had celebrated my transition to womanhood, had died of a fever the previous year.

It was late in the afternoon about five days after Clytemnestra had arrived that I began to suffer the first contractions of labor. Most assuredly I was unprepared for the force of the sensation. I thought I had been punched upward from the womb to the breastbone by someone with the strength of Heracles. For certain, the baby would end up springing forth from my chest. The contractions continued, forcing me into my bed, where, as I whimpered and moaned like a whipped dog, Aethra urged me to lie still with my feet drawn up together and my thighs parted. She soaked a cloth in warm olive oil and attempted to ease my labor pains by massaging my stomach and genital area with it. Then she laid the cloth, still warm, over my abdomen while she went to fetch sheep's bladders, which she would then fill with more warm oil and rest them on my stomach to soothe me for a longer period of time than the cloth might do.

Exhaustion from being so pummeled from the inside out sent me into a fitful slumber where I dreamed I had stepped into a raging stream during a rainstorm. My attempts to cross the stream were thwarted by the swift current that lapped around my ankles like lashes of rope, quickly swelling until the waters were swirling about my knees. Soon my thighs were engulfed by the angry undertow, then I was waist deep in water. Terrified, I awoke, screaming that I was drowning.

I was alone.

My bed had become the raging waters of my dream. The linens were soaked through and I was lying in a tremendous puddle. I grabbed one of the wooden bedposts and heaved myself into an upright position, managing then to stand and thus escape the watery grave of my waking nightmare. As I did so, more liquid poured from my body as though I were a human waterfall. I screamed again when I saw that the fluid was no longer clear, but a viscous yellow-green and tinged with blood. "I'm losing my baby!" I cried.

Aethra came running as fast as her bad hip would permit her, soothing me before she could attend to the flood in my bed and on the floor. "This is natural, Helen," she assured me. "It means the baby is ready to be born." She cleansed my body with cool clean water, helped me to sit on the bench by my dressing table so she could change the bed linens, and handed me a cloth to bite down on to stifle my cries of pain until she could locate Clytemnestra. She found her strolling by the blooming oleander along the reedy banks of the Eurotas and hastened her back to the palace. "You're about to give birth!" she whispered to my sister, ushering her into my room and barring the door.

"The stool!" Clytemnestra exclaimed. "We still don't have a birthing stool!"

My anxiety increased. Aethra had told me that if all else failed, she could deliver the babe while I sat up in bed. She urged me to try to recall who might be nearing her time or who had recently given birth. I had only one Spartan friend. Would Polyxo's midwife help us? "Tell her it's for the queen of Mycenae. Say the queen went into labor unexpectedly and that her nurse had traveled with her to Sparta carrying only her knife and her medicines. Say that her sister alone has been given permission to attend her, but that Clytemnestra forbids anyone but a Mycenaean to deliver her child."

With no one else we could take into our confidence, it meant that Aethra herself, with her slow and uneven gait, would have to make the journey to the outskirts of the city to locate Polyxo. She would remain absent from my childbed even longer while she went to find the midwife. If Polyxo was not at home, or if the midwife was not to be found or refused to relinquish her stool until such time as the queen of Mycenae saw fit to give birth, we were royally ruined. Even if the request came directly from the palace, the midwife might be reluctant to surrender her equipment indefinitely. Not only would she be deprived of the tools of her livelihood, but also other mothers might lose their babes or their own lives if their delivery was endangered.

"How long has she been gone? Where *is* she," I moaned. "Has she descended to Tartarus to get that stool? I'm going to die!"

"You're a daughter of Zeus," Clytemnestra replied. "You are never going to die if he has anything to say about it. Now breathe," she urged me.

The pain was more intense than I can possibly describe in words and still do justice to its enormity. "I can't. It hurts too much. I want to die."

"No, you don't. And you can't. You'll just have to accept the fact that you are fated to survive childbirth. Now, watch me." She urged me to breathe through my nose and showed me how to exhale in bursts, like the wind blowing a toy boat across a pond.

Once, my body had been athletic and strong, but the months in Athens followed by those in Aphidnae had provided me scant opportunity for sport. I felt like an ill-made vessel, too weak to be employed for the purposes for which it was designed. My body was drenched in sweat. Clytemnestra applied numerous linen compresses soaked in cool water and lemon juice to relieve my suffering, but she might as well have been trying to contain a flooded river with a wine kylix.

It seemed an eon before Aethra returned, carrying the birthing stool. My contractions were growing closer together. The stool was an odd-looking contraption, like a sturdily backed throne, closed on its sides from the crescent-shaped seat down to the floor, with armrests shaped like the letter *pi*—π—so I could grasp them during delivery.

Clytemnestra expressed concern that she and Aethra were the only ones to attend the birth. "I had three women in addition to the midwife, one on each side of the chair," she said.

"We two will have to be sufficient," Aethra said calmly, indicating with her tone that my sister was not to say things that might further agitate my already fearful state.

"In Pisa, they placed a hyena's foot on top of my own when I sat on the birthing stool," Clytemnestra continued heedlessly. "They say that if you place the right foot of the beast on the expectant mother's foot, it will ease the birth, but if you mistakenly use the left foot of the hyena, it will cause death."

"Tell her to keep quiet," I shrieked, as another contraction racked my body. They had seated me on the stool with my legs spread wide. Desperately, I wanted to believe that Clytemnestra was as fearful as I for my health and that of my child but that she handled her anxieties differently. I clutched the *pi*-shaped arms of the birthing stool, in too much pain to berate her or to beg her to keep her unhelpful thoughts to herself. I prayed that the baby would arrive before sundown as our small oil lamps might not provide enough light for Aethra to see properly.

"Get her another compress," Aethra ordered Clytemnestra. "And hold your tongue—if you can. I'm sure a healthy babe is as important to you as it is to your sister." Aethra demanded that I begin to count aloud, so that we could time the contractions. It was so hard to speak and breathe the way they wanted me to, in those short, swift exhalations.

"Have you pared your nails?" I panted, panicking.

"Of course I have," Aethra replied. "Now count."

When I could no longer get past the number fifty without experiencing another rebounding assault, Aethra said, "It's time." She told Clytemnestra to stand behind the chair with a clean folded cloth of the softest linen and to hold it beneath my buttocks, cushioning me while I pushed out the babe. If my sister could manage it, she was to use her other hand to sponge my face and upper body with cool, refreshing water.

"Shhhh," Aethra soothed, donning an apron. "All will be well. I promise you, Helen. Now, it's time to push."

"Push?"

Aethra explained how to work up a rhythm of breathing and push-ing, breathing and pushing, so that my body was working in tandem with the child's to expel it through my womb.

"I can't," I lamented, completely exhausted and soaked in sweat. "I've been pushing for an eternity and nothing is happening." How in all the gods' names was woman ever designed for birthing? *Push?!* It was like trying to push a boulder through the narrow opening of a perfume alabastron. I swore I was dying of thirst, and Clytemnestra held a cup of cool water to my lips, encouraging me to sip it slowly, be-fore resuming the pushing. "I can't do it anymore! Please don't make me!" I collapsed back into her arms.

"You must," she urged me, and began to mimic the breathing pat-tern she and Aethra had taught me. "I'll do it with you. *Push! Push! Push! Push!*"

"It's coming," Aethra announced excitedly.

"Push! Push! Push! Push! Push! Push! Push! Push!"

I thought I would be torn in two like the victims of Polypemon who stretched his houseguests on a bed of torture until Theseus killed him in the same manner. "Theseus!" I cried his name. "Theseus! Your child is being born."

"Push! Push! Push! Push!"

The agony became excruciating. I was not woman, not human, not Helen. I was Pain.

"The baby's crowning," Aethra said, and the news did not sound at all comforting. "She's too small to expel it." I saw her take the sharp knife from the pocket of her apron. "If I don't cut her, the child will die within her."

"Noooo!" I cried, and pushed with every dram of strength within my feeble body until all went black as Hades.

NINE

I had fainted for just a few seconds. The sound of a mewling child jolted me back to consciousness, and the cool compress on my face revived me almost immediately.

"It's a girl," Aethra said as I pushed out the rest of her tiny torso and limbs. I looked at all three of them—Aethra, Clytemnestra, and the little wondrous darling just removed from my loins—and wept.

My sister handed me the posset of dissolved dittany leaves and urged me to sip it slowly. I had no idea how its bitter taste would help me expel the placenta. Aethra determined that my infant girl was healthy in every way, from her lusty cry to the flexibility of her four limbs to the sensitivity of her skin to another's touch, to the normalcy of each of her tiny body cavities. She cut the umbilical cord with her sharp knife, gently squeezing the blood from it and ligating the end with a sturdy woolen thread; then she pressed the bent cord back into the umbilicus, covering the navel with a small piece of lambswool soaked in olive oil. She cleansed the babe of my bodily fluids with the mixture of salt, honey, and barley water, rinsed her off with warm water, and repeated the process until her skin was thoroughly clean. Finally, Aethra dabbed a bit of olive oil on another puff of lambswool and ever so gently washed the areas around my baby's eyes, ridding them of birth residue.

Aethra swaddled my daughter and laid her gently on the cushion we had secured for the purpose, and then she and Clytemnestra helped me back into bed. "I must hold her," I insisted, and Aethra brought her to me and placed her on my chest. She was warm and smelled of flowers. And she was beautiful, with her sweet little head lying between my breasts, gripping my finger with all the strength of Heracles. Now that she was clean, I could see that her soft corona of red-gold hair was indeed mine. When she opened her eyes, they were the green-gray-blue of her father's—all the moods of the Aegean Sea.

"Perhaps Helen should not suckle her," Clytemnestra said, "since I will be the one to raise her as my own. My breasts have been aching to nurse since I lost my own daughter a few weeks ago."

I looked to Aethra for comfort. Surely they would not take my little girl from me so soon. "But I have not even named her yet," I protested, protectively wrapping my arms around her tiny form.

"She was born with a name," my sister replied. "She is Iphigenia." Clytemnestra reached for Iphigenia and I roared at her like a mother bear deprived of her cub.

"It is for the best, Helen," Aethra said sadly. "Your sister is right. She, not you, must be the one to nurse Iphigenia, and the sooner she begins, the sooner your body will forget its purpose and begin to heal." I looked at her uncomprehendingly. "Now that you have just given birth, your breasts will ready themselves to produce milk; but without a babe to suckle, they will dry up sooner. Clytemnestra and Iphigenia must not even share this chamber with you, for when you hear your daughter cry, your breasts as well as your ears will respond."

"Iphigenia," I whispered to her, "I hope you will live up to your name and become the mother of a strong race. You are very like your mother, indeed—conceived during one ecstatic coupling by a father you will never know. Please—please—don't ever forget her." I lowered my arms and allowed my sister to take my precious girl into her own. My sobs filled the room. Iphigenia, brought into this world without a father present only to lose her mother in the blink of an eye. And as I had lost Theseus, so did I lose my firstborn child. It was as though the last year of my life had never happened.

~~~

I had lost the will to heal as well. For ten days I could not sit comfortably, nor during that time could I expel my body's waste without feeling as though I was giving birth all over again. Within two days after Iphigenia was born, although Aethra had swaddled my breasts with a close-fitting bandage, they became painfully engorged with milk and were hard as marble. Had I Aethra's sharp knife at my disposal, I would have considered attempting to slice them from my torso. Aethra removed the bandage and applied poultices of bread soaked in water and olive oil, and others that had been soaked in water infused with hydromel or fenugreek, but the agony remained excruciating. To relieve some of the pain as well as the milk, Aethra had me submerge myself to the neck in the terra-cotta bathing tub, in water as warm as my body could tolerate, while she massaged my breasts and milked me into the water as though I were a dairy cow.

"We must get you up and about as soon as possible," she said, once ten days had passed. "You must strengthen yourself. Your six-month period of penitence will end in just three weeks, and Tyndareus will begin to make the preparations for your marriage. Clytemnestra is departing today. It is time for you to leave all thoughts of Iphigenia behind and turn them toward becoming a bride."

While Aethra helped Clytemnestra prepare for her journey, I visited her in her room. My sister thought I should not have done so. She said I was making things difficult for all of us and creating unnecessary anxiety, but I could not bear to think of my daughter leaving Sparta forever without my kissing her good-bye. "She has none of your coloring," I remarked with quiet spite to Clytemnestra.

"But she has enough of Agamemnon's." There was a chill in her voice that frightened me.

I held my baby one last time before Clytemnestra left the gynaeceum to proudly present Iphigenia to her grandfather. That was a spectacle I would never have been able to withstand, so I returned to my room and barred the door until I heard the charioteer's crack of the whip on the horses that would speed my sister, and my new *niece,* to Mycenae.

~~~

"Call for a runner," I said to Aethra. "I wish to send a message to Theseus." I knew that by the time the runner delivered his message to another who would sail to Athens with it and deliver it to another runner who would make his way from Piraeus to the Athenian acropolis, it might be several days, but I refused to get out of bed until I knew that

Theseus would get the news. "We will tell him that on a recent visit to Sparta to see her younger sister, Clytemnestra the queen of Mycenae was blessed with a daughter, whom she named Iphigenia. The babe bears the russet-colored hair of the High King and her eyes are the color of the changing Aegean. Her grip is already so strong that she could grasp the horns of a bull and safely vault herself over its back—"

"Too much," Aethra said, holding up her hand to halt my extemporaneous dictation. "It's enough that you told him about the child's complexion. There is no need to refer to jumping the bull. My son is no fool. And you can never be too careful about a message falling into the wrong hands."

Reluctantly, I deferred to her wisdom. But my heart wanted to tell Theseus everything about our daughter. The sound of her cry, her placid countenance and peach-skin softness, her scent of wildflowers. I hoped that she would grow up in a world where she could have a husband of her own choosing, and where—unlike my poor sister—all of her children would be conceived in love.

Aethra insisted on my regaining my figure and my strength as rapidly as possible, pushing me to succeed as though I were an athlete preparing to compete in the games at the Festival of Hera. The irony of what we were doing—ridding my body of its childbed excess in order to enter a marriage bed for the purpose of *getting* a child—did not escape either of us. "I'll never love again," I said petulantly as I begrudgingly performed one of Aethra's calisthenic exercises.

"Don't be ridiculous," she scolded. "Of course you will. And there is nothing like a great love to make one forget one's first love." Once again she took pains to remind me that her advanced years bore testimony to her experiences, although I didn't believe she had ever lain with any man other than Aegeus.

A few days later, Tyndareus summoned me to the Great Hall to announce that preparations were being made to receive all the eligible chieftains of Achaea: If they were too old or already married, they would send their eldest son in their stead. There were to be two weeks of feasting and games, at the end of which time he would choose a husband for me. My cousin Penelope sat by his right hand. After my abduction, he had sent her back to live with her mother, but now he thought that her obedient nature and quiet pragmatism would make her an appropriate companion for me during this time, half jesting that I would do well to emulate her, since the lash of my Laconian tongue would invariably scare off my suitors. I suspected he had other things in mind. Tyndareus and his late brother Icarius, Penelope's father, had quarreled over the rights of kingship, and I was sure that finding pretty, dark-haired Penelope a suitable match from one of my leavings was in the forefront of my stepfather's mind.

His greed had the unintended effect of adding days to my postpartum recuperation schedule. There were so many suitors on his list that he had to enlarge the palace in order to accommodate all of them. He couldn't very well have asked them to pitch tents in the Eurotas valley! Laborers were brought in to give a fresh coat of whitewash to the inner walls of the palace, to patch up cracks and chinks in the stucco outer walls, and to displace any birds that had found within the orifices a convenient dwelling.

Craftsmen and artisans were hired to construct additional furniture. Ordinarily, Tyndareus and his honored guests dined at a table made from volcanic rock the color of onyx. But one table, although it was impressive in size, would be insufficient for the number of visitors he expected. We needed enough couches for all of those would-be bridegrooms to be able to recline at dinner. I watched the men construct the simple pieces from wooden frames and the webbings of cords or leather thongs, and then shape the legs of the trapezai, the three-legged stools that were placed in front of the couches and served as individual dining tables. I wondered why Tyndareus did not reduce his expenses by letting the men share long tables with groaning boards full of food. "I suppose he wants each one of them to feel like a High King and not a foot soldier," Penelope mused. "At least, with a little effort, the furniture can be dismantled and the timber and cords reemployed elsewhere, should it come to that."

"Tyndareus will probably sell them back to the very craftsmen who built them!" I said, only half in jest. I assumed that there would soon come a time when he would find a way to make me feel responsible for all these renovations. Viewed through the prism of Penelope's pragmatic gaze, the king of Sparta would receive bride-gifts that far exceeded the cost of his ameliorations. The chariots, livestock, grain, metals, textiles, spices—none of that would be bestowed upon the bride herself, but given to her *kyrios,* who would be tempted by them to reward the highest bidder. And the already legendary beauty of Helen of Sparta was certain to encourage an extraordinarily intense competition.

Competition. There would be games, too. My betrothal might as well have been an Olympiad. "Are you expecting to award me to the best athlete?" I asked Tyndareus. He reminded me of the value Sparta placed on the integration of body and mind, of strength and spirit. "If his body is insufficiently accomplished, so will be his judgment," he said. "Remember, Helen, now that Clytemnestra has left Laconia and dwells in Mycenae as its queen, and your half brothers have declined their birthright and have no wish to rule, *you* are the heiress to the throne of Sparta. The man you marry will be my successor. In choosing your bridegroom, I also choose a king."

~~~

The suitors descended in droves, as though they had come to collectively raid the Spartan treasury. In a way, they had. Tyndareus had already depleted his coffers of a hundred talents of gold in order to ransom me from Theseus. And within a year, he had gone to great expense to prepare for the arrival of the Achaean chieftains. The cost went far beyond the renovations and repairs to his palace. The suitors needed to be provisioned. Great stores of grain, wine, and foodstuffs were laid by. To flaunt the wealth of Laconia, Tyndareus served meat every night as though the suitors' sojourn was one long festival.

On the first night, I was summoned to appear beside Tyndareus so that the chiefs could admire for themselves the golden bauble they were vying for. That's truly how I felt; even my name—Helen—means *shining.* The men well knew that the kingdom was on the market, but I was on display as the most precious object among its vast assets.

It has been written by others that there were a dozen suitors—thirteen if you include Odysseus, who, as it turned out, had different motives for coming to Sparta. Not true. On the night of their arrival, dressed in a snow-white silk chiton with a golden girdle and matching amber necklace and ear dangles, my hair ringleted in the Athenian style, I stood beside the thronos of Tyndareus and counted *forty-five* heads, fair and dark, russet and silver, enjoying my stepfather's hospitality. Libations were made and the feasting, as well as the competition, began.

They seemed to me no more than a cacophonous muddle of masculinity, behaving as though they were on a military campaign rather than a wooing expedition and speaking loudly in their various Achaean dialects. If it had been up to me to choose, I would have sent every last one of them home.

"You can't pine for the one who will not come," Aethra murmured in my ear. It was the third night and not one of the suitors had paid me the slightest heed except to gawk at my breasts and buttocks and legs and act tongue-tied when they were compelled to look me in the eye and address me to my face. In my imagination, Theseus would stride into the Great Hall in the middle of the evening meal and whisk me away on horseback.

As the days went by, the suitors began to distinguish themselves from one another, not necessarily to their benefit. At first they were like a great tangle of weaving silks. Then I began to pluck out the individual colors, separating them from the giant hank of threads. I began by learning the distinction between the two men named Ajax. Ajax, son of Telamon, whom I took to calling Ajax the Greater because of his size, was a huge ox of a man with a brain no larger than a pomegranate seed and half as useful. Naturally, he excelled in the weightlifting events of what Penelope, Aethra, and I now called the Heleniad. I despaired of Tyndareus favoring him. Penelope reminded me that my bridegroom would eventually have to rule Sparta, which gave me some comfort. With more than forty alternatives, Tyndareus could surely find one who was capable of issuing a decree without first having to learn how to spell it.

Ajax the Greater was competing for my hand with his younger half brother, Teucer. I can't recall much about Teucer, other than that he was at least a head shorter than Ajax, dark haired, and the finest archer among the rivals. What I do remember about both sons of Telamon was that their mother was not Greek but originally from Phrygia. The one conversation I recall having with Teucer was about their mother Hesione, the older sister of Priam, who was now king of Troy.

"My father fell in love with her while he was in Troy on . . . on a diplomatic mission with Heracles," Teucer told me, his vocabulary strangely diplomatic, "but he was . . . unable to arrange marriage terms. For some reason, her family was reluctant to let her wed an Achaean. So he took her with him when he went back to Salamis!"

"Did they love each other?" I asked him. I suppose I wanted to learn whether Hesione had been kidnapped by Telamon or whether she had eloped with him. Naturally, it was all the difference between romance and rape.

He shook his head. "I don't know. I wasn't born yet, of course. I can tell you this, though. They have always seemed very happily married."

Teucer seemed more pleasant than many of his rivals, although I can't say that there was anything truly remarkable about him. Theseus was my secret touchstone against which all men would be judged and—with respect to my forty-five suitors—found lacking.

Ajax of Locris, whom I nicknamed Ajax the Lesser, was darkly complected, of middling height with a runner's build, and had a talent for spear throwing. This Ajax, who went everywhere with a giant serpent draped like a necklace about his shoulders and torso, was a very intense young man, quick to pick a quarrel with the other suitors. He gave the impression that a woman was as useful to him as an oinochoe, which, once emptied and his pleasure in its contents taken, was good for nothing until it was refilled with wine. Perhaps, since the people of Locris were still primarily a matrilinear culture that followed the old ways, Ajax the Lesser was determined to denigrate or despise womankind. "He frightens me," I admitted to Aethra.

"Not so much as *he* should," she said, discreetly pointing out the suitor from Crete. "Idomeneus." His handsomeness was marred by his demeanor, being a thin-lipped young man who never smiled. One thing I will never forget about Idomeneus is that his chestnut-colored hair didn't move with the breeze, even when he competed in the footraces.

"I think he must be an unnatural child," I giggled.

"Son of demons most probably," Aethra concurred. "Crete is also one of the last bastions of Goddess worship. Idomeneus has permitted the razing and torching of her shrines and has turned a blind eye to the ravishing and torture, even murder, of her priestesses."

"I will hang myself like my mother did if Tyndareus chooses *him,*"

I vowed. Aethra could tell that I meant every word I'd uttered, although she reminded me that any suicidal attempts would prove fruitless, despite my best intentions. "If these chieftains represent the finest of the Argives, I despair of the future of Achaea," I insisted. Worse even than Idomeneus was smug Menestheus—the same Menestheus whom my brothers had brought with them to Athens in the hope that the former exile would usurp Theseus's throne. I promised Aethra that I would fling myself from the summit of Mount Taygetos if I had to spend the remainder of my days in the arms of the man who would displace my darling. "I cannot even bear to look upon his face long enough to tell you whether it pleases me," I insisted.

Not only did I despise at least half of these rivals, but I also had no favorite among them. The fair-haired Patroclus of Thessaly, cousin to Ajax and Teucer of Salamis, was sweet-natured and gentle but lacked the makings of a king. At age fourteen, he was even younger than I was, the merest slip of a boy; besides, conversing with him was like talking to Polyxo, except when he rhapsodized about Thessaly's fields of golden grain, its fertile plains, and the herds of galloping wild horses that thrived on its hilly grasslands. Lycomedes, king of Skyros was too old, and I could have sworn that he was already married, with several concubines as well to keep him warm at night. He had no need for Helen of Sparta to grace his bed. Philoctetes caught my attention because he exhibited little use for human contact. Penelope and I once encountered him at the edge of the plain feeding a field mouse to a snake. He jerked his hand away just in time, for the serpent nearly bit him. Then, there was beetle-browed Diomedes of Argos, who made lovestruck cow eyes at me whenever I passed. I think he believed himself deeply in love with me, although he was always too shy to address me directly.

In addition to the athletic contests, Tyndareus interviewed each of the suitors more than once, and the rivals vied to see which of them could offer Sparta the most wealth and bring her the greatest glory should he be chosen. My heart sank when Idomeneus offered the superior seamanship of the Cretans, and my spirits plummeted further when Menestheus promised an alliance with Athens. Tyndareus had no need to be reminded of the advantages of such a union.

The two weeks quickly passed, and my stepfather was at a loss to settle on a winner for my hand. His larders were diminishing, the men grew quarrelsome in their cups, and he feared that if such minor disputes could erupt over dinner, imagine what might happen once he had made his decision! The rejected rivals would tear bridegroom and *kyrios*—and Sparta—to pieces. What was to be done? The days dragged on. The lavish feasting and games and petty arguments continued. It would not be much longer before the palace stores would be completely depleted and the great wealth of Sparta revealed to have dwindled to a precarious pittance.

Penelope had accompanied me to several of the sporting competitions and had taken a fancy to one of the strangest of the suitors. Odysseus, chieftain of the remote and rugged land of Ithaca, had not even bothered to arrive in Sparta with bride-gifts. He dressed in plain, homespun garments with no pretense of adornment. His complexion knew the rigors of a life outdoors, but Penelope was right in spotting something about the man's manner that was more remarkable than that of any of his rivals. For one thing, he spoke well, and it was evident that he gave much thought to his words before he uttered them. "I believe he enjoys being underestimated," I remarked to Penelope. His legs were so much shorter in proportion to the rest of his body that he looked nobler sitting down. Certainly, there was nothing about the man that would make anyone look at him twice, and yet Odysseus almost dared you to give him your full attention.

"I find him absolutely fascinating," Penelope confessed. "I would rather hear anything he had to say than watch another stupid wrestling match or weightlifting contest." On that point, I concurred. And yet, I was relatively sure that Odysseus had not come to Sparta to sue for my hand. He respected my beauty, most assuredly, but unlike his rivals, he was not overwhelmed by it.

The presence of Odysseus was the first puzzle to be solved. The second was the mystery of Agamemnon's. I had not numbered him among my forty-five suitors. I overheard Tyndareus speaking with him, reminding him that he was married already to Clytemnestra and that in fact he had petitioned quite vociferously for her hand. Despite his status as High King, he should not dare to expect that Tyndareus would permit him to dispose of one princess of Sparta in order to espouse the other.

"The Mycenaean alliance with Sparta is an old and honored one," Agamemnon said, his voice ever so slightly colored with threat. "Were my younger brother Menelaus to become Sparta's ruler, our families and our kingdoms would truly become forces to be reckoned with on the Peloponnese."

Tyndareus acknowledged the strength of the argument and promised Agamemnon to give it his full consideration. I tried to recall anything about Menelaus that might separate him from the wolfpack of suitors. *Taciturn* was the first word that came to mind. At least, as many of the other men did, Menelaus didn't salivate lecherously at the Laconian women, whose mode of dress in comparison to that of other Achaean women would best be described as scantily clad. He did not indulge in the suitors' scatological jokes or drunken games. Either it marked him as more of a gentleman or else he better hid his baser nature. But what I noticed most about him at the time, a quality that stood out above any other, was his lack of overt response—if not something of a tight-lipped disapproval—regarding any form of sexuality.

His looks neither fascinated nor repelled. Menelaus had the same russet-colored hair as Agamemnon, a shade that the superstitious believed had destined them both to be kings, but he lacked the imposing stature of his older brother. His hair was cropped much shorter than Agamemnon's leonine mane. His eyes were not the blue-green shade of Agamemnon's but were a dark gray as though they had perpetual storm clouds scudding behind them. Menelaus was well formed, although there was nothing about his person that would encourage a young girl's heart to quicken its pace. With regard to his achievements in the Heleniad, I recall that in every event for which he was appropriately suited—omitting such contests as weightlifting, for example— he placed a solid second. In short, he was not my best hope, perhaps, but he was far from the worst.

My numerous suitors had descended upon us during the month of the grape harvest with the intention of remaining with us for two weeks. By the time Tyndareus wearily announced that he would render his decision on the following day, bellicose tempers were thin as membranes, tensions ran high, and the rivals for my hand had bled Sparta's resources dry for more than two months.

∾ T E N ∾

Idid not sleep that night. Aethra offered to infuse some poppy juice into a tisane for me, but I had already lost enough control of my destiny to hand it over to Morpheus. After all, this would be one of my last nights in my own bed, free to focus my thoughts solely on my beloved Theseus and my beautiful Iphigenia. The muffled sound of men's voices drifted across the pergamos into the gynaeceum, and I strained to hear their words. Unable to clearly discern them, I threw on a cloak and stealthily made my way toward their source.

A knot of men was clustered around the volcanic table at the head of the room. Tyndareus sat on the throne, surrounded by Menelaus, Agamemnon, and one other man, whose identity I could not glean from the rear view. I waited patiently for his voice to give him away. It was wily Odysseus, whom my cousin Penelope was secretly sweet on. "I have a possible solution, if you are willing to entertain the humble suggestion of a man from such a lonely and impoverished outpost as Ithaca," I heard him say.

The sons of Atreus exchanged glances with Tyndareus. All three spoke in low tones, conferring among themselves before Odysseus was favored with a reply. "No matter whom I choose," Tyndareus said tensely, "there is the good possibility of war. None of us can afford that. My intention, as you know, gentlemen, is to find ways to unite, not divide, the Achaeans."

"We all ride the back of the same horse," Odysseus said, nodding in agreement. "Naturally, I would require a comparatively modest recompense in exchange for my counsel."

I held my breath, anxious to hear both the Ithacan's suggestion and his terms. Just then, a fly seized an opportunity to buzz around my head, landing in my hair. Startled and repulsed, I batted it away, but it persisted, attracted perhaps to the perfume I had been wearing or to the olive oil that gave my tresses their gloss. After the tenth such assault, the mite had become my primary focus; and unthinking, I emitted a cry of frustration, which immediately disclosed the presence of a stranger in their midst.

"Who's there?" Agamemnon called, his hand quick to his dagger. I remained silent, rooted to my hiding place behind a pillar. The High King repeated his question. I decided it was more prudent to reveal myself than to risk a nasty puncture if Agamemnon started poking around pillars with his unsheathed weapon.

I emerged from the shadows, clutching my cloak about me. "Helen!" Tyndareus exclaimed. "Go back to bed. This does not concern you."

I looked from man to man. "I think it does," I replied. "I think you must secure the strongest possible political alliance for Sparta, which can only be done by marrying Helen to the man with the most advantageous connection. If I am not mistaken, you would not be having this conversation with the Atridae and the Ithacan chieftain if you did not mean to wed me to one of them. One of the men who stands before me is already my brother, being the husband of Clytemnestra. Please sheathe your dagger, Agamemnon, I mean you no bodily harm, no matter how tenuous your affection for my sister." In a rare moment of humiliation, Agamemnon returned his knife to his belt. Odysseus chuckled at him as I continued to address Tyndareus. "One of the men at your side journeyed to Sparta without bride-gifts, a clear indication that I am not the prize he seeks to gain. Therefore, reason and logic tell me that you wish to further strengthen your ties with Mycenae."

"Reason? A woman's not supposed to have reason!" Odysseus said in mock horror.

"Or logic," Agamemnon concurred in all seriousness. "Good luck, brother," he added, clapping Menelaus on the back in soldierly fashion.

The High King had confirmed it. Menelaus was to be Tyndareus's choice. I admit that I was unsurprised. And unmoved as well. My husband-to-be appeared neither distressed nor overjoyed. The more I saw of him, the more I determined that he was a man who had always been a follower, perfectly satisfied to heed the wishes of those who were older or more powerful. This second son of Atreus was as useful an appendage to Agamemnon as his brazen-hilted dagger.

"Helen, I commanded you to go to bed!" Tyndareus thundered. No man appreciates being shown up by a young woman, particularly a young and extraordinarily beautiful one. I had bested the lot of them, with the possible exception of Odysseus, who seemed more amused than put out by my presence, although I had not yet learned the details of his scheme to avoid a war once Tyndareus announced his selection. "Tomorrow," Tyndareus declared, "when the chariot of Helios is at its zenith, I will reveal my intentions to everyone." That was clearly the end of the matter tonight as far as I was to be concerned. The men held their tongues, attending my exit from the Great Hall before resuming their deliberation.

~~~

Aethra chided me for fidgeting so restlessly while she dressed my hair the following morning. In just a few hours, the details of my fate—and that of the kingdom over which I would eventually be queen—would be disclosed. There was little doubt in my mind that within a year's time I would be breeding the issue of the house of Atreus. "One daughter married into that accursed household was enough," I lamented. "Why both?"

"You know very well why," Aethra responded, curling a lock of my hair with the metal wand we had brought back from Athens. "I'm perfectly aware that my son opened your eyes to the intricacies of diplomatic negotiations and strategic alliances."

"The sons of the House of Atreus have been cursed with bringing ruin on their fathers and upon their households," I argued. "Every generation has been punished by its own hubris in thinking it could escape the curse laid upon it for their ancestors' sins of cannibalism. Cousins turn upon one another, nephews kill their uncles."

Aethra dosed me with my own medicine. "I thought you were the one who believed in the exercise of free will. Curse? If that's what you choose to believe, then it must be true. But men don't need to blame gods they created for the arguments they invented to explain why claimants to a ruling family's throne engage in bloody feuds."

I chose a chiton of aqua-colored silk and a shawl of Aegean blue embroidered with *melissae,* golden honeybees. My bracelets, necklace, and earrings were of hammered gold so exquisite that Hephaestus himself could not have done half so well on his godly forge.

Penelope and I walked down to the valley where the spectators' benches had been erected for the athletic contests. Tyndareus was already there, sweltering in the blazing sunlight, clad regally in garments of deep plum. The suitors began to straggle onto the plain, also attired in their finest robes, with the usual exception of Odysseus, who looked like he had arrived fresh from the plow. Once everyone was assembled, Tyndareus began to address the gathering. He commenced by praising the suitors, finding something laudable to say about each of them. This canny prologue, which I suspected was coached by Odysseus, regained the men's loyalty and primed them with a coat of compliance.

Tyndareus reiterated the sentiment that I had heard him express the night before—his goal of uniting the Achaeans. Divided and feuding, the Argives were no match for the powerful kingdoms of Egypt and Asia Minor. To that end, he demanded that each of the suitors swear an allegiance to the future king of Sparta, the Oath of Tyndareus, which would commit them to defending my future husband—whomever he would be—should I ever be abducted from his household or harmed in any way by another, whether Achaean or barbarian. "Well, I know," Tyndareus continued, "that there may be those among you who will nurse a grudge against the victor, believing that Helen's unrivaled charms are rightfully yours. You will look for the chance to topple his reign in Sparta and take Helen to your own bed by seizing her from him. The Oath of Tyndareus will bind you all to uphold the rights of her husband. My choice remains a secret and will not be divulged until every one of you has taken the oath."

I scanned the faces of the suitors. Some seemed reasonably acquiescent to Tyndareus's proposal; others grumbled and frowned. I noticed Menelaus about to come forward, but Agamemnon stopped him, grasping his younger brother's forearm to pull him back into the crowd.

After several moments, Odysseus was the first to step away from his supposed rivals. "I will happily subscribe to this wisely drafted pledge," he said.

I was so sure that he had devised the oath himself that I almost whispered it to Penelope. I saw her hold her breath while he spoke. "He must know something the others don't," she whispered.

Despite her astute speculation, I decided not to let on how much I surmised. One by one, the suitors stepped forward to express their acquiescence to the pledge. The last to swear his allegiance to the Oath of Tyndareus was Menelaus. Agamemnon did not have to take the pledge as he was not one of my suitors.

Tyndareus declared that the oath must now be solemnized. He headed the procession of suitors to a corner of the field, where a small stone structure, which Tyndareus called the Horse's Tomb, had been erected. A large black Mycenaean stallion was kicking up the dust, impatiently straining at its halter.

"I can't look," I told Penelope, and lifted my hands to my eyes. The horse uttered a final defiant whinny and gave up its brave life to the sharp blade of Tyndareus's knife. From the stifling, metallic odor in the air, I could tell that the steed's warm blood had stained the altar and rendered the ground below it incarnadine. Into forty-five equal portions the flesh was divided, each suitor receiving his share. Forty-five cavities were made in the fertile earth, ringing the perimeter of the temple. Every suitor placed his right foot upon his bloody portion of horseflesh and formally reiterated his oath. Then each man buried his share, raising a small mound above it.

Now there was a renewed crackle of energy in the air. The moment of revelation was imminent. The knot in my stomach was not the progeny of suspense but was born of the realization that my entire life would be forever altered by my stepfather's announcement. All eyes were focused on Tyndareus. I stood beside him, scanning the faces of my suitors.

Then Tyndareus spoke. "My choice has been a difficult one, which is why you have enjoyed my hospitality for so long. Many factors were measured, not the least and most practical of which was the consideration of the wealth and resources that would enure to Sparta in the marriage."

He made no mention of what would enure to Helen.

"I mean therefore to enrich my kingdom by wedding Helen to a man of means who has the makings of a strong leader."

At this point, my brothers, who stood beside Menestheus, discreetly shook hands. Polydeuces gave him a nudge in the ribs. Menestheus was clearly their choice for my hand, and the words of Tyndareus had given them reason to suspect that they might be rewarded.

"You have all sworn the Oath of Tyndareus to stand by, support, and defend Helen's husband in the event of her abduction, rape, or injury. The man who each of you will guard and protect with your ships and spears under those circumstances and in such occurrence is Menelaus of Mycenae, son of Atreus."

Menelaus stepped through the hubbub of murmurs and whispers and knelt before me while I placed an olive wreath upon his close-cropped russet curls. He brought my hands to his lips and kissed them in a gentle show of formality, then I elevated him to his feet. After a few moments of awkward silence, Odysseus raised a cheer. Not to seem peevish already, the other men lifted their voices as well to congratulate Menelaus. Agamemnon came forward and enveloped his brother in a fierce bear hug.

While the others talked among themselves regarding preparations for their individual departures, Tyndareus asked Odysseus to approach. Before the sons of Atreus, he agreed to the terms that I had heard the Ithacan allude to the night before and granted him the hand of Penelope in marriage. Weeping and trembling with joy, my cousin embraced Tyndareus, thanking him for seeing her so finely matched. She looked back at me to praise my newly announced union, but she quickly turned away, her expression guilty. She knew that mine was in no way a love match, where hers was very much the product of a mutual admiration.

I looked forward to the day when I would no longer be subject to the will of Tyndareus, although I wished that I could have found more to cheer me about becoming Menelaus's bride. As soon as the Achaean chieftains and their kinsmen left us, the preparations would begin for my wedding. Tyndareus seemed inclined to host the grandest celebration imaginable—more lavish than Clytemnestra's, even—because with my nuptials the Spartans would be welcoming their future king.

My brothers' disappointment was evident. They thought that Tyndareus should have selected Menestheus as a way of thanking them for rescuing me from Athens. But if I viewed things from my stepfather's vantage, Menestheus had not yet succeeded in dispossessing Theseus from his throne and thus could not guarantee Tyndareus the wealth of Athens, while Menelaus could doubly assure him the Mycenaean resources with his brother the High King married to my older sister.

The issue of who would succeed Tyndareus would not have been important if Castor and Polydeuces had desired to claim their birthright. They would have jointly ruled Sparta, but neither wanted to be kings, informing Tyndareus years earlier that they much preferred their freedom to the trappings of royalty and the demands of tending to affairs of state. Nevertheless, they did not want to hear explanations or equivocations as to the selection of Menelaus over Menestheus. They were already feeling restless. Rather than remain in Sparta while the wedding preparations were under way, they decided to set off on a cattle raid, promising to return in time for my marriage. I felt sorry for their wives. A woman wedded to an Achaean adventurer spent many months alone.

I haven't written of my brothers' wives yet, nor of how they got them, primarily because my two sisters-in-law are footnotes in my own life; I never knew the women well. Sets of twins run in my family as does enmity among cousins. Castor and Polydeuces always had a competitive relationship with Idas and Lynceus, their twin cousins from neighboring Messenia. All four of them suffered from a horrendous case of mimetic rivalry; if one set of twins desired something, the other set coveted it as well. Lynceus and Idas were betrothed to two sisters named Phoebe and Hilaeira, who were also cousins of the Messenian twins. My wild brothers took a fancy to the girls and abducted them! Castor married Hilaeira, who bore him a son, and Polydeuces took Phoebe to wife; she gave him a son as well.

I have always remained angered by the irony that my brothers could abduct women at will, while they sought to punish Theseus for kidnapping me. Livid that they had brought retribution along with the ransom, I had found the courage to confront them about this dual standard during our voyage back to Sparta.

"One day you'll understand, *koukla*," Castor had said affectionately. "Right now you're too young."

"It's love," Polydeuces had added. "Love makes all the difference in the world. We abducted Phoebe and her sister because we loved them. Theseus took *you* like a pirate—for love of *gold*."

I held my tongue on the subject after that. But like a good pupil and a dutiful younger sister, I committed my brothers' life lesson to memory.

Now, several months after that conversation, I stood between the men of the House of Tyndareus and the House of Atreus. My brothers had just informed my stepfather of their intentions to leave Laconia as soon as practicable. Menelaus began to express his disappointment, saying he had hoped to enjoy their company in the coming weeks before the festivities, but Agamemnon once again manned the tiller of his younger brother's ship, gripping his forearm to forestall his too-effusive tongue. "Let them go," Agamemnon advised Menelaus quietly. "Their absence will ease your transition from supplicant to sovereign." His manner chilled me, the same way it had done the first night I encountered him, when Clytemnestra was pleading to be released from his control. There was always something about the magnificent Agamemnon (I might characterize it as a kind of charisma) that made people want to obey him for fear of the consequences. Looking back, I see it was the charm of a madman, brutal and terrifying.

Three days after Menelaus had been announced as my bridegroom-to-be, my brave brothers departed for Messenia. If I had known then what I would come to learn within weeks of our mutual parting, I would have given them a fonder farewell.

ELEVEN

The wedding preparations lasted for months. Nearly a year passed from the announcement of Menelaus as the winner of my hand until our nuptials were solemnized. One morning, a few days before the celebration was set to commence, a messenger came to the palace leading a snow-white mare, a wedding gift to me from Theseus. "I know how much pleasure you derive from riding," said his missive. He went on to tell me that the milky-colored Arabian was bred by the Troyans in Asia Minor, the finest horse breeders known to man. He apologized for not being able to attend my wedding. He was leaving Athens for Tartarus, fulfilling the pledge he had made with Pirithous to capture a daughter of Zeus for him, too. I thought the journey to the underworld was a foolhardy mission, but Theseus was a man who refused to be daunted by difficulty.

Aethra easily divined my expression as I received her son's message. "You can ride that mare all the way to Gythium," she said sadly, shaking her gray head, "but the *Minotaur* will not be waiting for you there." She urged me to forget about her son and to focus my thoughts on becoming a daughter of Mycenae as well as one of Sparta.

That afternoon, while I was working at my loom on a bridal shawl, a rider approached the palace at full gallop. He reared his horse, whose whinny announced the urgency of the matter. A servant came running through the gate and was told by the rider to fetch the king immediately.

I left the gynaeceum and was right on the heels of Tyndareus when he crossed the pergamos. Clytemnestra and Agamemnon, who had returned to Sparta for my wedding, arrived at the gate a few moments later. The rider threw himself at my stepfather's feet as though he feared retribution for his news.

The youth had not uttered more than a few words before Tyndareus raised his arms to the skies and let out a wail so piercing and so piteous I thought the stones beneath his feet would crack with grief. "My sons!" he wailed. "Tell me, how did it happen?"

Castor and Polydeuces—*dead*? My brain, my heart, my soul would not believe it. The rider must have misunderstood. It was commonly believed that Polydeuces was only partly mortal, like myself. He could not die without the intervention of great Zeus.

"They were raiding cattle with their Messenian cousins, Idas and Lynceus," the rider said, "when a dispute arose over who was the rightful owner of the stolen livestock. The set of twins who could devour an entire cow first would gain every head. Idas ate his cow first, then helped his brother finish his beast, thus winning the contest. As they drove the cattle back to Messenia, Lynceus of the sharp eyes determined that the Dioscuri—your sons—were following them. Lynceus and Idas ambushed Polydeuces and Castor. Polydeuces—the boxer—killed Lynceus, but Idas then felled Polydeuces with a rock, gravely injuring him, and killed Castor with his spear. Polydeuces, who barely breathes, says he has no will to continue living without his twin. He begs for an unusual kind of mercy—to be allowed to die, rather than be cured of his wounds."

Tyndareus wept and tore the hairs from his white beard. "Their bodies must be returned to Sparta," he told the man. The souls of the dead could not pass to their final destination, whether it was to be Hades or the Elysian Fields, without the proper funeral rites and lamentations. "What are we going to do about Polydeuces's wishes?" my stepfather asked me. It was me he turned to that day, not his beloved Clytemnestra, for he knew that this time, as a mere mortal, she would not be able to help him. The shock of our loss had suddenly rendered Tyndareus an old man, feeble and fearful, and for the first time in my life, even as he used my arm for support, I pitied him.

"Bring my brothers to me and I will anoint them," I said to the messenger. "And tell Polydeuces that Helen of Sparta, daughter of Zeus, will attempt to intercede for him with their great father."

Our plans for a celebration became preparations for ten days of mourning. Menelaus questioned whether we should not postpone our nuptials but was advised by Agamemnon to observe the appropriate solemnities for the Dioscuri and then marry as soon as possible. By nightfall, the twins' broken bodies had reached the palace. Lifeless Castor, black hair streaming over his shoulders, looked pale as marble, his bloody wound a gaping gash of carmine and brown. Polydeuces's head was split open; he scarcely breathed. I kissed his trembling lips, which seemed capable of uttering but one word: his brother's name. Would there come a time, I wondered, when I would sue to Zeus for the same relief as I now would have him grant my older brother— when immortality would become a curse and not a blessing?

By torchlight, Polydeuces and Castor were borne on litters to our family tomb, a stone building that resembled a beehive. I bade the mourners wait outside while I poured a libation and offered a prayer to Zeus, asking him to see his way to a compromise.

The Dioscuri were born from the same egg, yet it was commonly believed that Polydeuces's remarkable invincibility in all things, even when compared to his brother, surely made him a demimortal. Polydeuces, they averred, must be the child of Zeus, like his half sister Helen. How one son could be sired by the king of the sky gods and his twin be the progeny of the merely mortal Tyndareus, challenges the rational mind. I believed that Polydeuces might not be fully mortal; and yet I confess not to have been entirely convinced that he was a son of Zeus. After all, Leda had never mentioned any visitation of the great white swan prior to the coupling that had produced me. But faith is one of the most fascinating elements of human nature: the belief that something is true can make it so.

Somehow I found strength within my despair. It was not Polydeuces's death I would plead for, but Castor's immortality. "Almighty Zeus," I murmured, "accept Castor for your son as well. Take them both to your bosom." Alone, in the musty darkness of the royal crypt, I watched in silence for several minutes, waiting for my father to accept my offering and heed my prayer. Then, as I gazed upon his beautiful pale face, framed by hair as black as Castor's, Polydeuces ceased mouthing his brother's name. He emitted a little gasp of breath, then a sputter of air, and his lips moved their last, settling into a relaxed half smile that not so much resembled death as sleep. Both twins were now as still and silent as statues.

I exited the tomb into the velvet night and gazed toward Olympus to thank my celestial father. High in the firmament blazed two identical stars that I had never seen before, shining more brightly than any others.

Tyndareus was too overcome with grief to make the blood sacrifice, so for the first time in my life, I wielded the knife that shed the sacrificial blood. I had thought to breed Castor's favorite horse—the milk-white Mycenaean stallion—with my Arabian mare, but in the course of a few brief hours, everything had changed. I ordered the horse brought to me and forced myself to look into his proud face before delivering the fatal stroke. But I was no Clytemnestra. After I had done the deed, I turned away and was sick all over the paving stones.

Dirges and lamentations were sung by all of Sparta. Nine days of feasting and funeral games would follow, after which we would resume the preparations for my marriage to Menelaus. It was hard to think of celebration when, with every fresh memory of my brothers, my eyes were newly washed with tears. Clytemnestra and I were expected to cut our hair in mourning, but with the wedding festivities imminent, we divested each other of only a few locks.

Clytemnestra would now serve me as I had served her when she readied herself to wed Tantalus. She had left Iphigenia in Mycenae in the care of her nurse, claiming that my daughter was too young to make the journey to Sparta. My sister sweetly said that an infant should not be exposed to funeral rituals and that as my wedding days were supposed to be happy times, she didn't want to upset me by bringing my little girl to see me, only to take her away again a few days later. I think the truth of it was that she enjoyed vexing me. She was fully aware that a prebridal state of joy was never a factor for me. I was not anticipating my wedding night with girlish giggles, sighs, and blushes.

On the day of my *proaulia,* Clytemnestra bathed me with scented water and anointed me with oils and perfumes. She dressed me in shades of burnt orange and arranged my hair in cascading ringlets. I processed with her and Polyxo and Aethra to the temple of Artemis to make the *proteleia*—the proper sacrifices to the goddess of virginity and transition: little clay goats and deer to represent animal sacrifice, a lock of my hair, and symbols of a childhood I would leave behind— a toy rattle I played with as a baby and a short tunic I had worn as a young girl. Clytemnestra nudged me and whispered, "The *zemia!*" We had made that payment when she married Tantalus, as all maidens are supposed to do before their weddings, a bribe to the goddess to ease the bride's passage from virginity. Other Spartan girls had followed us to the temple, with wreaths of flowers in their hair, clicking castanets while they accompanied their holy song on flute and cithara. We had an audience that had to be propitiated almost as much as the deity, and of course Polyxo knew nothing of my willingly sacrificed virginity.

"She is overwhelmed by the magnitude of her wedding celebration," Clytemnestra said, straining her words through a condescending smile. My sister removed a gold ring from her finger and handed it to me to place upon the altar for the *zemia*.

We offered a loaf of bread to Demeter and left a basket of barley groats at the shrine of Aphrodite, then continued to celebrate my *proaulia* day with the burnt animal offering prior to the feast. At the temple of Athena, two calves were ritually slaughtered. Menelaus drew back the victims' heads and slit their throats. Then he skinned the beasts, cutting away the meat from the thighs. These he wrapped in fat, taking care to make the proper double fold, then lay shreds of the calves' flesh on top of them. These tributes were burnt on a cleft stick and wine was poured over them. The thigh pieces were burned, and Menelaus and I tasted the vitals, after which the remainder of the calves' bodies were cut into pieces, spitted, and roasted.

When it came time for the feasting, I dined with Tyndareus and Menelaus at the great volcanic rock table. Menelaus fed me honeyed dates and made a great show of enjoying my company, but the eyes of the man who was in the process of marrying the most legendary beauty, the most desirable woman in the world, gave me the impression that he would have preferred to be elsewhere. He was doing his best to pretend to a passion he evidently did not possess.

There was singing and the chanting of hymns, blessing our union and wishing us many healthy children. Menelaus listened to them with a strained expression while I tried to guess at the source of his anxiety.

The following morning, on my *gamos,* the actual wedding day, my bath water was brought by a dark-haired little girl with the face of an angel. This chosen child reminded me so much of Castor and Polydeuces that I burst into tears at the sight of her, frightening her so much that she dropped the *loutrophoros,* spilling half its contents; then, weeping herself, she fled the gynaeceum. "You must put on a brave face," Aethra soothed, massaging my shoulders and neck with her strong hands.

"If I can do it, you can," Clytemnestra added, filling the terra-cotta bathing tub. She scented the water with sprigs of lavender to becalm me. I closed my eyes and tried to relax, but the more I sought to push away thoughts of my recent losses—my brothers, Iphigenia, Theseus—the more those memories sought to intrude on the temporary idyll I hoped to create as I bathed.

Clytemnestra and Aethra dressed me, adding a veil, much against my wishes. "My mother used her veil to hang herself," I protested, "and I'll have none of it."

"It's customary for the virgin bride to wear the veil until the wedding night when her husband lifts it," Aethra reminded me.

"You forget I'm not a virgin."

"You should forget it yourself," Clytemnestra said, and secured the veil.

I regarded myself in the silver-backed mirror I had brought back from Athens. "I look like I'm going to *my* death in this thing." I fussed with the veil's gauzy softness, which kept tickling my nose and making me feel as though I needed to sneeze all the time. My sister had to sit me down again to readjust it.

We left the palace with Menelaus and offered our final sacrifices to the wedding gods. That night, during the biggest feast of all, Menelaus looked particularly distressed. He was afraid to drink too much wine for fear, I believed, that he might fall asleep on his own wedding night; and yet, he was afraid *not* to partake for fear of being too fearful on his wedding night. If I hadn't felt a bit sorry for his nervousness, his anxiety would have been almost comical. After dinner, another libation was made before the singing, when, once again, our procreative capabilities were much prayed for.

The songs over, it was time for the final procession. According to custom, Menelaus grabbed my wrist in mimicry of a symbolic capture of the bride, and Tyndareus officially announced that "in front of witnesses," he was giving me to him "for the production of legitimate children." Then the *amphithales,* a little boy whose parents were both alive, representing good luck and prosperity, was chosen to escort me to the king's quarters of the palace where Menelaus was going to be installed. He wore a crown of thorns and nuts to remind Menelaus and me of the proximity of nature in all her wild and dangerous glory, the acorn being the food of primitive man. The boy ran alongside us, carrying a torch as we rode in a chariot drawn by four white horses.

In the absence of my mother, I had selected Aethra to be the *daidouxein,* which was essentially the maternal role in the proceedings. Her honor was to carry the torches beside the *proegetes,* the leader of the procession, a role filled by Clytemnestra. Agamemnon served as his brother's *paranumphos,* the groom's attendant.

Other runners, maidens, carried torches to light the way, while young boys, the *paides propempontes,* danced along the path, whirling madly to the sound of flute and lyre. Spartan women carried baskets filled with apples and quince, violets and roses, even sandals. At the king's quarters, my *amphithales* retrieved a basket of bread that had been specially placed there and distributed morsels of it to the wedding guests. The basket represented nature tamed—civilized agriculture—while the bread was a symbol of the final product of my union with Menelaus: a child. Another child placed a grain sieve at the entrance to the king's quarters, where a pestle and a grill for toasting barley already lay.

Announcing my arrival at what would be my new home with Menelaus, the *amphithales* declaimed, "I fled worse and found better." Menelaus lifted me down from the chariot. Had his mother been alive, she would have been at the entrance to greet us. As the next step in the ritual, I ate a quince taken from one of the baskets, and then burned one of the chariot axles to signify the preclusion of a journey back to my former home. Since I was born and raised in the Spartan palace and was going to reside in it as the queen for the rest of my days, I thought the axle-burning a bit silly. The gesture was, however, also meant to indicate a renunciation of the past, and that, I admit, was something that was indeed painful and difficult for me to achieve.

Finally, I was offered a plate of dried dates, figs, and nuts, from which I daintily partook; and in front of all of the wedding guests and witnesses, Menelaus lifted my veil. I was now his. He offered me his arm and I favored him with my warmest smile. Before all, I had promised to renounce the past. He was my future, and *our* future was about to begin.

We were alone now in the bridal chamber. Oil lamps provided a gentle glow. Then, for the first time since we had been introduced, Menelaus took me in his arms and kissed me. His lips were soft and warm and tasted of Rhodian wine. It was a gentle first kiss, an affectionate one. I hoped that his desires would teach his body how to obey them. Virgin that I was supposed to be, I could not take the lead, nor were my passions at such a height that the urges of my own body preempted all else. Outside, women began to sing. The lyric was meant to reassure the bride on her passage to womanhood and to encourage the newlyweds to produce a boy.

"Can we shut them up?!" Menelaus whispered. I began to laugh. Then he began to laugh, and finally, we looked each other in the eye with the full realization that for better or worse we were now partners. Still laughing, we collapsed in each other's arms upon the bed.

A bride's girdle is tied in a special way. Only the bridegroom is supposed to be able to untie and remove it, just as only a midwife can undo the special knots in the girdle worn by a woman about to give birth. Our mirthful response to the chanting on the other side of the wall relaxed both of us, but poor Menelaus just couldn't untie my girdle, and thus undress me. "I suppose I could just pull my chiton up to the waist," I joked.

"I have a better idea," Menelaus said. When he unsheathed his knife, I hoped he didn't mean murder. There I was on the marriage bed, a sacrificial ewe on the altar. "Killing the queen of Sparta would not be an auspicious way for the new king of Sparta to begin their marriage," he said, then raised me to my feet again and deftly sliced through the girdle. When I frowned at the wasted beauty of the now-useless accessory, he added, "Well, you weren't planning to wear it for another marriage, were you?"

He undressed me and laid me down on the bed and then removed his own garments. He was a well-formed man, and as he turned around to face me, he looked quite handsome in the lamplight. He stood by the bed for a moment or two, examining my naked form with a stunned expression on his face. "My god, Helen, you are truly as beautiful as they say." He slid into bed beside me and confessed that until now, he had tried to conceal his feelings for me for fear of mockery by both men and gods—to have gained all only to lose it when he awoke from what revealed itself to have been but a beautiful dream.

"Not 'til this moment have I dared to believe it was all true," he murmured. "I have never won anything in my life. Agamemnon has always been the favored one. Now the gods have seen fit to smile upon *me*."

He kissed me on the mouth and placed his hand on my breast, leaving it there as though he was not sure what to do next. I could not guide him. I could make no suggestions without giving myself away. Given his confession of a moment earlier, a man like Menelaus did not want to learn that his young and beautiful wife had even the minutest degree of experience in the arts of love. Perhaps I had not sufficiently propitiated Aphrodite or had forgotten to ask her to grant my *husband* both proficiency and prowess in the bedchamber. Just as Menelaus began to become confident in his own nature, there was a terrible ruckus outside the door.

"What in Zeus's name is *that?*" he exclaimed, completely startled out of his burgeoning desire.

"Oh, gods," I moaned. *"Ktupia."*

"What's *ktupia?*"

"They're banging on the door to scare away the spirits of the underworld. Those obscene songs they're singing and the scatological jokes, that's all part of it. I forgot to tell you. Clytemnestra told me to expect this."

"Can we kill them?"

"Unfortunately not."

After several minutes, the cacophony died down. The guests must have finally decided to return to their homes. I thought it would not reveal too much if I just kissed Menelaus, so I nestled into his arms and tasted his lips again. It was not long before his ardor was kindled, and with scant attention to preliminaries, he mounted me. "Don't worry, little Helen," he said to me, "I, too, have never made love. Together, we will learn to please each other." He took his pleasure quickly, keeping his gray eyes shut tight as if the vision behind their lids was more magical than the vision of the woman who lay beneath his loins, receiving his seed as the dry earth does the spring rain. "My Helen, my queen," he cried, covering my mouth with kisses when he reached the pinnacle of ecstasy. I smiled up at him and gently wicked away the sweat from his brow, smoothing a recalcitrant copper curl off his damp forehead.

His passion spent, Menelaus kissed my lips once more, then rolled over into a deep and satiated slumber. My own desires unsatisfied, I gazed at the ceiling, listening to his muffled snores. *And thus my new life begins,* I thought. Yoked like oxen, together we would pull the plow of a royal marriage, plodding dully through our days. I watched Menelaus deep in the spell of Hypnos and thought about what he had told me—that he had never before won anything until Tyndareus awarded him my hand. I recalled how he had consistently taken second place in the athletic contests and how he always looked to Agamemnon for guidance, forever walking in the larger footprints of his older brother.

I propped myself on an elbow and watched Menelaus for several minutes, wishing I could forgive myself for so quickly passing judgment on my new husband. Wishing that I, too, was able to enter the land of Sleep, if only to quiet my brain of a single increasingly distressing thought: If destiny ruled our lives and the three Fates determined its outcome, had I, Helen of Sparta, been born to marry mediocrity?

Menelaus and I were awakened by another serenade. The rowdy men and women who had sung outside our door the night before had returned to celebrate the final day of the wedding festivities, the *epaulia,* named for the bridal gifts I would receive during the day. Once again, the odes focused on my transition from maiden to woman. I had barely slept and had a headache from all the Rhodian wine, which had not been as watered down as it usually was, and was in a mood to open the door and tell them all to save their breath. They would have done better to sing to Menelaus about becoming a man.

"Good morning, wife," Menelaus said to me, smiling and kissing my cheek with the kind of benign amiability that was better suited to long-married spouses well after their initial passion had died. With Menelaus and I, there *was* no initial passion. When I embraced him, he responded, but his caresses were clumsy. I had never considered that there might be men who lacked the natural ability to make love. It stunned me, and I tried to suppress my surprise. Was it still his fear of losing me that held him back from committing fully to love's commands? A person may be taught a dance if they are already possessed of an innate grace and a sense of rhythm. Menelaus was five and twenty. It was astonishing enough that he had never before made love to a woman, particularly since his older brother numbered lechery among his several excesses. Was this how it would be every night from now on? I was sixteen years old and despaired of spending the remainder of my husband's days in a disappointingly passionless marriage.

I thought about the message of congratulations that I received from my cousin Penelope. It had not cheered me. She and Odysseus had remained in far-off Ithaca, rather than journey to Sparta for the wedding that her husband was largely responsible for orchestrating. Where I saw the conniving Odysseus as the architect of my connubial misfortune, he was likewise the clever engineer of her conjugal happiness. The simple lifestyle of Ithaca suited her well, she informed me, and Odysseus was much beloved by his people for retaining his humility as a ruler. Then Penelope shed her pragmatic mantle and revealed what was beneath her serene, resourceful, and reliable exterior. She and Odysseus were deliriously in love with each other, so much so that he could scarcely bring himself to quit her presence even to plow his fields. She rhapsodized about the enormous bed he had built for the two of them, carved from the trunk and branches of an olive tree that still grew in the middle of their bedchamber. Of course I envied her. But I had to accept that our destinies were as different as our natures.

Foolish people have a way of confusing extraordinary beauty or immense wealth with a concordant happiness. Beauty was bestowed upon me from birth. I inherited wealth. But it was a permanent happiness—the kind that Penelope had found—that I would always continue to seek.

I propped myself up on one elbow and addressed Menelaus. "Today you will become a king, my lord." I gently raked my nails through the matted russet curls on his chest, and he responded to the caress with an appreciative murmur. In that instant, I silently pledged to make every effort to see our marriage succeed. Thus far, although I was aggravated by his reliance upon his older brother and disappointed by his limited lovemaking skills, Menelaus had done nothing to earn my enmity. It was not meet for me to punish him as though he had done me some injury. From now on, I would banish self-pity from my life as I had earlier banished shame.

The hour had come for us to rise, bathe and dress, and then greet Tyndareus, who would formally hand the kingdom of Sparta to my husband. As their queen, my people would look to me for guidance and wisdom, even for leadership. I knew how important it was to show a brave and lovely face to the world, regardless of my true feelings. The time for public mourning for my brothers had passed. My private sorrows must now be reserved for my solitude and the solace of my loom. In my present sadness, I realized how much I must have resembled my mother as I remembered her most.

I wore golden robes and a brazen girdle. My sojourn in Athens had given me a taste for silks above any other textiles; the sensation of its softness against my bare skin was incomparable. But as it was coronation day, my jewelry was cunningly crafted from Krokeai lapis, as I wanted to demonstrate my love for Sparta. Menelaus donned a tunic of purest white linen. Agamemnon and Clytemnestra were waiting for us in the Great Hall. Tyndareus entered the room, wielding the silver-studded staff with the carved heads of the lion and griffin that echoed the relief work on his throne and that were emblematic of the Spartan king. He looked tired and somewhat relieved to be passing the scepter. My stepfather had not been the same man since the Dioscuri had met their death. He seemed defeated, a shadowy figure who had lost the will to concentrate on affairs of state, instead discoursing frequently on the improvements he sought to make to his orchards.

Tyndareus handed Menelaus his staff, speaking the words "A double bind is doubly blessed," a reference to the kingdoms of Sparta and Mycenae now being ruled by brother kings and sister queens. We led a processional to the temple of Zeus, followed by several dozen of our countrymen and women. Along the road they danced, their dexterously manipulated castanets accompanying the songs of praise for Menelaus and me as their new rulers. Proper libations were poured at the temple, and the blood of a ram was spilt to ensure Menelaus a lengthy, strong, and secure reign, free from invaders and inner strife. It would have been a grave error not to have propitiated Eris, goddess of strife, along with the other gods we honored that day.

That morning, my husband held his head high, and I, too, prayed that he would prove every inch a king. It amused me to notice the difference in the way the Spartans treated me. The girls who had played with Clytemnestra and who had so rudely snubbed and even ostracized me just a few short years ago now strewed my path with petals.

There might come a time when they would need to petition the royal family, to settle a dispute, for example. Their smiles, they believed, purchased my leniency. Had I been Clytemnestra, I would have relished the opportunity for retribution. But on that day I smiled, too, for I knew I had already gained it. I wore embroidered silk where they clothed themselves in flax and woolens. I adorned myself with gold and precious gems where they lacked the means to purchase much in the way of ornamentation other than leather and local stones. Moreover, I was now Sparta's queen and had the power to affect their lives in far graver ways than being shoved into gorse bushes or excluded from girlish games.

An official tour of the palace stores was part of Tyndareus's formal abdication. For all my stepfather's miserly griping about Sparta's dwindling treasury, I had expected to see scant quantities of provisions. We could not hope to rival Mycenae for wealth, but what Tyndareus showed us far exceeded my anticipation of our holdings. He pointed out enormous amphorae of wine and olive oil, numerous tubs of barley and wheat, and bronze ingots that would be traded as currency or for smelting to forge armor and weapons and to fashion ornamental plate, jewelry, and accessories. There were kraters of alum used in dying textiles, amber for funeral rites, and stores of ivory, tin, copper, silver, and gold, in addition to items such as carved chests and footstools inlaid with these precious commodities. In a corner of the storerooms were the clay tablets containing the records of all barters and information regarding our import, export, and ownership of the weapons, seeds, and all other merchandise and supplies that were the property of the Spartan royal household. In another area, collecting dust, were the many bride-gifts that had been bestowed upon Tyndareus by Menelaus's rivals in anticipation that my stepfather would offer my body and his kingdom as a fair exchange: more chests, chariots, quantities of fabrics, metals, perfumes, and spices. Menelaus was especially enamored of an ebony footstool adorned with coral-colored shell that had been artfully inlaid to represent a hunting scene: A red-bearded man was chasing a deer with a bow and arrow. He ordered it brought up to the Great Hall where he would make good use of it from his throne.

I, too, found items of delight among the stores, ordering lengths of fabric and perfumes and cosmetics from Egypt and the East to be delivered to our private rooms.

"I do not like the way he looked at you," Menelaus said to me after the servant had brought us our treasures. "That man could not take his eyes off your body. He was too familiar. I will not tolerate such behavior in my court."

"He merely smiled at me, husband. I would not call that over-friendly or overreaching his status." This was a difference in opinion that—much to my distress—would remain unreconciled.

Later that morning, Menelaus and I journeyed into the countryside so that the Spartan people could officially welcome us. In fact, the excursion afforded us the opportunity to visit the farms and inspect the output of crops, livestock, and grain. It was a lovely drive. The air was scented with the sweet yet pungent fragrances of olive and oregano, and the sun peeked through the clouds to kiss our bodies with its golden warmth. There was no rush, the day was glorious, and I asked the chariot driver to slow his pace so we could enjoy the idyll. A gentle breeze rustled through the reeds along the riverbank; and beyond the palace's shadow Menelaus relaxed his grip on his tightly held sense of formality.

Farmers harvesting their olives waved as we passed. One man was culling them directly from his perch amid the lush verdant branches; others were beating the branches with long sticks to knock the ovoid gems to the ground, while young boys and girls merrily scampered to retrieve them.

The reaction of the Spartan men to my appearance among them was not lost on Menelaus. "I trust they understand that despite your making this progress by my side today that Sparta will be governed by a king, and it is to me they will look for guidance and leadership."

"Then you will require this, my lord." I removed a gilded cuff from my wrist and handed it to him, receiving an uncomprehending look in reply. "It appears that you desire nothing more than a glittering bauble to accessorize your reign. You forget that you will now warm the Spartan throne not because you have inherited it, but because you are married to Helen." He began to respond but I had not finished my thought. "I suppose you intend to go off on raiding parties like your brother."

"I intend to go on raiding parties *with* my brother."

I let that response pass unremarked for the time being, but said instead, "Then who do you expect will govern Sparta in your absence?" Before my wedding, Clytemnestra had drawn me aside and quietly informed me that during Agamemnon's frequent freebooting expeditions, she had become High King of Mycenae in all but name. Although her husband was largely ignorant of the extent of her influence, while he was away, my sister heard petitions, mediated disputes, and controlled the stewardship of the wealthiest realm in all Achaea with the efficiency of a military commander. Still, between the lines, it was evident that she was not a happy woman. She had hated carrying the seed of Agamemnon in her belly and was not as sorry as I had originally believed that her womb had rejected the baby, given the alacrity with which she accepted my Iphigenia. Her second husband was a rough lover, quick to take his pleasure of her body without seeing to hers. And yet he slaked his sensual thirsts on serving women when it suited him. Adultery was a crime punishable by death, the retribution often sought by the legitimate offspring of the transgressor, but when one is High King of Mycenae, the rules of conduct do not apply. Or at least that was the way Agamemnon behaved, to read Clytemnestra's words. Not only that, but he was also a warrior and a raider, and it was common knowledge that plundering a village included the pillage of the treasures between any woman's thighs. My sister confided that she bore her disgrace with outward dignity and had mastered well the art of patience. There would come a time, she disclosed, when Agamemnon would be punished for his numerous infidelities.

I glanced at Menelaus and wondered if he would follow his brother down the same adulterous path. He looked to Agamemnon for guidance in all things, much to my disgust. A single night in my husband's bed had taught me that he was nearly indifferent to the nuances of sex, although that was no indication whether he might force his inept attentions on others. Yet his temper was quick to rise when he perceived that I had encouraged the glances of strangers. I, too, was a gilded possession to Menelaus. And he was not a man to be despoiled of his riches.

When we returned to the palace, the charioteer sprang from his perch to assist me in descending. Along the path to our rooms,

Menelaus grasped my upper arm, pinching the tender flesh. "What do you mean by this?" I demanded of him, wrenching my arm away. A discoloration the size of his thumbprint marred the paleness of my skin. At least, owing to my demimortality, the mark would soon disappear.

Menelaus stalked about the room like a lion deprived of his prey. "That man touched your breast!" he said to me angrily.

"What are you talking about?"

"When he lifted you down from the chariot, his hand brushed against your breast. Don't deny it, Helen. I saw it."

"I felt nothing," I said, stunned by his jealous reaction to an act I was not sure had even occurred. "I don't believe he touched me improperly at all."

"That is not for you to determine," Menelaus said, his choler increasing. "I will be the laughing stock of all Achaea if I permit any man to handle my wife, to avail himself of her charms—particularly a common charioteer."

I had to plead with him not to whip the poor man. "What would you have me do?" I asked Menelaus. "I will not shut myself indoors and shun the world because *you married Helen!*" My tears and rage began to get the better of me, and I came dangerously close to indiscretion. "There are men far better than you who would be happy to consider me an asset, rather than a detriment, to their lives."

A scowl darkened my husband's countenance. "Did he take you to his bed?" Menelaus nearly choked on the question.

"Who?" I asked, although I was sure I knew the answer.

"Theseus. You were not much more than a girl then. Did he rape you?"

Was that the only way the Atridae thought that men took their sexual pleasures? I was angry with his presumption. Not only that, I would defend my first love forever against any attacks on his character and aspersions on the nature of our relationship. I acknowledge that Theseus did not have the most noble reputation; but where I was concerned, his behavior was irreproachable. True, I would have gladly become his bride, but I knew that he had no plans to wed me when I slipped into his bed and urged him to make me a woman. I faced Menelaus and irately met his steel-gray eyes. "No, my lord, Theseus did not rape me," I said tensely, measuring every word. "And you will never ask me that question again." Whatever had passed between myself and the king of Athens had happened months before Tyndareus had chosen Menelaus as my husband. I owed the son of Atreus nothing and chafed at his audacity to claim a proprietary interest in me before he had even met me. Already I was regretting the vow I had taken only hours earlier—to look for joy in my marriage. It was the hardest promise I had ever made. And then, there was this . . .

From the flat delivery of his words, I could not discern the primary meaning behind them. Was Menelaus angry or confused? "There was no blood on the sheet this morning," he said.

He had looked? "I have ridden horses since I was old enough to sit upon them. Do I need to explain to you the effects of horseback riding on a young girl?" I bit my words. Clytemnestra had been right about marrying a son of the House of Atreus. They were all cursed, and it seemed that their wives would be likewise doomed to unhappiness.

Menelaus let the matter drop. But I had been warned. Our union was on rocky shoals and we had been wed less time than it took for Helios to make a single revolution.

T he months went by, during which Menelaus occupied himself chiefly with his plans to remodel the palace and extend its grounds. Tyndareus seemed perfectly complacent in his orchards, never interfering with Sparta's governance, as I had suspected he might do. Given his parsimony, I was certain that he would be quick to express his displeasure over what he ordinarily considered unnecessary expenditures. New rooms were to be built, the Great Hall enlarged to rival Mycenae's throne room, and Menelaus had hired artisans to paint every wall with elaborate frescoes of battle and hunting scenes or to illuminate them with brightly colored borders of flora and fauna. Most of the floors were to be tiled with rich mosaics, utilizing as much Laconian lapis and porphyry as possible. It was not difficult to see that Menelaus was trying hard to outdo his older brother. Now that he had the prettier wife, his next step was to have the prettier palace.

I would spend many hours at my loom in conversation with Aethra. We both agreed that my husband's behavior was childish at best, and, at the other end of the spectrum, churlish. "It's because he has no war to fight," Aethra said, helping me card a fresh basket of wool. "Men need an activity, a project to occupy them or they go mad. They have no ability to be idle, if only for a moment."

"Indeed, since a modicum of contemplation might make them think twice about what it is they're about to destroy," I agreed curtly. Menelaus had made it no secret that he longed to be on a raiding party. As I understood it, for men like my husband and his brother—

in fact, for all the Achaean chieftains, according to Menelaus—there was nothing like the fever that I tartly termed *plunderlust*. To hear him rhapsodize about these expeditions, neither wine, nor women, nor even the chewing of hallucinogenic laurel leaves (as the Pythoness at Delphi did before she made her oracular predictions) could provide a man with the same thrill as sacking a city or town and despoiling its inhabitants and its property in every way.

And this was the man who was going to be a father in a few moons. It took longer for my body to show the obvious effects of pregnancy this time. But I was more ill than I had ever been when I carried Iphigenia. I vomited so often in the mornings that it seemed as though I spent the entire afternoon eating parsley by the bushel to sweeten my breath. All the chamomile tisanes in Achaea availed little. And yet, in the evenings, I had a tremendous appetite for physical affection. At first, Menelaus was happy to comply with my voracious needs, and I looked forward to his caresses and to feeling the sturdy warmth of his body entwined with mine. I pretended to blame my pregnancy for my boldness when I finally achieved the courage to show him how to touch me. I tried to teach his fingers, lips, and tongue to learn my body. Sometimes he was an eager student; on other occasions he expressed impatience and questioned the scope of my desires, calling them unnatural for a woman and branding me a sybarite. I honestly think that he was embarrassed to have a wife who was such a wanton in bed, and the frequency with which I urged him to perform made him ill at ease. The Fates had played a cruel trick on me. Menelaus had married the most beautiful woman in the world; how many men would gladly have exchanged places with him! There were nights when I would humiliate myself begging him to pleasure me. Naturally, he also assumed that I had developed my appetite between Athenian sheets.

As I came closer to term, Menelaus refused to share our bed for fear I would compel him to make love to me. He was certain we would injure our unborn child. I believe he thought I was seeking a way to miscarry because pregnancy temporarily marred my perfect figure. He must truly have thought me a shallow woman. I was not trying to expel my babe prematurely, and any man who thinks a woman takes such a decision lightly is an uncomprehending fool not worthy of being called a man.

My sister, however, did everything she could *not* to carry Agamemnon's babe, but to no avail. Clytemnestra sent me word that despite her frequent use of pessaries made from lambswool soaked in lemon juice, her husband's seed was more powerful than her prophylactics, and she was, unfortunately, with child again. Her hatred for him was as strong as ever. My older sister was never prone to forgiveness; but since the man whose bed she warmed—if he wasn't with one of his serving women—had slaughtered her husband and baby boy in front of her, I admit that I sympathized with her revulsion. When Tyndareus permitted Agamemnon to wed Clytemnestra, she gave up all faith in the power of love. From that day forward, her concentration was focused on power itself as a means to an end.

It was nearly time. A small, low cot was brought into my rooms to ease the first pains of labor. I lay flat on my back with a soft cushion beneath my buttocks, my feet drawn up together, but with parted thighs. As my cervix began to dilate, Aethra introduced her finger, generously coated with olive oil, at the too-tender opening. I yelped in pain. "It hurts! Cut your nail!" Aethra showed me how short her nails indeed were, but still I acutely felt her efforts to encourage the widening of my womb. When she was satisfied that my cervix was dilated to the size of a hen's egg, she and Polyxo assisted me in moving to the birthing stool.

Aethra had obtained her own stool so we would never again have to scramble around Sparta to borrow one from another midwife. After Iphigenia was born, I had sent a basket of dates and pomegranates to the generous soul who had laid aside her business to loan us her stool. This time, two palace serving women and Polyxo, who had come all the way from Rhodes just to be with me for the birth, stood by in attendance, so we had the full complement of ladies surrounding me. Polyxo was in a happy mood. She had put on a deal of weight in the past year or two, but she had retained her optimistic spirit, reflected in the warm and genial glow of her moonface.

With your birth, Hermione, my body remembered its lessons, and although I might as well have been standing under a waterfall, so drenched was I with sweat, I found the pushing less of a travail.

And with the element of secrecy removed, I assumed—incorrectly—that there was less of a danger with this birth. I breathed and pushed and screamed and screamed and pushed and breathed, and as your head breached my elastic walls, the room fell silent, save my cries of struggle to expel you. I realized then that there was something terribly wrong. I looked down at Aethra's grave expression. "What's the matter?" I thought of Clytemnestra and her stillborn babe. Was I giving birth to death? It had been prophesied that this would be so.

"The cord is wrapped around the baby's neck," Aethra said, her voice betraying her level of concern. "You must hurry to push the child from your womb, and I will do my best to save it." With all the strength I had, I forced my body to obey Aethra's commands, and a little girl, more blue than pink, was delivered of me. I held my breath and watched Aethra as with all due speed she sought to unwind the umbilical cord from around your tiny throat without causing you further injury. You may not believe this now, Hermione, but I despaired of losing you from the moment you first came into this world. *Dear Eileithyia,* I prayed to the goddess of childbirth, *let her live.* I begged her not to punish me for the daughters of Leda's lack of sympathy toward the sons of Atreus. If my babe survived, I would propitiate the shrine of Eileithyia every day for a month.

After many agonizing moments, Aethra prevailed, and soon your skin began to regain its proper rosy hue. She inspected your every cavity for signs of damage or marks upon your person, and although you looked quite battered and bruised from your ordeal, she pronounced you fit to take your place in the world as a princess of Sparta. As an honor to your father, I waited until he returned from a hunting trip, assuming that he might wish to have a say in selecting the name for his first child, although girl children were considered inferior to boys.

I feared Menelaus's reaction to the news that his firstborn was a daughter. The House of Atreus, through the Houses of Tantalus and Pelops, were known for begetting strong sons—so strong that they overpowered each other's families to the point of murder. What use, I thought, would my husband have for a tiny girl? But Menelaus surprised me greatly. By the time he returned to Sparta, he was presented with a daughter who resembled him in so many ways that I sought in vain to find a trace of myself within her, for you possessed the russet curls and freckled skin, particularly across the face, arms, chest, and throat, that was pure Menelaus. And he was delighted with this miniature female image of himself.

I told him of the terrifying moments accompanying your delivery in every particular and how you bravely fought for breath. "Would you like to name her, my lord?" I asked Menelaus.

He grew thoughtful, running his fingertips through the short hairs of his beard as though it would aid his decision. "I will give her a name of my people," he said, referring to his ancestors, the tribes of Aryan horsemen who came down from the northern plains, overwhelming the agrarian Goddess worshippers with weapons of hammered bronze. "Hermione. It means 'strength,' for that she has aplenty to have withstood her mother's near strangulation upon her birth."

All of my goodwill evanesced in an instant. "Dare you insinuate that I tried to kill my own daughter in the very act of giving birth to her?!"

"I know nothing of childbearing, Helen. I can only arrive at a conclusion based upon the information you have yourself provided me."

I have never been quick to violence like Clytemnestra, but I admit that even in my severely weakened state, I used my last bit of strength in an attempt to claw out my husband's eyes. Aethra tried to soothe me. "It will do your health no good to anger now. Your body is as battered as Hermione's. You must rest, my lady." She glared at Menelaus.

And so, you became the apple of your father's eye, always more his daughter than mine. Even when our first son, Pleisthenes—named for both a brother and a cousin of his father's—was born a year later, your star was not dimmed. After another year, the twins, Maraphius and Aethiolas, entered this world, and Menelaus's dotage over you never ceased. There were jokes about the palace that Sparta's ruler had been weakened by a female no higher than his knee. As for my role, I felt like nothing but a brood mare those first few years of my marriage.

Clytemnestra commiserated. She had given birth to a daughter shortly after I was delivered of you, Hermione, and named her little girl Electra for her amber-colored locks. Electra resembled Agamemnon as much as you were the mirror image of your father. The year my twin boys were born, Clytemnestra had another daughter, Chrysothemis, a yellow-haired child whom she said favored me most in looks for her golden coloring. My sister confessed in the most couched terms that she found it difficult to love the children of Agamemnon, adoring Iphigenia more than she could ever bring herself to care for little Electra and even tiny Chrysothemis. The reason was clear: Though no child of Clytemnestra's, Iphigenia had not sprung from her husband's vile loins.

Over the years, Menelaus had let his beard grow long, a sign that he had given up the notion of battle, as a long beard was an enemy target in close combat. For a few years our region enjoyed a relative peace, although my husband still participated in piratical raids whenever he claimed that our treasury was depleting. The realm had settled into a kind of placid complacency, but during the fourth or fifth year of my marriage, the mood on the Peloponnese began to shift and darken. Talk of war became a frequent topic of discussion among the Achaean chieftains. Penelope gave birth to a son whom Odysseus named Telemachus—Final Battle—as though it were a portent of things to come. She wrote to me that on Telemachus's birth, an oracle had predicted that his father would go off to battle and not return home for twenty years. This news put my pragmatic cousin into a panic, and the wily Odysseus was equally concerned. No one dared dispute an oracular prediction.

When I had Menelaus's ear, I asked him if he thought the Greeks would go to war. Troy was the territory most often mentioned in their discussions of battle and of the weakening economy, but sometimes there was talk of Ilios, and a few times I heard the name Wilusa bandied back and forth.

"They are all the same place," Menelaus replied. "The Hittites of Anatolia call the great city Wilusa, which is Ilios in our dialect. We would invade Troy if we can find a good enough excuse," he added gruffly. "King Priam controls the Hellespont—the narrow entrance to the Black Sea—and collects a duty on all goods that go in and out of the channel in both directions: to the north and south."

"What does that mean for us?"

"It means that my brother—among others, of course—is tired of paying tariffs to Priam on the corn, spices, hides, silks, and other goods that pass through the Hellespont. After all, the name of the strait is not an Asian one. It's Greek. Comes from Hellas. We are the Hellenes and that part of the world is rightfully ours."

Clytemnestra had confirmed it. She had sent me word on more than one occasion that Agamemnon was itching for a fight. He had a warrior's spirit and was not content to remain in Mycenae for any length of time. She often told me that he wasn't happy unless he was hacking and slashing and conquering things. Ironically, my sister was more like her brutal husband than she thought, or would perhaps admit. A taste for blood and a volatile temperament were qualities they shared in abundance.

"Do you think we will go to war with Troy over customs duties?" I asked Menelaus. I knew that if his older brother was contemplating a raid of major proportions, Menelaus was certain to be right beside him. By now my husband had grown accustomed to my interest in politics and diplomacy. In that, I confided to him, I had indeed been schooled by Theseus. Menelaus was never sure what to make of my desire to fully comprehend what he was quick to remind me were manly arts; although he had to acknowledge, begrudgingly, that the queen of Sparta was no foolish girl content to ply her loom and play with her cosmetics and her babies all day.

"I have opened negotiations with Priam for better trade concessions, but we are at an impasse," Menelaus said. "He keeps promising to dispatch an envoy, but it is hard to credit his commitment to diplomacy when no such man has appeared."

"You are content to settle the matter by diplomacy, then?"

Menelaus fixed me with an unfathomable gaze. It was often his way, I learned, and for years I struggled to penetrate his inscrutability. What tempests lay behind the storm-cloud gray of his eyes? "You think me too much like my brother, Helen. I would talk first, and when that fails, use the sword. Agamemnon has always done the reverse. To answer your question, we are fully aware that Mycenae and Sparta alone cannot take Troy. The city is far too powerful for two small Achaean kingdoms to challenge its superiority; and Priam's vast wealth, which dwarfs that of my brother's, enables the old king and his fifty sons to outnumber us with weaponry and with warriors. I am my brother's right hand wherever he chooses to venture, but the other

Achaean chieftains have far less reason to risk all in order to topple Priam's stronghold. Agamemnon knows that they would require a very compelling reason to join forces with Argos and Laconia."

Our discourse was interrupted by the arrival of a messenger from Mycenae. He had been dispatched by Lycomedes, king of Skyros, to bring news of great import to the High King concerning the future of Athens; Agamemnon, upon hearing it, had sent the runner to us.

As was the custom, food and drink were ordered and consumed, and the herald was treated as an honored guest before he was permitted to perform the duties for which he had been engaged. Anxious and impatient, I awaited the delivery of the youth's news. Finally, after a dessert of honeyed figs, Menelaus permitted him to discharge his office.

It was delivered in few words and with no show of emotion. Theseus was dead and Menestheus was now the Athenian king.

The news caught me with such force, it was as though a hand had grabbed me by the throat, crushing my windpipe until I could no longer breathe. The room swirled out of focus before my eyes, and I sank to the floor, sliding from my seat by Menelaus's throne and sending my footstool toppling off the platform. My next memory was of a servant bathing my forehead with a moist cloth and offering me a drink of wine. "Tell me what happened," I begged the messenger.

"He has done his office," Menelaus said tersely, evidently having received the particulars while I lay between wake and sleep.

"Please, you must tell me," I insisted, becoming hysterical. "The queen of Sparta commands you!"

At this, the young runner could not fail to repeat his message. "After a four-year sojourn in Tartarus, Theseus returned to Attica to find his kingdom in a shambles. In his absence, the usurper Menestheus had gained a stronghold. Although he struggled mightily to restore order and to regain the confidence of the Athenian people, Theseus could not recapture their support. They were all for Menestheus; there was nothing he could do. Theseus therefore went to Skyros where he had property in the rocky kingdom, thinking to live out his days in solitude. But an accident befell him while he was walking along the cliffs of his estate, surveying his lands. Losing his footing on a loose stone, he stumbled and, pitching forward, plunged to his death in the churning waters below."

It was almost the same way his father had perished. And there was something about the image that disturbed me deeply. I found it too much to believe that after all his extraordinary exploits, where Theseus had met danger and faced it down with the courage of a leopard, that he would lose his life in the simple act of taking a stroll. I refused to believe it, refused to accept that there was not some foul play involved. But all my suspicions would not bring him back. My only love, the father of my firstborn child, was gone.

To escape the quotidian dullness of my Spartan existence and my loveless marriage, I had often allowed my most private thoughts to travel, daydreaming of an alternate universe where Theseus would come for me; we would leave everything else behind and create a new life for ourselves, subsisting exclusively on love. Now, even my fantasies had been cruelly destroyed. No more would I hope to see the crinkles at the corners of his eyes and the smile lines that heralded his amusement. Those orbs that changed their color to reflect the myriad shades of the cool Aegean would never look upon those waters again. The muscled body in whose arms I only once found the greatest delight a woman can know would decay into dust; only his shade would wander the underworld, returning to Tartarus sooner than he had ever anticipated.

"Was there any word from my sister?" I wanted to know, speaking through my tears.

"The queen of Mycenae said that Argos grieves for Theseus and libations were made in his memory."

Was that what I wanted to hear? I thought of poor Iphigenia, barely seven years old, robbed forever of the father she never knew. I had hoped that Clytemnestra would give me a hint, however thickly veiled, that she had done Theseus some special honor for the child's sake. But all the spilt wine and blood in the world would not wash away my sorrow, and all the offerings of milk and honey could not sweeten it.

Once the messenger had departed, Menelaus chided me for my unseemly behavior. "Any fool would think you were in love with Theseus," he scolded. "How dare you shame me—and Sparta—and the House of Atreus—in the presence of a lowly messenger!" My husband was enraged, but my ire was perhaps even stronger.

"What will it avail you to know whether or not I loved him? What can it change? Nothing! But since you have always been so keen to know the truth—yes, I loved Theseus! Deeply. More than that, you have no need to know. He cannot touch you now, nor ever could have, save in your jealousies. You know me to be a faithful wife. My memories, however, are my own. I beg you to leave me in peace with them." I swept from the Great Hall and retreated to the shadowed solitude of my rooms.

Summoning Aethra, I disclosed to her, with an aching heart, the most devastating and sorrowful news a mother can ever hear. Aethra keened and cried loud enough for the sky gods on Mount Olympus to hear her lamentations. She tore clumps of hair from her old white head and rent her garments. For several hours afterward, I held Theseus's grieving mother in my arms as if she were my helpless babe.

That night, Menelaus took me with such a fevered passion, it felt as though he was trying to flood my body with his seed in an attempt to purge it forever of all thoughts of Theseus.

⊱ FOURTEEN ⊰

L ittle Nicostratus was the issue of that near violation. By the eighth year of my marriage, he was learning to walk, possessed of a toddler's insatiable curiosity and indefatigable energy. Aethra spent half her days running after him in an effort to prevent him from doing himself some injury through one of his exploratory perambulations. By that time, you, Hermione, were beginning to blossom into a very grave young lady. I remember the way you would walk by your father's side, your strawberry-colored hair tousled by an errant breeze, barely speaking yet absorbing everything. It seemed as though you were storing away each recollection, every nuance of human action and interaction, every conversation. Pleisthenes, having reached the age of seven, was taken by the Spartan elders into the *agogi* system to receive the ritual indoctrination and rigorous training demanded of a hoplite, our elite warrior class. Next year, the twins would be sent away as well.

The parents of sons training to become hoplites would not see their boys again until they attained their majority. Losing Pleisthenes was very difficult for me. I had barely gotten to know my firstborn son and he was being ripped from me. I had finally remembered which butterflies were his favorites, had nearly cured him of his childish lisp, and he was just beginning to learn the lyre, musicianship being considered an accomplishment for Achaean boys. The elders were taking away a little boy who still tripped over his sandal laces. Pleisthenes would return to me a strong and stoic young man who I was sure I would scarcely recognize. Menelaus was more resigned to the farewell. It was an honor to the family. In my view, we were honored enough, by virtue of being the royal household. But there was nothing I could do to prevent Pleisthenes's departure even if I had wanted to. It was the Spartan way and I was Sparta.

Menelaus consoled himself for his loss by favoring Hermione all the more. He rarely spent time with Maraphius and Aethiolas, figuring that the twins would be taken from us in another year, so there was no reason to make their loss any greater by getting to know them. I disagreed and sought to compensate for their father's dwindling affections and increasing love for Hermione by lavishing more attention on the twins. Besides, they reminded me so much of my twin half brothers. Their dark curls and their sportive, highly competitive natures were Castor and Polydeuces in miniature.

As the years wore on, I became increasingly disaffected: not only with the dullness of my daily existence, but also with the entire ethos of the Spartan culture. Pleisthenes being taken away from me to be raised as a warrior not too many years after he had learned to run, encapsulated the Laconian virtues of pragmatism. I remembered how much pride Theseus had taken in his Athenian cosmopolis. In marked contrast, we Spartans had no art to admire and no architecture to take one's breath away. We were a culture focused on a solitary aim: to be prepared for war at a moment's notice; and even more to the point, to be possessed of the most advanced and best-trained elite forces ever known to the civilized world.

I had endured Menelaus's continual jealousies, often in silence. Yes, all eyes were upon me when I appeared in public, but I was their queen: where else should my subjects gaze? Yet in every look he interpreted desire. This, too, I will acknowledge was most likely true, but never did I encourage a man to act upon his thoughts. My husband blamed me for my beauty, and many times in the presence of others he rued the day when we were wed, for he had not known a moment's peace since our *epaulia*. Dark dreams of infidelity tormented him, and he shrugged off my repeated sweet assurances that he was being plagued by mere fantasy. The climate in the royal household was always tense. Whenever I was in the presence of my lord and others, I felt the watchful gaze of his gray eyes, their ever-present downward slant of disapproval. I did my best to love him and harbored guilt when I admitted how difficult that was. I honored Menelaus and did my duty by him, but I knew the difference between dignified tolerance and a genuine passion. How greatly my union contrasted with that of Penelope and Odysseus. After the same number of years of marriage, the flame of their love still blazed as bright as it had done on the day they left Sparta. On that day, Penelope, riding off in Odysseus's chariot, lowered her veil to shield her face from her family as a sign that she was choosing her husband over them.

It was also in the eighth year of my marriage that the fetid stench of war's hot breath threatened our realm. And yet, my husband did not speak of it with me directly, nor did he bring me into his official counsel or take me into his private confidences. One morning as I was making my toilette, two of the armed palace guard violated the sanctity of my rooms by entering my chamber unannounced. Nico, afraid of the burly metal-clad giants, immediately burst into frightened sobs and scurried for my skirts like a terrified puppy.

"What does this mean?" I demanded as they searched the room. "Look, you have frightened the young prince!"

"We have come for the bronze, Your Majesty." One of the soldiers grabbed the mirror in my hand and tried to wrest it from me. Nico's wails grew louder and more agonized seeing his *mitera* so rudely handled. "The king's orders," one of the men insisted as we struggled for the ornament. He was bruising my wrist with his grip, which was of course much stronger than my own. The mirror flew out of my hand and landed a few feet away. Like thieves, the guards ransacked my rooms, clearing my dressing table with one swipe, spilling pots of ointments and cosmetics. They informed me that they had been ordered to investigate every room in the gynaeceum for items containing even the smallest scrap of bronze.

Wasting no time, I dispatched Aethra to find my husband and bring him to me. Two of my maids immediately threw themselves to the floor to recover as much of my precious makeup as they could, but most of the powder had been ground into the stone by the soldiers' sandals, staining it carmine, lapis, ochre, and black.

Within minutes, Menelaus appeared in the doorway. "Explain yourself!" I commanded. "Why have you sent the palace guard to my rooms to rummage through my personal effects, behaving like common sea raiders? Where is their respect for their queen? They barge into a woman's private chambers unannounced. They request no audience with me and then have the audacity to plunder my possessions!" By now I had to raise my voice to be heard above the sound of Nico's terrified bawling. "Look what they did to your son!" I said, scooping the toddler into my arms, trying to soothe him with honeyed whispers and soft caresses while around me chaos reigned.

"Matters of state," Menelaus muttered, tugging at his beard and looking somewhat sheepish.

His answer was unsatisfactory to me. I accused him of speaking even more laconically than native Laconians. "For Sparta's sake you would let the elders take my *sons;* is not that enough? Will you rob me of everything that is precious to me? I am not some serving woman or farmer's wife. I am the queen!"

"This is only the beginning," he said as any artifacts of bronze— my mirrors, combs, hairbrushes, jewelry—were tossed into woven sacks by his loutish soldiers. "The High King is planning a raid of great proportions and is in need of more weaponry. He has called for bronze from all sources to be collected and melted down to forge armor and armaments."

"Then let the High King find his bronze elsewhere. Sparta is not some petty, frightened village to be despoiled at will by your brother's ambitions. Let him pillage where he always does—from the coast of Anatolia, from the Cyclades, or from Egypt."

"Helen, I must," Menelaus insisted grimly. "It will take more than a few women's trinkets to arm hundreds of men. Agamemnon has commanded me to collect all the bronze to be found in Sparta. He is not depriving you alone of your little baubles. The entire kingdom must contribute."

"Do you intend to send your guards house to house?" When Menelaus nodded but did not expound, my heart grew heavy in my chest, for I feared that something dreadful was still to come.

"Not just the homes, but the temples as well."

"The temples? Your brother would have us despoil our own sacred sites?!" I was aghast. Even Agamemnon could not intend for the shrines to be plundered, for the sacred images of the gods and goddesses whom he believed controlled our destinies to be treated as scrap metal.

"And the tombs, Helen. Including the royal tomb." Menelaus looked as though he wished there had been a way to break the news to me more gently, but his voice had assumed a tone of finality that after eight years I recognized all too well.

"You would desecrate the tomb of the House of Tyndareus for your brother's ends?!" If I had not been holding our son, I would have hurled a perfume alabastron at my husband's head. I was not prone to fits of temper; that was always *Clytemnestra's* way of handling betrayal or disappointment. My ferocity lay within me like a lion slumbering in the summer heat, but now it was awake and eager for blood. "Is there no end to the hubris of the sons of Atreus? My brothers—national heroes—whose helmets and shields, their breastplates and their swords, lie as tributes to them in the royal crypt—these you would turn to molten bronze to satisfy the whims of a power-mad tyrant?" My tears flowed like hot rain down my cheeks and throat, splashing little Nico, who still clung to my breast. Hubris is more than mere pride: it encompasses inappropriate violence against the innocent, including the dead. It includes insolence—which Agamemnon possessed in abundance—and impiety—as exhibited by the High King's order to desecrate altars, shrines, and temples. Not even Tyndareus, a man well known for his covetousness, would have dared to challenge the gods, but the ethos of the House of Atreus was all about the complete subjugation of everything to personal power.

"If you believe that your brother is in the right, you are as mad a man as he is, and I despise you for it," I told Menelaus. "And if you disagree with his commands, yet execute them nonetheless, you are a weak man, and for that I despise you even more. If you do not believe that hubris leads to *atē*—ruin—then you are as foolish as you are weak and unfit to rule any kingdom, let alone Sparta, the strongest realm in all Achaea."

I dismissed him from my sight. Unable to calm Nico, I gave him to Aethra, whose soothing voice and healing hands always produced the desired effect, while, with the help of my serving maids, I reassembled the remaining items of my toilette.

~~~

I remember being summoned to the Great Hall the following morning and noting the irony in that the throne room, which Menelaus had so ostentatiously enhanced in order to rival that of his brother's in Mycenae, was now being stripped of any bronze fittings by many of the same laborers who had been engaged to install them. Menelaus took me aside and told me to dress and adorn myself as if for a state occasion. "You took all my mirrors," I responded tartly.

"You have plenty of servants to be your looking glass."

I surmised that Menelaus was secretly pleased that his brother's orders meant that I would spend fewer hours at my toilette. I struggled daily to come to terms with my husband's *philia-aphilia,* his love-in-hate for my beauty. He swelled with pride when other men congratulated him on my loveliness, as though he were somehow responsible for its existence; yet inwardly he fumed, fearing at any moment that the selfsame exquisiteness would somehow bring him to ruin.

Later that day I returned to the Great Hall, attired all in white, my ears, throat, and bare arms glittering with precious stones. "Do not make me do this," I begged of Menelaus. "I am the daughter of a long line of priestesses." When he became king, he made me relinquish all vestiges of the old ways. Now, the Atridae sought to desecrate the new religion as well. The sky gods they revered would surely take their revenge, and I, as injured as the rest of my people by Agamemnon's hubris, wanted no part of their wrath. "The Spartans look to their queen to respect and preserve their shrines," I insisted. My pleas may as well have been shouted into the wind.

As I expected, our procession was marred by jeers and taunts. How different was this progress from the one Menelaus and I enjoyed some eight years earlier when we toured Sparta together for the first time as its king and queen. On the day we rode out to supervise the stripping of the shrines and temples, we were pelted with olives, and one distraught woman even threw a rock, which grazed Menelaus on his upper arm. He ordered one of his guard to arrest her, and I pleaded with him to try to understand how angry she must have been to assault the king. "These people—your people—are true believers in the gods," I warned. "The gods *you* want them to worship. To take their idols and defile their altars implicates them in your crimes. They fear retribution."

"They should fear *Agamemnon's* retribution if they attempt to prevent us from complying with the commands of the High King."

"*This* is your religion! Bronze! War! You worship the power to take, not what you can receive." Perhaps, I thought fleetingly, that is the fundamental difference between man and woman. The man takes the woman, who receives his seed. That day, of all days, made me rue my birthright. "Would that I had never been born in Sparta," I spat. "Would that I lived in a realm where every day was not given over to war—talks of war, threats of war, training for war, plans for war— where death was not the grandest reason for living."

To the earsplitting sound of women's wailing commingled with men's insults and children's taunts, bronze mixing bowls for libations and sacrifices were taken from the temples, along with the statues depicting their respective patrons. Artemis, Aphrodite, Zeus, even Athena, all were seized to become weaponry for Agamemnon's upcoming raid. Supplicants' gifts that had been left upon altars to propitiate the various gods were snatched up as well. Mycenaean greed recast itself as Spartan pragmatism. Menelaus, evincing neither love nor sympathy for his subjects, proclaimed that there were greater riches to be found within the temples than in the palace treasury and that there was no need to enrich the priests and priestesses at the expense of Sparta's security.

Our people followed us as we then journeyed to the beehive tomb that was the family crypt for the House of Tyndareus. Menelaus might just as well have sliced through my breast and taken my beating heart when he insisted that I be the one to desecrate my own ancestors' resting place.

I balked, refusing his command. I wept and tore off my jewels, flinging them at my husband's feet, begging him to accept them in place of my forbears' dignity. "To insist upon this piracy reaches far beyond the humiliation of Sparta's queen; it is an insult to Sparta herself." I tried to run, but two of the king's guard impeded my escape, and the words of Menelaus stunned me.

"Helen, if you continue to defy my order, these men have my permission to compel you to obey it. I urge you to spare yourself—and the Spartan people—any further indignity."

With a sorrow I had not known since their deaths, I removed my brothers' armaments and my mother's jewelry from their monuments and gave them, with trembling hands, to the palace guard.

I was a broken woman that day. I could not stand before my people and tell them outright that my husband, their king, was a traitor to his religion and to his subjects, that he only worshipped his elder brother, the High King, and all that Agamemnon's political ambitions could bring them. I did not say that I condoned his actions, and yet, by my very presence, robed and gowned and jeweled and coiffed as though it were a state festival, despite my tears, I had been complicit in his crimes.

Old wounds had been reopened and bled afresh. I mourned anew for my mother and half brothers. That night I looked heavenward and asked the twin stars what they thought of Agamemnon's decree and the resulting desecration of our sacred sites. I asked the Dioscuri to intercede for me with Zeus, my father. "Punish the Atridae," I prayed.

What had become of my life? Where Clytemnestra wielded power on the Mycenaean throne, I was but a cipher on Sparta's, no more than ornamentation for Menelaus. If I had been forged of bronze instead of flesh, I, too, would have been destroyed only to be recast as a helmet or the hilt of a dagger for one of Agamemnon's minions.

Love had eluded me as well. I had long since forgotten my promise to make the best of my marriage, to cherish Menelaus. By now, we viewed each other with the kind of *philia-aphilia* that I was all too accustomed to receiving from Clytemnestra, Tyndareus, and, often, the women of Sparta. I continued to honor Menelaus—in that I had never been unfaithful—but I could no longer will my body to desire his, to yearn for his touch in the night. Despite many years in my bed, Menelaus never became practiced in the arts of Eros. I had borne him five children, and we had both lost interest in actively seeking to beget any more of them. I could not love a man who respected the will of his power-mad brother over the wishes of his queen and the needs of his people. Therein lay much of the problem, I thought as I continued to ruminate over my husband's actions. The Spartans were only his people by virtue of a royal marriage. I was the true Spartan, while Menelaus had remained in all but proximity a Mycenaean.

I began to pay regular visits to what remained of the shrine of Aphrodite, leaving her offerings of milk and honey, combs of tortoise shell, and baskets of pomegranates. Daily, I entreated her to grant me love. I had so much to bestow and nowhere to confer it. I prayed for her to turn my husband's heart away from his kin and toward his wife. I implored her to fill my heart with affection for Menelaus; to fill my spirit with the *philia* of loving amity as well as Eros and Himeros—the lust and desire—that my loins so desperately craved.

But the gods are as capricious as the men who exercised their free will to invent them. As I made my daily ablutions and paid my tributes to the goddess of love, Aethra—who often acted as my conscience— would shake her head and wring her hands, murmuring, "Be careful what you wish for."

FIFTEEN

The gods did answer one of my prayers. But in punishing Menelaus for desecrating their temples, the rest of Sparta suffered as well. Not too many days after my husband carried out Agamemnon's wishes, the southern Peloponnese was shattered by a violent splitting of the earth. Zeus was angry and visited his wrath on the homes and the people of Laconia. At first, when we heard the rumbles, we thought the great sky god was merely threatening us with his thunderbolt. Rain would have been much welcomed. For months, we had endured a drought that had withered the crops on the vines and in the fields, starving many of our citizens, who then came to the palace stores seeking handouts. Menelaus and I dispensed grain, olive oil, and wine to the needy and thought we had ameliorated matters, if only temporarily, but the effects of the drought were nothing compared to the aftershocks of the defiling of the temples.

I was at my loom when I felt the first tremors. Hermione, you were at my side, stitching a little tapestry of your own. I thought little of it until a chunk of plaster as big as a date landed beside my right foot, and a dusting of powder sprinkled my shoulder. I remember glancing up very cautiously and discovering that there was a small hole in the ceiling.

A second tremor sent my dressing table sliding toward me, and Hermione, I recall as if it were yesterday how you flung your arms about my waist. I leapt up and, taking your hand, making you promise not to let go, we went in search of Nico and the twins. Aethra had herded the boys to the plain beyond the palace walls where nothing could fall upon them. Fortunately, they were too young to realize the potential for disaster. "Look, *Mitera!*" they called to me; full of mirthful giggles, they danced around in a circle, thinking that the earth had turned into a giant pony that was bouncing them about.

The royal family was lucky to escape unscathed, but when Menelaus joined us in the field, he took me aside and told me with fear in his eyes and sorrow in his heart that we had lost a young serving girl and one of the palace guard who had been crushed by falling debris. My husband was more distressed than I had ever seen him. All his grand improvements had now been rendered for naught. The pillars in the Great Hall were in danger of crumbling completely, ceilings had collapsed, the eastern wall of the treasury had all but disintegrated into dust, and our marital rooms had been utterly destroyed by the earthquake. Even the servants' quarters had suffered. Only the gynaeceum had remained primarily intact. It would take numerous masons several weeks, if not moons, to make the palace habitable again.

"We must inspect the damage in the rest of the city," I insisted, and leaving the boys and Hermione in Aethra's care, we commanded the equerry to saddle our horses.

I was not prepared for the devastation. In the town, the houses, comprised primarily of dried mud, had tumbled like dominoes upon one another, the weight of one damaged dwelling causing the destruction of its neighbor, and so on, often for several yards. Men and women, too dazed to flee or to aid in a rescue sat by the edge of the road, their panic and fear etched deeply into their frightened faces. We bore witness to the lifeless forms, looking as though they had been rolled in wheat flour, dragged from where they fell, crushed by falling plaster, wood, and stone. The bodies of children—too many to count—were lifted onto wagons to the earsplitting accompaniment of their keening mothers. The air was filled with the sounds of grief and the pungent onset of decay. Livestock, too—chickens and goats—had been felled by Zeus's wrath. There were so many bodies that it would have made individual funeral rites an imposition on the priests.

An old woman, swaybacked and struggling under the weight of a corpse no bigger than a rag doll, spat in the dust in front of Menelaus. "You! You, in your fine palace with your beautiful wife and your fine robes and your fine food and drink, what care you for the common people of Sparta? You are to blame for this!" she cried, shoving the inert bundle at the king. I left his side to comfort her, but she turned her invectives on me. Was this carnage indeed great Zeus's vengeance for the hubris of the Atridae or for something else entirely? It had been foretold that I would bring death to my countrymen; and now the prophecy, like a wayward bird on the wing, had come home to roost. Was this then the revenge of the Goddess for my having forsaken her? Tearful and trembling, I beseeched the sobbing crone to permit me to relieve her of her burden, and taking the dead infant from her, I cradled him in my arms. Surely, I should be made to bear some of the weight of my destiny. It could well have been Nico instead of some commoner's grandson.

Menelaus gathered together the members of the mourning families and suggested that a single state funeral be performed for all of the fallen. It was the least he could do to atone for a loss that might have been prevented, in our subjects' view, had he and his brother not flouted the gods. I believed that I had my own transgressions to cleanse, and I stood by him. In that moment, Menelaus was not a politician. He comported himself like a ruler and a diplomat and his offer was a genuine response that came from the heart. If he could one day establish an identity independent of Agamemnon, I was certain that the goodness within him would reveal itself in time. But if he remained in his brother's thrall for the rest of his days, Sparta and her neighbors were permanently imperiled as well.

~~~

There was much to be done to repair the destruction of Sparta's dwellings and to heal the rift between the people and their king, for we depended on their loyalty as well as their respect. Menelaus had promised them that all would be made new again before the celebration of Kronia began in the late summer.

Kronia was an annual festival lasting eighteen days that embodied what I liked to think of as the light and dark in our culture. Nine days of religiously sanctioned outrageous excesses of all kinds were followed by another nine days of strict abstemiousness and atonement, during which no coupling was permitted, no entertainment employed, no fighting could occur, and all formal battling ceased. The celebration—particularly the first half of it, where men and women were free to relieve their sexual mania in any way they chose, including adultery and homosexual encounters—was always greeted with great anticipation. It was a ritual that bore echoes of a more primitive time, when the Peloponnese was peopled by quiet agrarian villages whose inhabitants were close to the land and respected both the bounty and the power of the earth that was the source of their life and their livelihood. Occasionally, of course, there were those, like Clytemnestra, for whom neither mania nor atonement held any allure. My sister worshipped power and had little use for popular frivolities and their inevitable aftermath and counterpoint. I had always enjoyed the idea of the festival, for it appealed to my lustful nature; even the staged mock battles and sporting competitions were tinged with erotic excitement. Before I was abducted by Theseus, I was too young to indulge in the sexual excesses of the celebration, and once I was married to Menelaus, I resisted all temptation, although my licentiousness would have been perfectly permissible under the laws of Kronia. As for my husband's conduct during Kronia, I cannot say, but he never shamed me with it before our subjects.

The Spartan people had much to celebrate that year. The drought had finally ended and their homes had been speedily repaired following the death and devastation wrought by the earthquake. For the next nine days, their mourning would be ameliorated with banquets, games and contests, and libidinous mania bordering on mayhem. Garlands were hung from every window, perfuming the air with a fragrant headiness that whispered "lust." Men and women, and the most nubile of the Spartan youth, bedecked themselves in their finest garments, oiled their hair and perfumed their limbs, the better to be prepared for any amorous encounters. Young girls happily demonstrated to any willing spectator why they had earned the sobriquet *thigh-flashers*. Boys in the throes of adolescence availed themselves of freedoms conferred upon them by the festival to press their advantage with girls they were too timid to approach during the rest of the year. At night, lanterns would be strung across rooftops or left dangling from poles placed in the fertile earth to light the way to carnal paradise. Passion flowed like wine.

Menelaus had charged me with decorating the Great Hall for Kronia. To that end, fertility statues of both sexes graced the entrance to the throne room, and I had commissioned a new fresco to depict the courtship and ritual capture of the sea nymph Thetis. After Thetis led King Peleus on a merry chase, many times shifting her shape to elude him, he overcame her and eventually wed her at the greatest nuptial feast ever known. It was the last time men dined side by side with the gods. In their story, where a mortal man claims an immortal woman as his consort, there was something of my own lineage in reverse and it secretly pleased me. Menelaus offered no comment other than to say that he liked the theme of man and god in harmony. He found the premise soothing after the summer earthquake had followed so hard upon the desecration of the sacred sites.

I was directing the servants as to the placement of the incense braziers that would fill the room with the pungent aromas of jasmine and sandalwood when Menelaus entered, followed by two of his palace guard and two strangers, foreign-born, as evidenced by their garb of elaborately embroidered saffron and crimson-colored silk. "Welcome to Sparta," he told them, approaching his throne and ordering two chairs to be placed beside him for his guests.

"It is not the custom of Wilusa to speak of diplomatic matters in the presence of women," said the shorter of the two men. He wore his sand-colored hair to his shoulders and sported a long, though well-trimmed, beard.

"*This* woman will gladly inform you that she is an exception, Aeneas," Menelaus replied, and summoned me to stand beside him. Honeysuckle perfume trailing in my wake, I glided to the throne with an excess of queenly grace and dignity; after all, it was Kronia and excess in all things was the custom. "Before you stands the most beautiful woman in the world," Menelaus added, speaking the words with pride for the first time in my recollection. "Queen Helen of Sparta."

The two men bowed low and reverentially, and when they stood again, my eyes locked with those of the taller of the two, like and yet unlike his companion: clean shaven, with a fine strong jaw and a head of golden curls that made me believe that I gazed upon Apollo incarnate. He wore the aura of clear, crisp mountain air like an invisible cloak. It reminded me of the days when I used to ride and run wild in the hills of Mount Taygetos without a care for weighty affairs of state and wifely obligations. The young man smelled like freedom, and such a man had never visited Sparta in my lifetime. "My queen, before you stand two ambassadors from Ilios: Aeneas, son of Anchises, and his cousin, Prince Paris Alexandros, son of Priam."

I could not take my eyes from this ambassador of masculine perfection. My heart had been punctured by an arrow of Eros as surely as those in Alexander's quiver could inflict lethal damage on a hart or hare. From that first moment, I desired him. Thoughts of luscious impalement caught me unaware and imprisoned me as though I had been ensnared within a fisherman's net. Paris Alexandros. His very name was music and flowed like liquid silk across my tongue. "You have caught us at a most auspicious time," I told him. "Our festival of Kronia begins today." And then, I remember so well, my mouth went dry, my words tumbling out like pebbles kicked up by the wheels of a chariot. The queen of Sparta had been robbed of speech by a stranger.

Menelaus laughed. "We Spartans pride ourselves on being excellent hosts, but during Kronia, you will receive more honors than you have dreamed of. The finest of everything is at your disposal. We will hear of your errand tomorrow, after the First Night's feast. For now, enjoy a respite in your quarters and we will look forward to seeing you again at the banquet tables this evening."

The Troyan prince and his cousin were escorted from the Great Hall and shown to their rooms; they would remain in Sparta until their diplomatic mission had been concluded. Messengers were sacred to the gods and were always treated well. Ambassadors such as these from Ilios would not even be permitted to discuss their business until they had feasted at the elbow of their host. And I . . . I was undone. Never before, not even with Theseus, had I experienced a connection so immediate and so powerful. I was on fire. Great conflagrations raged within me that I could not quench no matter how much water I consumed. I retired to my rooms and bathed again to rinse the sweat from my burning skin.

Aethra thought I was unwell; perhaps the first flush of another pregnancy. But I knew that could not be the case. Menelaus and I had enjoyed separate sleeping quarters since the desecration of the temples. Despite his attempts to mollify the people of Sparta after those raids, I could not forgive him for cavalierly despoiling my family's tomb. Besides, if I was carrying another child, by now my figure would have begun to show the signs. No, these sensations were something altogether unfamiliar, a sea change within me that I was unable to contain, desired not to confess, and over which I had no control. A religious person would have said for certain that Aphrodite had taken possession of my body at the moment I saw Paris Alexandros, and from that instant I became her servant, willing or no. But Aphrodite was ever my patron goddess; and the embers that lay banked inside me from birth, flaring only once when I chose to visit Theseus's chamber, now flamed even higher and burned hotter and more brightly. If the Fates had delivered the ultimate temptation, it rested with me to choose whether to accept or reject the gift, however exquisitely wrapped.

～～

Aeneas remained quiet throughout much of the First Night meal. His spirit was less boyish than Alexander's, although I guessed that they were about the same age. The cousin had the air of a settled man: thoughtful and perhaps even taciturn when necessary, whereas Paris Alexandros possessed the exuberance of a wild stallion. In some ways he reminded me of my brothers, who brought their passion for the untamed beauty of the countryside into the cool and stately chambers of the palace.

The Troyan ambassadors were surprised to find the women eating alongside the men during the banquet. In Ilios, they explained, the women ate in a separate hall, joining their men to enjoy the entertainment once the meal was over. I found myself surprised that in such an advanced city as theirs, far more cosmopolitan than Sparta, such backward views of women prevailed. "Then you rob yourselves of pleasant and soothing company to aid in your digestion," I teased. "Here in Greece, our men are never deprived of our companionship at mealtime."

"And more's the pity!" exclaimed some loutish friend of Menelaus, with particular reference to the short-skirted flute girls who had just entered the Great Hall. "Are we never permitted a moment's peace from your flapping tongues?"

"Then, for the first time in twenty-six years of life, I regret that I am not a Greek, for the flapping tongue of the queen of Sparta would be pleasant enough company during any meal."

My heart stopped. Time stopped. The motions of the serving women and the flute girls . . . all . . . stopped.

"You are fortunate to be a guest during the celebration of Kronia, my man," said Menelaus, clapping Prince Paris on the back in a hearty display of camaraderie. The servants resumed their bustle. The musicians recommenced their melody. I exhaled.

Smiling gamely, I supported my husband. "You are fortunate indeed, Paris Alexandros—the laxness of Kronia or not. Were you not an ambassador from foreign shores, you would not have enjoyed such a mirthful response for so boldly referring to the person of the queen and the wife of your host."

"A thousand pardons," Paris said, humbled and blushing. "I am still unused to the ways of the court."

"I thought you were a prince," Menelaus said, his eyes glazing over from the quantities of Rhodian wine he had consumed thus far. He called for his favorite liquor, a potent mixture of wine tinged with pine resin, then became momentarily distracted by the entrance of the acrobats. The lightly clad serving girls passed plates of honeyed figs, leaning forward as if to invite the diners, male and female alike, to sample more than the confections they carried. It amused me to watch how hard they tried to gain the attentions of Paris Alexandros. He spoke to Menelaus when directly addressed by him, but for the rest of the evening he had not taken his eyes from my face and form. I admit that I did nothing, my tart comment aside, to discourage his attentions. I remember how he admired the new fresco I had commissioned and, pointing to the goddesses depicted among the wedding revelers, murmured, "Remind me to tell you a story about them." He smiled as though he held a secret the way a young child traps a butterfly within his cupped hands.

"I *am* a prince," Paris said after the acrobats took their bows. Menelaus himself refilled his guest's golden wine goblet and offered him a taste of the retsina as well. "But we Troyans are a superstitious lot and the royal family lays great store by dreams. My mother, when she carried me in her womb, had a prophetic dream one night that she gave birth to a burning brand that brought destruction to Wilusa in a holocaust of smoke and flame. It is quite a story and makes for a good after-dinner tale. Nevertheless, Queen Hecuba believed the nocturnal visions that had visited her, and after giving birth to me, she and my father, King Priam, handed me to a trusted retainer, a shepherd named Agelaus. Agelaus was ordered to leave me on Mount Ida to die, but the old man and his wife took pity upon a helpless infant and raised me as their own. I grew up a shepherd boy in the mountains beyond Troy, and even today," he added with a boastful grin, "no man is better than I am with a bow."

"Then how did you discover you were really a prince?" I asked him.

"Last year, King Priam's representatives came to Mount Ida seeking prize bulls for their annual festival games. Agelaus and I had raised one, a perfect white specimen of which we were particularly proud, but I was reluctant to let the king's men rob us of our best beast with only meager compensation. We were mountain people and did not live as they did. We bred our livestock and survived on what we hunted or slaughtered. We were expected to consider ourselves honored that our bull had been chosen for the sacrificial centerpiece, as bulls are the sacred emblem of the city you call Ilios. Seized with what I can only describe to you as wanderlust, I insisted, despite Agelaus's vehement protestations, on leaving Mount Ida and accompanying our prize bull to Troy. There I beheld the festival games and could not resist entering the sporting competitions. As a poor shepherd, ill-accoutered and meanly attired, I incurred the mockery, and then the enmity, of the great princes Hector and Deiphobus, the latter being particularly intolerant of outsiders. And yet I bested them all. I shamed them in the footraces, wrestled all comers into the dust, and with my bow, I easily outshot them."

I glanced at Menelaus. Where I had feared he might feel overmatched by this golden prince, he was instead impressed, a reaction that I admit completely surprised me. I believe he decided right then that he had found a protégé in Paris Alexandros. "You will wrestle *me*, young Troyan," Menelaus said. "Mock combat is one of the chief diversions of Kronia. You came at the right time, my new friend!" Was it the

wine speaking, or had my husband truly found a prospective companion for the next few days? I had never seen Menelaus so animated. "I
am eager to learn the end of the tale. Go on," he urged Paris Alexandros.

"The spear, alas, has never been my best weapon, and there, the
first and third sons of Priam triumphed."

"The spear is *my* weapon as well," my husband interrupted excitedly. "The spear-famed Menelaus, I am called."

"Then I am heartily sorry you were not there to have come to my
defense," Paris Alexandros replied. "For Deiphobus played me false
and ordered the doors of the arena bolted shut so there was no escape,
and then he aimed to kill. After both spears were thrown, he blocked
my exit and had drawn his knife to strike the fatal thrust when old
Agelaus created an uproar by hobbling onto the field, waving what I
thought was a white flag of surrender."

"It wasn't?" I asked. It didn't matter to me what the old shepherd
carried. All I cared about was that Paris Alexandros had obviously survived and was here to speak of it. To my ears, his words were like the
sweet golden honey that coated my fingers after devouring the figs.

"It wasn't, my queen. Agelaus brandished the cloth in which I had
been swaddled when he was charged with the errand of leaving me to
die atop the harsh summit of Mount Ida. He insisted that King Priam
and Queen Hecuba hear him out before Deiphobus made another move
to strike the stranger whom he held at knifepoint. The story of my
childhood and my youth was disclosed, and I was immediately embraced as the lost prince. I have since taken my place as the second son
of Priam. Although I must confess," Paris demurred, "that my elder
brother Hector is still the idol of my parents' eye. Sometimes it is
hard to wear the mantle of a second royal son and still make a name for
oneself!"

With those words, the fate of Paris Alexandros as a kindred spirit
to Menelaus, second son of Atreus, had been sealed. My husband
raised his goblet to the gods. "Helen," he exclaimed, "our guest's
arrival is fortunate indeed. And may this Troyan prince show *me*
how to distinguish *myself* from the much vaunted achievements of a
renowned older brother!"

❧ S I X T E E N ❧

The following day, while Aethra bathed me with fragrant essences, I lazed in my tub with my eyes closed, the better to summon images of the magnificent Troyan prince. After dressing in shades of lapis and turquoise and setting a golden diadem in my hair, which I had ringleted in the Athenian style, I descended to the Great Hall, answering a summons from Menelaus.

"Prince Paris has requested your presence this morning," my husband said, leading me to the chair beside his throne. "I had assumed his errand regarded the trade concessions I had spoken of with his father, King Priam, but it appears that he comes to talk of other matters entirely."

Then Aeneas spoke up. From his expression, I could tell that he found the situation uncomfortable. "Ordinarily it is not for a woman—even the queen—to hear our embassy, but as it directly concerns another woman, we hoped that you would be more inclined to find sympathy for King Priam and might be persuasive in helping to make the case to King Menelaus."

I was intrigued by his words. Paris Alexandros then spoke eloquently for one who had so recently led a sheltered shepherd's existence. "Many years ago," he began, "when my father was only a boy, the renowned Heracles attacked Wilusa, damaging part of the western wall of the citadel, sacking the city and pillaging our possessions." He went on to explain that the great Heracles rewarded one of his most valorous warriors, his cousin Telamon of Salamis, with a captive Troyan princess as his bride. The young woman was Hesione, elder sister of young Podarces. "Heracles was planning to enslave Podarces, but Hesione, who was granted one parting wish by the conquering Achaeans, purchased Podarces from Heracles with her golden veil, and then set her brother free. Podarces, reaching his majority, called himself Priam and claimed his birthright, the throne of Ilios." Although Hesione had been gone for decades, bearing sons to Telamon, including Teucer, who was one of the unsuccessful suitors for my hand, Priam still viewed his sister's absence as having been brought about by abduction and force. Now, he insisted upon her return. Paris and Aeneas had come to Sparta to seek the aid of Menelaus in the form of ships and men pledged to join forces with a Trojan armada that would invade Salamis and recapture the aged Hesione.

"We have little to spare," replied Menelaus after several minutes of grave consideration of the Troyans' request. He told them about the depletion of our stores during the drought, the necessity of requisitioning all items of bronze to be found anywhere in Sparta to satisfy his brother's orders, and the expenses of repairing the dwellings, including the palace, that were damaged or destroyed in the earthquake. "Much as I would like to entertain the particulars of your embassy, my first allegiance is to Sparta," he continued. Catching my dubious expression, he added, "Although . . . my brother Agamemnon frequently exercises his fraternal prerogative, as well as asserting his status as High King, in requesting Sparta's aid and support in supplying men and materiel for his ventures."

"You were right to request the ear of the queen," said Aeneas, smiling at his cousin. "So, what says Helen of Sparta?"

What would Theseus do, were his counsel solicited on such a matter as this? I remembered the Dioscuri demanding my own release and forfeiting the requested ransom; although, unknown to them, I would have happily remained in Athens. But Theseus had staged a legitimate abduction. I was not a spoil of war, as was Hesione of Troy. I recalled Hesione's son Teucer's version of events when we had spoken nearly a decade earlier; back when he had been one of forty-five suitors for my hand. *They have always seemed very happily married,* he had said of his parents. The echo of his words now filled my ears.

"Has King Priam ever sued for Hesione's release?" I asked the Troyan ambassadors. "Ever sailed to Salamis before now to negotiate her return to Anatolia?" Paris looked to Aeneas, who shook his head. "Has Hesione ever sent word to her brother, however couched, indicating her wish to return home? Perhaps she now calls Salamis her home and has no desire to come back to Troy. Perhaps she is quite happy to be Telamon's wife. Has King Priam considered that he may be funding an expedition for a fruitless quest and that it might be *he* who would be abducting Hesione after all these years have passed?"

The Trojans could not answer my questions. I was reluctant, I told them, to spend my credit with Menelaus by encouraging him to aid in rescuing a woman who in all likelihood had no wish to be rescued. No doubt she had despaired of her lot at first, being taken from her homeland and given as a captive bride to a man she didn't know or love; but since that time, many decades had come and gone. By now, Hesione's children had children of their own.

Paris bit his lip in disappointment. He had been so certain of my support. But in all good conscience, I could not see committing Sparta's resources to endorse his father's venture. "Well, it cannot be said that the woman doesn't speak her mind," he said.

"Laconian women are renowned for their outspokenness. It is something my Mycenaean husband has, after nine years of marriage, finally begun to accept!" For different reasons, Menelaus and I had come to the same conclusion regarding the Trojans' petition. My husband claimed we lacked sufficient capital at this difficult time, where I believed that Priam's mission was self-serving and that the interests of the woman at the center of the controversy had not been taken into account and would not be honored by it.

Menelaus was more reluctant to let his new princely friend depart in haste than he was to aid King Priam. Learning that they had no comparable festival in Ilios, he insisted that the Trojan ambassadors remain for the duration of Kronia, or at least through the first nine days, where one lived for nothing but pleasure. This, too, I supported, though once again for entirely different reasons.

"I understand you Trojans know something of horses," I said, recalling the white Trojan mare Theseus had given me as a wedding gift. "Perhaps you two would like to ride with me later. I will show you the mountains where I played as a girl."

Aeneas demurred, preferring to talk of politics with Menelaus.

"We are the best breeders of horses in the world," boasted Paris Alexandros. "In fact, my brother Hector's nickname is 'Tamer of Horses.' "

"My late brother Castor was called the '*Breaker* of Horses'!" I said with a laugh of recognition that quickly metamorphosed into a nostalgic stab of pain. Everything I had just wished for was everything I most feared. Only Paris and I would ride out together. As it was Kronia, it was not considered unseemly for the queen to be seen alone in the company of another man, particularly a foreign ambassador.

We sent a servant to fetch our horses and walked out into the sunlight. "The Spartan king surprised me," Paris said as we waited for our steeds.

"Why? Did you really expect him to give you the ships?"

"Yes. But that's not what I allude to. He is a livelier man than I had been led to believe. And fonder of his wife, too, than I had imagined."

"It is you, not I, who has brought my husband's conviviality to the surface. He sees in you a kindred spirit. And his mood is doubly light because he adores Kronia. For nine days a year he permits himself to be a boy again. It is the sporting contests and the mock combat that he most enjoys," I added, hoping to convey my subtext: that it was not Kronia's sexual libertinism that appealed to Menelaus. "And when his heart is light, he even praises me. For the rest of the year, he is a victim of his jealousies, and he does not hide from me how burdensome he often finds it to be married to the most beautiful woman in the world. I am a weighty possession then, but now he sees his chance to flaunt Sparta's greatest treasure before a prince of powerful Troy."

A hawk circled far above us, its silhouette black against the cerulean sky. "Do you think he already sees his prey?" I asked Paris Alexandros. "Or do you think he is looking for something to kill?"

"I think he is admiring the view below him; a vision in blue and gold. Traveling on the wind, the tales of Helen of Sparta reached his mountaintop aerie and he had to come closer to the earth to find out for himself if she was indeed as beautiful as they said."

"And what does the hawk think?"

Paris Alexandros offered me his hand so that I could mount my mare with ease. Our hands kissed, palm to palm, and I felt his soul, his *thymos,* enter mine. "He is enchanted by her loveliness. The songs of the bards do not do it justice. He is cursing the fate that made him a bird and wishes himself a man so that he might make love to her."

"He does not wish *her* a bird so that she might fly away with him?" Our hands were still joined, and Paris brought mine to his lips and kissed it before helping me up. Our flirtatious exchange confirmed my greatest hopes and fears: The Troyan prince desired me as much as I did him. This situation was as new to me as were the sensations that had overtaken my body and mind since the moment our gazes first met. Exquisite and charming Paris Alexandros, with his honeyed speech and overt attentions, swooped down and took hold of my heart before I had time to stop for breath. So long unaccustomed to affection from my husband, and never anticipating the possibility of onslaught from another quarter, it was an undefended citadel, vulnerable to attack from an outsider.

We rode toward the outskirts of the city, and I pointed out the modest mud and brick farmhouse where my childhood friend, Polyxo, had grown up. The prince was surprised that the legendary Helen had played with commoners. "My sister Clytemnestra was a cruel playmate and convinced the other girls to shun me," I told him. "I never desired to be any different from my playfellows, and yet I never felt as though I inhabited their world. Even adults would remark upon my beauty in a way that made me feel I was not human. True, my father was the great Zeus, but although I am demimortal, I am my mother Leda's daughter as well: made of flesh and fueled by emotions that are as vulnerable to injury as theirs. All through my life I have tried to put myself back among other people to make sure I have not missed any elements of a normal life by being Helen. From the very beginning, Polyxo was the only one who had enough courage and goodness to seek to befriend me."

"Then I should like to thank her for her courage and goodness."

"You want to meet Polyxo?"

"Why not?"

"You would need to leave Sparta then, for she married a Rhodian, Tlepolemus."

The day could not have been more beautiful. First I showed Paris Alexandros the reedy banks of the Eurotas, where we waited for a tortoise to cross our path. The creature seemed to enjoy the warmth of

Helios as much as we did and took his time before ambling into the rushes. The Troyan prince pointed toward Gythium, where his ships lay moored. His men and Aeneas's had erected tents, dwelling there until their commanders completed their diplomatic office. "How I wish you could see my ship!" he said. "The great bull of Troy graces her prow, and her hull is the color of pomegranate seeds." It sounded remarkable indeed. As exotic as the vessel's master, who wore fine robes and bedecked himself in gold and brazen bracelets and earrings like an Achaean woman. "This is the fashion for well-born men of Wilusa," he explained to me. "At first I was astonished by it. But it did not take long for this former shepherd lad to grow acclimated to the custom. I have always appreciated beauty in all its forms."

I felt the heat spread from my hairline to my cheeks, along my throat and chest, taking up residence between my thighs. "Come," I said, "I will show you where my brothers taught me to ride." I led him up the slopes of Mount Taygetos, past eucalyptus, cypress, pines, and acacias. Our route was a riot of color. Like the golden narcissus, my precious anemones were long gone, their blossoms of red, violet, and indigo children of the spring; but we were greeted with cyclamen, carpets of fragrant lavender, and patches of sweet veronica. Asphodel and iris paid court to the Spartan queen and her consort for the day. As we rode through a shady spot, a gentle breeze carried the crisp scent of mint to our nostrils.

Not in nine summers' time had I felt so free. The heavy yoke of marriage, motherhood, and responsibility had been lifted from my neck; unhaltered, I embraced my renewed unrestrained state like a lover. The terrain became rockier the higher we climbed, and as we neared a plateau, Athena, my mare, stumbled on something and nearly threw me. Paris Alexandros insisted that I dismount immediately, which I did, and he alit from his mount as well, the better to ascertain whether Athena had been injured. With the same expert tenderness I had seen my brother Castor display with one of his horses, the Troyan prince examined Athena's left front leg and, somehow convincing the massive beast to raise her foot, discovered a stone caught in her hoof.

"I thought you told me your brother Hector was the tamer of horses," I said, admiring Alexander's talent for calming the mare and gaining her trust.

"That *was* his nickname—before *I* returned to the family fold!"

His ego was as healthy as his complexion and physique. Modesty did not become this prince. At any rate, his inclination toward boasting set aside, in his management of equine matters he was indeed as skillful as he claimed. "She should rest for a bit," Paris Alexandros said, having just removed the stone. He gently guided Athena's hoof to the ground, and she gave a little shake and tested her leg. "And so should we. Rest." He removed his cloak, also the color of pomegranate seeds, and laid it across a patch of earth.

In order to avoid acknowledging our increased physical proximity, I found myself complimenting the richness of the winedark shade.

"The red dye comes from the safflower," he told me, "and we set the color in salt from the plant's ashes. That is why, through wind and wear and weather, it remains a true red, rather than eventually fading to an orangey hue."

"Ahhh . . ." I found it hard to look at him because I feared, even then, and even though it was Kronia, that I could not remain responsible for my actions. Once I walked through the fire, there was no returning. *That* I knew as well. We gazed across the fertile Taygetos valley, past all the dwellings, and out to the Great Sea. Suddenly, I thirsted for it again, as I had done that day at the beginning of my fourteenth year when Polyxo and I had hiked up the mountain and were set upon by Theseus and Pirithous.

"You were going to tell me a story about the goddesses depicted in the mural in our Great Hall," I reminded him. I lay down on the pebbled ground, protected only by the fabric of Alexander's mantle.

"The wedding of Thetis to Peleus." Paris Alexandros sighed deeply and reclined beside me. His skin smelled of sunlight, but I could not hold my breath forever to avoid its intoxicating effect. "All the gods and goddesses were invited to the feast . . . but one. Eris."

"Well, who would want the goddess of strife at their wedding banquet?" I interjected, aware that Lady Discord had not received an invitation.

"To overlook Strife, whether deliberately or unintentionally, is to court it, of course. When traders came to Mount Ida for livestock, after dinner they would regale us with stories about the renowned and mighty. After one such evening in the company of a particularly loquacious trader, I dreamt about this famous wedding. And in my dream, the uninvited Eris appeared at the feast, leaving the happy couple an enigmatic wedding gift. She tossed a golden apple marked 'for the fairest' at great Zeus himself and challenged him to judge which of the greatest goddesses merited the prize. As his own wife Hera was among the three contestants—the other two being Athena and Aphrodite—he refused to be the arbiter, naturally disinclined to unnecessarily incur her ire. So he sent Hermes the messenger god to my humble dwelling on Mount Ida, demanding in the name of Zeus that I act as judge. Naturally, I could not refuse an offer from the king of the sky gods, and reluctantly I rose to the task. Athena and Hera tried to bribe me. The latter offered me tremendous wealth and power, and the former promised me victory in battle. I was happy with my simple life and had no desire for Hera's gift, and as I was a hunter and not a warrior, saw little value in Athena's bribe. But more to the point, as the apple bore the words 'for the fairest,' it was a *beauty* contest I had been asked to adjudge, not an assessment of the goddesses' relative merits. *Of course* the fairest among them was the goddess of beauty herself, Aphrodite. But to tempt me further to award her the glittering orb, she promised that the most beautiful woman in the world would be mine. My consort, my lover, my wife."

A shiver, like little sparks of flint, crackled along the length of my spine, and I felt robbed of breath.

"You see?" Paris said, propping himself on one elbow. "We are destined to be together. The gods themselves have ordained it. Do you not believe in *anake*—in fate?"

"*Anake:* what has to be." I tried to see the situation with Spartan pragmatism: for someone to insist that your union is favorably starred is nature's way—perhaps even the Great Mother's way—of saying that they want you very much at that moment. It's not too distant an emotion from that of the young child who sees a brand-new plaything or a starling that spots a shiny object and thinks *mine!* But I was neither a child nor a bird; I lacked their freedom to follow my desires so unequivocally. I had loved Theseus with an all-consuming passion and still reserved for him a special chamber in my heart, although he had been dead for four years. How then could I accept that Paris Alexandros was fated to be my perfect lover: the *only* man for me in a lifetime?

From my own experience, that was not true. What *is* true is that a great love, like lightning, can strike twice. Once, I thought my destiny was Theseus. Looking at Paris, I realized that as our personalities develop, and our devoted hearts break and attempt to repair themselves, our destinies are not as final as we believe them to be.

Love and loyalty were separate entities as well. In a good marriage, they combined to form a single centaurlike creature: half one and half the other. In a union such as mine with Menelaus, only loyalty warmed itself at our hearth. I had believed that my destiny was not to be permitted to embrace both.

"You are silent, Helen. What do you think of that?" Paris Alexandros asked me, twining a tendril of my hair around his finger.

"You have a way of robbing me of words . . . of . . . incommoding me. I do not know you, and yet I have never before been so drawn to a man. You are a foreign prince from an exotic realm, which is enchanting enough . . . and I am the queen of a somewhat powerful, though provincial, city . . ."

"An orchid among weeds—"

"—That is hardly fair."

"Among common wildflowers then."

I smiled. "Wildflowers have a unique beauty, too. But you could still be the shepherd youth on Mount Ida, or here on Taygetos. It is your spirit and your words . . . and *your* beauty that move me."

Paris inched closer to me. Our bodies were nearly touching. His mouth was so close to mine that I could taste his breath. "Let me make love to you, Helen."

The words formed themselves on my lips and escaped from my mouth as though my body had no power to restrain them. "Not now."

"When, then?"

"Soon." The bargain had been made; the pact sealed. On my honor as queen I could not renege, and so, I would dishonor Menelaus. Perhaps Paris Alexandros was right. That our destinies were meant to be thus joined. A religious person, upon hearing his retelling of the story of the Judgment, would certainly agree that Zeus and Aphrodite had conspired to plan the fate of Paris Alexandros, a fate to include Helen of Sparta as *his* golden apple. Zeus was my father and Aphrodite my spiritual patroness, a godmother of sorts. Was it not reasonable for me to concur that my Olympian family desired the best for their shining daughter? It offered an unassailable explanation, should I choose to follow the path as allegedly preordained.

I was terrified of the power within me. It was as dangerous as a conflagration or a tempest-tossed sea. Although it dwelled inside me, contained by the flesh and sinew of my body, I knew it could consume me.

Paris Alexandros removed one of his earrings and pressed it into my palm. "Here is my promise: to give you all that is mine. Will you pledge the same to me?"

I gazed upon the small golden hoop for several moments, then with great deliberation and a tiny pinch of pain, handed him one of my own. Each of us now was in possession of a mismatched set. "A pair and not a pair," I breathed.

Rising to my feet, I adjusted my skirts. I held out my hand to Paris Alexandros and led him back to our horses. "We should begin our descent," I said.

And so we did.

ertain that my secret promise covered my face like a veil, I was grateful that Menelaus monopolized Paris Alexandros at the evening banquet. All he could talk about was the wrestling match he had planned for the following day. I asked Aeneas to tell me all about Ilios. "Was it like Sparta?" I asked, knowing that the cities bore little in common, but as the hostess I wanted to give the other Troyan ambassador the chance to shine. The Dardanian-born Aeneas bloomed with pride for his adopted city, boasting that its highly advantageous location at the mouth of the Hellespont made it the center for world trade. From the summit of its twin-towered citadel, King Priam controlled the flow of commerce from the Black Sea to the north and through the Aegean to the south.

"Wilusa has the best of everything," Aeneas averred. "The finest goods from the Adriatic, Achaea, Egypt, and the Hittite kingdom are at our fingertips. Most important, ships bearing copper from Cyprus and tin from Central Asia pay their tributes to Priam in the form of tolls as well as goods."

"Why are those ships the most important?" I desired to know. This was something in which Theseus had not completely schooled me.

"We are living in the age of bronze," Aeneas replied. "And bronze is an alloy. One part tin combined with ten parts copper makes bronze. He who controls the flow of bronze, controls the world."

"And your King Priam from his towered city on a shining hill sits atop that world."

"Until someone topples him. Even the great Heracles tried . . . and failed. And Priam was only a boy then."

I caught Paris Alexandros looking at me. He peered over his wine kylix and touched his lips to the cup as though the lip of the kylix were my own. Momentarily flustered, I lowered my eyes, then raised them to meet his again. *Not now,* they told him. I touched Menelaus's arm and favored him with a warm smile. He accepted my gift with an inclination of his head and resumed his impassioned discussion of wrestling.

∼∼

Menelaus had wanted to stage their mock skirmish out on the pergamos, but I feared that the injuries both men might suffer on the hard paving stones would be anything but sham. Enduring their taunting and chiding, I convinced my husband to move the bout to the field beyond the palace. I found it amusing in an almost pathetic way: two grown men—one of whom was a hunter who had never been in a real battle, and the other an experienced soldier who for several moons had been nostalgically pining for the thrill of blood and drums and clash of bronze—playing at war.

The patch of earth was ringed by spectators, all cheering for Menelaus, as they would never dare to cross their king even during Kronia. This did not seem to daunt the foreign prince, who twice pinned the older, slower Menelaus within the first few seconds of the match. Embarrassed to be losing on his own territory, particularly after having so vociferously insisted upon the face-off, Menelaus found his strength and skill and turned the tides. Paris gamely rallied but was clearly not as committed to the bout as was his adversary. For the Troyan prince, it was little more than an entertainment in which he happily humored his host. Physically, the men were not well matched. Paris Alexandros was younger by a decade and a few inches taller; but the stockier physique of Menelaus was more suited to that of a wrestler, and my husband was able to use it to gain the advantage. Or had the Troyan prince diplomatically allowed his host to best him? The two men wrestled well enough so that I could not be certain whether Menelaus had legitimately won.

He rose and offered his hand to Paris Alexandros, pulling the prince to his feet. They embraced and brushed the dust from their loins, and Menelaus complimented his opponent on being a worthy competitor. "Come! I will send our loveliest serving girls to bathe you and tonight we will feast again!" My husband asked me to attend him in his bath and I could not refuse. Some kings might have sent the queen to bathe their guest as a gesture of the goodwill they bore him; such a thing was well within the bounds of tradition, but Menelaus, ever alert to even the most innocuous communication between another man and me, would certainly never have made such an offer. During the past three days, either Menelaus had been too focused on his own newfound amity with the Troyan prince, or I must have concealed my blushes well, for they went undetected by my husband.

A messenger was waiting at the palace gates when we arrived. He had come from Crete to inform Menelaus that Catreus, his mother's father, had died. Another runner had been dispatched to Mycenae with the same sorrowful news. "I must go," Menelaus said grimly. "It is only fitting that my brother and I are present for the funeral rites and games." He made no delay in arranging for his immediate departure, although at least he allowed me to bathe him first! "You must entertain our guests with all the hospitality I would accord them had I been able to remain for the duration of their stay in Sparta," he charged me. "And I will not hear that you shunned them, as you are often wont to do." I did often take pains to avoid our guests, it was true, but only because Menelaus would scold me for what he considered was conduct too warm and too familiar. I was expected to be Helen but not Helen. There was no way to win; and therefore, I did my best to try to remain aloof and distant. Now, even that behavior was being held up to censure and scrutiny.

Nine days' observance was the funerary custom. Menelaus would be gone for at least that long, and it would take him an additional couple of days to travel. Taking two of the palace guard and a small retinue of servants, he made for his flagship at the port of Gythium, giving me a cursory farewell. I did not know whether to look upon his absence as a blessing or a curse. I wanted to remain a good wife, and yet desire was fast becoming a more formidable opponent than fidelity was my ally. Then there was the wild and foolish promise I had made to Paris Alexandros on Mount Taygetos. I entered the guests' quarters where a dark-haired Egyptian serving girl was bathing the Troyan prince. "Leave us," I said.

I knelt beside the tub and drenched the sea sponge in the fragrant water. "You honor me, daughter of Zeus," said Paris as I leaned over him to wash the dust from his chest.

"The honor is mine. *You* are beautiful enough to be a son of Aphrodite."

The prince smiled. "*That* honor belongs to my kinsman Aeneas."

"Truly?"

Paris Alexandros nodded.

I drizzled water over his shoulders and watched the rivulets trickle down the sunkissed plains of his chiseled torso.

"The goddess took a fancy to his father but made him promise never to tell a soul about their coupling. However, the ecstatic Anchises couldn't keep a secret like *that,* and so she left him."

"Your kinsman hides his beauty with his beard." Unlike Paris, who was irresistibly exquisite.

Drawing me closer, he clasped my wrist, plunging my forearm into the water, guiding my hand to the most evident source of his desire for me. "Join me," he whispered, his eyes daring me to meet the challenge.

"Not here," I said, but I could not release my prize. "By all the gods—and by the ancient Goddess, too—you will undo me."

"You will be your own undoing, Helen, if you do not believe as I do that we are each other's *anake.* If you agree that we are destined to be lovers, then your fate is beyond your own grasp. You are powerless to control it or to alter your destiny."

"It is too convenient an explanation for me to embrace with ease," I told him. "Forgive my Laconian pragmatism, but I am not convinced that I should trust in dreams, particularly when they do not come to *me.*" By my own reckoning, it was *technē*—the combustible fusion of my free will, my imagination, and my power—and not my destiny, that compelled me to explore his flawless anatomy with my licentious hands. Never was a man so thoroughly and lovingly bathed.

"When?" asked Paris Alexandros, breathless.

"Tonight."

"Here?"

"No. Not in the palace. That I cannot do. I will take you somewhere else."

And so, after the Third Night feast, disguised as Kronian revelers, I brought Paris Alexandros to the sacred grove. And on the remnants of the altar where my mother received the seed of Zeus, we consummated our lust.

We needed no torches to light our way. Selene, the goddess of the moon, was full-bellied, silhouetting the trees against the sky. The cool and gentle breeze that rustled through the leaves made them whisper like illicit lovers. I unclasped the brooches that closed my chiton and let the fabric puddle to my feet. Alexander's fingers fluttered like swallow's wings across my throat and breasts as he explored their contours, bringing me to the brink of ecstasy with his kisses alone, each impression from his soft mouth creating a delicious burning as though they were imprints of gently warmed wax. With our lips and tongues we honored every atomy of each other's bodies. With his fingers and his mouth, Paris Alexandros worshipped at the altar between my thighs, drinking the sticky-sweet nectar he elicited as a tribute to the undulations of his tongue. When he entered me, his sex reminded me what it meant to be a woman and to give and receive the greatest bounty known to mortals. For hours, I swam in the winedark waters of Eros and Himeros, receiving the seed of Alexander's loins. Our fingers danced in each other's golden hair, creating tingles of ecstasy like fractured bolts of lightning. My lover took my strawberry-tipped nipples into his mouth, nibbling them into a ripe hardness, and my womb became ready to embrace his length once more. "You have robbed me of words and now you rob me of breath," I told him, crying my pleasure yet again into the crisp night air.

A rustle of leaves and murmured voices warned us that we were in danger of discovery if we did not quit the grove immediately. The ruined temple of the Goddess was a popular spot for romantic assignations, particularly during Kronia. We dressed in haste, redonned our disguises, and slipped between the trees, where Selene's cool gaze could not penetrate. I explained the deeply personal significance of the sacred site to Paris Alexandros. "The progeny of Leda and the great swan, I was conceived upon that plinth. It was there that Zeus ravished my mother in a consecrated ritual honoring the Goddess. And it was there, too, where as a child I found her pendant body, her final offering to the source of all life. The grove is my favorite place in all of Sparta and the only one where Menelaus cannot disturb my peace." I told the Troyan prince that my stepfather had ordered the shrine demolished after he discovered my mother's unusual infidelity, a decision that was fully sanctioned by Menelaus once we were wed. "My husband even desecrated the temples of his own gods," I added, disclosing to Paris Alexandros how he had ordered the bronze to be stripped from all the shrines and altars. "But after he dared to rob the tomb of the House of Tyndareus of its brazen treasures, I refused to share his bed. I never loved Menelaus, but I always showed him proper wifely respect. When he despoiled my family's tomb, he lost that as well. Such a man was no longer deserving of my honor. The Atridae live for personal gain and aggrandizement. At any cost."

Arm in arm we walked across the valley toward the palace. "Menelaus *was* right about one thing," whispered Paris Alexandros, breathing softly into my ear.

"And what is that?"

"That if I stayed in Sparta for your Kronia festival, I would receive the best of everything."

～～～

For the next few days, Paris Alexandros and I were nearly inseparable. We swam naked in the cool waters of the Eurotas and feasted on cold roast meats and olives in the open air. We returned to the plains below Mount Taygetos with our horses and rode through the mountain trails. In every desolate location, we made love. At night, we would return to the sacred grove and anoint the altar with the spendings of our desire.

The first half of Kronia was drawing to a close. Soon, Menelaus would be returning home, the nine days of Kronian abstinence and atonement having already commenced by the time he arrived in Sparta.

"I must leave in two days," Paris Alexandros told me as we lay satiated in each other's arms in the coolness of the grove. "Tomorrow morning I will give the order to my men to be sure the ships are prepared to sail."

"I wish you never had to leave," I confessed, blinking back the moistness in my eyes. "I wish that every day could be the beginning of Kronia."

The Troyan prince was silent for several moments. "It can be," he said, nibbling at my lips. "Come with me."

"You can't be serious!"

"I have never been more so," he replied, gazing directly into my eyes. "You are Aphrodite's greatest gift. To mankind and to me."

"I am a married woman, Paris. With children. Nico is all I have left of my sons; in a few years' time, he, too, will be taken from me and I shall never see him again until he is taller than his father. And Hermione . . . I cannot abandon my young daughter. She is barely nine summers old. Insofar as my husband's treatment of me, he has been everything from merely neglectful to overtly hostile . . . perhaps I can conscience leaving him, as there is nothing left for me in our marriage except a dull and doleful stalemate of affections. But I cannot abandon my children." I began to weep, thinking of Iphigenia. "To rip either child or mother from each other before the child is fully grown is against the laws of nature."

⁓

Aethra clucked and chided when I confided my dilemma. "I want to go with him," I said.

"Do you love this barbarian prince?" she asked me.

"Beyond all measure. Beyond what I ever imagined it was possible to feel. Perhaps Paris Alexandros speaks the truth. Perhaps it *is* my destiny and I am free to fuss and fret and try to fight it, but not to change it or alter its course." Reason and desire warred within my psyche.

Aethra spared no love for Menelaus, but she counseled me nonetheless to remain in Sparta. "If nothing else, you owe a duty to your people as their queen," she reminded me. Perhaps she was annoyed, despite her old ambivalence about my love for her son, that another man had displaced Theseus from his aerie atop the summit of my affections. "It will come to no good end," was all she added. It was then that I recalled the words she had spoken on the Athenian pergamos when I was saying my final farewell to Theseus. He had promised me that one day a man would come who would love me as much I did him. Aethra had inserted her unsolicited oar with a portentous invocation. *And may the gods help you,* she had said.

I reasoned myself into the elopement. The gods were punishing Menelaus for his desecration of their temples. The arrival of Paris Alexandros, who had been promised by Aphrodite that I would be his, was proof of their vengeance. If I took little Nico with me, it would be a further embarrassment to the royal family, depriving Sparta of another future hoplite. Hermione's remaining behind was the only way to assure Menelaus's security on the Spartan throne. He was king only by virtue of his marriage to me. If I was gone, my children would provide his tenuous link to power. I could deprive my husband of my body and my presence, but I could not bring myself to deliver the blow that would strip him of his right to rule Sparta. Besides, Hermione was the shining light in Menelaus's eyes, his favorite child, and to take her to Ilios would be to blind him. Even Aethra could not accompany me because she was needed to stay behind and care for the children. They loved and trusted her, and she would have to be the bulwark between them and any attempts by Menelaus to punish the offspring of my loins for my transgression.

My pacing must have worn a path in the cool stone flooring of my rooms. Like my father Zeus, I was ruled by my sudden, almost violent, sexual passions, so how else could I be expected to behave when all was said and done? In disobeying my lawful husband, I was only obeying my nature.

Clearly, we had to leave before Menelaus returned; his absence made my departure—and the choice to abscond at all—an easier one. I would be relieved of having to find a way to say good-bye. But how would I bid farewell forever to my children? This prospect terrified me; I rethought my decision to leave them in Sparta many times over. Hermione, you were always far closer to your father than you ever were to me, so I don't believe you can begin to imagine how painful my determination was. I had hoped that as you grew to womanhood I would teach you its secrets and our bond would finally strengthen. In making the agonizing decision to abandon you, I knew I was risking your hatred for the rest of your days. Never had I anticipated that a man would come from across the sea and imprison my heart. I had no choice but to follow it, for without it I was an incomplete soul. Had your mother remained in Sparta, she would have been a heartless woman. My immortal beauty has been called perfection, but in all things I am not perfect. They reflect the half of me that is all too human.

I went to Paris Alexandros and told him that I would sail with him for Troy. He was overjoyed. Coming to him had the effect of strengthening my resolve. Held by his gaze, and in his embrace, I was once again spellbound and could not imagine spending life without him, condemned to an existence of modest and passionless comportment in a loveless royal marriage, deprived of my sons by the Spartan elders, and raising a daughter who cared little for me.

On the Ninth Night of Kronia, I kissed my children good night and enveloped them in my arms with an even greater tenderness. Nico was too young to realize that he would most likely never see me again, so there was no point in trying to explain that his *mitera* was leaving him. To you, Hermione, I remember saying simply, *I am going on a voyage.* I tried to keep the tears out of my voice. You shrugged and did not ask when I might return; but like a dutiful daughter, you let me embrace you and kissed my cheeks before clutching your doll and shuffling off to bed. To Aethra, I reaffirmed my trust in her wisdom and her affection for my young children.

I had packed my robes, my cosmetics, and my jewels. Paris Alexandros warned me that there was not enough room aboard his ship for all of my possessions as well as the trunk that had belonged to my mother. I despaired of leaving her legacy behind and reluctantly selected a few items that were most precious to me, including the garments she had worn as a priestess, her jewels, and the swan's feather that remained on the altar after my father flew away from the sacred grove. The rest I left in my rooms, consoling myself by reasoning that as Leda was a true daughter of Sparta, she belonged there and not in Troy.

Yet I, too, was a daughter of Sparta, as well as its rightful queen. I cursed the gods for placing before me a temptation so irresistible that I became willing to forfeit not only my family and my crown, but also my homeland—to bid farewell forever to my beloved Mount Taygetos and the muddy banks of the sparkling Eurotas . . . to never again seek the solace of the sacred grove. My heart ached with sacrifice.

Under cover of darkness, Paris Alexandros, Aeneas, and I rode to Gythium. I took Aeneas's horse while he carried my trunk in a chariot belonging to Menelaus, which he had managed to covertly liberate from our stables. By the water's edge lay the pomegranate-hued hull of the Troyan prince's ship and another belonging to his kinsman. Aeneas boarded his vessel and Paris carried me onto on his pentekonter like a conquering hero. At his command, the sail was raised and fifty oars in unison sliced noiselessly through the winedark waves of the Great Sea. The wind captured my veil and claimed it as a forfeit. Enfolded in his embrace, my mouth met Alexander's in a lingering kiss. The only sound to penetrate the silence of the night air was the slapping of the water against the bloodred hull that drew me farther and farther from Achaea, from marriage and motherhood, into strange and uncharted territory.

⤛ EIGHTEEN ⤜

W hat country is this?" I asked upon waking, stiff and groggy-eyed from an uncomfortable night in cramped quarters. I had not recalled the *Minotaur* being as claustrophobic as this vessel was. Perhaps it was, but I was a mere slip of a girl then and sea voyages were a new and exciting adventure. The terrain just beyond our bow was similar to the Peloponnese. Surely this could not be the bustling port that bestrode the eastern and western worlds.

"This is Cyprus," answered Paris Alexandros. "The Hittites of Anatolia, who claim it as their territory, call it Alasiya. We will anchor here before we continue on to Wilusa. I wish to make sacrifices to Aphrodite on the island of her birth. She must see how pleased we are at the fulfillment of her promise."

His desire to propitiate our patron goddess made sense, although I would have preferred to have been heading straight for Troy. Having made the agonizing decision to go to Ilios with Paris Alexandros, I now wished to get there as soon as possible. "How long would it take if we were to have sailed directly from Gythium?"

"From Gythium? Four days, perhaps five if the winds were favorable." Paris Alexandros steered my gaze back to the prow of his ship. "See the dolphins leading our way? It is a sign that we are favorably starred."

I seemed to recall that Theseus and I had enjoyed a similar escort and things did not end well for us. "If you lay such store by superstition, then what of the omen that warned your expectant mother that you would bring ruination upon Troy—the portent that caused your parents to expel you from Ilios when you were but a few days old?" I was already allowing fear and regret to tinge my love for the Troyan prince. Perhaps the stop in Cyprus was a good idea after all. I would pray to Aphrodite to guide me. Yet how could I place the bounty of my trust in her when I was not certain I had done the right thing in accompanying Paris Alexandros to his homeland?

We remained in sunkissed Cyprus until the moon was once again full, then hoisted the sail for Anatolia. Or so I thought. We were beset by heavy seas and a great north wind that blew us off course; within two days, we had landed in Sidon, well to the south of our intended destination. I had heard tales of the great Phoenician port and of the land renowned for its cedarwood, used in vast quantities to build the greatest navy ever known to man. Sidon was a bustling center of commerce, even larger than Piraeus was, as I remembered it from my travels with Theseus. After so many years in peaceful, provincial Sparta, I was unused to such crowds, the cacophony of man and beast—and the filth. The entire city wanted a good whitewashing, from the facades of the tightly packed dwellings to the dirt-encrusted skin of the ragamuffins who prowled the port seeking to relieve its visitors and denizens alike from their pouches of gold and precious stones.

I noticed that Paris Alexandros did not appear terribly inconvenienced by what I believed was an unexpected detour. "Why are we here?" I asked him. "Was the seduction of Helen merely a stop along your trading route?" I was not feeling terribly well; life upon my beloved sea was not as companionable as it once had been, and I admit to having been extremely irritable then. I had not abandoned my homeland and children for this. "Was that your true embassy? Woo the queen of Sparta; propitiate Aphrodite for having enabled you to do so; buy ships and lumber?" I accused my lover of being as insensitive as Menelaus, and stung by my words, Paris Alexandros promised to conclude his business with the Sidonian merchants as quickly as practicable. He sought to appease me by securing several elaborately wrought robes for my wardrobe; nevertheless, we spent nearly two moons there before we were once again under way for Troy.

Under a favorable west wind, we sailed past Samos, Chios, and the leeward side of Lesbos. But the closer we got to Ilios, the stronger the headwinds that tried to prevent us from safely reaching the port. Passing the isle of Tenedos off the Anatolian coast, I noticed many ships with colorful sails moored and bobbing on the white-tipped waves.

"The north winds can blow for weeks," Paris told me. "And until the winds change, the ships must bide their time in this sheltered strait, paying my father for the privilege to remain in Wilusan waters, rather than risk lives and precious cargo by challenging the wind."

Finally, with the northern tip of Tenedos safely at our stern, we approached the Hellespont. Off the starboard side was the bay of Ilios. My heart was drumming wildly within my chest as we rounded the beachhead. The rowers raised their pinewood oars, allowing the tide to pull us onto the sand. From the shore we could not even see the vessels waiting out the south winds off Tenedos.

So this was the fabled Troy: the jewel of the East, glittering hub of trade from all corners of the world. Paris Alexandros carried me off the ship and onto dry land. The breezes off the bay immediately took hold of my cloak, whipping it about, and swirling the sands about my ankles. My lover's horse was taken from the vessel, and Paris lifted me onto the stallion's back and swung into the saddle behind me. Beyond the bluffs, we came upon a defensive ditch, perhaps as deep as a man's waist and twice as broad. On horseback, it was impossible to cross without a running jump to breach it, which the terrain did not permit. A chariot never would have been successful. It would even have been difficult for a man to cross it on his own; he might have jumped into the ditch with relative ease, but climbing back out would have slowed his progress immensely, particularly if he was armored.

Paris Alexandros led his mount to a cut in the ditch where planks might be laid and removed, permitting the Troyans ingress and egress to the city limits. "I wondered how you were going to bring a horse into Ilios," I said as we crossed the cut and approached a high stone wall. Paris drew a horn from his belt and blew a long blast. The huge gates swung open for us, and we passed through them into the lower city. Now, finally, I had the first glimpse of the Troy I had imagined: the tree-lined winding lanes, some wide and sunny, others narrow and shaded; the well-spaced dwellings along the broader avenues, homes to wealthy merchants and traders; and the more closely configured homes on the smaller streets those of common laborers. Thrushes sang sweetly from the fruit trees in the private gardens; the air was redolent of sea brine and fragrant spices. Unlike the crowded and smelly Piraeus and Sidon, this port city gleamed. The citizens, recognizing a son of Priam riding through their midst, waved and bowed and called out his name. He was clearly a favorite among the ladies. Women tossing flowers from their upper windows at the handsome prince turned to one another when they spied me, their expressions conveying both curiosity and envy. "Do they know who I am?" I asked.

"The most beautiful woman in the world needs no introduction. Even the slaves in Wilusa have heard the tales of Helen of Sparta."

The city was at least as vast as Athens; perhaps even more so. Excited, anxious, and somewhat fearful, I rode toward the citadel, the roads of the lower city sloping gently upward, their twisting configuration most often describing the shape of a thunderbolt hurled from the walled upper city. The ramparts were crenellated like saw teeth or like an undulating wave that wrapped protectively around the royal dwellings and temples. From one massive tower, one could look across the Hellespont north to the Black Sea and to the fingerlike Thracian peninsula; the other tower, its perfect twin, afforded a clear vista south to the Aegean. I had never seen anything like it. With such a triple fortification, it was little wonder to me that no one had ever successfully subdued the Troyans. Between the two unadorned towers lay a massive gate set within the walls: high but surprisingly narrow for its size. Two blasts of his horn opened what Paris Alexandros called the Scaean Gate. Before us lay Priam's palace, by far the most impressive edifice within the citadel.

Paris dismounted and lifted me down. "I can't wait for my family to meet you," he murmured, claiming my mouth. Hand in hand, we climbed the two grand tiers of steps and entered the palace.

You could have put at least two of Sparta's Great Halls within the Troyan one. I was sure that it was even finer than Agamemnon's in Mycenae. Paris Alexandros and I traversed the length of the room to the accompaniment of so many whispers and murmurs and buzzing that I felt like I was in a field of wildflowers hosting dozens of honeybees amid their fragrant petals. The court was an exotic one. Men and women alike wore robes of silk, brightly colored, embroidered and brocaded, smelled of musk and ambergris and hyacinth, and adorned themselves with extravagantly wrought golden jewelry.

Suddenly, all went silent. An elaborately robed graybeard in a horned headdress shaped like the head of a bull—the Trojan Bull of Heaven—rose from the throne. Priam. Beside him, a majestic-looking woman wearing a golden wreath atop her silvery black tresses, glared malevolently at Paris Alexandros. "What have you done?" she breathed. She would have said more but was silenced by her husband.

"I didn't believe it was true," he said to Paris.

"It is," the prince replied, feigning indifference to the hostile reaction he was receiving. "King Priam, Queen Hecuba—Father and Mother—this is Helen. Helen of . . . Troy."

Before Priam could respond, a young woman in priestly robes, her hair flying wildly about her shoulders, burst into the Great Hall. "Death!" she shrieked, pointing at us. The glaze in her eyes was no doubt induced by laurel leaves—chewed by prophetesses of the temples before issuing their oracular decrees. "Blood! I see blood and death! The blood of our fathers and brothers, husbands and sons, shed for the harlot of Sparta! Every house in Wilusa burning to ash for the sake of her perfect breasts and honeyed thighs." She turned her invective on Paris Alexandros. "How dare you have the hubris to flout the words of the seers? You have no business being alive. Our parents should have slaughtered you ere you left Hecuba's womb and not trusted your death to other hands." My lover was visibly shaken. Priam ordered the girl removed from the Great Hall.

"She is so pretty," I whispered to Paris Alexandros. "It is a shame she is mad."

He quickly explained the situation. The hysterical woman was Cassandra, his younger sister, a priestess and prophetess at the temple of Apollo. It was believed that Apollo himself once fell in love with her and asked her to be his consort, to which she happily agreed. But when he kissed her, she reneged on her promise, and so he spat in her mouth; thereafter, any prophecy she uttered was doomed to be dismissed as folly. Her twin brother Helenus was also a seer and a priest, but his oracular predictions were uniformly accepted as truth and had invariably proved correct over the years. "Were he here to buttress Cassandra's wild prognostications, I might have reason for concern. My little brother is nowhere to be seen, however, and so I see no cause for despair." Still, Alexander's eyes betrayed what his voice did not.

"We had visitors while you were gone," Priam informed his second son. "A delegation from Achaea: cunning Odysseus the Ithacan, old Nestor of Pylos, and King Menelaus of Sparta, who claimed that you had abducted his wife." Priam looked directly at me, then returned his focus to Paris Alexandros. "They demanded her immediate return as well as the treasures you stole from the Spartan palace."

"Treasures?!" I blurted. "We took nothing but my own personal effects and some things belonging to my late mother."

"I told Menelaus that we were not harboring Helen," continued Priam. "That she was not in Wilusa and had never arrived on our shores. But I was disbelieved. As the Spartan king had also entertained Aeneas, and Aeneas was standing beside me, Menelaus thus reasoned that you and Helen must have returned as well and that I was either feigning ignorance or was being obstinate. I am indeed obstinate. 'Had Helen been here,' I told the Achaeans, 'I would *still* shelter her within Troy's walls in retaliation for the abduction of my sister Hesione by *your* countrymen.' Upon hearing my final words on the subject, the flowing-haired Achaeans fumed and threatened and promised to return with an armada that would reduce Wilusa to rubble and smoldering ash. 'Then come!' I told them. 'And Troy will face you down and turn your great warriors into carrion for the crows!' "

Hecuba's eyes blazed with angry fire. I had heard that the Hittite queens were renowned for their formidability, and this Anatolian sovereign appeared to be no exception. "Listen to your mother's words, Alexandros," she said, her voice the low rumbling warning of impending storms. "You were ever destined to bring ruin to your homeland. It is not for men to question the gods or to circumvent their designs. You tried to cheat them once, but it only purchased you some time. That woman," she added, rising and pointing imperiously to me, "will be *your* ruin and the downfall of Troy. It is not too late to send her back to Sparta. Let her husband do with her what he will; it is none of my concern. My cares are for the welfare of the men of Wilusa and the women who will be widowed by your lust."

A swarthy-complected man, tall and well muscled, supported the queen's position. "Should we be compelled to defend our homes because my elder brother can't control his passions?" he scowled, a hand upon his silver-hilted sword. "Since our parents were too craven to kill you at birth, they should have let me do it with my spear." I guessed that the speaker was Deiphobus, who appeared also to be ruled by his passions, although his were fueled with anger. He was the one who had tried to kill Paris Alexandros during the athletic games. Alexander's return had displaced the third-born Deiphobus as heir apparent to Hector's glory, and it was evident that Deiphobus bore him no fraternal affection. I took an immediate dislike to him. His manner was rough and his demeanor coarse. In some ways he reminded me of Agamemnon, but without the undeniably imposing regality of the Mycenaean High King or Agamemnon's striking looks.

Then spoke a darker version of Paris Alexandros, bearded, handsome, and noble. "I have no burning hunger for war, brother, being newly a father. But I will not hesitate to take up the spear for my family and for Troy if called upon to do so. I am more of our father's mind. It is no secret that the Achaeans have long sought to possess Priam's domain and plunder its riches. Mycenae is a city rich in trade and Wilusa is enriched beyond all measure by taxing it. The presence of the Spartan queen within our walls is a political subterfuge no doubt designed by the crafty Ithacan and endorsed by the High King of Mycenae in order to convince the Greek chieftains to rally in defense of the sullied honor of Menelaus. If the Greeks come to take our city and seek to control the Hellespont, it will not be because of Helen."

I remember not knowing what to make of all this discourse. Was the Troyan royal family friend or foe to Helen?

With the situation remaining unresolved, we left the Great Hall, and Paris Alexandros brought me to his palatial rooms, arranging for a Thracian girl, Xanthippe, to be my maidservant. She spoke no Greek.

My first evening in Ilios was awful. Although the food was plentiful and well prepared, and the wine and water were consumed from golden goblets, as Paris and Aeneas had asserted when we hosted them in Sparta, the Troyan women did not dine with the men; consequently, I was entirely friendless among those who took no pains to welcome me, flashing looks of resentment when they bothered to make eye contact at all. They spoke the Phrygian dialect, which I barely understood, catching an odd word here and there that sounded similar to a cognate in my own tongue. When I tried to speak with them, they did not understand me, or at least pretended not to. Priam, Hecuba, Hector, Aeneas, and Paris Alexandros all spoke good Greek. Surely some of the twelve daughters of Priam or the wives of whichever of his fifty sons had wed, spoke decent Greek as well. In this cosmopolitan metropolis, I had heard many dialects when Paris Alexandros and I rode through the streets; thus, I was hard pressed to believe that everyone in the royal women's dining hall spoke only Phrygian. I was horribly lonely and could not wait to be reunited with Paris in our bed, where no jealousies could touch us and where it was clear that I was desired.

~~~

"I fear I have made a dreadful mistake," I told Paris Alexandros as I lay in his arms. "I am not wanted here."

He brushed the hair from my brow with a gentle caress, then kissed me full on the lips. "I want you. I want you here. Here. Beside me forever."

"Except for you, I am all alone here in Ilios. The women hate me. Even your mother hates me."

"Her opinion is inconsequential to me. She still believes I should be dead. When I cheated the omens, my father embraced me like the long-lost son I was and called for a festival in honor of my homecoming. My mother did not rejoice. My father accepts you; and my brother Hector, the noblest man on earth, welcomes you as well."

"His wife, Andromache, was one of the rudest of all. She is determined to detest me. I went to embrace her as a sister and she cursed me with almost as great a furor as your sister Cassandra. I had heard that Andromache was a woman of great dignity. But not when it comes to welcoming Helen, I fear. I am a daughter of Zeus, and I have been a queen. If they refuse to respect my birthright, can they not at least welcome me as their brother's beloved?"

I wept in Alexander's arms, bedewing his chest with my hot tears. I had not anticipated such antipathy. But in those strong arms I found a solace and a satiation I had never known until we'd met. Paris Alexandros gave me a reason to exist, and wherever we dwelled, as long as we were together, I could endeavor to endure the taunts and insults of the envious.

Days turned to weeks and weeks became months. Time and distance continued to diminish any homesickness I still might have harbored. Three of my boys by Menelaus were in the *agogi,* and I would not have seen them for many more years, even if I had remained in Sparta. You, Hermione, had always reserved your affections for your father. I did miss little Nico, but soon he, too, would be taken by the Spartan elders to become a hoplite. There were moments when I longed for the wild beauty of my Laconian countryside, but I did not pine for the Spartan lifestyle or for my abandoned husband. I resolved anyhow to look forward to what might lie ahead rather than dwell too much in what I had chosen to leave behind. I was reminded of the future every day. A new life now throbbed within my womb.

Apart from meals, Paris Alexandros and I spent every moment in each other's company. And no Achaeans stormed the port with their black-hulled ships. One day we rode out to Mount Ida. As I had brought Paris Alexandros to Mount Taygetos where I roamed as a girl, he yearned to show me the countryside where he was raised as a shepherd lad by Agelaus. We crossed the river Scamander and wended our way up the mountainside, where the air was cool and sweet. By that time, I should point out, the Troyan prince was referring to me as his wife, for I was in every way; indeed, it was how I had come to see myself, although Priam and Hecuba had refused to host a formal wedding feast. Hecuba, particularly, had tried her best to ignore my pregnancy.

At the sound of hoofbeats, the mountain villagers came out of their humble abodes. Agelaus welcomed us, insisting that we join him for a meal of roasted lamb. He seemed pleased to meet me; and his love for Paris Alexandros was undeniable, a far warmer affection than Priam had conferred upon his prodigal. Yet most interested in our visit was a dark-haired nymphlike girl, whom Paris, with some trepidation, introduced to me as Oenone, his favorite childhood playmate, exceptionally skilled in the arts of healing. Oenone looked me in the eye, then turned her gaze on my obviously swollen belly. She bit her lip and blinked back tears.

"Are you still such a genius with that bow of yours?" Agelaus said hastily in an attempt to alter the dampened mood of their reunion. "Or has your new life on silken cushions softened the boy I raised?"

Paris Alexandros slung his bow across his shoulder and wordlessly pointed to a circling hawk. Drawing an arrow from his quiver and laying it across the bowstring, he squinted, took aim, and let his missile fly, bringing down the predator in a single shot. "Now show me a hare or deer, bear or boar, and their first taste of my arrow will catch them on their final breath."

Agelaus laughed and embraced his foster son. "Finest marksman on Mount Ida! In all of Troy and Dardania, too! But don't think his skill is limited to the creatures of the woods and sky. He could bring down a man the same way, if he had a mind to."

"If I had a mind to," Paris Alexandros echoed. "I have no love for killing, except to put food on the table. I am a hunter, not a soldier like my brother Hector."

~~~

My anxiety was reawakened; I could not hold my tongue as we rode back toward Ilios. "You loved her," I said to Paris of the dark-haired girl Oenone. "And she still loves you. Tell me why you left her."

He had followed the men who took his prize white bull to the city and became swept up in the athletic games at the festival. Suddenly, his birthright was revealed, and he was welcomed back into the bosom of the royal family. There was no turning back; he was no longer a carefree man of the hills, free to consort with and marry a simple mountain girl. Paris Alexandros assumed the regal mantle; with some regret for leaving Oenone among her people on Mount Ida, he moved on, embracing his new life as a prince of Troy. "Are you jealous?" he asked me. The sensation was new and terrifying; that I, the most desirable woman in the world, should fear losing her lover—her new husband—to anyone else, least of all to a lowly shepherdess. I despised myself for my vanity, but I could not deny its existence. "You are the only woman for me," Paris Alexandros soothed. "I want to live every day of my life in your love and to die in your arms."

"Pretty words."

"You disbelieve me?"

I touched my belly. "It must be my condition," I replied, trying to embrace his assurances. "We are starting a family of our own now."

It was the first time I truly felt like Helen of Troy.

NINETEEN

Gradually, I became acclimated to my adopted homeland. I insisted that Paris Alexandros teach me the Phrygian dialect and instruct me on the customs of his country. I was afraid to make even the slightest misstep, for I knew that people were closely watching, eager for me to fail at something or to make an utter fool of myself. Priam's household was vast. While Hecuba was his queen and sole official wife, he had ninety-nine concubines, many of whom had borne him children. Several of King Priam's fifty sons and twelve daughters were already grown, or nearly so, and had families of their own, all of whom resided in connecting rooms within the palace bordered by smooth-stoned cloister walks. The king's kinsmen were called "the great family" and enjoyed special privileges, which they constantly exploited. Priam's third son, Deiphobus, was particularly abusive. I remember one night after dinner, I was nestled on a cushion at Alexander's feet, as was my custom, my head in his lap while his fingers entwined themselves in the tendrils of my hair. Deiphobus had been in an angry mood that day, although I must admit that I never saw him when he appeared to be content, or even sanguine, about anything. He was in his cups, too, as far as I could tell and had Eumetes, one of his personal slaves, in attendance simply to keep his golden rhyton filled with wine. The bard had been singing for many minutes; in honor of my Troyan husband he was weaving the yarn of the Judgment of Paris. The story of Alexander's dream had quickly become the stuff of legend, embellished by the bards. When the blind man sang of Aphrodite's promise to Paris Alexandros, Eumetes turned to gaze upon me as he went to refill his master's goblet. In the youth's inattention, he tripped over my cushion, causing him to stumble and spill the wine all over Deiphobus.

In one swift motion, the scowling prince rose and grabbed the young slave by the wrist, drawing the silver-handled dagger he always wore at his waist. The oinochoe flew out of Eumetes's hand and clattered to the floor, splashing wine, like a river of blood, across my lap. Cursing Eumetes for his clumsiness, Deiphobus was about to sever the youth's hand from his body. White with terror, Eumetes pled for mercy before his master could strike the disfiguring blow. I held my breath. Surely such barbarism was not common to such an advanced cosmopolis as Ilios.

Suddenly Hector was between them, his body shielding Eumetes from Deiphobus and his own knife at his younger brother's throat. They argued openly, Deiphobus asserting his right by law to punish his slave, Hector attempting to convince Deiphobus to see reason: The punishment clearly did not fit the crime.

Paris Alexandros leaned forward to whisper in my ear. "In Wilusa, if a slave displeases his master, the master may punish him by maiming or even killing him—or her. Not only that, it is also within the master's rights to subject the slave's relatives to the same punishment, even if they are entirely blameless." I was stunned. In Achaea, a life of slavery was not without its perils, but we did not hold an entire family to account for the misdeed of a single servant.

"I will not stand by while you torture Eumetes," said Hector. "The boy knows he did something wrong. Accept his apology and that will make an end of it."

My husband explained that slaves were forgiven if they admitted their transgression. After all, they were not deemed fully human and therefore could not be held entirely culpable. "In Anatolia, a slave is considered only half a person, and if he commits an offense, he is therefore liable for only half the amount of the penalty, whereas his master, should he commit the same offense, would be responsible for the entirety."

I was still confused by their laws. "But if the penalty includes mutilation, like the removal of a hand, how does one cut off only half a hand?" I wasn't sure I really wanted to learn the answer. I resolved, however, to observe the slaves more closely, particularly those who served Deiphobus.

Hector skillfully diffused the conflict and Eumetes remained unscathed, but not before Deiphobus fired off a final insult. "You love to play the hero, don't you, brother," he taunted Hector. "Brave, spear-famed Hector. Noble Hector. You and our dog of a brother mock me because I remain unwed: you with a wife who is the epitome of loyalty, and Paris with one who is the quintessence of beauty." It was clear that he was aiming to wound each of his elder brothers by intimating that each of their wives lacked what the other possessed in abundance.

Hector, with his dignity and quiet strength, was always kind to me. Never had I met a man with a stronger sense of decency. Where I was concerned, he was not one to be swayed by the inconsiderate behavior and unpleasant opinions of others, including his loving wife, Andromache, to whom he was utterly devoted. Although it pained me greatly, as the moons waxed and waned, I learned to live without the affection of Alexander's kinsmen and women. Most of them made a deliberate show of ignoring me, which was preferable to outright hostility. I was not at all at ease around Deiphobus and tried to avoid his company whenever possible without appearing blatantly rude. He made it quite clear to me that he did not consider my marriage to Paris Alexandros a legitimate one—after all, Menelaus still lived, and it was *I* who had cast *him* off, and not the reverse. In Deiphobus's eyes I was nothing but a sweet-smelling, glorified whore, ripe for the taking. I confided my anxiety, even fear, to Paris Alexandros, who assured me of his constant protection; if I encountered Deiphobus alone, he counseled me to continue the course of action I had already undertaken. Paris Alexandros understood my predicament all too well. After all, the xenophobic Deiphobus had been willing to spit him upon his spear when he believed him to be a mere shepherd who had bested him in an athletic competition.

∼∼∼

I had been in Ilios for a little over a year when we received extremely disturbing news. King Priam could never be certain that the information provided by traders was reliable, but my intelligence arrived from an impeccable source. Ominously addressed to "The Widowmaker of

Troy," my ordinarily placid cousin Penelope sent word that in his capacity as High King, Agamemnon had invoked the Oath of Tyndareus, by which all of my former suitors were compelled to come to the aid of Menelaus. The very plan that her husband Odysseus had craftily designed was coming back to haunt him. Aware that he was about to be tripped up by his own scheme, and having been warned by a seer that if he went to war at Agamemnon's behest, he would not return home for twenty years, the Ithacan chieftain feigned madness. Thus, when Agamemnon and his kinsman Palamedes came to rocky Ithaca to recruit him, Odysseus was found sowing his fields with salt instead of seeds, his plow pulled by an ass and a cow. Only a madman would salt his own soil. Salting was so devastating to the land that it had even become an effective military tactic: An army might salt the fields of their adversary, rendering the earth completely infertile for generations to come. Without the ability to grow crops, the enemy and their families would starve. And here was Odysseus risking the utter destruction of his estate, his tiny son's inheritance. Palamedes, who could be even wilier than Odysseus, had snatched Penelope's infant Telemachus from her arms and laid him before Odysseus's plow. While she and their baby shrieked with terror, Odysseus made straight for the child, and just before the ill-matched livestock were about to crush Telemachus under their hooves, he steered the plow away. Odysseus's reaction had been my cousin's greatest relief, but also her greatest sorrow, for it meant that her clever husband had been overmatched by Palamedes and had no choice but to abide by the Oath of Tyndareus. His ruse revealed, Odysseus then attempted—unsuccessfully—to weasel out of his pledge by reasoning with Agamemnon, holding up a mirror to the High King's motive for war and arguing that if the Achaean chieftains abandoned their homes to plunder Ilios, their own cities would thus be ripe for the taking while they were miles away in Anatolia.

"Your lust has robbed me of my beloved," Penelope said, "and my son will grow to manhood never having known his father. How many other men will you rip from the arms of their wives, from the eager grasp of their children, from the handles of their plows, from their forges, and from their cobblers' benches?"

Although I loved Penelope, I was less sorry for her than might have been expected. I respected Odysseus's mental agility and knew that he was a man to be feared because of it. But had he not devised the Oath of Tyndareus, which effectively sealed our individual and collective doom? Had there not been such a pledge, I might not have been married off to Menelaus. Had there not been such a pledge, Agamemnon would have had a far more difficult time convincing the leading Achaean chieftains to commit themselves and their subjects to a protracted war with Troy. At whose feet then, should the guilt for "widowmaking" be laid? I was prepared to accept my share of the blame, but it was not mine alone.

This was only the first taste I was to have of the wrath of my own countrywomen. Naturally it stung, but Penelope's words were doubly painful because she was my kin: a friend from childhood who became a woman I admired, if not envied, for the abiding and passionate love she shared with her husband. *Widowmaker.* The word tasted bitter and metallic, as if I had laid a knife across my tongue. It clutched at my heart like the talons of a hawk.

According to Troyan spies, the Achaeans continued to ply their trickery in their efforts to strengthen the Greek forces. Agamemnon claimed that it had been foretold that he could not conquer Ilios without the aid of the young Achilles and his father Peleus's elite army of Myrmidons. To that end, he had sent the crafty Odysseus to the kingdom of Lycomedes in Skyros. The Ithacan's errand was to smoke out the valiant youth who had been squirreled away on the rocky island by his mother Thetis, disguised there among the old king's fifty daughters, one of whom had secretly become Achilles's lover and had borne him a son, Neoptolemus. Like Hecuba, the pregnant Thetis had also experienced a prophetic dream: Her son would end up either dying gloriously in battle, or, if he never went to war, would enjoy old age in the bosom of his family. Thus warned, Thetis sought to protect her boy from the clash of bronze and the pungent stench of winedark blood and rotting flesh. Because his mother was said to be a sea nymph, the young Achilles and I shared a demimortality. I felt another unusual connection to the youth, although we had never met. In the now-famous dream of Paris Alexandros, it was Achilles's parents' wedding feast that Eris had interrupted with the golden apple. In the story, Eris's appearance had led to the Great Judgment of Paris Alexandros, which led to my union with the Troyan prince.

And now Paris Alexandros and I had a son of our own: little Idaeus, as affectionate as his father. Like Thetis, I despaired of him ever going to war. No mother rejoices in her son's thirst to die young. I had already lost my other boys to the rigorous Spartan military training program. Now it seemed that my destiny was to bring the Achaean warriors to Anatolian shores. Would my newborn babe one day be called to fight against my old countrymen—and perhaps his half brothers—to defend his family and his own homeland?

A personal attack on family honor had escalated into an international crisis. Several of the chieftains were bound by the Oath of Tyndareus because they had sworn it personally; but their soldiers were held by no such pledge and needed to be convinced to leave their homes, their fields and farms, and their families to sail to distant shores for the sake of one man's marital honor. Agamemnon's strategy, wrote Penelope, was to convince the common man that if the home of the powerful King of Sparta was not safe, and his hospitality so flagrantly breached by an honored houseguest, then no Achaean home was secure from such treachery; no wife's fidelity nor daughter's chastity could be taken for granted or guaranteed. To fight for Helen was to fight for all of the women of Achaea.

Recalling Theseus's words—*men do not go to war over a woman*—I despaired of the High King's manipulation of so many trusting and malleable souls. If I could not explain to Penelope, who was the most intelligent and rational woman I knew, that the misogynistic Agamemnon would never wage war for the sake of a woman, not one, not thousands, then how could I make the case to women who had even more cause to despise me?

⁓⁓⁓

According to the news we received from Achaea, it took nearly two years from the time I eloped with Paris Alexandros before the High King was able to amass his coalition. Odysseus and Achilles—who had never even sworn the Oath of Tyndareus, having been a mere boy at the time and far too young to have been my suitor—had both been tricked into going to war. A thousand ships, which meant fifty thousand men to man their oars, were now assembled on the mainland at Aulis on the Euboean Strait, but already there was dissension within the ranks. The chieftains who were among the first to join their own forces with those of Agamemnon's had been waiting many months for him to decide that he had amassed enough soldiers to successfully sack Troy. In the meantime, there was no one left at home to till their fields and tend their flocks; and their families, abandoned indefinitely by men who had never even left Achaean shores, were starving and suffering. The men themselves were going hungry in their makeshift tents in Aulis. Threatening mutiny, they demanded that Agamemnon slaughter the hundred bulls he had intended to sacrifice as a hecatomb to the gods for a safe and successful voyage to Ilios, using the meat to fill their groaning bellies instead.

Fearing rebellion, the High King reluctantly capitulated. The men were fed and the wind kicked up—a sure sign that warriors' stomachs merited the precedence over the Olympians—but no sooner had they sailed through the Euboean Strait than a contrary high wind, a norther, blew them back to port. Once more, they laid in wait for favorable conditions.

And then . . . when we finally received word that the Argive host was again ready to sail . . . the winds off Aulis became uncooperative and died.

Apparently, the High King was placing great store in the prognostications of a man named Kalchas, a Troyan priest gifted in augury. Kalchas had been sent by Priam as a trustworthy emissary on a peacemaking mission but had defected from his errand and elected to serve Agamemnon instead. After seeing a snake devour a mother bird and her eight nestlings, Kalchas foresaw a nine-year siege outside the walls of Troy. In the tenth year, he claimed, the city would finally fall. Agamemnon sought to keep this news from his army. Should they learn that the quick skirmish they had expected would drag on for a decade, their chieftains would surely seek to withdraw before hoisting a single sail.

No wind. A reason for every man, woman, and child in Ilios to exhale. Depending on one's belief, either time or the gods were truly on the Troyan side of the imminent conflict.

And then . . . the most devastating news of all.

Clytemnestra, with whom I had not communicated since I'd left Sparta, sent a message through a Troyan silver trader she encountered in Aulis. She laid the lengthwise warp of her missive and with each sentence wove a crosswise strand of the weft until the entire hideous picture was before me: The climate at Aulis was stagnant, the winds absent, and the soldiers, many of whom had been encamped on the beaches for several moons waiting for the order to sail, were impatient and demoralized.

Agamemnon, bolstered by yet another vision from Kalchas—prophecies that Clytemnestra believed were paid for by her husband—claimed the gods had told him that the only way to awaken the winds and ensure a victory in Ilios was for him to make the ultimate personal sacrifice as High King and leader of the Achaean armada.

Sharing his evil secret with no one, not even Menelaus, Agamemnon summoned Iphigenia to Aulis on the pretext of marrying her off to young Achilles, the Greeks' most promising warrior. My sister could not comprehend why her husband did not want her to be present for this prestigious union and contrived to accompany Iphigenia to Aulis nonetheless.

The story was becoming darker. Each word of Clytemnestra's tasted more bitter than the last.

Achilles, too, knew nothing of Agamemnon's plans, other than that he was to be the bridegroom to the eldest princess of Mycenae. According to Clytemnestra, he resented the High King's orchestration of his future. Achilles's sword thirsted to spill rivers of Trojan blood because, as his mother foretold, his martial prowess would be immortalized by the bards; he did not fight for the sake of Agamemnon's overweening greed.

Thus, were the colors laid by Clytemnestra.

"She is gone!" were her next words. "My Iphigenia! How soon she went from blushing and expectant bride to courageous victim, baring her breast according to custom so that the blow would be clean. Her flawless beauty stunned the soldiers into silence. I wept and tore my hair as a woman already in the throes of mourning. Several times I threw myself between them and tried to stop the brute, but Agamemnon shoved me to the ground as though I were no better than one of his bandy-legged serving girls.

" 'Don't butcher my baby for Helen's sake,' I pleaded. 'Perhaps the whore doesn't *want* to come home!'

" 'This pains me more than it could ever injure you,' he swore, and knocked me once more onto the dusty earth.

" 'And if Menelaus is as brutal as you are, I wouldn't blame her!' I spat, ignoring his feeble disclaimer.

"Agamemnon himself wielded the knife that made the fatal incision across Iphigenia's milk-white throat. Her blood, as bright as berries, drenched her yellow bridal dress and speckled my body and my garments. The blood of the only child I ever loved was on my hands as well as his. My virginal daughter, slaughtered on the altar like an animal! For the sake of favorable winds. For Athena and Poseidon the earth-shaker and Zeus who, while created in man's image, have no love for humankind. For the sake of my faithless whore of a sister, no paragon of female perfection in my eyes, but merely another bastard child of Zeus who could not keep her legs together and whose lust has brought shame and ruin on our house and an unnatural death to my beloved Iphigenia!"

Iphigenia? *Her* Iphigenia? *My* precious, beautiful daughter was no more, cut down like a yearling upon the altar! With the "sacrifice" of Iphigenia, the war between Achaea and Ilios had already begun, and the first blood to be shed was that of a child. *My* child, though unbeknownst to Agamemnon, who believed he had willingly butchered the first fruit of his own repellent loins in exchange for victory. Villains will bedeck their lies in the finery of clever words, but the stench of their rotten deeds will soon destroy their silken dressing, revealing the ugly truth beneath. Still, Agamemnon's self-serving and deliberate deceit of his troops did not alter the cold fact of death: Iphigenia, by his hand, now dwelled in Hades.

What had I done? A scream escaped my body as though I had been speared through the heart. Was this the gods' revenge for my transgression of love? If the gods controlled my destiny, wasn't I fulfilling it according to their plans by eloping with Paris Alexandros? Or was Agamemnon's invocation of the sky gods merely a convenient excuse for his overarching hubris—to demonstrate to fifty thousand angry and impatient warriors that he was willing to make the ultimate sacrifice for his country and that the very least *they* could do was to lay down their *own* lives for Achaea. Iphigenia must die for Hellas, the demon had argued, and who is she, a mere girl, to deny Greece? The

High King would rather shed his "daughter's" blood than surrender his own illusions, much less compromise his vainglorious imperial and military career. He had invented the idea of Hellas—a unified Achaea—as well as the view of the cosmopolitan Troyans as "barbarians," whose very existence, he convinced his troops, were an affront and a threat to young Hellenic girls like Iphigenia. Agamemnon had crafted a kind of "demophilia" or patriotism, to conceal the shabby, all-consuming self-interest and thirst that he shared with Menelaus for more: more land, more power, more goods, more slaves. There were two sacrifices that horrible afternoon in Aulis: my Iphigenia and Truth. The way I saw it, the High King had to invent the lie, then had to force himself to believe in the atrocity of Iphigenia's sacrifice as a moral, national, and religious obligation; for the alternative was to admit that a father could murder his daughter for the sake of his own ambitions. And yet, according to Clytemnestra, her husband's final words to his army as the winds whipped up and the soldiers made for the ships, were, "Let our wars rage on abroad with all their force, to satisfy our lust for fame."

I sank to the floor and unleashed my fury at the Olympians and at the High King; I lashed out against my own celestial father who had permitted this brutal chieftain to commit the most heinous of crimes in his exalted name. I had to stuff my fist in my mouth to prevent the slaves from discovering my secret, which made the mourning a hundred times more painful. My baby. My beautiful, innocent girl of the red-gold hair. Conceived in love and first child of my loins. Now I would never see her again, never hope nor dream that our paths would cross once more, and the woman she believed to be her aunt would embrace her and bedew her damasked cheeks with tears only a mother can weep.

I was full with child again, and the news of Iphigenia's death made me violently ill, so much so that it was feared I would expel the baby prematurely. My body had suddenly become too weak to bear it. I could confide in no one: Not even Paris Alexandros knew the secret of Iphigenia's conception and her birth. The Troyans thought I mourned for my niece, and there were murmurs, even among my slave women, that my grief was excessive under the circumstances, that the Spartan harlot played upon the hearts of others with her high drama, the better to win their sympathies.

I was alone in my suffering. No one could reason me out of my lacerating guilt. My adoring Paris Alexandros was unable to ease the aching in my heart; and in my depleted physical condition, I was unsure whether I would be delivered of a healthy babe.

Not even when I was taken from Theseus's arms by my brothers, nor when I learned of their horrific deaths, nor when I received the news of Theseus's surprising demise, had I felt such complete and overwhelming sorrow, such eviscerating pain. How I wished to die myself, but my demimortality doomed me to live forever with the fatal damage my misdeeds had wrought.

Perhaps the most painful knowledge of all was that the death and devastation had not even truly *begun*. Clytemnestra had written that as soon as the lifeless body of Iphigenia was taken from the altar, a strong wind churned up the waters of the Euboean Strait and the order was given to hoist the sails. The oars of a thousand ships were lowered into the white-tipped waves of the winedark sea. The Greeks were on their way.

I n the throes of my grief, and in the terror of the impending invasion, I was delivered of a baby girl. There was a part of me that wished to name her Iphigenia, but I knew that another Iphigenia, no matter how much love I gave her, could never replace the angelic infant I had held in my arms and who all-too-briefly had nestled on my chest thirteen years earlier. So I permitted Paris Alexandros to name our daughter Helen. I was delighted to have another girl, finally, and in celebrating a new life, I felt able to rob Death of the full measure of his triumph.

Already the high house that Paris had commissioned from the finest laborers and artisans in the wide Troad seemed too small. Still, I was glad to be liberated from the emotional discomfort I had endured in Priam's vast palace where his numerous too-proximate offspring dwelled in interconnecting rooms, yet refused to acknowledge Idaeus and little Helen as legitimate members of the royal family. I was relieved to be freed from the unkind remarks of the wives of Alexander's brothers, from Hecuba's disapproving scowl and Andromache's diffident air of superiority. In our new home at the summit of the citadel, with its lavishly frescoed and intricately tiled greeting hall, courtyard, and sleeping rooms, I could at last be Helen: the Helen my beloved Paris Alexandros cherished, the Helen who never allowed a day to pass when we did not set aside the time to pleasure each other, tasting every sensual delight we could devise. Nearly three years had passed since we eloped from Sparta, and our mutual affection had never diminished. Our openly passionate union was yet another source of envy among the royal household. Once Paris Alexandros and I became parents, they seemed to expect our passion to wane. Although she and Hector certainly had an exceptionally loving marriage as well, Andromache often made it clear that our inability to refrain from touching or caressing or kissing each other in public was unseemly, undignified, and thoroughly disgusted her.

When Paris Alexandros and I moved into separate quarters, Andromache had sent us a house gift: one of her own slaves, a girl from the island of Lesbos, widely known for its beautiful and skilled women. It had been Andromache's fondest hope, I am certain, that Myrrhine's fine looks would entice my husband from our bed, a wish that was doubly insulting, for Paris Alexandros never so much as noticed another woman from the moment we had met; and no one—no matter how charming and beautiful—could ever supplant my own desirability. She would have to have some special talent indeed, one in which I lacked all skill, to gain Alexander's attention. Thus far, such a woman did not exist.

The House of Atreus, and I, having made the ultimate sacrifice, the Achaeans should have reached our shores within a week's time now that the winds had become favorable. But day after day passed and their sails had yet to be sighted from the towers. Some Troyans were lulled into complacency by the delay, believing that the warnings had been dire, as the fleet had not materialized. Others heeded the suggestions to stockpile food and water, filling huge amphorae with wine, water, oil, and grain and burying them beneath the floors of their dwellings, which, thus "paved" with jar lids took on a cobbled appearance. Confident that his walls were impregnable, but taking no chances, Priam ordered the entire defensive ditch to be studded with wooded stakes, designed to impale man or beast who attempted to breach it. Citizens of the lower city hoarded sling bullets and arrows.

I was nursing Helen when I was interrupted by the sound of wailing and shouting in my courtyard. Andromache, paying her first visit ever to my home, cursed my name and called for me to come out of my chamber. With my daughter still latched on to my engorged breast, I stepped out onto the balcony. Hector's wife displayed none of her customary dignity. Her dark hair was disheveled, hanging loosely about her shoulders, and her dress had been rent to shreds. "Whore!" she shrieked, "harlot of Sparta, whore of Troy, you are to blame for this!"

Little Helen, terrified by Andromache's hysteria, bit my nipple. Wincing in pain, I called for Xanthippe to take her while I sought to communicate with Andromache. I knew she bore me no love, but she rarely allowed herself to show it in any way other than deliberately shunning me. She was never one for direct confrontation. For me to welcome Andromache—who had come to excoriate me for some offense that I could only assume explained her unkempt appearance— merited a swallowing of my pride. I descended the stairs and urged her to sit with me in the courtyard, but she slapped away my arm, a gesture that enabled me to swiftly reclaim my honor. "Your Greeks have taken Thebes," she told me, each word choking in her throat. "They have not yet come to Wilusa because they were pillaging the cities along the coast. Achilles himself, with his battle-mad Myrmidons, destroyed a dozen towns and plundered their spoils. Lyrnessus is now rubble, Mynes slain, and his queen, Briseis, taken by Achilles to warm his lustful bed. And Thebes . . ." Andromache added, so distraught that her hands clutched at the air as if to feed her lungs with a fistful of it, "was entirely razed. My seven brothers. My father, King Eëtion, my blameless mother. All slain by Achilles's hand. There is nothing left of once-powerful Thebes. And I . . . have . . . nothing." She lunged for my throat and ended up grabbing a hank of my unbound hair, jerking my head forward. My golden diadem clattered onto the smooth stones. "You have brought this sorrow . . . this torture . . . to my soul. Unfaithful shrew, who deserves not to see another day's sunlight. May your immortality be ever your curse. You, who can never know the touch of Ker—the evil death—like my beloved kin tasted at the tip of Achilles's spear. May the memory of those whom your unslakable thirst for eros has slain haunt you like the shades of the unburied."

I had no words of comfort. What could I possibly say that would be believed, or received, by Andromache as an offer of condolence? The sacking of every city from Aulis to Anatolia during a voyage to ostensibly claim revenge for Helen's marital infidelity was proof itself that they were not fighting for Helen at all, but for power and plunder, for land, for precious metals, for supplies, and for slaves—but no one would listen to my voice of reason. I empathized with Alexander's sister Cassandra. But even she would have nothing to do with me. She claimed to see the blazing holocausts of the future, but she focused entirely on the outcome and not upon the motive.

Polemos, war, was now imminent; we in Ilios could feel the hot breath of Ares on the backs of our necks.

The winds brought the Achaeans to our beaches, their black-hulled ships already bursting with the ill-gotten spoils of plunder.

We watched with trepidation as each crew lowered and stowed their sail, let down the mast by the forestays, settling it into the mast crutch, and then rowed the rest of the way to the shore. Vessel after vessel was dragged onto the beach, and the Greeks made camp beside them, erecting their tents and, according to our spies, adorning their interiors as though they intended to remain indefinitely. They had brought nearly all the comforts of their homelands, including furniture, gold and brazen mixing cauldrons, tripods, goblets, fleeces, and finely woven blankets. Captive women, willing or no, the victims of the Achaeans' raids en route to Ilios, were taken to the tents for the pleasure of the Achaean chieftains while the common men slept on the ships and adhered to the soldiers' vow of celibacy. The Greeks had brought their horses and chariots, too, as well as livestock most likely stolen from the pillaged cities within Ionia, Lydia, and Phrygia.

And the fighting began, on a windy plain just beyond the city walls and down by the ships near the Greeks' encampment. The Troyans preferred to clash on the broad plain, enabling them to employ their light chariots, which were by far the Wilusans' best weapon. Their chariotry was second to none in the known world.

The members of Priam's great family would gather on the ramparts of the citadel to watch the daily clashes. His young grandsons, uncomprehending of the terrors of battle, would admire the warriors' armor: the silver-hilted curving blades favored by the Troyans and the straight-bladed swords employed by the Achaeans; the battle-axes and ash spears and the elegantly curved bows like the one Paris Alexandros prized; the fancy bronze helmets with their horsehair plumes, whose earpieces and noseguards obscured the wearer's identity; the great rectangular shields of the Troyans, some shaped like a broad double axe; and the enormous round shields of the Achaeans. I remember the first time I recognized the shield of Menelaus. The Gorgon head emblazoned in its center was designed to strike fear into the hearts of his enemies, for it was believed that the Gorgons turned all who looked on them to stone. It certainly filled me with dread. I was terribly shaken. Suddenly, the conflict spun into sharp relief, like the silhouette of a black hawk against the cloudless sky. The fighting was so terrible, so fierce, that it was hard for me to believe that what I was watching, what I was living, was real and not an awful dream, a never-ending vision visited upon me by the vengeful gods. The sight of bellicose Menelaus, an identifiable figure in the midst of the fray, sent me crumpling to my knees on the smooth stones of the battlements. If the Achaeans emerged victorious, that butcher and his brother would bring me back to the Peloponnese—or torture me right here in Troy.

According to military custom, the armies clashed during the spring and summer, when the weather was most favorable. The summer season, when the earth was baked as dry and brown as unleavened bread, was also used by both sides for foraging expeditions. Owing to their proximity to Ilios, the villagers of Mount Ida and other nearby towns were the first to suffer losses; raiders from both armies would appropriate the produce of their fields, orchards, and vineyards and steal their livestock in order to feed the troops. As the Troyans quickly cut off the Achaeans' access to fresh water and a ready supply of food, the Greeks also took to raiding the northern Cyclades and Anatolia's coastal cities for fresh supplies. Strategically, it was in their best interest to go farther afield, for they risked alienating the neutral inhabitants of cities near Ilios. If they angered them enough, as Achilles had done in Thebes, the citizens would enter into an alliance with the Troyans, if only to seek revenge.

In the autumn and winter months, when the winds blew ever colder from the Black Sea and the plains were bitten with frost and blanketed with snow, an official ceasefire was universally observed. During the winters in peacetime, the king presided over numerous festivals. In Ilios, we celebrated at least eighteen different festivals annually. Once, there had always been a reason for celebration. Then, when all began once more to become sweet and green, when the warblers sang and the buds burst forth into achingly beautiful riots of color, the carnage would resume.

Down in their encampment, life was hard for the Achaeans. For those who slept out of doors, the morning dews soaked their clothes and filled their heads with lice. The men who made their foul beds on the ships suffered impossibly cramped quarters. In the winter, the snows came down from Ida. The summer heat was sultry and windless. The weather alone might have caused many of the miserable souls to consider raising the anchor stones and sailing for home. It was commonly said that the seas were like a shifting gray shade, salty from all the tears shed by the wives left behind upon the Achaean shores.

We were in a state of unending siege. Our walls remained impenetrable and our city protected, but the fighting continued in earnest nonetheless. During the first few years, the Troyan and Achaean armies were evenly matched, which meant that a vast amount of men, some scarcely older than boys, were slain in equal number on both sides. Agamemnon's and Priam's royal households each received daily reports, sometimes more often, of the status of the fighting, wherein the heralds would recite to their respective commanders in chief the names of the men who had been wounded or had perished, and by whose hand the felling blow had been delivered. All too soon it became a numbing recitation of the departed. The casualties were staggering. And gruesome: a tongue punctured by a spear entering through the throat or neck; a limb or head lopped off with one swipe of a blade; sliced tendons, shins; arrows piercing nipples and groins. And for every name a face, for every face a soul, for every soul, a wife or mother, sister or daughter who mourned the senseless loss. I recall hearing the herald name Tlepolemus of Rhodes and remembered that he was the husband of Polyxo, my girlhood playmate. A friendship I had always treasured as emblematic of childlike innocence was now dead, too. The war had come right to the doorstep of my memories and laid its bloody issue at my feet.

Each year, the sweet fragrance of the spring air grew fetid with the stench of death. Bodies frozen in their final moment of agony might for several days remain strewn across the plain or down by the ships, mangled, twisted, despoiled, and defiled by dogs, crows, or their enemy who had stripped their armor, robbing them of their dignity, even in death. On some nights, the funeral pyres, piled high with corpses and tributes to the fallen—their cherished possessions and perhaps a favorite horse or dog, sacrificed for the occasion—blazed as high as Olympus itself, blowing the acrid soot toward the sky gods as if to demand that they take note of the butchery below. According to custom, livestock were also slaughtered as part of the sacrificial ritual, their fat wrapping the bones of the departed, while the soldiers, who could have used the meat to fill their complaining bellies, went hungry. We lit braziers filled with brimstone so that the medicinal fumes might clear the air of the nauseating scent of gore and blood.

Each army was convinced that certain gods were on their side. When the fighting went well for them, they propitiated their Olympian patrons; when it went badly, they blamed those who aided their enemy, thereby avoiding both responsibility and accountability. Supporting Ilios were Aphrodite (assuredly, since she was the one who had brought Paris Alexandros to me); her sometime lover Ares, god of war; and the brother and sister archers: golden Phoebus Apollo, whom Alexandros resembled, and brave Artemis, who was angry that Agamemnon had murdered the virgin Iphigenia, for she was the patron goddess of unmarried maidens. It was also said that Agamemnon had further angered the chaste Artemis by killing one of her sacred deer before he sailed from Aulis. Throwing their protection and support to the Achaeans were Poseidon the earth-shaker as well as Hera and Athena, to whom Paris Alexandros in his dream had denied the golden apple. The most powerful god of all, great Zeus, my own father, must certainly have been on *our* side, as I now thought of the Troyans after so many years in their midst. Without a doubt, he wanted to see his daughter happy. But there were those who believed that he could not openly take our part because he despaired of incurring Hera's insistent and unrelenting wrath. Even if there had never been a contest for the golden apple, even if Paris Alexandros had never been born, or had indeed died on Mount Ida, my very existence was proof of Zeus's infidelity. For that alone, Hera surely believed she had cause to aid the Achaeans.

After a couple of years, when it was evident that no end to the conflict was on the horizon, and the Troyans' ranks were being decimated,

Priam emptied a goodly portion of his treasury and hired mercenaries. From the East came the Khita horsemen, sallow complected, small and fearsome, hairless but for their thin black beards, long mustaches, and flowing raven locks. Hatred blazed in their almond-shaped eyes. Even their horses were no larger than our Troyan ponies, but they managed to cut through the Achaean flanks, never flinching from the ceaseless clash and thud of leather, bronze, and wood.

In what might have seemed a joke, were it not that the deadly business of war had brought them to fight for the same army, the proud Nubian warriors led by Memnon, their glorious chieftain, were as tall as the Khita were diminutive. Rumor had it that the Nubians had marched to Ilios on foot all the way from their land well to the south of Egypt. These colorfully clad warriors, who fought bare chested and whose skin was the shade of carob pods, were renowned for their prowess with the spear. It was for that reason that Priam had solicited their aid, but things did not fare as well for them as the old king had expected. For one thing, the Nubians and the Khita distrusted one another, although both mercenary armies were fighting for the same side. The Achaean infantry were also far more formidable against the Nubian spears than any of the Troyans had imagined. And in what proved to be the most crushing blow of all, prideful Achilles cut down the giant Memnon with his great ash spear, the gift from his father Peleus, leaving the Nubian warriors entirely demoralized and subsequently vulnerable.

The situation was looking more dire for us by the day. And then one evening, I felt the bottom drop out of my world.

long with the other Troyan royal wives, I had joined the men in their feasting hall and was approaching Paris Alexandros to take my customary position at his feet and to recline my head in his lap. He always looked forward to my appearance; it was his favorite part of the evening, when I would glide toward him with all eyes upon me, and he would favor me with a look that was loving and proud and desirous, as if to say to his kin, *This is my woman, this vision. Can any of you dare to believe himself as fortunate as I?*

But that night, he did not look in my direction. He did not even glance when I entered the room. His gaze was fixed upon another with the same passionate intent that I remembered transfixing his face on the night we met. He was rapt; his full attention given to an extraordinary-looking woman. And she was everything that I was not. In fact, I did not even realize that Paris Alexandros was listening to a woman until I drew nearer to them. Her dark hair was shorter than most of the men's locks. Her body, even seated, was long and lean, like that of a runner: supremely athletic. Her attire was more manly than feminine as well. And yet she wore an air of feminine danger as if it were a cloak made from the skin of a mountain lion. How had this woman been permitted to dine with the men? And why was she here? Moreover, how had she so enchanted my husband—the man who continued to risk everything for my love?

Suddenly I was assaulted by an enemy I had never truly known:

jealousy. It came upon me like a laurel-winning wrestler, grasping me about the midsection and leaving me gasping for air. This was no fleeting tinge of anxiety about the shepherd girl Oenone. The room swirled in and out of focus, and I nearly lost my balance. Had the last few years of my life led me to *this*? I had given up home, homeland, and family; I had abandoned my children. Was this my punishment, this woman the gods' revenge for my infidelity to Menelaus?

She was everything I feared. I had always known that no woman could compete with my immortal beauty and my desirability. The gods had made sure that it would be so. No other female who might also have embodied every womanly charm had a chance. But somehow I sensed that one day there would come a woman who would personify everything I was not: lean where I was soft and curvy, boyish where I was feminine, and a fighter—where I was a lover.

I had to make a grand show of clearing my throat in order to secure Alexander's attention. He looked up and clasped me by the hand, bringing it to his lips and kissing the tip of each lacquered fingertip. I felt a bit better. "Who is your new . . . lady acquaintance?" I inquired, my words honey coated. "Forgive my confusion, love, but I have been under the impression ever since you brought me to Ilios that women were not permitted to dine amongst the men."

"No doubt you have heard of the Amazons," said Paris Alexandros, still caressing my hand. Now I sensed that he was overcompensating and my terror returned. "They have volunteered to fight alongside us to defeat the Achaeans, as there is no love lost between them."

I suddenly recalled that Theseus's great love, Antiope, had been an Amazon princess. Were Amazon women always to come between me and my two great loves?

"This is Penthesilea, queen of the Amazons. Their archery is unsurpassed by any man, including myself," he added, favoring the woman with a reverential gaze. "She has brought twelve of her warriors to join the Troyan forces on the battlefield."

A warrior. Of course. She dined with the men because they somehow did not regard her as a woman. I was quite certain that all of her feminine charms were, however, perfectly functional; for those who believe that the Amazons lopped off a breast, the better to pull the bowstring, they are mistakenly deluded. Penthesilea had high, small breasts, barely larger than an adolescent's, that assuredly would have presented no impediment to her marksmanship.

∼

"You are fond of her," I remarked to Paris Alexandros as we readied ourselves for bed. I had dusted our sheets with finely milled talcum scented with bergamot and left the oil lamp still burning so that we could see every plane and curve of each other's anatomy by its golden light. In the gentle glow, Alexander's eyes glittered like polished onyx.

"Is my Helen envious?" He reached out to brush a tendril of hair from my forehead.

I could not tell whether he was mocking me or truly incredulous that such a thing might be so. "I won't give you the satisfaction of knowing the truth."

"You are!"

I turned my face away from him and hid my head. Embarrassment was something I had banned from my life when I banished shame so many decades earlier. Now it crept back like a pest that bedevils the grain stores.

"You can't mean to begrudge me an admiration I have for a fellow warrior?"

"You are wrong on both counts."

"I have no idea what you mean. Helen, you confound me sometimes."

"I'll parse it out for you, then. First, I know you better than anyone has ever known you, and you looked at the Amazon with an 'admiration' that went far beyond an appreciation for her military and athletic prowess. I was once quite an athlete, too, if that's what strikes your fancy nowadays. Second, you are not a 'fellow warrior.' In fact, you never cease to remind me—and your noble brother Hector, who has often urged you to don your armor—that you are a hunter and most emphatically *not* a warrior."

Paris Alexandros released a defeated sigh. "All right, then. If I admit my attraction to Penthesilea, will there be an end to this silliness?"

He reached for me and I bristled at his choice of vocabulary. "Oh, no, my darling. I'm afraid it will be only the beginning."

"My love, my life—my wife—Helen, there is no other woman in the world I would rather be with. Now, or ever. I swear by all the gods!"

I touched my finger to his soft lips to end the discussion. I wanted him to bed me right then, to reassure me; and yet, that seemed like the desire of a desperate woman. I was too proud for that. And so, for the first time since that life-altering night in Sparta's sacred grove, Paris Alexandros and I did not make love.

~~~

Despite his apparent infatuation with Penthesilea, which I thought would have led the two of them to form a redoubtable partnership of archers, Artemis and Apollo incarnate, Paris Alexandros remained reluctant to engage in combat. He knew that the Troyans were at war not because of our love, but because of Agamemnon's greed and Priam's stubbornness. Maintaining his belief that battle engendered nothing but death, Paris stayed above the fray. My husband found no harm in bringing down a beast with his great curved bow but saw no reason to kill a man.

But not too many days after she first dined in Priam's hall, the Amazon did convince Paris Alexandros to make an appearance on the battlefield. I was terrified; if I lost my beloved, I lost everything. My own future, and my safety, were inextricably tied to his. I reminded my husband that it was not cowardice to abide by his beliefs. He was girding for battle not because he suddenly agreed with Hector that he was honor-bound to fight for his country, but because Penthesilea had challenged his manhood. The great siege of Ilios had become, for Paris Alexandros, an archery competition.

He excelled, however. Having witnessed his marksmanship on Mount Ida, I did not doubt but that he could bring down an Achaean with equal skill. My fears were not that his arrows would fly wide of the intended target but that my love himself would be felled by a bloodthirsty Greek. Once they could identify Paris Alexandros on the dusty plain, not even Hector could protect him. Word spread throughout the enemy camp that Paris had finally come out to fight, and nothing could surpass their hatred for him. With Paris Alexandros on the field, not even Hector, the greatest Troyan warrior, had as big a bounty on his head.

The twelve Amazons were formidable and fought valiantly for the Troyan side, but they were no match for an entire army of Achaeans. One by one, they fell, and their sisters-at-arms took their corpses from the field before the Greeks could defile them, until only their queen remained.

Amid the endless casualties and fatalities, the bloodcurdling battle cries, the thundering hoofbeats, and the harsh clang of bronze against bronze, amid the ugly symphony made by the sounds of dying men—death rattles, moans, the choking gurgle of blood emitting from the throat or frothing from a festering wound, and the smell of rotting or burning flesh—Paris Alexandros and I sought to take comfort in each other. Daily he reassured me of his love; knowing that he would be girding for battle the following morning, I feared that each night would be our last. Our bed was piled high with the softest fleeces, rugs, and sheets of purest linen. It became a haven, a safe harbor, from the horrors that surrounded us. In the midst of all the death, we celebrated life, exalting the beauty and sensual grace of each other's bodies while below us on the plain, where horses once were pastured, men saw their final glimpse of Helios before they blinked their last and their eyes were closed forever.

How inextricable were the intimacy of battle, the passionate grappling and entwined limbs, and the intimacy of bed. How fascinating, and frightening, that the word which describes the collective frenzy of an army on the brink of war, or trapped within its throes, is the same one that defines a burning sexual passion: *eros.* Carnage and carnality were sons of the same sire, both words born in blood.

When Paris Alexandros fought, I was torn between watching his performance from the battlements and clinging to the shelter of my loom, pretending the world outside was a far different one. To occupy my darkest thoughts, I would prepare and scent his bath myself to welcome him home from a grueling day in the service of Troy. Even the slightest scratch I attended to with a potion of milk mixed with the juice of figs to ensure that the blood clotted properly and that his beautiful skin would fully heal.

My envy did gain the upper hand where Penthesilea was concerned. It possessed me like a dark spirit and suffocated all reason, like a fantastical creature that warps the psyche and distorts the mind, and I finally understood what drove Clytemnestra all those years.

After all her sister warriors had been killed, Paris Alexandros took it upon himself to look out for Penthesilea, something which, it pleased me to note, did not sit well with the fiercely independent Amazon queen. She was quite a sight on the field, her muscled golden body shown to advantage in her short tunic; her long legs laced into high sandals, protected by decorated greaves. Her quiver, too, was elaborately decorated, and she wore a crested, plumed helmet like the men. Indeed, she was a brave and admirable warrior, possessed of a courage that was daunting. But Paris Alexandros could not prevent the inevitable.

Achilles was on the plain, cutting down the Troyans and our mercenaries as if they were complacent cattle. I had heard that he admired Penthesilea almost as much as Paris Alexandros did; but to the spear-famed Achilles, the warrior queen was a glittering battle trophy. One afternoon, as the departing Helios cast his passing shadows on the open plain beyond the city walls, the last Amazon tasted the brazen tip of Achilles's spear. From the south tower I watched her fall, her taut body crumpling to the dust. And then, the unthinkable happened.

As Penthesilea appeared to be gasping her final breaths, the powerful Achilles claimed his prize. Despite the clamor raging about them, the Achaean knelt; and straddling the Amazon's broken body, forced himself upon her, spilling her virgin blood as the winedark lifeblood poured forth from the wound in her chest. Stripping the fallen enemy's armor as a spoil of battle was an accepted custom. But where in the rules of engagement was it written that a warrior could rape the dying—or already dead—body of his opponent?

I was sick. It was not the overwhelming summer heat that made me vomit all over the smooth paving stones. I would have killed Achilles myself and vowed to do so if I ever had the opportunity.

Penthesilea's death and defilement at the hands of brutal Achilles drove Paris Alexandros deeper into the fighting. Where the entire Greek army thirsted for his blood, because—under Agamemnon's exhortation—they accepted our elopement as a personal insult to every marriage in Achaea, Paris Alexandros, with a murderous rage I had never seen, took the violation of Penthesilea as a deeply personal affront and cut down every Achaean who came within range of his arrows.

There are no "good" days during a war. Even when your army claims to have inflicted more injuries and caused more fatalities than they have suffered themselves, it is not a fit time for rejoicing. Every one of those mangled bodies, while anonymous to the rest of us, had a mother who pushed that once-tiny, nearly helpless being through her narrow loins, screaming from the agonizing pains of childbirth; her body should not have had to experience such pain anew at the loss of the son whom she was doomed to outlive.

By that time, if my son Idaeus had been a Spartan, the elders would have already whisked him off to the *agogi*. I was glad that no such system existed in Ilios, where the emphasis was placed on nurturing families rather than on breeding soldiers.

Andromache was a wonderful mother, lavishing affection and attention on her young son Laodamas, without turning him into a spoiled little boy. For this she was much admired by her many sisters-in-law, and I sought to emulate her maternal behavior with Idaeus. In truth, I treated Idaeus with no less love than that which I had so happily bestowed on my Spartan sons; but I somehow reasoned that if I was seen by the royal household to be as good a mother as Andromache—as wise, as benevolent, as doting—that my children and I would finally gain their favor. I was more concerned for my children than for myself. Idaeus and little Helen suffered from ostracism similar to that which I had so painfully endured as a girl. I understood their sorrow as well as their outrage.

Hector, the voice of reason, commanded tremendous respect, and it was to him I quietly sued. Of the royal multitude, only Hector somehow managed to find the time to make my children feel as though they were part of his enormous family. He would teach Idaeus how to build a toy boat, or he would carve a doll for little Helen; and for his generosity of spirit as well as his gifts, I was grateful. But Hector could not influence Andromache or the other women of the great family to emulate his gracious, avuncular behavior. Queen Hecuba and Andromache held sway in the domestic sphere, and their comportment in all things concerning home and hearth was roundly imitated by the other wives and mothers.

My outcast children were innocents, caught in a web fashioned by their own extended family. The Troyans' behavior was of course designed to torment me and Paris Alexandros as well. My beloved petitioned his parents to put a stop to the cruelty. Priam, who was usually kind to me and who bore my children no particular ill will, laughed at his son for daring to trouble him with such trivialities. Hecuba, their own grandmother, replied that Idaeus and Helen only got treated as they deserved. In denying our children their royal birthright, Hecuba was still punishing Paris Alexandros for living. Fated to bring ruin to his homeland, he was supposed to have died on Mount Ida. Had Paris Alexandros perished there, the queen maintained, perhaps the Achaeans would not be butchering his brethren outside the city walls.

Hecuba was punishing me for being faithless. In her eyes I would always be the Spartan harlot, still wed to Menelaus. She outranked her son and me, and thus could wield her power over us. The indomitable Hecuba placed the utmost store in marital fidelity. How, I wondered, had she made her peace with the daily reminders of her husband's dalliances, in the persons of Priam's numerous bastards sired on his concubines? Those offspring did not suffer the humiliations that my children did at the hands of their own relations.

I tried to make up for the companionship they had been denied, but when I visited them too often in their quarters, their nurse warned me against smothering them. "Too much maternal affection and they will never grow strong and independent," Xanthippe cautioned. I worried about their future. Would Idaeus and little Helen become resourceful and strong, or would they eventually turn bitter and resentful, blaming their ill-starred parents for their ostracism?

My hope was that they would reap the best the world had to offer: to live well, marry for love, and treat others as they would themselves be treated. However, it almost seemed like too much to ask; with the war raging outside the city and no end to the violence in sight, I amended my wish to the simple prayer that my darlings survive it.

~~~

Several years into the conflict, both sides suffered a devastating blow that none of us could ever have imagined or anticipated. It was now the ninth year of the never-ending siege. There had been no rainfall all spring. Crops withered and died on the vine. The wheat and barley fields were scorched and sere. Animals dying of thirst were slaughtered to end their slowly increasing misery, but the Troyans feared consuming the flesh of a sickly creature. For season after season we had burned the corpses of our warrior dead, the pyres producing an odor more repulsive and nauseating than any I have ever breathed, but now we were destroying our beasts in their own beds of flame. The gods' anger with all of us was deemed to be the source of the drought. Never in anyone's memory, even aged Priam's, had there been a dry spell so lengthy and so deadly.

The Olympians had to be propitiated. Queen Hecuba sought to appease Athena with some of the elaborate robes that Paris Alexandros and I had brought from Sidon. A stream of gifts was brought to the temples, blood and wine spilt in libations. The irony was that in making these offerings, more citizens starved. The food and drink left for the gods was, by religious order, on no account to be shared with any layman or woman. Naturally, the offerings most favored by the gods were the choicest: the first fruits of the season; the unblemished yearling. Children and their grandsires, soldiers and farmers, artisans and laborers, all sacrificed their best and finest. Oxen, sheep, and goats, pomegranates, apples, dates, and figs: all were delivered in desperate abundance to the temples. And the children and their grandsires, soldiers and farmers, artisans and laborers—royalty and commoner— went hungry night after night. The only people getting fed—and getting fat—off the drought were the priests and priestesses.

Down on the beaches, the hulls of the Achaeans' high-prowed ships swelled and cracked and the Greeks starved, too.

But the anger of the gods was neither appeased nor assuaged by the myriad sacrifices offered to them by Troyans and Achaeans, soldiers and civilians, the high and lowborn. They tested us even further. Thanatos, god of death, knew no limits.

The dryness of the plain, the blinding sun, the hordes of black flies that settled on the dead, rotting corpses, and the scarcity of food and fresh water, all contributed to the further decimation of Greek and Troyan alike. The gods turned away from us, and the drought continued with no end in sight.

And then the pestilence came.

Although the people of Ilios were taken in great number as well, the Achaeans claimed that we were responsible, that a Hittite merchant admitted to their encampment, his wagon piled high with finely woven, brightly colored robes and attractive trinkets designed to delight the vanity of the camp followers and concubines, had contaminated his goods with plague.

The slave girls immediately bedecked themselves with the Hittite's finery and, within a day, seemed to be expelling their vitals from every bodily orifice, gasping their last only hours later. To their lovers, indeed to anyone who had touched their tainted garments or bodies, they brought an equally speedy and painful end. Somehow, Agamemnon and Menelaus cheated Thanatos, as did Agamemnon's concubines, including his favorite, the golden-haired captive Chryseis. The girl was the daughter of Chryses, a priest at the temple of Apollo in Chryse, one of the cities near Ilios that the Achaeans had sacked before they reached our shores.

There were those in the Greek camp who believed that the Hittite trader was only an agent of Apollo, that it was the god of light himself who had visited the plague on the Greeks to punish Agamemnon for kidnapping his priest's daughter and forcing his lustful attentions upon her. Chryses had even come to Ilios to beseech the High King to return his child but was greeted with derision and scorn and sent back out to sea empty-handed.

While we burned our infected dead and buried their bones, down by their ships the Achaeans quarreled amongst themselves. Agamemnon in his hubris refused to return his captive to her father. He loved her, he claimed. She pleased him more than his own wife and satisfied him greatly in his bed. For that reason alone, despite my prickly relationship with Clytemnestra, I would have stolen a knife, sneaked into his tent, and stabbed the adulterous High King in the heart.

For shame! The war that he claimed was entirely predicated by the lustful actions of a faithless wife was being waged by a commander in chief who was himself false to his own marriage vows; and not just with one lover as I had been, but with slave girls within his Mycenaean household and with every woman he captured as a spoil of war. The man who convinced fifty thousand others to fight for his brother's dishonor, dishonored my sister every day with women who did not deserve to scrub her floors.

Thus it was with great interest that I followed this dissension among the most formidable Achaeans. While Agamemnon remained obstinate, his men and their whores continued to die. I wondered how he might explain to a mother that her son was dispatched to Hades by disease while he stubbornly satisfied his brutal lust.

After several days, Odysseus, considered the voice of reason among the Achaeans, finally persuaded Agamemnon to return his captive to her homeland. The crafty Ithacan sailed with Chryseis back to Chryse and delivered her into the hands of her father, offering the hecatomb of one hundred oxen at the altar of Phoebus Apollo in the hopes of propitiating the great archer and golden god of light.

Until the advent of the plague had temporarily halted the fighting, the casualties had been fairly evenly distributed. The discord within the Achaean ranks had benefited us as well, allowing our battle-weary warriors to begin to recoup their strength. Now that Chryseis had been returned, the Greeks were once again prepared to rally around their High King.

And at the temples within the walled citadel, the Troyans, exhausted and fearful, slit the throats of Priam's yearlings and prayed to the sky gods for a little more time.

TWENTY TWO

T hey heard us. Or perhaps it was Agamemnon himself, whose subsequent actions after the loss of Chryseis inadvertently contributed to our military advantage. Our spies informed us that Agamemnon had demanded that *Achilles* forfeit the woman *he* had taken during the sack of Lyrnessus and deliver her to the High King as a replacement for Chryseis. Priam was overjoyed to learn that Achilles had refused, whereupon Agamemnon took the girl anyway. In retaliation, the spear-famed Achilles immediately withdrew his support for Agamemnon and ordered his fearsome Myrmidons to refrain from fighting as well. Achilles himself, we had learned, was sulking in his tent, playing his seven-stringed lyre and singing sweet lays of heroes past to his kinsman Patroclus while the rest of the Achaeans took to the field.

Employing the lessons in which Theseus had so assiduously schooled me, I surmised that this quarrel between the two most influential Achaeans had little to do with either of the two slave girls, much as this entire bloody conflict had little to do with my flight from Sparta. The real prize was power. Agamemnon was High King and commander in chief of the Achaean host. His godlike stature was undeniable, but he did bully men into following him. Achilles embodied the Greek concept of *arête*—heroic excellence. He was younger, stronger, and eminently admired for his extraordinary skill by foot soldier, charioteer, and chieftain alike. He fought not for Helen, but as a mercenary fights: for his own glory and all the plunder he could amass for himself. As Achilles was not bound by the Oath of

Tyndareus, he saw no reason to bow to Agamemnon's commands and abide by his military strategies. The Thessalian was further angered by Agamemnon's behavior during the coastal raids before the war began. He had been unleashed to handle the dirty business of battle while the High King languished on his flagship. City after city fell under Achilles's spear while Agamemnon ravaged only slave women. The final insult to the young warrior was Agamemnon's demand that all of the spoils be delivered to him.

Something else was at work here, too. Having been raised in the Achaean culture, I understood what the Troyan herald could not: the other reason that the unfortunate Briseis could not have been one of the genuine causes of the present quarrel. For Achilles to forfeit Briseis to Agamemnon at the High King's whim or command was tantamount to an acknowledgment of Agamemnon's supremacy, something the prideful Achilles bristled at, believing himself the better man in every way. It was arrogance, not love, that fueled the fire between the two warriors. I did not doubt that Achilles had bedded the girl, nor doubted his affection for her. But *love,* the love that accompanies passion and loyalty and friendship, as well as the pleasures of the flesh, the kind of love that the *erastes* bears for his *eromenos,* Achilles reserved for another.

I had never met Achilles, but I remembered his cousin Patroclus from a time when life was more innocent; when I thought nothing in the world could be as evil as an arranged marriage. The gentle, fair-haired Patroclus had been one of my suitors. I recalled his fine-boned features and his tender disposition, his love of horses. I had been fond of the boy, though not in the way a woman desires a man. Patroclus was not cut out for war. Although he was my bitter enemy, I hoped that the powerful Achilles would safeguard his *eromenos,* his beloved. Of all my former suitors, Patroclus was the only one whose survival I prayed for.

By now the war had dragged on for so long that the young sons left behind by their fathers were grown men themselves and had sailed to Ilios as reinforcements. Now father and son might find themselves fighting side by side. I tried to discover whether my Spartan sons had reached our shores, but received no word. Even little Nico would have been nearly old enough to become a soldier. I didn't want to imagine my boys on the battlefield. Did they think they would be fighting *for* their mother when they wielded a sword or spear under the command of Agamemnon, seeking to slaughter a member of my adopted family, or—even more unbearable—one of their own half brothers, my sons by Paris Alexandros? By now we had two more boys, Aganus and Bunomus, lively toddlers barely a year apart, whose curious natures rivaled even that of Nico's at their age. When these two were on the loose, nothing breakable was safe, no matter how securely Paris Alexandros and I had placed it out of reach. Everything fragile or sharp seemed to find its way into their clumsy grasp or, just as often, into their mouths. All three of my Troyan boys were too young to fight, but still I feared for them every day.

I received word from Clytemnestra. Nico's parentage was being falsely claimed by one of my Spartan slaves, a covetous girl named Pieris, whom Menelaus had taken into his bed after my departure. Clytemnestra told me that Pieris had borne him a son, who they named Megapenthes, but maintained that Nico was her child as well. Why else, she boasted, would the boy have been left behind? And many believed her.

I raged at Menelaus's betrayal. It galled me that marital infidelities were winked at or shrugged off when instigated or committed by a husband, but a wife was branded a harlot for her indiscretions. Clytemnestra apparently agreed; fully aware that her own husband was a dog, she willfully flouted these unwritten rules. Almost as soon as Agamemnon had sailed for Ilios, my sister took a lover; wily political animal that she was, it was not just any man who satisfied her fancy. Her chosen consort, Aegisthus, was a first cousin to Agamemnon and Menelaus. The curse of the House of Atreus was on him as well. He had spent his youth in exile, fearing that if he returned to Mycenae he would be killed by the Atridae. Their father had stolen the throne from Thyestes, Aegisthus's father, supplanting Thyestes as High King. For years, Aegisthus bided his time, waiting, serpentlike, for the right moment to strike. I could not be sure whether my sister seduced Aegisthus or if it had happened the other way around, but the two were united in more than white-hot lust. They shared a common hatred for Agamemnon. And Clytemnestra, who was always bolder than I, flaunted her lover before the people of Mycenae. Aegisthus did more than bed Agamemnon's wife. He sat on Agamemnon's throne, wore his robes, and ruled his kingdom at my sister's elbow. And she reveled in her vindication.

While Mycenae flourished under my sister's rule and a conniving slave girl who could not keep her legs closed promenaded around Sparta like its de facto queen, the people of Ilios began to starve. The drought and the plague had decimated our crops and livestock and had contaminated the water supply. The hoarded stores buried in the earthen floors of the lower city dwellings had been exhausted. The residents were seeking higher ground; many of the homes nearer the base of the slope had been subject to pilfering and rampant theft, and sometimes violence, by marauding Greeks who scaled the wall and sneaked into the lower city under cover of darkness. The robbers were often caught and killed, but their loss did not seem a great deterrent to others.

Although there were some night raids that met with limited success, the Achaeans could never have taken the lower city. It was too well defended by archers on nearly every rooftop as well as atop the wall that ringed its perimeter. No one would have been able to survive the deadly hail of arrows that would have greeted the attempt.

Nevertheless, in the upper city, inside the Scaean Gate, Priam undertook a massive construction project. Gone were our wide avenues in favor of cramped, closely spaced buildings of mud and brick that lacked all glamour. As the looting increased during the ninth and tenth years of the siege and as the fighting grew fiercer, residents of the lower city, particularly the women and children, were decamped to the newly erected quarters where they would be safer and better protected. One now had to look hard for a tree or a patch of greenery to soothe the eye.

One morning I stood beside Priam on the battlements. A breeze caught my trailing robes and whipped them about my ankles; I clutched my wreath-shaped diadem to keep it from being blown off and bestowed by the wind on some unsuspecting warrior like a golden laurel. The men were fighting just below the walls. Lately I had grown accustomed to avoiding the position of spectator, preferring the solitude of my home, the warm embrace of Paris Alexandros (who had hung up his bow after the death of Penthesilea), the companionship of our children, and the comforting routine of my weaving. When I ascended the walls, I was reviled as being solely responsible for the carnage below. But I was condemned no matter what I did. When I remained indoors, I was roundly criticized for hiding from the ugliness I was accused of sparking.

From the south tower of the ramparts I could readily identify the Spartan hoplites in their tightly formed phalanxes. They fought differently from their other Achaean brethren, advancing in seven or eight rows, fifty abreast, the man to the right protecting the one to his immediate left with his enormous shield. Unlike other armies, in Sparta it was a privilege to be in the front rows. That was where the sons of the richest and most powerful citizens marched, with the sons of the lower orders bringing up the rear. The rear flanks provided the traction, pushing the vast human killing machine toward the enemy until they were close enough to destroy them. The men in the first three rows of the phalanx were perforce the bravest. They were the fighters who were within range of the enemy's spears, once the forces engaged.

The Spartan discipline was legendary as well. A hoplite was never permitted to relax his left arm, which bore the twenty-pound shield covered with several layers of tanned ox hides embossed with a family insignia (such as a lion, bull, or snake), and embellished with bronze. For a man's shield arm to falter was considered not only dangerous, but also unmanly.

A few of the greatest Achaeans were distinguishable from where I stood, and those I identified to aged Priam. "See there? The tallest of them; a near giant among the men. No, there—with the bare head, bald, and no breastplate. That's Telamonian Ajax. Ajax the Greater, his men call him, for his incomparable size."

"Then his father was Telamon?" Priam asked.

I nodded my head. "The very same Telamon who once took Ilios under mighty Heracles. His sons have returned to seek their own glory."

"Then Ajax—the Big One's—brother, Teucer, is my nephew. My sister Hesione's son. Where is he?" Priam looked bewildered. "Should he not be fighting for his mother's people?"

I did not know how to reply. The aged king remained silent for several moments. Finally he returned to our earlier conversation. "He who wears the helm plated in boars' teeth and fights so skillfully against my men, who is that?"

"Odysseus," I said. "You have met him before—without his unusual helmet. When he and Menelaus sailed here so long ago to demand my release. And there is Menelaus." I pointed out my former husband, grown squatter and more barrel-chested over the years, his russet beard now threaded with strands of gray. We watched intently as his Gorgon-emblazoned shield repelled a thrust from the sword of brave Aeneas. "And there, his brother Agamemnon," I said, pointing to the imposing High King, his long red hair streaming from beneath his crested helm. Not only was he distinguished by his height and lion's mane of hair, but his armor was unmistakable for its embellishment and for the size of his shield.

The corselet, a gift from King Kinryas of Cyprus, was adorned with circlets of cobalt, gold, and tin. Toward the throat, on either side, three serpents, also wrought of sea-blue cobalt, reared up and twisted their bodies to gaze at one another from across the High King's broad chest. The round shield was large enough to enclose his entire body and was fitted with concentric circles of bronze and knobs of tin and cobalt. At its center, a Gorgon's head dared the enemy to look upon her. Even the shield strap was ornately fashioned with silver findings and a three-headed cobalt snake whose faces twisted back to fix on one another. The four-horned, crested helmet befitted a high king as well. Priam was amazed that a warrior could fight so well and wear so much, for the armor alone was equivalent to the weight of a man. Many of the Troyans went bare-chested and bare-headed into battle, which was something I never understood. The unhelmed Troyan fighters kept their hair out of the reach of their enemies by plaiting it waspwise into beadlike cylinders of gold and silver.

"I am glad Achilles does not fight today," Priam said quietly. It was clear that the long war had taken its toll on him, even though he had never girded for battle. Of the fifty sons Priam had sired, few remained. Several had already been killed by the Achaeans. During the years when he was fighting alongside the other Greeks, Achilles had taken some of them prisoner and sold them into slavery across the sea.

It was the warrior's way of showing respect to a prince. Yet a few had escaped their bondage and returned to Ilios. The second time Achilles encountered them, he was not so lenient. With each son's death, King Priam lost a piece of himself, like a dying plant that loses leaf after leaf until it is completely barren, bereft of the greenery that lent it life.

"When will it end?" he groaned, grasping my arm as though I were a staff. His voice was barely audible.

That afternoon, Hector visited our home. "The Achaeans want to end this as soon as possible," he told my husband. "And the Troyans cannot continue to sustain such losses either."

"What would you have me do about it?" replied Paris Alexandros.

"That question should not even be dignified with a response."

Paris Alexandros sat silent for several minutes, his face an anguished mask of pain. "Tell Menelaus I will meet him on the plain tomorrow. The quarrel rests between us alone. When the sun is highest in the sky, he and I will fight, and the outcome shall determine everything."

Trembling and robbed of breath, I waited to see if he would say more.

"If I should kill Menelaus, Helen remains in Wilusa. But if he should . . . if he should . . . defeat . . . me, Helen must return with him to Sparta."

"No!" I gasped, and flung my arms about him.

"My precious love, there is no other way. I should have made this challenge long ago, but I despaired of—"

"You will not lose!" I insisted. I couldn't bear the thought of his being willing to forfeit me, or the thought of losing him to the icy grip of death.

"You must endeavor to be brave, Helen," Hector said gently; then turning to his brother, he added, "I will go myself to the Achaean camp to tell them of your challenge. And may the gods grant you victory tomorrow." He embraced his younger brother, clasping him tightly to his chest. They held each other for several moments, and then Hector, with an awkward nod to me, departed our chamber.

"I won't let you go!" I said, flinging myself upon Paris Alexandros. I pulled him to our bed as though it were a charm that could bind him to my side. "What if . . . ? What if you . . . ? Menelaus is the fiercer warrior. He lives for it. You know that. No!" I drew him even closer to me. "I cannot live without you. If I must return with Menelaus, I will kill myself."

Paris Alexandros claimed my lips. "You are forgetting something."

"I can't die. Oh gods!" I cursed my fate, cursed Zeus my father.

My husband caressed my tearstained cheeks. "These men, all of them, Troyan and Achaean alike, believe that they are fighting for Helen. Thousands have died in the name of an argument that should properly be settled only by the parties affected by it. Helen, it's the only way to end the bloodshed. Nine years—more than nine—have passed with no end in sight to the conflict."

"Do you truly believe that all of these warriors are fighting for Helen?" I sobbed.

"Do I? No. But they do."

"Do you love me?" I asked Paris Alexandros.

"You know how much I do. That's what nearly a decade of death has been about—so they believe."

"If you love me so much, then you would never forfeit me. Never enter into an arrangement where that might be the outcome." I kissed his forehead, eyelids, mouth, and cheeks, in the hollow of his throat, his collarbones, and the broad plains of his chest. "Don't go tomorrow. Don't leave me alone. Please. Don't. Leave. Me. *Alone.*"

Paris Alexandros caressed me gently. "How little faith you have in my soldiering!" he teased. "I will come back to you, I promise. And there will be an end to everything. The Achaeans will go home and we Troyans will rebuild our lives."

I wept into his chest. "I have never loved anyone, not even any of my children, as much as I love you."

"The feeling, my sweet love, is mutual," he murmured, holding me so tightly that our bodies nearly became one.

That evening, two lambs, one black, one white, representing the earth and the sun god, were slaughtered, and the pledge that Paris Alexandros had made was sealed before the chieftains. Old Priam himself, taken down to the Achaean camp in a chariot, vouched for his son's honor in the bargain, because the Achaeans refused to trust the promise of the Troyan princes.

After dinner, I could not wait to return to our home so that my love and I could once more—perhaps for the final time—be alone.

Paris Alexandros unclasped my girdle and removed the brooches that fastened my gown.

We made love as though it might be our last night of passion, savoring the scent and taste of each other, our kisses and caresses lingering longer. I wanted to make sure that the feel of him between my fingers and lips, the way he filled me, the sensations produced when his lips and tongue worshipped my sex, when he suckled at my breasts, would be seared forever into my memory. The years had never diminished our desire nor slaked our mutual passion. Again and again that night we gave, and took, our pleasure in each other.

I watched my beloved slumber, believing that the longer I remained awake, the more time we had together; when I finally was overcome by sleep, the first of my nightmares came. The new homes within the citadel had become repositories of squalor and filth; our citizens wandered the streets in rags, begging for a scrap of edible food. Ilios crumbled and burned, and amid the stench of destruction, the cries of the helpless echoed in my ears.

When the gentle glow of Eos heralded the morn, Paris Alexandros, stirring, held me to his chest, his hand cupping my bare breast, his hardness swelling against the hollow of my back. I nestled against him and stifled a cry into my fist. My tears spilled down my cheeks, bathing his strong arm.

"I'll be back soon. I promise," whispered Paris into my hair.

I helped him dress, dreading every moment, especially when he insisted on wearing his leopard skin instead of a proper corselet. It brought him luck, he insisted. It was the skin of a beast he had killed on Mount Ida when he was merely a youth. I despaired and wrung my hands and tried not to harangue him. The only warrior I ever knew of who had emerged victorious wearing an animal skin instead of armor was the great Heracles. But Paris Alexandros would not hear reason. By the time I laced his leather boots, I admit that I believed my own days in Ilios were numbered.

TWENTY-THREE

I walked out onto the battlements. Priam and Hecuba and a number of their daughters and their sons' wives were already there; Hecuba clasped her veil to keep it from blowing away in the high winds. Hector, too, had climbed the walls in order to gain a better view of the plain below, before his brother met the Fates and Menelaus. I watched him survey the terrain, his chin resting against the rim of his enormous shield. It was an action he often repeated in repose, so it bore a gentle, chin-deep dent, and the ox hide that formed the outer layer of the shield was stained with sweat. Andromache had brought their second son, the infant Astyanax, up to the ramparts and was cooing to the little boy as she held him, pointing to his brave papa in his glorious battle gear. When Hector leaned toward them to reach for the child, the usually sweet-natured Astyanax shrieked in fear. I have never ceased to marvel at how so small a child can make so huge a sound. The babe could have frighted the shades in Hades with his bawling. I realized that it must have been the plume on Hector's shining helm, the nodding, wind-blown movement of the giant horsehair crest, that somehow terrified him. I pointed to my head and Hector removed his helmet, handing it to me. Astyanax instantly ceased his sobs and willingly went to his father's waiting arms. "One day," Hector crooned to the baby, "you will overmatch your papa in valor and become an even greater warrior than he. Do you know what your name means? Astyanax: lord of the city. And, one day, you will rule mighty Wilusa and survey all you command from where we stand at this very moment."

I was immeasurably moved by the tenderness of this great hero for his tiny son, and for the depth of affection and respect that Hector and Andromache felt for each other. How many families, I wondered, had been shattered by the carnage of this decade-long conflict? How many sons and daughters would nevermore nestle in their father's strong embrace?

Hector kissed every inch of his little son's face, then drew Andromache into his arms as well, before bidding her good day. I blinked away a tear and handed back the brazen helm to Hector. He descended the steps toward the plain.

Andromache pointed toward the west. "The Achaeans tried to scale that part of the citadel wall three times," she said, her voice betraying no emotion to me. "The two Ajaxes, Idomeneus of Crete, the Atridae, and Diomedes. They must have known something."

Was she hinting that I might have betrayed to the Greeks the weakness of the western section of the battlements? I told Andromache everything I knew about the wall, adding for good measure that I had had no contact with the Achaeans in almost thirteen years. "The father of Ajax the Greater was Telamon, who fought against Ilios with mighty Heracles," I said. "It was Telamon who discovered, quite by accident during the fighting, that the wall was weak at the spot you indicated. I agree that the Achaeans must be in possession of some special intelligence, but I can assure you it did not come from me. I would look to great Ajax instead."

Below us, the sand swirled about in angry eddies. The armies were beginning to gather as though a sporting competition was about to take place. Hector and Odysseus, representing each combatant, met and measured out the distance of the battleground. Two lots were placed in Hector's helm, and the first to be shaken from it was Alexander's; Hector stooped to fetch it from the earth and waved it toward the battlements. My heart was in my mouth. It meant that Paris Alexandros would be the one to strike first.

My love walked out onto the field and greeted his elder brother, who looked upon him in horror. An argument ensued between them. Clearly, Hector disapproved of Alexander's battle garb. From the disheartening look of things, it appeared that Paris Alexandros was not taking the impending contest seriously; he could not have made a graver error. He had re-attired himself since I'd wished him good fortune, and he now wore a kiltlike garment and a wide belt, in which his brazen-hilted dagger was sheathed. Instead of a helmet, he had draped his precious leopard skin over his head like a cowl; rather than wear an armored corselet, over his woven tunic he had clad himself in his heavy leather hunting jerkin. His silver-studded sword was slung over his shoulder. At least his heavy, many-layered shield met with Hector's approval. I was certain I could hear the snickering of the Achaean warriors from where I stood overlooking the field. I saw Hector approach one of the Troyans, who nodded his head and relinquished his breastplate and silver-buckled greaves, along with his crested helmet and his spear, which Hector handed to his brother, insisting that he remove the jerkin and cowl and don the armor.

With a sinking heart I noticed that the borrowed helm was too large for Alexander's head, and the chin strap could not be sufficiently adjusted to tighten it. Was there no other warrior who was willing to help my love with the loan of his helmet? Then, with a spasm of panic, I remembered the time when Menelaus and I had hosted him in Sparta and how Paris Alexandros had admitted that the spear was not his best weapon. I recalled too well that Menelaus excelled with it: the "spear-famed Menelaus," he was called. I crossed my arms and dug my nails into my flesh to keep from weeping. O, how I wished Paris Alexandros could have brought his bow, but it was not an acceptable weapon in the formal rules of one-on-one combat. Had it been allowed, the contest would have been over in an instant and my future in Ilios would have been secure.

Menelaus was armed with a short sword as well as a long blade. Impatiently, he paced the field in his bronze cuirass and polished greaves. The horsehair crest of his helmet undulated majestically in the light breeze. I could tell that he was anxious to begin—and to put a swift end to—the combat. I wondered if the men remembered their wrestling match during the Spartan celebration of Kronia so many years before. What innocents we all were then!

The opposing armies had now gathered on opposite sides of the measured area and were menacingly shaking their spears at each other, assailing their adversaries with barbed taunts. The two combatants strode into the space between them. My heart was in my mouth. I couldn't watch—and yet I had to. Did Paris Alexandros look anxious, or confident? I could not see his face beneath the huge bronze helm. Beside me the royal family clutched their garments or one another's hands. Queen Hecuba's face was implacable. What was she thinking, that mistress of inscrutability? Surely any mother would pray for her son to survive . . . and yet, I could not be certain of her will.

Paris Alexandros loosed his spear and his aim was true. The shaft headed straight for the stalwart Menelaus, but lodged in the layers of his sturdy shield, the spearhead bending back from the blow. I bit my lip.

Up on the ramparts we held our breath.

Menelaus removed the damaged javelin and tossed it behind him. It was his turn now. Releasing his earth-splitting war cry, he let fly his spear. As though borne by the will of Poseidon, the shaft headed straight for Paris Alexandros, who deflected the blow with his shield—but it was not enough. The shaft smashed through its eight layers of tanned ox hide, piercing the borrowed corselet where it joined, slicing straight through Alexander's hunting jerkin and tunic. I screamed. My love grimaced and staggered back. Hector rushed over and examined the puncture. He waved at us and collectively we exhaled. The tip had only grazed his flesh; he did not bleed. Tears of joy spilled down my cheeks, staining my silken robes. The Fates had been kind to us.

The spears having been used, Menelaus drew his long sword and charged at Paris Alexandros. Once, twice, thrice, four times, he struck at the horn of Alexander's helm as the Troyan prince sought to parry the blows. And then, to our amazement, the great sword of Menelaus, the silver-studded weapon of which he was so proud, broke apart in his hand and clattered in two pieces to the earth, of no more use to him than an elm twig.

Paris Alexandros raised his sword and lunged at Menelaus. The men were so close, body-to-body and nose-to-nose, that in another time and place they might have been engaged in a wrestling competition.

Pressing his shield against his opponent's right hand, Paris forced Menelaus to drop his short sword.

Then Paris Alexandros thrust home.

Menelaus let out a roar and Paris Alexandros withdrew his short sword, drawing blood from a chink in Menelaus's cuirass. My beloved turned toward us on the battlements, raising his gore-smirched blade as if to prove his victory.

He turned to leave the field. First blood. Game over.

But it was no game. This was not the sham wrestling match of thirteen summers ago. First blood was not the agreement.

The agreement was death.

The winds churned up the sands, and some of the warriors raised a hand to shield their eyes.

Then a great cry rose up from the Troyan ranks as Menelaus, like a rampaging bull, charged at Paris Alexandros from behind, grabbing hold of the majestic horsehair plume and whirling the Troyan prince around to face him. Now Menelaus the wrestler proved himself the wilier combatant. He managed to lay hold of the sagging chin strap on Alexander's borrowed helm and spun my beloved around and around amid the swirling sands.

Unable to strike, Paris Alexandros was losing his balance and Menelaus was choking him. All formal rules of engagement had been thrown to the winds, but the fight raged on in earnest.

Then the chin strap snapped and the shining helmet came off in Menelaus's hands. Both men staggered backward. It was difficult to follow the action as the sandstorm buffeted the men down on the open plain. I saw the broken helmet sail toward the knot of Achaean troops as Menelaus attempted once more to charge his enemy, fighting the temporary blindness caused by the roiling silt.

But where was Paris Alexandros? I had lost sight of him. Below, the armies ducked for cover, raising their great shields against the pelting sands.

Clutching my skirts, I descended the wall, frantically searching for him, stopping everyone I encountered to ask if they had news of him, but they could tell me nothing. I raced home, fighting for breath, my heart pounding inside my chest as though it would burst its confines.

On reaching our bedchamber, I gasped at the sight. There was Paris Alexandros angrily releasing the silver buckles of his borrowed greaves, tossing the shin guards across the room.

"My love!" I flung my arms around his neck and clasped him to me. "Closer. Closer. I don't want to ever let you go again." A million kisses I bestowed on his perspiring brow, cheeks, and lips. I called for servants to fill the enormous silver bathing tub, which I scented with fragrant, healing elixirs, then fashioned a poultice soaked in fig juice and milk with which to bind his wound once he had bathed.

He grumbled as I lovingly undressed him. "They will brand me craven because I left the battlefield. But only a fool would remain there in the middle of a sandstorm, blindly thrusting at an unseen enemy. The gods were kind to both of us today. Myself and Menelaus."

"Sh-shhh," I soothed. "If it salves your conscience, Menelaus played you false, coming up behind you like that and grabbing your helmet. But you miscalculated him. He is not a gentleman on the field of battle. He fought to win at any cost, but fought dishonorably." I helped my husband into the bath and sponged the dirt from his flaw-less golden skin, caressing each part of his body as though its mere existence was a gift to me. And then I stripped bare, letting my robe and gown puddle about my feet in a swirling eddy of sea-green silk and climbed into the great tub opposite the owner of my heart. I wrapped my legs about his waist and drew him toward me. "Thank you for staying alive," I whispered into his mouth. And when I felt the greatest manifestation of his mortality pierce the soft flesh between my thighs, his life had never been dearer to me than at that moment.

Later, lying on scented sheets, our idyll was interrupted by a messenger bearing urgent news: Paris Alexandros having fled from the field, Menelaus had proclaimed himself the victor, striding pridefully through the Troyan ranks, taunting them for their prince's cowardice and demanding my immediate return. Although they bore no love for Paris Alexandros, Menelaus's gloating so angered the Troyans that one of their number, Pandarus, a master archer, took aim at the son of Atreus and let loose a deadly shaft. It hit the target but did not bring death, merely wounding Menelaus in an unprotected area of his shin.

It was enough to reignite the battle, bringing to a swift conclusion the all-too-brief ceasefire. That day, Ajax the Greater and noble Hector fought to an exhausting draw. Diomedes, a butcher with his sword, twice slashed the valiant Aeneas, Alexander's kinsman, one blow slicing dangerously close to his eye, the second gash leaving a deep wound in his chest.

Lying on the battlefield surrounded by the clash of arms and hovering between life and Elysium, Aeneas had a vision of his mother Aphrodite lifting him from the fray. But no sooner had she borne him aloft than Diomedes lunged for the goddess, slicing open her soft white hand. The dark ichor spilled copiously from her wound, causing her to release her precious burden. As Aeneas plummeted toward the bloody earth and his injured, sobbing mother soared home for Olympus, the dying Troyan was sure that the lord of light, Apollo himself, had descended into the skirmish and swept him to safety, for Aeneas could not recall how he came to be brought home to his bed.

Paris Alexandros and I prayed for his swift recovery; a few days later we were gladdened to learn that Aeneas, although still feverish and in tremendous pain, had cheated Thanatos from his mortal grip. Yet I derived no consolation from believing that the life of loyal Aeneas had been spared so that he might once again set foot upon the open plain.

For those who still seek to blame me for all the years of carnage, I wish to remind them that just once, for a few terrifying moments under the blazing Anatolian sun, did the only two warriors with a genuine stake in the conflict take up arms to fight for *Helen*.

✖ TWENTY-FOUR ✖

And the violence continued to escalate with vertiginous speed. Achilles still refused to fight; and his pride, which served us well, cost the Achaeans dearly. Hector had never been fiercer or more formidable. Numberless Greeks were silenced by his spear, demoralizing the enemy even further. There was rejoicing within the walls of Ilios the day our herald reported to Priam that Agamemnon was considering decamping and returning to Argos. His men had been decimated by death, casualties, drought, lice, and plague, and still the Argive host was no closer to their goal. Ilios remained impenetrable.

What the Achaeans did not realize was that this shining citadel of their warlike dreams no longer gleamed. The quarters Priam had constructed to house the citizens from the lower city had quickly become repositories of filth, stench, and squalor. The lower city was now almost empty of its residents, and in the low buildings within the upper city's battlement walls, several relatives, and sometimes more than one family, dwelled in a single room.

Food was rationed. Decisions were made to cease leaving cuts of meat at the sacred altars because the people needed it more than the gods. The *pithoi* that contained the hoarded stores were dug up from the floors of beaten earth where they had been embedded in order to make room for the dead. The tiny bodies of stillborn babies or those who died soon after their birth, were buried by their mothers beneath the floors. Pregnant women prayed to Athena to send them boy children only, for life had become so hard that girls, who of course would never become soldiers, were considered unnecessary mouths to feed and were taken to the mountaintops and abandoned.

Nearby villages and islands, having been plundered for years by both armies, had become so depleted that they had no more bounty to yield. After such a lengthy siege, with all supplies of grain and produce, dried meat and fish, wine and water having dwindled substantially or become fully exhausted, the citizens of Ilios were slowly starving. Neither was the royal family immune from deprivation. Silks and brocades, perfumes and unguents, gold and jewels, could not fill our bellies, nor could they be sold to purchase food that simply did not exist.

As a military strategy, we endeavored to hide our condition from the Achaeans.

Old Nestor of Pylos tried to convince the demoralized Agamemnon to remain in Troy. The Greeks had suffered so much for so long: How could they return home with nothing? He was sure that the Achaeans were losing the war because the High King had angered Achilles. If the proud young warrior and his fearsome Myrmidons would fight once more, the tides would most certainly turn in the Achaeans' favor. After a great deal of agonized deliberation, Agamemnon heeded his aged confederate's counsel. Choking on his own hubris, he made grand overtures to Achilles in front of the entire army, offering him numerous lavish gifts of goods and slave women, including Briseis, if he would return to the field.

High in the citadel we held our breath, awaiting the young hero's response.

Achilles said no.

Zeus was on our side. Or so we believed.

~~~

Many of the Achaean ships had been damaged over the years by the weather. The devastating drought had further dried the wood until the hulls cracked and split. Hector elected to hasten their demolishment, organizing a campaign to burn them. And it was sweet music to the Troyans' ears to learn that Achilles still refused to fight unless his own vessels fell victim to the Wilusan torches.

Down by the ships, the skirmish begun in darkness raged on. Fire-brands shot from the beachhead under cover of the tamarisk bushes immolated some of the desiccated hulls. The sailors slumbering on board awakened to terrified cries of "Fire!" Rubbing the sleep from their encrusted eyelids, they raced on deck with their bows and spears. By dawn, Achaean and Troyan alike stained the golden sand with their winedark blood.

By Hector's orders, Achilles's ships were spared. And the proud and petulant Thessalian warrior, true to his word, remained in his tent, strumming his lyre and serenading his flowing-haired kinsman, the sweet-natured Patroclus.

We had lost many men on the beach, but the Achaeans' deaths greatly outnumbered ours, and Priam was jubilant. Hector had carried the day. The most glorious news of all was that Achilles had decided to take his ships and his Myrmidons and sail home on the next day's tides.

But war is a fickle and unpredictable monstrosity. The battle on the beach resumed the second day at first light, but this time there was no cause for celebration. Priam's herald reported the worst. It appeared that Achilles had changed his mind.

Hector had been in the thick of the skirmish when a shout rose up among the Achaeans. Bearing down on the Troyans like a fiend released from darkest Tartarus was their greatest nemesis, his unmistakable bronze armor glittering in the bright sunlight, the majestic horsehair crest on his shining helmet nodding defiantly in the sea breeze.

The Troyans seized their opportunity to vanquish their most formidable adversary, and, nearly to a man, set him in their sights. But Achilles was a fighting machine that day, and countless Troyans were felled by his two spears and his silver-studded sword of bronze. Toward dusk, one of Hector's men, Euphorbus, wounded the great Achaean warrior with his spear, finding a chink in the great breastplate just below the collarbone; as Achilles's weapons failed him, Hector himself struck the fatal blow with his sword, plunging the blade to its hilt into his adversary's belly.

The splendid helmet toppled to the bloody earth. Its wearer

collapsed in the dust, and noble Hector released an anguished cry. For it was *not* the spear-famed Achilles who had succumbed to death at the point of Hector's sword, but his kinsman Patroclus.

Believing that once the enemy glimpsed his armor, they would draw back in fear, thus giving the exhausted Achaeans a chance to regroup, Achilles had acquiesced to Patroclus's request to don his elaborate arms and go forth amongst the Troyans. And once in the thick of the fray, the young man who had seen little of the battle, having reluctantly remained under the aegis of his cousin, had become a force to be reckoned with. It was as if the very act of wearing Achilles's armor had somehow given Patroclus his kinsman's near-mythical skill and strength as a warrior.

Nothing is simple in the heat of battle. Although Patroclus had decimated our number with demonic fury and thrice attempted to scale the citadel wall, Hector in fact repented delivering the final, fatal blow. "It should have been his better," he said of the lesser warrior whose courage that day had admittedly been nothing short of daunting.

But no one within Troy's walls grieved for Patroclus as I did. Indeed, he had slaughtered men I'd known, granting them neither mercy nor reprieve, and for that I accounted him an enemy. But in a corner of my mind, perhaps even in a tiny chamber of my heart, there was a place where dwelt the memory of a gentle youthful stripling, not much older than a boy, not yet a man, who was the only person I had ever known who I can truly say possessed a spaniel's unfaltering loyalty. Even though Patroclus was a few years older than his cousin Achilles, he had always been happy to submit to the stronger man's will; happily reversing custom to be the *eromenos* to the younger man's *erastes*, looking up to him as a superior and following his lead with devotion and constancy. So clearly I recalled our conversations of nearly a generation ago when Patroclus had rhapsodized about his beloved wild horses that galloped so proudly across the Thessalian plains. Despite his butchery on the battlefield, I would somehow forever remember him as a gentle spirit.

My tears angered Paris Alexandros. He believed them treacherous and thought that they bore out my true allegiances. I remember the bitter words that flew from his mouth; how they stung me like nettles.

"Go to them, then, your Greeks! And see if they welcome the woman they call 'Helen the harlot of Sparta' the way the Wilusans have embraced you all these years."

"My people are here, within these walls," I insisted. "How can you possibly doubt my love for you, for your father, and for noble Hector? As for the rest of your kin and countrymen, I look upon them as my own and have done so for many years, despite their reluctance to accept me, despite their vicious accusations that I am the scourge of their existence and the author of this savage war. Have I ever given you cause to question my fidelity to you and to all of Ilios?"

Begrudgingly, he acknowledged that I spoke the truth.

"I mourn a time of innocence and lost youth as much as I grieve for Patroclus," I added. "This war has changed all of us. I am not the woman I was when I left my husband and homeland for the ecstasy of your arms. I thought then that I would never know a greater pain than the one I felt at having chosen to abandon my children. Since then, I have seen, and heard, of loved ones slain, the blameless slaughtered." I thought of poor Iphigenia and was racked once more with sobs. "You have been by my side every day. I have no greater confidant; yet you can never comprehend the depths of despair to which I have on occasion descended. To now challenge my love and loyalty is to give me even a moment's regret for my decision. It is an unwise test at best."

He was silent for several moments. Then Paris Alexandros reached for my hand and gently drew me close. He was never one to remain vexed; certainly not with me. His anger would flare like a lightning bolt but diffused nearly as swiftly. He drank my tears of anger, tears of sorrow, and made love to me so gently that night it was as though he were afraid that I might snap apart in his arms.

~~~

My tears for Patroclus were but drops in the blue Aegean compared with those of Achilles. And his fury knew no bounds. We learned that he had rent his garments and torn his hair like a woman, blaming himself for permitting Patroclus to don his all-too-recognizable armor. Although the High King had finally returned Briseis to him, Achilles no longer needed Agamemnon's bribery in order to take up arms once more; in fact, he thirsted for Troyan blood, especially eager to spill

Hector's. Spoiling to fight and vowing a bloody and swift retribution, Achilles paced in his tent like a tiger, impatiently waiting for another set of armor, for Hector had stripped the corpse and now wore Achilles's armaments as his own, a customary spoil of battle.

After a day and a night had passed, Achilles emerged, wearing such spectacular armor it was whispered that the god Hephaestus himself had forged it as a favor to Achilles's immortal mother, Thetis. The elaborately wrought shield depicted in minutest detail scenes of city life and pastoral idylls. It had a triple rim, five folds thick, and was constructed of gold and silver, bronze and tin. Even his shield strap had been cast from silver. The corselet gleamed like the sun; his leg armor was fashioned from pliable tin. The magnificent helmet was massive in size but fitted close to the temples with a golden ridge along the top. It, too, bore lovely and intricate tool work. His weapon of choice was the ash spear of his aged father Peleus. It was longer and had greater heft than other javelins, and only Achilles was said to be able to throw it, for it was too unwieldy for any other warrior. Fascinating to me, who knew nothing of soldiering, was that despite the ornate carapace that protected nearly inch of his body, Achilles, like the other Achaeans, preferred to fight in sandals rather than in sturdier footgear, such as the boots worn by Paris Alexandros and many of the other Troyans.

With Achilles's return, the morale in the Achaean camp increased a hundredfold, and the Troyans, led by noble Hector, struggled to maintain their resolve. Never, he reminded the warriors, could the residents of Priam's glorious city countenance their subjugation by the Achaean High King, whose greed knew no bounds. And as long as the men of Ilios fought so fiercely to defend their homes and families, I was safe, despite my fears.

Andromache despaired more than ever for her beloved husband's safety. She took to remaining at home, all but clinging to her loom, rather than venturing out on the wall to observe the warfare as she had so often done before. She was weaving a lavish bloodred robe and insisted, in the faraway tone a woman takes when her mind is troubled and unwell, that she had to finish it before Hector returned home from the field. Although her elder son Laodamas, who was nearly thirteen and still too young to fight, spent much of his days in the company of his numerous cousins, Andromache no longer left little Astyanax in the care of his nurse, but kept the baby beside her all the time, singing softly to him in his carved wooden cradle as she skillfully worked the warp and weft of the carmine-colored cloak. Naturally, she shunned my overtures to ease her spirit. Every day we feared the worst for our lords and should have been able to cleave to each other like sisters in our time of anguish, but Andromache still wanted nothing to do with me.

Of course, my own sister had never provided any loving reassurance or a calming touch, and I suppose I always craved that kind of affection, having lost my mother when I was too young to fully appreciate the bounty of maternal love. Aethra had been wise, but ever judgmental, and once we left Aphidnae in the company of my brothers, she had become my inferior. From time to time I wondered what had become of Theseus's mother. She would have been well advanced in years by now. Had she crossed the river Styx or did she still dwell among the living? Was she well? I had not received news from Sparta in years.

∼∼∼

During the first morning of Achilles's return to battle, several brave Troyans gasped their last, having tasted the tip of his Pelian spear or the point of his sword. One of those who lost his life was Polydorus, the youngest of Priam's fifty sons. Years earlier, Achilles had encountered the youth; impressed with his beauty, and out of respect for his noble lineage, he had spared him, selling him into slavery instead on the isle of Lemnos. But Polydorus had managed to escape his masters and return to Ilios; and in their second encounter on the banks of the river Xanthos, Achilles, in his rage and grief over the death of his beloved Patroclus, was unmerciful. The great Achaean vowed, too, that he would behead twelve young Troyans and pile their mangled corpses on his kinsman's pyre as a fitting tribute of his love.

It went hard for our warriors all day. Helios, passing above us in his chariot, scorched the earth with his blistering rays, dehydrating the men, who had neither refuge nor respite from the sweltering heat.

In mid-afternoon, the encounter that everyone on both sides most anticipated—and most feared—finally happened. After ten agonizing years, after countless men had fallen to the dusty earth, choking on their own blood, the greatest Achaean and the finest Troyan, both wearing Achilles's armor, faced each other.

Hector's supreme nobility and bravery, even in his direst moments, were a credit to his unimpeachable honor and that of the House of Priam, for in the thick of the fighting he drew Achilles toward him, allowing the Troyan ranks to take cover behind him and retreat to safety within the city walls. Paris Alexandros then climbed the wall and joined me on the battlements. After every one of his warriors was inside the great Scaean Gate, Hector stood his ground and faced down his most worthy adversary. His giant ash spear was formidable to behold: eleven cubits long, with a shining bronze tip and a ring of gold to hold it. His massive shield was covered by an entire ox hide. His young son Laodamas, eager to prove himself a hero, once tried to lift it and collapsed under its weight.

Clutching Alexander's arm, I watched the standoff from the wall, alongside the fearful Priam and Hecuba. Andromache, having willfully retreated to the safe little world inside her mind, remained at home. We held our breath. Queen Hecuba was gripping her husband's hand, her knuckles clenched so tightly that her skin had turned a bluish white.

Suddenly, like a mountain hare, Hector began to run, sprinting around the high walls with Achilles in hot pursuit, the Achaean unable to unleash his great spear for fear of missing his moving target. They passed below our watching point and headed for the windy fig tree. Around the walls they raced as we scrambled to follow their progress, dashing across the battlements from one side to the other. By the river Scamander, two natural springs, one hot and the other cold, jetted up the salty waters, the warriors swiftly passed them, flying toward the stone hollows where, in peaceful times, the Troyan women did their washing.

As fleet as Hermes, Hector led Achilles on a harrowing chase. After a second circuit of the citadel walls it was evident that he wished to tire his enemy before the combat began in earnest. The noble Hector then began his third revolution, maintaining just enough of a distance between himself and his pursuer to prevent Achilles from throwing his javelin.

But—to our dismay—Achilles did not flag, and on the ramparts we clutched our robes, or one another, and called upon the gods to maintain Hector's strength and grant him victory.

By the time Hector had passed the wellsprings for a fourth time, he was clearly spent. He halted, staggering, and called Achilles's name, daring the Achaean to do his worst.

Achilles unleashed the great Pelian ash spear, and Hector, ducking from its trajectory, dropped to one knee. High above them on the sun-baked wall, terror gripped our throats. Perhaps we looked away for the briefest of instants and shielded our eyes from witnessing the unthinkable, as if to prevent its occurrence, but somehow Achilles's spear, though it had fallen wide of Hector's body, was now back in the Achaean's hand.

Hector rose to his feet and opened his arms. He taunted his opponent, telling him that he would meet his spear head-on, and then let fly his own. Hector's aim was true, and peeking through parted fingers, we watched it sail toward Achilles.

Thumph! The javelin struck the Greek's enormous shield, lodging in its center. Hector called for another spear, as if another warrior stood beside him waiting to do his bidding. But there was no one else on the dusty ground except himself and his nemesis, and with his life in the balance, not another moment could be spared.

His spear gone and lacking another to replace it, Hector drew his sword and lunged for Achilles, hoping to swoop beneath him and discover a vulnerable chink in the elaborate armor.

He continued to slash and Achilles jumped back, increasing the distance between them. And then . . . as if each fractured movement had been slowed by time . . . Achilles raised his arm, his gazed fixed on Hector's corselet—on the very hole near the collarbone that Hector himself had located two days earlier, enabling him to dispatch Patroclus to Hades.

The brazen head, so sharp, so deadly, plunged into Hector's pliant flesh, his blood erupting from the puncture as though it were a crimson geyser. I flung my arms around Paris Alexandros; cleaving to each other, we wept bitter, anguished tears. Hecuba shrieked and sank to the paving stones, clasping her aged husband about the legs like a suppliant. Priam raised his fists, roaring and raging at the sky gods as though his own life were ebbing from his lungs. His firstborn son's final words echoed off the city walls. "Give my body to my family," Hector gasped. "You must permit them the proper funeral rites. And Priam will give you riches beyond measure, slave women . . . gold . . ."

And that was all.

I saw Achilles shake his head and toss his spear beside Hector's lifeless body.

The noblest man I'd ever known had met his end. I was not the only one in the city who believed that as Hector went, there went Ilios. The Achaeans began to gather around the fallen hero and gaze upon him as if he were a mythical curiosity, like a centaur, half man, half beast. I could have killed Diomedes with my own hands for sneering that the worthy Hector was not so formidable after all.

Someone summoned Achilles's chariot and I thought that perhaps, if for no other reason than for the respect he bore him as a warrior, the victor had decided to honor Hector's dying request. But hatred had taken up residence in Achilles's heart. With the tip of his spear, he bore holes straight through Hector's tendons between the ankle and heel. He unbuckled his fancy tin greaves and unlaced his sandals far enough to rip off two lengths of ox hide, which he fashioned into thongs, threading them through Hector's mangled ankles; then he secured the defiled corpse to the axle of his chariot. This accomplished, he stripped the armor from Hector's body and tossed it in to the horse-drawn car.

Hecuba had staggered to her feet, using her husband's feeble form to help regain her balance. At the crack of Achilles's whip, the horses bolted forward, dragging noble Hector's body across the dusty plain, and the proud queen tossed her headdress upon the paving stones and tore out fistfuls of her hair.

I reached out to embrace her. I, too, knew what it was like to lose a child to brutal death, although I had not witnessed my Iphigenia's slaughter. Hecuba and Priam had seen most of their sons cut down by the Achaeans, but the firstborn Hector, dearest son of all to Hecuba, had been the hope of Ilios, and now his light was dimmed forever. Cruelest of all was Achilles's vengeful debasement of his body, conduct unbecoming the Achaean's illustrious reputation. And yet I should not have been so surprised at Achilles's behavior, given his brutal rape of Penthesilea as she breathed her last on the blood-soaked field. Hector and Achilles were indeed the finest warriors in each of the two opposing armies, but Achilles was as dishonorable as Hector was noble.

Someone had to tell Andromache the devastating news. Priam and Hecuba still clung to each other in horror as they watched Achilles savagely drag their son's corpse around the walls of the city in hideous mockery of the chase on which Hector had led him just prior to their combat.

"I will go," I said, cradling Alexander's face between my hands as if to search there for some sign of Hector. "She cannot despise me any more than she already does. And perhaps I do deserve the full measure of her fury and her grief."

"Let me accompany you," insisted Paris Alexandros, his eyelids already swollen with weeping for his beloved brother. "As I am now the first son of Troy, it should be my duty to bear the bad tidings."

As we descended the wall, he momentarily lost his footing and stumbled into me. I steadied him, and looking into his eyes, saw that they were still misted over with tears. We lingered several minutes on the steps, and I held my husband close, his anguished tears drenching my breast. "I wish I had known him all my life," he said between muffled sobs. "I never believed I had missed anything by growing up on Mount Ida, but now I realize how much I lost. There never was a better man, a better warrior, a better father, than Hector."

"And a better friend," I added, for surely no one else in Ilios had befriended me when I arrived so many years ago. I, too, loved Hector like a brother. "Let's dry your tears," I suggested to Paris Alexandros, "before we enter Hector's home." We did our best, but our red-rimmed eyes betrayed the dreadful outcome of the combat.

We found Andromache at her loom, weaving elaborate figures into the bloodred robe. Beside her, little Astyanax fretted in his cradle, but she appeared deaf to his whimpering. "I heard the hue and cry from the walls," she said numbly, not turning from her weaving. "I must hurry up and finish." Her fingers worked the weft at a feverish pace. "I must be ready to greet Hector when he comes home."

U nfortunately, Andromache had too much time in which to complete the garment that would become her husband's shroud. The next day, Achilles once again hitched Hector's broken body to his chariot and dragged it over the sand, around the pyre he'd erected for the fallen Patroclus. At dusk, he dumped the battered corpse outside his tent, beside the monument. At sunup the following morning, he repeated the day-long defilement.

Meanwhile, beyond the walls of Troy, the battle raged on, and down by the ships, the Achaeans hosted funeral games for Patroclus. Prizes taken from the spoils that lay stored within their vessels' hulls—weapons, cauldrons, and tripods, as well as horses, cattle, mules, and even slave women—were awarded to the victors.

Perhaps an understanding of the nature of warfare is necessary to admit this irony: that a man heralded as a paragon of gentleness and compassion can be a bloodthirsty demon from dawn to sundown on the battlefield. That which the vanquished call butchery is considered valor by his comrades-in-arms. Over his anointed body, Patroclus's loving spirit and unshakable loyalty were lauded by his countrymen. It was said that even his two beloved horses wept at his death.

True to his dastardly promise, Achilles slit the throats of twelve Troyan youths and piled their bodies atop the pyre. Two of Patroclus's favorite dogs and four horses also forfeited their lives to grace the tomb. Finally, the funeral mound was torched, and when the acrid flames died out, the pyre was doused with wine.

Above them, all of Ilios was devastated by the loss of our greatest warrior. Even I, whose love for Paris Alexandros never wavered, could admit that Hector was our finest man in every way. The loss of twelve boys, innocents in the conflict, further angered and saddened us. But there had been no greater insult to Troy than Achilles's repeated and prolonged debasement of Hector's body.

Andromache chopped off her flowing chestnut tresses and walled herself within her home, refusing to step outside or to speak to anyone. Even Priam and Hecuba could not console her.

During the nearly thirteen years that had passed since I'd come to Ilios, Hecuba had never been more than civil to me, and often far less than that; but though we had never made peace with each other, I sought to mourn with her, hoping she would accept my words of condolence. However, she rebuffed my overtures, berating me for cutting only a few locks from the ends of my hair, rather than submitting myself to be shorn like a sheep, as was the custom for women in mourning. Even when my beloved brothers died, I did not divest myself of my flowing tresses. That was never my way. I did not appreciate my devotion to the dead being questioned or challenged by those who sought to dishonor me as well.

Priam, having scarcely slept since Hector's death, looking even more aged and defeated than I had ever seen him, rolled himself in dung and refused to bathe or change his garments. He cursed his surviving sons, including Deiphobus and Paris Alexandros, berating them for their ineptitude as warriors and wishing they, too, had been killed alongside Hector. He had sent his herald to Achilles's tent to offer him untold wealth; and the youngest Troyan princess, Polyxena, who had once fancied the illustrious Achaean, having discovered that he loved wild horses as much as she did, sent word that she would bestow Achilles her golden bracelets as a keepsake, or else as an offering for Patroclus's tomb. But Achilles was deaf to Priam's overtures and entreaties by proxy. For twelve days he drove his chariot around his kinsman's pyre, dragging the corpse of Hector behind it.

I was in the Great Hall when Priam decided to make his petition in person. I remember how Hecuba railed at him for his foolhardiness. "How simple would it be for that butcher to run you through with his spear? If he lacks all respect for Hector, how do you think he will treat the hero's father who never once took the field himself and now comes to him like an ancient stable boy reeking of manure, imploring the mercy he has so flagrantly denied us for a dozen days?"

But Priam would not hear reason, not even from his beloved wife, who undoubtedly wanted her son returned as much as he did. Hecuba retreated to their living quarters, and Priam dismissed his counselors and remaining sons, including the pugnacious Deiphobus, who looked less sorry about Hector's demise than I thought he should. I told Paris Alexandros that I wished to take a moment to speak privately with his father, promising to meet him at home as soon as our talk had been concluded.

The aged patriarch, who once appeared so regal and imperious now seemed dwarfed by his great throne and his bull-horned crown. He looked very much alone. Inured to the stench of his person, I approached him, divulging only the portion of the plan to ransom Hector that I had so painfully devised. I had not made such an agonizing decision since I had resolved to abandon my children in Sparta. Neither were choices I had made lightly, and each time the risks were at least as great as the reward.

"Relieve your herald of his duties tonight. I will make the journey to Achilles's tent with you," I told him. "The young warrior and I are both Achaean, both half mortal. Because of that common ground, I expect that he will hear me out. No one but you and I—not even my beloved Paris Alexandros—will know that I have accompanied you. Nor can they ever learn the truth. Sire, you have always been kind to me," I added, lowering myself to kiss the foul hem of his besmirched robe. "I ask you to trust me now. Hector was a brother to me, my first and only true friend in Ilios. For the sake of the love I bore him, I want to help you reclaim his corpse."

Reluctantly, Priam agreed to my request. But I could not be certain that its secrecy would be honored. The king's age as well as his grief made him prone to babble.

Ordinarily, it is a blessing when spouses are so well in tune that a husband can easily detect the slightest anxiety in his wife's countenance, in the sound of her voice, and in the nearly imperceptible shift in the language of her body. But Paris Alexandros most of all had to remain ignorant of my design. I had never been dishonest with him, never given him cause to doubt my love or my devotion, but I knew he would despair if I had told him that I was going to enter the Achaean camp with Priam. He might even try to prevent my leaving, or insist on joining me, thereby putting his own life in jeopardy.

I boiled a handful of Anatolian poppies, distilling the liquid into a tisane. Since Hector's death, Andromache and Hecuba, seeking solace from their grief, had consumed such a brew in abundance. Before we retired for bed, I brought a cup of the tisane to my beloved lord, holding him until he was carried off by Hypnos into a peaceful and innocent slumber.

Then I anointed my body and hair with fragrant oils, perfuming my skin with an irresistibly aromatic elixir and artfully applying my cosmetics. My softest silk chiton floated over my bare skin like a whisper. Over that I donned a robe the color of night and covered my face and shining hair with a heavy woven shawl. Carrying my sandals, I noiselessly crept out of our home and met Priam outside on the pergamos.

Another lifetime ago, once or twice I had managed to convince Menelaus to let me drive one of our chariots. The experience had not especially prepared me to manage a mule cart; but I could not permit a servant, or even Priam's herald, to see me leave the citadel and descend into the Achaean encampment; therefore, I had to take the reins myself. Priam had loaded the wagon with the treasure he intended to give Achilles in exchange for Hector's release. We hoped to be able to bring back his battered corpse on the emptied cart.

When I arrived at the wagon, it had already been laden with a dozen each of robes, mantles, blankets, white cloaks, and tunics. Added to that were ten talents of gold, a pair of shining tripods, four copious cauldrons, and an ornately wrought Thracian goblet.

Suddenly, I heard a sound coming from the direction of the palace, and I darted for cover amid the darkness.

Hecuba came running down the steps with a golden cup and a mixing bowl. "You must first pour a libation to the gods," she implored. "In our grief, we must not forget to propitiate them." Priam mixed the wine with water and spilled it on the paving stones, staining them purple. The queen threw her arms about her husband's neck, and kissing his forehead, eyelids, mouth, and cheeks, and then what must have been every hair in his long white beard, she urged him to be ever vigilant on his most dangerous errand. "For the Achaeans are treacherous and untrustworthy," she reminded him, "and would not think twice about seizing their opportunity to murder you or to detain you in their camp and hold your enfeebled body for ransom."

Priam managed a brave chuckle. "After so many years of marriage, you have so little faith in the king." Once more he embraced the weeping Hecuba. I watched her climb the palace steps and waited until she was safely indoors before I emerged from my hiding place into the silver-blue moonlight; then I helped the old king onto the wagon.

Priam's guards opened the Scaean Gate, and we passed through its enormous jointed limestone blocks. We crossed the plaza where Hector had so bravely met his end, the dust now still and silent, unyielding of its secrets. I could have approached the Achaean encampment from the south, driving across the plain whose thirsty earth had absorbed the winedark blood of so many thousands of warriors over the years, but I chose to drive the wagon through the lower city instead. It had been so long since I had visited the winding narrow streets, the houses densely set together, the marketplace. I was shocked to find it so deserted. I realized that the town was quiet not because its residents slumbered, but because most of the homes themselves had lain empty for ages. The wind hissed eerily through tattered sheets that had been hung to dry several seasons ago. The clatter of our wagon as it rolled and bounced along the cobbled lanes echoed off the mud and brick walls of the abandoned buildings and surely would have disclosed our presence had there been souls to hear it.

When we reached the second gate, Priam gave a signal and it was opened by his guards. Another group of royal guards bridged the trench with wooden planks, and we drove over it and descended the bluffs, riding down the beach into the Achaean camp. The Greeks had fenced themselves in with pickets and a bolted gateway. Our wagon was halted and Priam identified himself. He was scoffed at, disbelieved, and we were ordered to wait. Many agonizing minutes passed until, finally, we were approached by one of the commanders.

"Who comes from Ilios into our encampment?" he demanded.

The voice was one I could never forget no matter how many years had come and gone. It was Menelaus who had spoken. My heart leapt from my chest into my throat. I turned away so that I could not be identified in any way. My former husband did of course recognize Priam. "Who is that?" he asked the king. He must have been inquiring about me.

"No one. A slave," answered Priam. "Once he has delivered me to the great Achilles's tent, he will not stir from where he sits. I give you my pledge."

It nearly broke my heart to hear the proud king refer with veneration to the butcher of so many of his sons. How much he adored Hector to so abase himself!

Menelaus let us continue on our errand but walked silently alongside the wagon as though he were an honor guard. I wanted to look at him, to see from a closer vantage than the walls of Ilios how the years had changed him, but I dared not even toss so much as a single glance in his direction.

We then encountered Odysseus, who exchanged a few words with Menelaus about Priam's visit; then Menelaus turned away and headed for his own tent, leaving us in the company of the crafty Ithacan. Time had not altered my opinion of that man. I still mistrusted him.

I drove on until we came upon the tomb of Patroclus, ringed with flaming torches that had been planted in the sand. Facedown beside it lay the dirt-encrusted body of noble Hector. Even in his death, the gods must have looked upon his form with favor, for his face and limbs had not been disfigured by decay.

Priam wept openly when he saw his son's corpse thus abused. I halted the mule beside a clump of tamarisk bushes, and Odysseus helped him descend from the wagon. Achilles's tent was the one closest to his kinsman's pyre. A fire blazed from a hearth at its center, and through the fabric I discerned the forms of three men and a woman.

The king told Odysseus that he needed to give his slave some orders, then approached me where I sat atop the wagon, the reins still in my hands. "Pray for my success," he murmured.

"You go in alone," I whispered to Priam in the Phrygian tongue. "I'll stay by the wagon as you promised them. I can see and hear everything from out here." I never intended for the Achaeans to know that Helen was there, not unless it was absolutely necessary— something I feared might come to pass.

Odysseus parted the leather flaps, and Priam stooped to enter the pavilion. The shadow of Achilles rose to greet him. A few moments later, Odysseus, two warriors, and the woman, who I guessed was Briseis, left the Troyan king and the Achaean hero alone.

Achilles's shadow brought forth a stool for Priam, and the king seated himself. I heard him commence a recitation of the wealth that lay in the wagon just beyond the tent, offering it to the young warrior as a ransom for Hector's body. Achilles shook his head, and Priam buried his between his hands. Then, like a suppliant, he prostrated himself before the slayer of his sons; taking Achilles's callused fingers in his own trembling hands, he kissed the killer's knuckles.

"Think of aged Peleus," he pleaded. "If your father came to Hector, came to me, and implored us to return your body to your family for the proper honors, we would not hesitate to grant his request." Seeing Achilles appear to soften at his words, Priam embellished his entreaty. "I sired fifty sons," he told the hero. "And all fifty of them are dead, many at your own hands. I have no more sons to give to this bloody cause. At least give me Hector's corpse so that his mother and I can say farewell before he journeys to Elysium."

Whether from grief or hope, the ancient king had said too much. Achilles commanded Priam to rise. "Where then is the craven Paris Alexandros? And the warlike Deiphobus? Where is Helenus the seer? Where is Polites? And young Prince Troilus has yet to celebrate his twentieth year. You had my sympathies just now, old man, but I will not be dealt with falsely. Hector's body will remain here and will feed the crows ere long. And do not presume to waste my time again." He dismissed Priam from his presence, and the Troyan king, stumbling forward in the sand, unseeing through his tear-dimmed eyes, collapsed beside our wagon.

I leapt from my perch and helped him to his feet, and then, although he would befoul them with his stinking garments, I cleared a place among the sumptuous textiles where he could rest. "Wait here," I cautioned. "Sleep if you can."

I tiptoed to the tent and let myself inside it. Achilles turned when he heard my footfall, and I removed my shawl. "Shhhh," I whispered, putting my finger to my lips. I pointed to the stool where Priam had so lately sat. "Sit there." More stunned than surprised to see Helen in his tent, he obeyed me.

"Achaeans and Troyans believe the same thing," I said. "We both know that the soul of a dead person cannot pass into Hades without the proper funeral rites and lamentations. You do yourself a disservice with the gods by violating their laws. A man's immortality is assured by the glory won and honor done on earth, deeds the bards will sing about for generations to come. And even if a man or woman is not blessed with demimortality as we are, they can live on in legend long after their bodies have been entombed and burned. Do you desire the brilliance of your legacy to be forever tarnished by this?" I asked, pointing toward the area outside the tent where Hector's corpse lay in the sand, his shade wandering between this world and the next. While I spoke of weighty things, I favored Achilles with the full measure of my charm, renowned for softening even the hardest hearts.

The Achaean listened to me, his expression inscrutable. I could not yet discern the effect of my words. I continued to measure them, careful not to overstep as Priam had. "Achilles, we have much in common, being half mortal. But even *we* are not above the sky gods, nor should we even imagine ourselves their equal, for there is no greater hubris."

"You speak well, daughter of Zeus. And were it a contest between us for immortality, we have fought to a draw. You have bested me on lineage, however. The progeny of the king of high Olympus far outstrips the son of a sea nymph. But make no mistake: Zeus was as smitten with *my* mother's beauty as he was with yours. But the Oracle had prophesied that Thetis's son would become greater than his father, so the powerful Zeus smothered his lust for her." Achilles's volubility and change of humor was proof enough that my magnetism had put him off his guard. He pointed to an enormous golden cauldron. "To this I owe more of my godliness than anything else."

"I don't understand," I whispered, smiling, as though we demimortals shared some secret joke.

"Imagine old Peleus's face when he saw my mother plunging my tiny newborn body into the roiling contents of this cauldron." Achilles took a small bronze statue of a young man, a kouros, from a low table and gripped the figure by the left ankle, plunging it into the pot. "My father thought my mother was drowning me. He pulled her away from the cauldron before I was scalded completely, then chided my mother for what he thought was an act of attempted murder. Furious that he did not believe that she was ensuring my immortality, as she had done with all their other demimortal children—my six brothers—Thetis abandoned him forever."

I suppressed a chuckle. "And yet the bards immortalize their marriage and not their separation."

"The surprise appearance of Eris at their wedding changed their destiny," Achilles said curtly.

"The arrival of Lady Strife that day changed *all* our destinies," I reminded him. I stood above him so that my perfume wafted gently toward his nostrils. "It is said that I am the most beautiful and desirable woman in the world. You are perhaps the greatest warrior of our age. Regardless of the truth, the bards will invent a new destiny for us: a marriage of the bravest and the most beautiful in the history of all Achaea. Ares and Aphrodite incarnate."

The proud Achilles looked somewhat startled.

I rose and moved toward him, so close that he could feel my breath upon his face. "I will offer you a trade," I said. "Hector's body . . . for mine. Helen of Troy, the fantasy of every man who knows her name, is in your tent, offering herself to you like a humble supplicant." I dropped my cloak and unclasped the brooches that secured my gown. The liquidy silk pooled at my feet. Entirely naked and vulnerable, I stood before him.

Our gazes met. Achilles licked his lower lip involuntarily, enjoying the humiliation in my eyes. "Kneel."

Trying to disguise the trembling in my legs, I sank to my knees and raised his finely woven tunic past the origin of the line of nut-brown hair that snaked up the center of his abdomen. Like a lowly camp follower or a slave girl captured as a spoil of war and taken home to warm her master's bed, I took him in my mouth. I wished I had been able to pretend it was not me, that it was another Helen, who had willingly submitted to this degradation.

Achilles clutched my hair as my lips and tongue worked their magic, but after a minute or so, he jerked my head away. "Kneel," he said again. It took a moment for his meaning to penetrate my benumbed brain. Achilles shoved me down onto the floor.

He took me like a boy.

It is frightening how history can be distorted to serve the poets.

The tongue of man is a twisty thing indeed. Hermione, if you ever hear that your mother was "married" to Achilles, read my words and learn the truth.

I remember kneeling on all fours, trying so hard not to cry out and thus betray my presence. The excruciating pain, the humiliation, and the shame that I endured that night to earn the release of Hector's body will always be imprinted on my memory. I will forever remember another thing, too. That the only place for me to fix my gaze was straight ahead, where Achilles's armor lay. I focused on his leg greaves of supple tin, with their shining silver buckles, the lowest of which when fastened would fall about three fingers' width above the heel.

First I would redeem Hector's body.

And soon I would exact my revenge.

TWENTY SIX

W ordlessly I rose to my feet. It was easy to locate a hand mirror among the amenities in Achilles's tent, and I availed myself of it, drying my tears and washing away the rivulets of kohl that had trickled down my cheeks. While I performed these perfunctory ablutions, Achilles strummed his lyre, paying me no more heed than he would to a common slave girl.

I dressed and covered my head with the midnight-blue shawl. "Priam will be overjoyed to learn that you have agreed to exchange Hector's body in return for his wagonload of treasures. I will send him to speak with you directly about the particulars." Achilles gave no indication that he had heard my words, but skilled at reading men, I understood that was his way. His immortal fame was a certainty, but his earthly goal was power. That was how he derived his pleasure, and I had permitted him to dominate me. King Priam and his family would never know the depths to which I descended to win the battered body of their most beloved hero.

With halting steps I approached the wagon and gently awakened the Troyan king. "Hector will come home," I told him. He did not ask how I achieved the mission at which he had so miserably failed. I suppose he assumed that my earlier hypothesis, which posited a common understanding between Achaean-born demimortals, had succeeded. The vilified Helen turned out to be of use to Ilios after all.

I hid behind the wagon while Priam once more entered Achilles's pavilion; a few minutes later both men emerged. Achilles ordered two of his Myrmidons to unload the cart and carry the ransom to his tent.

Then he commanded a pair of slave women to wash Hector's corpse and anoint it with olive oil.

"You must be hungry, old man," Achilles said, this time referring to Priam's age with the cocky respect begrudged by a beloved son. The great warrior slaughtered a sheep and spitted it, then made the Troyan king partake of it with him, according to the customary laws of hospitality.

As they ate, they spoke of diplomatic matters. Priam requested a unilateral ceasefire to allow for a proper period of mourning for Hector. "I will hold off an attack for as long as you bid me," Achilles replied. The hero then parlayed with Agamemnon, exchanging but a few words with the High King, and the aged Troyan ruler's request was honored.

After they had feasted, Achilles ordered the serving women to bathe Priam and make up a bed of soft fleeces and purple linens as an honor to his royal status. "You have endured much this night, especially in your enfeebled condition," Achilles said. "Sleep here until sunup, and I will personally guarantee your comfort and your safety." Nothing was said about Priam's "slave," but I was well aware that the undertaking of this unheralded driver had brought about Achilles's stunning volte-face.

I had slept in the shelter of the tamarisk bushes and awoke, sore and aching, at the first rosy light of Eos. Without the cover of darkness, my disguise was no longer as effective. I crept behind Achilles's tent and, lowering the timbre of my voice as much as possible, I called to Priam in the Phrygian dialect and told him to rise and hasten.

He emerged from the tent, Achilles following and giving orders to have Hector's anointed body placed upon the mule cart. As soon as the corpse of the Troyan prince was in our care, and Priam seated on the wagon beside it, I drove us out of the camp as swiftly as the mule could take us over the sands.

The royal guard at the lower gate rejoiced to see the wagon returning and blasted their horns to announce our success to the keepers of the Scaean Gate. Those soldiers at the entrance to the citadel trumpeted our accomplishment as well, and now all of Ilios knew that Hector had come home to his family.

Cassandra was the first to see her brother. At the second blast of the horn, she came running out of Apollo's temple, her hair streaming down her back, tears of joy commingled with those of grief staining her rosy cheeks. She threw herself upon her father and then upon the lifeless Hector as though her embrace could bring him back from the dead. Andromache and Hecuba flew down the tiered steps of the palace and with the utmost tenderness lifted Hector's body from the wagon. Queen Hecuba was as jubilant to see her husband alive as she was to see her dead son restored to her.

Just inside the Scaean Gate was an enormous altar. While there were individual temples to several of the sky gods within the walls of the upper city, this central altar served as the sacrificial site to all of the Olympians in the name of Ilios. The elevated altar was surrounded by six pedestals, and a few yards beyond lay a cult house for burned sacrifices. Hector's mother and his widow had his body placed atop the great altar, resting on a sumptuously carved bed.

Later that day, the royal family gathered around the altar to deliver our eulogies. Paris Alexandros and I had quarreled about the appropriateness of our children being present. Idaeus was now twelve years old and had adored his uncle, hoping to follow in his footsteps as a great and noble warrior, so I did agree that he could be present. I thought the spectacle would be too much for our daughter, though. Young Helen was a painfully shy child who hated crowds and loud noises, as introverted as her mother was convivial; and I tried to keep her as far away as possible from the horrors of the war and its aftermath. Despite Alexander's protests, I left the little girl in the care of her nurse, who would watch Aganus and Bunomus as well. Those two little mischief-makers, who had seen but four and three summers, respectively, were far too young to be exposed to funeral rites.

Andromache, who was the first to speak, approached her husband's body. Clutching her left hand was their elder son Laodamas, the very essence of his noble father in miniature, and cradled in the crook of her right arm was the infant Astyanax. "You were the light of all my days, my beloved. When all alone I came to you from Thebes, you were father, mother, brother, and husband to me; and after my family was slaughtered there, you became even dearer. Now, Achilles has killed everyone I ever loved, save my children. I see no hope for Wilusa now. I fear your sons will not fare well, never grow to manhood, never claim their birthright. For myself I see no future beyond a life of slavery and toil . . . and crave the day when my broken spirit will be reunited with yours." Even as her voice wavered, she tried to comfort her children, and in her grief I saw no greater dignity.

Queen Hecuba approached the corpse and offered her parting words. "Dearest—and bravest—of all my sons, you did not deserve such foul treatment at the hands of mighty Achilles, for there were other princes—brothers who could not hold a torch to your magnificence and your integrity—who were dealt with far more gently. The Achaean demon captured and sold them into slavery in Lemnos, Imbros, and Samnos, but he was never so brutal, never showed so little respect or accorded so little honor as he did with you." She was more angry than tearful, seeking to lay blame, and unconcerned at how her obvious bias for Prince Hector might fall upon the ears of her surviving sons.

Of course, one of her sons, Deiphobus, was not a lovable man. He walked about bemoaning his unmarried state, but it was certainly evident to me why women would have nothing to do with him despite his regal lineage. I glanced at Paris Alexandros to gauge his reaction to his mother's bitter words. He seemed stricken, truly wounded by them. With overwhelming sympathy, I met his gaze again and whispered that I loved him. I knew too well what it felt like to be the less-loved child, regardless of my accomplishments.

A murmur undulated through the crowd when I stepped forward. It was clear they felt that I did not deserve to speak. I chose to address that situation rather than ignore it. "After nearly thirteen years I am still regarded as an outsider in Ilios. Of course you are entitled to your thoughts, but the man for whom we grieve did not share your opinion, and to dishonor Helen is to dishonor noble Hector. I lost my brothers many years ago, when I was no older than Polyxena," I said, referring to Priam's youngest daughter. "And when my beloved Paris Alexandros brought me to these foreign shores, although my beauty had been much vaunted, I myself was vilified; reviled by those who thought the love my Troyan husband bore for me would come to no good end. Although King Priam is a gracious man who always treated me with respect, it was Hector first—and only Hector—who looked upon me with a kindly and forgiving eye. It was Hector first—and only

Hector—who understood the true reasons why the Achaeans might sail to Ilios in Helen's name. It was Hector first—and only Hector—of all my husband's royal brothers, who became a brother to Alexander's wife. Although he was the greatest warrior in Troy's illustrious history, he had a gentle heart. You had only to see him at play with his infant son to see how tender he was, how mild and sweet his words. Hector fought so valiantly *not* because his commander, his father, *told* him to. He was a marvel on the battlefield because he was driven by *love:* for his family and for Troy. His reverence and respect for his religion, his compassion, his sense of honor, and his modesty of spirit were unparalleled by any man. He was indeed the embodiment of the concept of *aidos.* I have never known the heroic Hector's equal and expect I never will."

The pergamos was silent, save for the cry of a bird winging past the sun. I slipped my arms about Alexander's waist and we held each other and wept.

Then Priam spoke and eulogized his son, declaring afterward that a twelve-day ceasefire would be observed by the opposing armies so that Hector could be properly mourned. He called for the men to bring timber for the funeral pyre. It was considered a great honor to help build it.

Nine days of mourning followed, during which noble Hector's corpse lay in state, wrapped in a purple-bordered robe and crowned with a wreath of myrtle. Day and night, singers, ringed around the altar, chanted the funeral dirges and sang lamentations. On the tenth day, the pyre was lit and Hector's body was burned until nothing but his white bones remained. The flames were then doused with wine and the bones of the great warrior were dipped in oil and wrapped in the finely woven linen tunic that had been worn by Hector on the day he wed Andromache. Hecuba brought forth a golden casket into which Priam gently placed his son's bones, bestowing a kiss upon the cloth before closing the box. The entire city was then invited to a lavish feast, old Priam having sent emissaries to our allies, charging them to scavenge and scrounge, to empty their larders, fields, and farms in noble Hector's honor.

On the morning of the eleventh day, Andromache draped the elaborately wrought red funeral shroud over the coffer; alongside

Hector's parents, she set the casket in a hollow grave, which they piled over with enormous stones laid close together. Each of Priam's surviving children and their wives laid down a stone until the great grave barrow was complete. Priam set up watchmen all around it in case the Achaeans broke the truce and tried to defile the newly raised tomb.

Then, on the following day, when Hector's name and legacy had entered the realm of legend, the fighting resumed.

Paris Alexandros, now the eldest prince of Troy, felt it his duty to assume Hector's mantle. How far my husband had come from insisting that he was a hunter and not a soldier! "I want Achilles," he said as he lay in my arms the night after the ceasefire was lifted. "I want to be the one to make him pay for Hector's life. For Penthesilea's. I have become a man obsessed. It's said he is not fully mortal, and I believe it. How else could he have remained untouched even in the thick of battle? He appears invulnerable to arrow, spear, and sword."

I traced his jawline with the tip of my finger, then brought my lips to his. "The Troyan warriors are aiming for the wrong place."

"We have aimed everywhere!"

"Not quite," I whispered.

I recalled how Achilles, having unwittingly lowered his guard in my presence, handled the kouros. "Remember the story you once told me about the marriage of Peleus and Thetis?"

"Of course."

I nestled into his arms. "I have one, too." I could not tell him how I learned it; Paris Alexandros was surprised that no Troyan seemed to ever have heard it or surely they would have taken better aim. I told him the tale of Achilles's near immortality: how Thetis had held her newborn son by the left ankle and dipped his tiny form into the cauldron to boil away his mortal parts, thus leaving the rest of his body completely invulnerable to death or injury; how Peleus, coming upon her and thinking, mistakenly, that she was trying to kill their baby, had pulled her away from the cauldron; how Thetis, still holding Achilles by his left ankle, had never dipped that part of his body into the boiling waters of immortality; therefore, his left foot up to the ankle was as mortal as any man's.

"His sandal covers his foot, but his greave ends just above his ankle. The tiny patch of flesh would not be easy to reach with a sword, and a spear would strike the dust before it struck Achilles, but it is supremely vulnerable to an arrow's tip." I straddled Paris Alexandros and kissed him passionately, feeling him grow hard between my legs. "For an archer as skilled as you, no target is too small."

He slipped inside me. "Are you sure that what you told me of Achilles is true?"

I shook my head. "But you have everything to gain by taking aim." My hair tumbled over my breasts and down my back as I rode him. Our lovemaking was fierce and feral, an even greater passion gripping us that night: the raging mutual desire to extinguish the Achaeans' brightest light.

～～

"I go to kill one man today," said Paris Alexandros the following morning as I helped him don his armor. "I have no urge to see any other Achaean fall."

Never before had I encouraged Paris Alexandros to set foot on the battlefield. Although I'd been in Ilios for years, my life was still completely tied to his alone. Without him, neither I nor our children were entirely safe from harm. Every time he shouldered his great curved bow, I felt like I was holding my breath for hours until his return. And when he returned home safe and unscarred, I was even happier to see him than I had been the day before. I regretted that Andromache had always rebuffed my repeated overtures of friendship, for we were truly sisters under the skin for the overwhelming love we bore our husbands.

Paris Alexandros checked his store of arrows one last time before leaving. I kissed him good-bye, holding him so close that I could feel his heartbeat through his leather armor, and wished him good fortune on the field.

Then I dressed as if for a festival in cloth of gold and crowned my head with a glittering diadem that resembled a wreath, studded with rubies to mimic wild berries. I climbed the steps to the ramparts and stood on the wall to watch the day's carnage. For the first time in my life I felt something akin to the way my sister Clytemnestra viewed the world, and it both thrilled and horrified me.

Below me, the fighting raged as fiercely as it did on any other morning. What a dreadful life a soldier had! I still saw no honor in dying on the field for a cause in which one had no personal stake, as had numberless Achaeans. By now, their warriors were half a generation younger than those who had sailed under Agamemnon. Most likely they hardly had a clue who Helen was and why so many of them were dying in order to recapture her. To them I was no more than the stuff of legend, though I lived among them.

I spied Achilles in the thick of the conflict. Hacking and slashing with his sword, he cut a deforesting swath through our army. Troyans staggered and fell on either side of his blade. He appeared invincible.

Crouched behind a crenellation, Paris Alexandros waited for open space before he drew his bowstring. The other warriors were too close to the mighty Achaean; the target was obscured.

Achilles did not lack for hubris, though, and I will always believe that his ego, as much as Alexander's arrow, contributed to his downfall. For a few moments, the great Greek warrior stood alone amid a sea of corpses, his leather sandals soaking up the lifeblood of the morning's victims. But, from where I stood, it appeared that one of the Troyan warriors was not expiring quickly enough to suit Achilles's temper. He raised his left foot to deliver a swift kick to the mutilated body.

With the instincts of an eagle, Paris Alexandros released an arrow from his bow just as Achilles made the slightest movement to raise his foot. My beloved's aim was perfect and deadly; the tip of the shaft penetrated the back of Achilles's leg, just above the heel.

Like a wounded boar, Achilles roared in pain. Perhaps it was my imagination, but it seemed to me that in that moment, every movement, every noise on the vast and bloody plain, ceased, leaving nothing but the echo of Achilles's final cry. The great warrior reeled and staggered, tearing off his helmet and raising his arms to the sky as if to rail at the Olympians who had failed to protect him. Blood poured from the sensitive mortal flesh.

With the massive momentum of a felled cypress, Achilles toppled to the earth, striking his bare head on a stone, becoming motionless in an instant as the dust around him billowed into a sepia-colored cloud. Troyan and Achaean alike were shocked to see the hero dead. Odysseus and Diomedes faced down the Troyan army, keeping them at bay, lest they try to despoil Achilles's corpse the way the fallen man had done to Hector's. Despite their collective hatred for Achilles, the Troyans had a certain reverence for him as a warrior and let the Achaeans bear him from the field undefiled.

It was not long before word spread throughout the enemy army that it was Paris Alexandros—fabled as a lover and not a fighter—who had dispatched the mighty Achilles to the Elysian Fields. They considered it an insult to the hero's glory that Achilles was felled by one who in their view could scarcely bear a candle to his brother Hector's light. In our culture, excellence on the battlefield was determined by one's skill with spear and sword (and in the Troyans' case, with chariots as well), but never with a bow and arrow. A man who needed distance from his target in order to be effective and who took cover behind the presumed safety of a wall rather than stand in the thick of an ugly skirmish, was seen as less than a true soldier. Bows and arrows were considered fine for hunting, but not for warfare. In the Achaeans' view, Paris Alexandros had killed the greatest warrior since the mighty Heracles with no more than a craven sportsman's toys.

I welcomed him home that day with a steaming bath strewn with rose petals. I lovingly bathed every inch of my adored husband and washed and oiled his hair until it shone like Apollo's, the Olympians' greatest archer. I smoothed fragrant lotions along every limb and plane of his beautiful golden body and decked him in his finest robes.

"Do you think that my mother might finally appreciate my return to Wilusa?" he quipped, but I could tell from the look in his eyes that he did not speak entirely in jest. Not only had Hector been his mother's favorite by far, but Hecuba still remained certain that the prophecy she dreamt of when she carried Paris Alexandros in her womb would still prove true and that her second son would live to bring ruin on Ilios.

To my view, the city—and the royal family—had already suffered the devastation predicted in her dream. Perhaps the worst of it had passed, that it had culminated in the death of Hector and that with Alexander's triumph over Achilles, the tide had finally turned in our favor.

That night we feasted well, amid much revelry. I thought, mistakenly, that some of my sisters-in-law would have congratulated me on Alexander's feat, or even sought to ingratiate themselves with me as the wife of Troy's new hero. But I was as lonely as ever until the meal itself was over and the women adjourned to the Great Hall to join the men.

I was so proud to languish at Alexander's feet; I never thought it an abasement to show my adoration for the man I loved, but Paris Alexandros called for a chair so that I could sit beside him. While he insisted on propitiating Apollo for his aegis that afternoon, my beloved alone knew how great a contribution *I* had made that day. The arrow that struck the seemingly invincible Achilles in the vulnerable mortal flesh above his left heel was not a lucky shot by any means, but the achievement of a master marksman . . . guided by the equally lethal tip I'd given to him during our lovemaking.

Priam stood and raised his elaborate golden wine cup. "I've always believed that Paris Alexandros was a fine warrior," he began, lest any snickers contradict the king. I could see that Deiphobus barely concealed a smirk behind the lip of his kylix. "And his lovely Helen has ever been a charming, gracious asset to Wilusa. We have not lost so many sons because Helen saw in Paris Alexandros what others were so late to acknowledge." I noticed that he glanced first at Hecuba and then at his daughter Cassandra. "To believe that men have died for Helen and the love she bears my second son, and now my heir, is to tarnish the name of glorious Hector—who understood what was truly at stake in this bloody conflict—as well as to discredit Alexandros. Let us drink to Paris Alexandros, hero to all of Wilusa and heir to the throne of Troy!"

My eyes misted over with joyous tears. Everyone drank to my husband's valor and continued health, and libations were mixed and poured to thank the gods for favoring us that day. And what a grand show it was of Priam's faith in and love for his son, to proclaim him heir before the great royal family! I think that was what stung Deiphobus most of all. Even though he was younger than Paris Alexandros, Deiphobus had convinced himself, I'm certain, that their father did not regard the man best known in Ilios for being the city's most scandalous lover, as fitting material for a king. Now the outraged Deiphobus had to swallow his anger as well as his pride and embrace his elder brother in a public show of affection and support.

Although Paris Alexandros had returned from Mount Ida many years ago, that night he felt as if he had finally come home; and when Queen Hecuba enfolded him in her arms, kissing first his right cheek, then his left, and then his right again, the tears that trickled down his face bedewed her lips. The plaudits of his peers and his father's approbation were thrilling, but his mother's acceptance was all the world to him.

Unfortunately, his euphoria was too short-lived. Late that night, after we had made love, I thought that Paris Alexandros had drifted off to sleep and was deep in the bosom of Morpheus dreaming of the day's triumph. But his eyes were wide open, sparkling in the moonlight and gazing at the frescoed ceiling.

"You realize, love," he murmured in a voice that froze my soul, "that from now on, I am more than heir to Priam's throne. My life is now the Achaeans' greatest prize."

lthough another ceasefire was not demanded, the Achaean chieftains decided that they needed to regroup. Achilles's death had been as much of a loss to their army and a blow to morale as was Hector's death to ours. Once more, though tragically, the opposing armies were evenly matched.

We gleaned much intelligence from our trustworthy spies. The Achaeans claimed that a seer had proclaimed that they would not be able to take Troy without the arms of Heracles. The famed warrior's great bow and arrows were bestowed upon his friend Philoctetes, who had been the only one brave enough to set the first torch to Heracles's funeral pyre. But when the Achaeans stopped en route to Troy on the isle of Tenedos, just beyond our bay, Philoctetes, suffering a serpent bite that soon became gangrenous, was abandoned there by his trusted fellow warriors.

Agamemnon thus dispatched a party to Tenedos for the purpose of bringing Philoctetes to Ilios and curing his wounded foot. It amazed me that they dared to imagine that the poor man might still be alive so many years later, particularly since their treatment of him a decade ago was almost as insidious as the gangrene.

It was also prophesied that the Achaeans would never conquer Troy if one of Priam's younger sons, Prince Troilus, lived past his twentieth birthday. The fact that the youth still lived was what Achilles had alluded to on the night that Priam came to ransom Hector's corpse.

In response to a third prognostication, Achilles's young son Neoptolemus had been fetched from rocky Skyros where he dwelled with his mother Deidamia, one of the daughters of the island's king, old Lycomedes. The boy was barely older than my son Idaeus; in my opinion, far too young to fight.

By now my first three sons by Menelaus would have been grown men about the age of Troilus and were surely on our shores among the Spartan hoplites. I still had no word of them, despite the requests I'd made to our Troyan spies. Perhaps they had never even looked for my boys or had learned something but withheld it from me. With the possibility existing that my Spartan sons were on the battlefield trying to kill my Troyan husband and his kin and countrymen—and with all the ambivalence about allegiances that this situation might engender—I suppose I could understand how the scouts would have wished me to remain in the dark.

The Troyans had fought well ever since Achilles's death, particularly since another of the great Achaean warriors had died soon afterward. The Greeks had quarreled among themselves as to which of their number was the greatest surviving warrior and therefore most deserving to inherit Achilles's armor. It had come down to Odysseus and Ajax the Greater: the first renowned for his cunning, the latter notorious for his tremendous strength. Agamemnon had been called upon to break the tie, and he awarded the armor to Odysseus, on whom he relied tremendously as a strategist. No one could have predicted that this act would completely devastate Ajax, but the battle-hardened warrior went mad over it and fell upon his sword. Ajax, too, had been one of my suitors all those years ago. I still remember how grateful I was that Tyndareus had not chosen him for my husband; but with his death, as with that of Patroclus, a piece of me, the girlish Helen of a gentler time, died as well.

There was much anticipation in both camps on the day that Philoctetes was well enough to set his healed foot onto the battlefield, for everyone believed that Heracles's arms bore a near-mythical power. Would they turn the hapless Philoctetes into a hero of his predecessor's stature or would he dishonor great Heracles's name by not distinguishing himself on the field? Naturally, we Troyans hoped for the latter.

The irony of the bow and arrow being suddenly sacrosanct in a world where spear and sword were the revered weapons was not lost on Paris Alexandros. Before this intriguing shift of popular opinion, at least in the Achaean camp, Alexandros had said repeatedly that he could not understand why a sane man would put his life and his family at risk by being in the thick of things when he could dispatch at least as many of the enemy from behind a bow.

The Greeks fought with a renewed vigor that day, despite the fact that Philoctetes had not yet had the chance to employ Heracles's massive bow. I watched the combat from the south tower of the citadel wall, where much farther along it, Paris Alexandros crouched, loosing his arrows in abundance.

I sighted Philoctetes in a chariot below the wall, perhaps at the same moment that he and Paris Alexandros spied each other. I drew in my breath as each man drew his bow. It was difficult to follow the two trajectories simultaneously. Alexander's arrow flew straight for Philoctetes, but the Achaean ducked, and the arrow stuck fast in the body of the cart.

But Paris Alexandros had not taken cover in time. Philoctetes's arrow pierced my husband's armor, lodging in his breast. Paris Alexandros staggered backward and collapsed upon the stone; his cry of agony could have been heard on lofty Mount Olympus. Clutching my skirts, I descended the steps of the tower and raced toward him along the wall until I was out of breath. I elbowed past the Troyan warriors who warned me that I was now in an area of combat and who tried to prevent me from reaching my beloved lord. "Let them hit me!" I cried, referring to the enemy below. "Would that I *could* die today!"

Someone had propped up Paris Alexandros so that he was seated with his back slumped against the wall, sheltered from the line of fire. His jerkin and tunic had been split open to avoid infecting the wound. Blood flowed like wine from his chest and his skin was deathly pale. I knelt beside him, ripping my gown to make a cloth to mop his brow. Shivering and trembling, he was covered in sweat. Sliding my arm behind his neck to cradle him, I whispered words of comfort. "Stay by me, my love," I urged him. "You will live to save Ilios from the invaders. You will be king one day, and our son Idaeus after you. All Troy relies upon your valor."

I don't know if he heard me. Paris Alexandros drifted in and out of consciousness, with one word on his lips: *Oenone.*

Could my heart die twice in a single day? Oenone was the nymph-like girl of Alexander's youth upon Mount Ida. In a moment of clarity, I recalled that he had once told me that she was exceptionally skilled in the arts of healing. Perhaps he only sought her as a nurse. Or was it more than that? I could not bear to think that might be true. But it was her name that he whispered, not Helen's, in what might have been his final breaths.

"Carry him home and send to Mount Ida for the woman Oenone," I commanded the soldiers. When they did not move with enough alacrity, I became hysterical. "Heed me! I am Helen! And when Helen speaks, you obey."

The warriors transported Paris Alexandros to our sleeping chamber and laid him amid the fleecy coverlets and silken pillows. With utmost tenderness, I removed the offending arrow and undressed him, treating the wound as I had cared for the lesser injuries he had suffered in the past, with a poultice of figs soaked in milk to coagulate the blood.

For hours my husband floated feverishly between darkness and light. I prayed to Aphrodite, who had brought us to this pass, to spare his life, and exhorted Zeus my father to be compassionate and merciful. I climbed up on our great bed beside Paris Alexandros and ever so gently slipped my arms around him. I would not let my flesh leave his, as though the constant touch of my hand or caress of my lips would bind him to this world. Softly, I sang to him and recounted the story of our mutual passion—from the moment we first laid eyes on each other to our first magical encounter in Sparta's sacred grove—and all the nights and days we had spent since in each other's embrace, holding out hope that the promise of countless passionate nights to come would seduce him into the light.

Late that night a Troyan warrior pounded on our door. "Oenone will not come," he said.

The wound was becoming infected despite my best ministrations. I nestled closer and softly kissed my husband's lips, then rested my hand on his sweat-drenched brow. "Oenone?" he murmured.

"She will not come. It's Helen. Helen, my love." Without Oenone's skill, I knew that it would soon be over. "Please . . . please, my beloved . . . my life . . . please don't leave me. You are all I have in Ilios." My sobs bathed the skin that once was golden bronze and now was white as chalk.

"Helen?" whispered Paris Alexandros in great pain, tilting his head to gaze directly into my eyes for the first time since I had brought him home.

I nodded. "Helen. Your Helen. Helen of Troy."

"He . . . len . . ." he whispered once more, and closed his eyes.

I was alone.

∼∼∼

I took a small knife from my cosmetics box and clipped a curl from Alexander's honey-colored locks, setting my treasure inside an amulet through which I slipped a golden chain and fastened it around my throat.

When Priam came to visit the following morning, he found me seated on a low, carved stool, ankle-deep in a mass of red-gold hair.

∼∼∼

The funeral honors for Paris Alexandros were nearly as lavish as those accorded Hector. Libations of wine and honey mixed with milk were poured, dirges chanted, and orations delivered. He was buried on Mount Ida, in a cave where in his shepherd youth he often liked to sleep and from where he loved to watch the stars. As voluble as I had been at Hector's pyre, with Paris Alexandros I was mute. I was too filled with emotion and passion to articulate my thoughts. It was universally acknowledged that the love I bore him was undying and irreproachable; it did not need to be restated.

I was as dead as Paris Alexandros, and yet I still breathed. I suffered as much as any mortal; how I wished I could die like one. I existed in a state of *eikasia,* seeing my own death in that of Paris Alexandros, wishing, hoping, imagining that I, too, would be taken by Ker or Thanatos—in a painful or a gentle death, it didn't matter to me anymore; yet I did not literally die. Not being able to join my beloved in the underworld was the cruelest trick of immortality, for in memory I would forever relive every moment of his slow and painful death.

To compound my grief, Hecuba refused to allow me to see my children, insisting that my hysteria might frighten them. In my disconsolate state, I was too weak to fight her will. Deprived of my babies, I had nothing left of my precious Paris Alexandros but my memories and a lock of his golden hair.

~~~

Over the following days, the most fascinating intrigue came to light. It began this way: Ilios, being situated in Anatolia, where inland of us the Hittite Kingdom held powerful sway, had co-opted many of the Hittite laws. One of them affected me most directly: If a man dies, his widow shall be married to his brother. Deiphobus strenuously asserted his right. He was now the eldest son of Troy and Priam's heir presumptive. He was also not above taking what he wanted, even where a human being was concerned. But Deiphobus had a rival, I learned to great surprise, for his much younger brother Helenus—the priest and seer—had scarcely glanced in my direction since I'd arrived in Ilios.

I would never have wed again, had that decision been mine to make. Despite the youthful bloom upon my demimortal face and figure, I was nearing the age of forty, and suddenly I felt like the sixteen-year-old Helen at the whim of the avaricious Tyndareus. Had the choice of husbands been mine as well, I would have opted for the unknown, far preferring the quiet Helenus to his savage older brother who still referred to me with leers and whispers, outside his father's presence, naturally, as the Spartan harlot.

But King Priam deferred to Deiphobus's seniority, and we were married in a ceremony that could not have been performed with greater haste.

Scarcely had the white bones of Paris Alexandros been buried on Mount Ida than Deiphobus appropriated our high house as his own, filling it with slovenly serving women who freely helped themselves to my perfumes and cosmetics and lived to do his pleasure at peril of their limbs. When it came to attending to my directives, they suddenly grew indolent.

But the apathy of my servants was insignificant compared to my treatment at the brutal hands of Deiphobus. "Open your whoring legs for me the way you did for my brother," he would demand, roughly parting my thighs and forcing himself upon me. When I did not do his bidding quickly enough, or when out of disgust or fear my lips and tongue or any other part of me went dry or became otherwise unresponsive to his touch and his commands, he beat me.

It was my curse that I was unbelieved when I threw myself at Priam's feet and disclosed with bitter weeping what went on inside this mockery of a marriage, for in my half-mortal state, no marks of roughness remained upon my person within a few hours of their infliction. Deiphobus had slapped me until my face resembled raw pork. He had bruised and pinched my limbs and raised welts on my sore buttocks. My every orifice had been violated repeatedly, not so much in a manifestation of his lust, but in a sick desire to destroy me. Straddling my body one night he even threatened to introduce the elaborately wrought hilt of his dagger between my splayed legs. In his presence, my fear and sorrow, and my suffering, knew no bounds. And the following night, when he determined I had displeased him in some way, he threw himself upon me, clasping my throat until I could scarcely breathe, and vowed, "I'm going to kill you, you filthy whore!"

I wished he had been able to do so, for I no longer desired to live. After Alexander's death, my life had become increasingly miserable. In a moment of desperation and weakness, I considered hanging myself as my mother had done to escape her marital torment; but I decided not to emulate the action Leda had taken in her shame. I'd heard Oenone had hanged herself after Paris Alexandros died. Perhaps that was another reason why I changed my mind.

So I prayed to Zeus my father to take me in some other way, for my demise had to be his decision, but he was deaf to my entreaties, as was Priam to my repeated confessions of his son's brutality.

After I was legally married to Deiphobus, Hecuba had relented to my pleas to be reunited with my children, but their homecoming was horrifyingly short-lived, for Deiphobus could not bear the sight of my offspring by Paris Alexandros and sent them to the temple of Athena to be raised as priests and priestess.

With nothing left for me in Ilios, I was ready for the Greeks to inflict their worst. No matter what Menelaus chose to do with me once the war was over, it would be preferable to this death-in-life of my present existence.

I soon discovered the source of all the recent prophecies by which the Achaeans had reconfigured their military strategy. It was the jealous Helenus. Unknown to Priam, he had been briefly captured by the enemy and had revealed the importance of regaining Heracles's great bow and lethal arrows. Helenus foresaw that with those weapons Philoctetes would kill Paris Alexandros, thereby clearing a path for this younger son of Priam to marry his rival's wife. But having lost his bid for me to Deiphobus, Helenus, believing that he lacked his father's love and respect, had turned willing traitor. Of all the perils they considered, the Troyans had never taken into account the dangerous vengeance of a jilted youth—a youth with the ability to see the future.

Helenus was a serpent: silent and deadly. It terrified me that he had bided his time all these years waiting for his chance to strike. I had been his secret passion, his fantasy. In his desire for me he lost perspective, even though as a seer, he had to know that as his wife or lover, I was not his destiny. And so he told the Achaeans how to destroy Paris Alexandros—and therefore, me. Hate is only love turned inside out. It is envy; it is wounded pride, both of which ultimately gained the better of Helenus. But all of us over the years, Achaean and Troyan, had become so caught up in a tide of events that was far greater than we were, that its momentum eventually engulfed us. We lost all clarity, all reason. Ruled by our passions alone, we were riding out situations over which we now, or perhaps ever, had little or no control.

Willingly, I contrived with Helenus to aid the Achaeans. I knew that I conspired with a demon, but every night I fell victim to a far greater monster in his elder brother.

Helenus reminded the Achaeans that if his younger brother Troilus survived his twentieth birthday, the city would never be taken. Within a few days of this "prediction," the prince's body was spitted upon an enemy sword. A city could also not be sacked as long as the statue of its patron god or goddess remained safely within its temple. For Troy, this icon was the Palladium, the statue of Pallas Athena.

Under cover of darkness, Helenus planned to unbolt a secret gate within the citadel wall and lead Odysseus and Diomedes through a clandestine tunnel that opened into the Temple of Athena. Diomedes would steal the Palladium, murdering its priestly guards, if necessary, and then Helenus would spirit the two Achaeans back out of the city.

A few nights later, Hecuba came calling. Deiphobus was out carousing as he did almost every night before staggering home to rape me. "There is a beggar outside who would speak with you," she told me. "He is probably one of the starving citizens who once dwelt in the lower town."

"I have no cause to converse with a beggar man," I replied. "Send him away."

"I have already tried that. He came first to the palace, demanding to speak with Helen. He says he must tell Helen something that no one else may hear."

After a few more minutes of talking in circles, I reluctantly agreed to see the beggar. Hecuba accompanied him to my chamber. "He insists you bathe him," the queen told me, standing back from the man's foul stench. "If I had told you that at the outset, you never would have admitted him to your home."

In thirteen years Queen Hecuba had never left the palace walls to escort someone to my home, least of all a flea-bitten, sore-encrusted vagrant. Something was amiss—but what? It seemed as though the queen was urging me in no uncertain terms to grant the beggar's boon and do his bidding.

So I summoned my serving women and had them fill the enormous silver bathing tub with warm water. They were more than happy to be dismissed after that single, simple task. I scented the water, and with extreme disgust undressed the man, dropping his reeking garments in a pile outside the door. I would give him one of Deiphobus's tunics after I had cleansed him. I did not expect my new husband to return shortly.

It suddenly occurred to me that perhaps it had been Hecuba's intention for her son to catch me performing such intimate ablutions for another man, knowing the consequences would be dire, retribution swift. But it seemed I had no choice. I must take the walk the Fates had planned for me.

The vagrant had not yet spoken to me, although he had communicated his errand to the queen outside my presence. As I scrubbed the filth from his matted hair, I attempted to engage him in light banter. On noticing that his Phrygian accent was inauthentic, I asked, "When did you come to Troy?" He told a clever tale, but I did not believe him. And when I bathed his body, which was not that of a spindly, half-starved beggar, but that of a strong and seasoned warrior, I was sure of his identity. His face, once shaved, bore a scar that dimpled his chin, and my suspicions were confirmed. That small disfigurement had often sent his adoring wife into raptures.

"So, you found a way to feel the caress of my soft hands on your bare flesh after all, you swine. What do you want from me, Odysseus? We bear no love for each other and never have. Were it not for you, I never would have been married to Menelaus and you and I would not be here."

"Complicity," he replied. "A blind eye. It will cost you little or nothing; I know you are unhappy now. You do not have to display *your* scars for me to see them." His words were well chosen and he knew it.

"So, you have Helenus, and now his mother, believing that it would be an act of mercy on the Troyans to end this bloody conflict now. What bargain did you strike with Hecuba for her to bring you to me?"

"Achilles wanted her youngest daughter, Polyxena, to be sacrificed upon his pyre. He knew she had once fancied him. In death, she will become his bride. From the Temple of Athena I went straight to the palace with that news. Hecuba entreated me to see that Polyxena was spared that fate."

"And you agreed?"

"I did."

"And in exchange for *my* . . . complicity . . . what do I gain?"

"We're both aware you have no friends within the walls of Ilios. You will see your enemies pay."

"My enemies lie on both sides of the citadel walls."

Odysseus demurred.

"Promise me my Troyan children will be safe. Deiphobus sent them to the Temple of Athena to be acolytes."

A silence so enormous that it could have swallowed me whole, filled the room. Odysseus rose and stepped out of the bathing tub, reaching for Deiphobus's tunic.

I knew the worst had taken place. "What have you done?!" I railed, clawing at his chest. My nails raised welts before he could clothe himself.

"Your children tried to prevent Diomedes from taking the Palladium. I am sorry, Helen."

"My babies?! All four of them?" The horror of his words penetrated my heart like an arrow. "Diomedes was to kill grown men if necessary, not to slaughter children!" My cries filled the night. I didn't care who heard me now. I had nothing left to protect. "I want you dead!" I screamed at Odysseus. "I want ALL of you dead! I will not weep for you or any of the Achaeans, nor will I shed a tear for a single Troyan. Sack the city. Raze it to the ground. Leave no man alive. And may every Achaean perish in the flames as well."

Odysseus collected his filthy beggar's disguise and, to my horror, donned it over his fresh clothes. "With your help, Helen," he said, before he turned to leave my home, "the gods may yet grant half your wish."

❧ TWENTY-EIGHT ❧

One morning, some days later, I was awakened by a cacophony of shouts and cries. Deiphobus sprang from the bed and ran down to our courtyard. Below us a crowd had gathered, shrieking gleefully that the Achaeans had gone. "Go down to the harbor," someone shouted. "There isn't a ship left!"

With Priam in the lead, the members of the royal family processed through the Scaean Gate and down the winding avenues of the lower city. When we reached the defensive ditch, it was evident that there was nothing left of the Achaean encampment—the tents and pots and cauldrons, the horses and mules; except for Achilles's funeral pyre, nothing remained. Even their refuse had been removed.

But where the tents had been erected and the vessels had been beached stood something truly astonishing: a giant horse, nearly as big as a ship and twice as high as my home. Set upon cart wheels, it was a glorious monstrosity indeed, constructed out of planks of polished wood and adorned with gemstones. Its flashing eyes were made of amethyst ringed in deep green beryl. The hooves were shod in bronze. Its mane was painted purple, tipped with gold, the open mouth—as if the beast were caught in the act of a defiant whinny—was set with teeth of ivory. The ears pricked up as if the creature was ever alert. Its great tail flowed all the way down to the rear wheels. The bridle had been fashioned of leather adorned with spangles of bronze and ivory; and the straps, bedecked with violet-colored flowers, all but invited the Troyans to grasp them and tug the magnificent creation inside the city walls.

"Wait, there's someone there!" said Deiphobus, drawing his ever-present dagger.

"Please spare my life," we heard, and from behind the horse an aging man clad in little more than rags, crept cautiously toward us, raising his hands in surrender. His body was covered in welts and sores, as though he had been beaten.

Priam's guards immediately placed his hands in restraints. "Who are you and why are you here?" the king demanded of his squirming prisoner.

"My name is Sinon," sniffled the man. "The Achaeans accused me of being a traitor and were going to kill me. They would make of me a human sacrifice to suit their will. But I escaped their wrath and hid here before they sailed away." He went on to explain that the wily Odysseus had contrived to tar an innocent man, Palamedes, with the brush of treachery.

I wondered if Odysseus had waited all this time to take revenge upon Palamedes for tricking him out of his feigned madness so many years ago, forcing him to honor the Oath of Tyndareus and come to Troy.

"Believing the Ithacan's crafty tale, Agamemnon put his own kins-man to death," the trembling Sinon told Priam. "I had been the good Palamedes's lieutenant, and when I spoke out about his blamelessness, Odysseus began to slander me as well." Sinon feared a similar fate to Palamedes's. "If you think all Achaeans are as ruthless as Odysseus, then kill me now," he urged. "And the sons of Atreus will thank you for ridding their kind of another traitor."

Priam considered the captive's words. In silence, we waited for his verdict. "We are not barbarians in Wilusa. You are welcome here," Priam told him, "if you speak the truth."

Sinon's words tumbled out of him like a waterfall. "It was no secret that for many years the Achaeans had wanted to give up and sail for home. Once Achilles and the High King quarreled, Agamemnon was quite prepared to quit these shores. After nearly ten years' decimation of their ranks, they finally decided to go home. But the winds were un-favorable and Agamemnon looked to Kalchas the seer for guidance. Having spilled human blood in exchange for fair winds before he sailed for Troy, the High King believed the same remedy might be necessary for them to leave these shores. Because I had already been tarred a traitor, I was to be their convenient victim. I throw myself now on your mercy!"

Priam ordered the removal of Sinon's restraints, and the Greek threw himself before the Troyan king and kissed his hem. Then Priam asked why the great horse had been left behind.

Sinon explained that after stealing the Palladium from the Temple of Athena, the Achaeans feared her wrath; to appease the goddess, they had built the horse, rendering it as grand as possible under such short notice. It was Kalchas, he said—reminding Priam that the seer was a Troyan turncoat—who had advised the Greeks to make it so tremendous that it could not be brought inside the city and thus gain the citizens of Ilios the renewed protection of Pallas. "If you allow the great horse to remain here on the beach, it is decreed that the Achaeans shall come back and capture Troy; but if you bring it inside the city walls before the Temple of Athena and present it to the goddess as a holy offering, then the enemy's task shall remain unaccomplished."

"It is a deadly fraud! He plays us false!" cried Laocoön, a seer himself and one of the priests at the Temple of Apollo. He and his two sons had hastened to the beach as soon as word spread about the great wooden horse. "Why should we believe the Greeks would bear us gifts? I say we fear this horse as we should still fear the Greeks. This is no tribute from the Achaeans; it is an elaborate siege machine," he insisted. To demonstrate his point, he threw his spear at the horse's belly, hoping to penetrate the wood and impale one of the men he was certain were hidden inside.

But then the most remarkable thing occurred. A wave swept in with the encroaching tide, its extraordinarily powerful undertow gripping Laocoön about the ankles like a monster from the deep, pulling him into the sea. In vain, his two young sons grabbed hold of his limbs, struggling to tug him back onshore, but the undertow snaked about the small boys' bodies as well and all three were dragged into the sea and drowned.

"You see, Poseidon is angry at such blasphemy of his sacred symbol," snapped Deiphobus angrily. "I say we spit in the Achaeans' face and bring the horse all the way through the Scaean Gate."

"Fools! You're all fools!" spat Cassandra, distraught at seeing Apollo's priest so violently slain. "White-haired Laocoön spoke the truth and for that he was destroyed. *This horse is not a gift; it is a trick!*" She grabbed her aged father by the arms and shook him. "Why do you heed the words of this foreigner, Sinon, instead of those of your own child? And if you will not believe me, believe poor Laocoön, a priest who always commanded your respect and who never uttered falsehood in his life."

At this Sinon increased the fervor of his entreaties, swearing oath upon oath to Priam that his story was no fabrication. "You see me on your shores, scared and bleeding. Where else am I to go? Either way, I am at someone's mercy. Would you return me to the tyrants who framed Palamedes, who stole Briseis from the great Achilles, who abandoned Philoctetes for a decade until he suited their purpose—to the High King who sacrificed his daughter for his own ambitions?"

My throat seized at Sinon's inference to Iphigenia. The man knew which notes to play so that his music would achieve the desired effect. His words were crafted in the manner of an orator, though not delivered as such. To me, it sounded almost as though he'd memorized a text. And I was now fairly sure of its author. The great horse was no doubt Odysseus's plan as well, or at the very least a collaboration with Helenus. Helenus had come down to the beach but was careful to offer no opinion on the matter. Hecuba, too, remained silent, though I doubted she had any real idea of the magnitude of her treacherous son's involvement in this conspiracy. The lone dissenter was Helenus's twin, Cassandra.

But Sinon's plea had worked its magic on Priam.

The king ordered the horse to be drawn into the city, and the men went to fetch ropes and pulleys. They built a sturdy bridge across the trench with planks of wood, then drew the monstrous horse through the lower gate, up through the winding lanes of the lower city, and across the dusty plaza where Hector's light had been so brutally extinguished. Finally the enormous Scaean Gate was opened amid triumphant fanfare, and the horse was wheeled inside the citadel.

The Troyan women, inspired by the floral adornments on the horse's reins, ran to the fields outside the city, going as far as Mount Ida to pluck wildflowers, with which they fashioned fragrant wreaths, climbing on ladders to fling them over the beast's neck. They wound garlands about its polished fetlocks and danced around it, chanting songs of celebration over the retreat of the Achaeans.

The events of recent weeks had changed me far more than everything that had transpired over the previous thirteen years. The death of Paris Alexandros, my repeated defilement at the hands of Deiphobus, and the slaughter of my precious children by Diomedes, had benumbed me. Like one who sleepwalks, I roamed through the rooms of the high house that Paris Alexandros had built for us. My passions that had once burned white-hot in the name of Eros were dead. Now I lived entirely for revenge.

I welcomed what the citizens were calling the Trojan Horse, not because I thought, as they did, that it was the Achaeans' guilty tribute to Athena, but because I believed the alarmist words of Laocoön. And if Odysseus and Diomedes were inside its polished carcass, that only brought them closer to the point of the dagger I now carried with me everywhere, cunningly concealed within my silken robes.

That night, the entire city, from Priam to the lowliest washerwoman, danced and drank as if there were no tomorrow. Never in my recollection had any festival's revelry been so grand or so joyous. No one heeded Cassandra's dire prognostications of holocaust. The woman might as well have been spitting into the Great Sea. Suspicions from any quarter were roundly dismissed as folly and the speaker as disloyal to Ilios.

No one questioned why the Achaeans had so suddenly weighed anchor. And by the time our warriors were in their cups, no one cared. The ships were gone; thus the story ended as far as it concerned them.

If Queen Hecuba regarded the horse as a trick rather than a tribute, her acquiescence to bringing it inside the Scaean Gate was an act of calculated suicide. Nearly all her sons were dead, including her unparalleled favorite. She bore little love for the vicious Deiphobus and the duplicitous Helenus. Priam was old and feeble, and the strain of the long siege had been killing him by degrees for years. Better to end it swiftly.

In the midst of all the carousing, Helenus cornered me and whispered instructions to leave a torchlight burning in my bedchamber once the citizens slumbered, overcome with wine. I agreed, but wondered if, when the time came, I would have the courage to go through with it. And could I keep from trembling in the presence of Deiphobus as he insisted that I spend the evening by his side? He was the most vociferous advocate of the Trojan Horse and I had to appear to support him.

Deiphobus believed that his rule of Ilios was now so close at hand that he could taste its extravagant sweetness. Old Priam would soon die, or better still, abdicate in favor of his wise, strong son. Control of the Hellespont would be his alone. And if the craven Greeks came crawling back, Troy would never again abide by the rules of formal military engagement that had wasted ten long years.

"To think the Achaeans are hidden inside the horse!" I teased, as arm in arm Deiphobus and I strolled around the massive tribute. "Your sister Cassandra is most certainly a misguided fool." My words were coated in honey. I behaved as though I could not wait to be Deiphobus's queen, and in his tremendous hubris the monster in man's flesh did not even notice how differently I was behaving in his presence.

"Oh, Menelaus, it is Helen," I taunted, looking directly at the horse's belly. "You thought that I would never be Troy's queen once Paris Alexandros was dispatched to Tartarus. How you underestimated the strength of his brother Deiphobus, whose bed I warm as his new bride. For Deiphobus is not softhearted as was Alexandros. He is a fierce man whose brutality is unforgiving."

Deiphobus laughed, accepting as a compliment what I offered as a veiled warning to others.

"And Agamemnon," I continued, mimicking the voice of my sister Clytemnestra, "your hubris will become your downfall. For Deiphobus does not quake at the merest mention of your name."

Deiphobus was delighted. At last his wife understood what a great man he truly was! Perhaps tonight he would not strike her after all.

"My sweet Odysseus," I teased in the voice of my cousin Penelope, "I fear you will not return to my white arms as quickly as you'd hoped. For Deiphobus the Fearsome may yet prove more cunning than yourself."

Deiphobus wallowed in my words the way swine frolic in mud and filth. He could not wait to return home to demonstrate the full measure of his appreciation. But Aphrodite, if no one else, was on my side that night, and no sooner had Deiphobus reclined on the fleecy coverlets than all the wine he had consumed delivered him directly into the arms of Hypnos.

At the sound of his strangled snores, I tiptoed to the chamber window, still fully dressed, my dagger within easy reach; after several deadly quiet moments of reflection tinged with fear and tremendous ambivalence, I lit the beacon.

Helenus had told me that Sinon would light one, too, as would he, and this would alert the Achaeans—who could see his window from the Trojan Horse's gaping mouth—that all was ready.

In the flickering light I waited for the Greeks to come. But my heart was not as cold as I had believed it to be. I knew the invaders would spare no one in their wake of destruction, and while my rage against Odysseus had been fully heartfelt, I never truly countenanced the death of women and children—especially children—for I had now lost at least five of my own to senseless slaughter.

Then the cries of panic began. Shouts of "Fire!" rang across the pergamos and echoed up from the lower city. Through my window I saw the last of the armored warriors descending a rope ladder suspended from a trapdoor in the belly of the Trojan Horse. Troyans, peering out of doors to wonder at the clamor, found themselves beheaded or run through with an Achaean sword or spear. The Scaean Gate had been thrown open and throughout the night, wave upon wave of soldiers marched through the lower city, torching the homes and massacring the residents who had been brave enough to remain there even in the final year of the long siege.

The Achaean ships must have taken shelter behind the isle of Tenedos, off our coast, in the very place I had remarked upon when I first sailed here from Sparta. As the nearby cove could not be seen from our beaches, or even from the towers atop the citadel, it was the perfect spot from which to launch a surprise attack.

Groggy and disoriented, Deiphobus leapt out of bed. "There has been some trickery after all," I told him in a panicked voice. "You must don your armor and save the city!"

My heart raced frantically when I heard shouts from my own courtyard and the heavy footsteps of the encroaching warriors.

Deiphobus had not dressed; his first thought was to punish me. "False whore!" he cried, throwing me to the floor. He straddled me and grabbed my shoulders, repeatedly slamming my body onto the cold hard tile. Seized with madness, he grabbed me by my cropped hair and throttled me, cursing my name and dashing my head against the floor. I screamed and clawed at him, unable to reach my dagger, but in his white-hot rage, Deiphobus was a man possessed by the Furies. All reason had deserted him, all thoughts of defending his city and his parents. He saw me as the treacherous architect of his demise, and for that I would pay with everything I had, including my dignity, before he threw himself amid the clamor to save Troy.

So dazed and battered was I from this brutal beating that I was barely aware of Deiphobus entering me, delivering each painful thrust with every dram of hatred in his body. His eyes did not see Helen; they saw everyone he had ever wanted to destroy.

In a blinding flash of inspiration, I realized that I might gain the upper hand if I timed my own movement to the rapist's rhythm rather than inertly succumbing to his punishment. Each time Deiphobus raised his body, I was better able to maneuver my right hand toward my dagger.

Not much longer than a minute had passed since I'd first heard the commotion below us; now everything seemed to happen in a matter of moments.

With Deiphobus's next downstroke, I thrust home as well, sinking the dagger into the center of his back.

Deiphobus released a startled cry. I dislodged the knife and stabbed again between his shoulder blades. He tried to raise himself just as the Achaeans burst into the room, but someone drove a spear into his back, and I felt his full weight as he collapsed on top of me.

"Get off my wife, you filth!"

Deiphobus's dying carcass was roughly removed from my body with a swift kick to his midsection.

From where I lay, bruised and trembling, I looked into the eyes of Menelaus. As ever, I could not tell what truly lurked behind their inscrutable storm-cloud gray. Behind him stood Agamemnon, who impatiently tried to elbow Menelaus from the doorway.

"No, brother. He is mine," said Menelaus. He glowered at the crumpled, bleeding body. "This is what Achaeans do to adulterers," he told Deiphobus. With one swipe of his sword, he cut off Deiphobus's nose. Followed by each ear. And then his genitals. In Greek culture, this was the ultimate dishonor to someone found guilty of adultery or incest. If I was the wife of Menelaus, Deiphobus had most certainly committed the former; and under Achaean law, a man could *not* marry his brother's widow, which, if I was the wife of Paris Alexandros, rendered Deiphobus guilty of incest.

In his methodical way, Menelaus then hacked off Deiphobus's arms, followed by his legs, and finally, beheaded him. Everything in the room, including the two of us, was spattered with the vicious Troyan's crimson blood.

"Now we kill the adulteress," said Agamemnon, and strode into the room, his sword unsheathed. I scrambled for cover behind my bed.

"No!" Menelaus cried, knocking his elder brother off balance. "That's never why we came to Ilios," he growled. "The mission was to *rescue* Helen, not to kill her. For ten long years, thousands of men have given their lives for this cause—the cause that you yourself devised to incite them to arms. You will not touch her, nor harm a hair on her head. The quarrel is not yours to resolve or mitigate. Not only that, if you injure her, you hurt your own wife's sister. Helen is my wife, and I will deal with her as I see fit."

I rose to my feet and took a few tentative steps toward him. "Then I hope you will see fit to kill me after all," I said, unclasping the brooches that closed my chiton at the shoulders. The silk tumbled down my body, baring my breasts. "I have made it easy for you. I will die as Iphigenia did, my bosom exposed and vulnerable to the fatal thrust. Come, husband. I beg you to end the torture I have lately suffered." I truly wished to die, for I could not endure any more pain. Dying would have been easy then. And preferable. It was living that was a far more painful fate.

Menelaus did raise his sword, but then he hesitated, gazing upon the perfection of my bosom.

"There is no impediment to your blade. Why do you wait and waste your brother's precious time? Surely he would love to see the harlot of Sparta, whore of Troy, dispatched with alacrity so he can get about the business of sacking Ilios and taking his pick of the choicest females to warm the bed he rightfully shares with my sister back in Mycenae."

Menelaus's eyes met mine, if only for a moment. Then he returned his gaze, as if bewitched or hypnotized, to my half-nude body. He sheathed his sword. "I cannot kill you," he said in a choked whisper. His eyes were dimmed with tears. He prodded the leering Agamemnon out of my chamber. "Now dress yourself and come with me," he commanded.

Outside, the Achaeans were everywhere, swarming like ants. The air was thick with smoke. No building had remained unscarred from their torches. Cries of Troyan souls expelling their final, defiant breaths filled the night. The Greeks had climbed the walls and had set fire to the twin towers, while below, the city burned like a giant bonfire, sending huge, choking billows of black smoke skyward. Citizens who had climbed the battlements, mistakenly believing they would find shelter there, threw themselves into the flames and roiling smoke when they saw their cause was lost. Better to choose to die than perish by the enemy's sword.

I looked up and saw Andromache, clutching the baby Astyanax. Beside her stood Odysseus and two Achaean soldiers who tried to wrest the infant from her grasp. She fought like a demon but was no match for the warriors' strength. Odysseus did nothing to help her. Andromache lost the tug-of-war, and under the crafty Ithacan's stern gaze, the soldiers threw Hector's tiny son over the wall, dashing his body on the stones below.

"Monster!" I shrieked at Odysseus, and then I saw Polyxena being dragged from the palace, no doubt being taken to Achilles's funeral pyre after all. Odysseus had played Hecuba false as well, breaking his pledge to see that the girl remained unharmed. Just as the long war had begun with the sacrifice of a young girl, so it would end.

Around me, all was chaos. When we'd left my house, Menelaus had grasped me by the wrist and refused to release his grip, but somehow in the confusion we had become separated. Buildings were collapsing all around me. The noise of human cries, tumbling masonry, bronze against bronze was deafening and terrifying. I sidestepped mangled bodies—among them, children with their unseeing eyes wide open as though death had taken them by surprise—and climbed over smoldering rubble, seeking shelter. I saw a girl no older than my little Helen, who ran out of her house to chase her fleeing pet, a frightened housecat, and was cut down with an Achaean spear that drove straight through her fragile body into that of her panicked mother.

I raced up the steps of the Temple of Apollo hoping to find sanctuary, but learned that nothing had remained sacred to the enemy. A woman's anguished screams echoed off the walls; following her cries, I found Cassandra, virgin priestess, legs splayed, suffering a brutal rape upon the altar. Her attacker, Ajax the Lesser, had been one of my suitors. I hoped my own scream would distract him, but I could not be heard above the clamor. An Achaean warrior then blocked my path, and I ducked under his arm, narrowly avoiding Agamemnon, who was entering the temple. As I hid in a darkened niche, I watched the High King haul the vicious Ajax from his victim's half-naked body, then drag Cassandra from the shrine himself.

An ear-shattering sound split the night, and I looked up to see one of the turrets atop Priam's palace being shaken from its foundation by dozens of men, Troyans, who, in a misguided effort to demolish the invaders, hurled painted tiles and gilded roof timbers at their enemy. In a final desperate effort to save themselves, they pushed what remained of the turret over the rooftop, crushing scores of people below. Soldier and civilian were leveled in the rubble.

The Achaeans weakened the doors of Priam's palace by hacking at them with their axes. Then a group of warriors took up one of the fallen beams and with it rammed the doors until they broke apart, bursting the great bronze hinge plates from their sockets. Charging over the debris, the Greeks entered the building before the Troyans could climb down from the roof.

Priam and Hecuba and the surviving members of the royal family had sought sanctuary by the altar of Zeus in the inner courtyard of the palace. They clung to one another, pouring panicked libations and offering their frightened prayers. Priam was girded in his outmoded corselet, his sword, the blade dulled with age and lack of use, hanging ineffectually from his side. For the first time since I had come to Ilios, Queen Hecuba embraced me.

"It's over," she murmured.

I took her tearstained face between my hands. She looked relieved, then reached again for Priam.

Suddenly, a group of Achaeans burst into the temple. I heard someone shout "Neoptolemus!" The unhelmed person they referred to was not much older than a boy, a mere stripling, but he had his father's swagger and was in feature the very likeness of Achilles.

The warriors charged in, heedless of the sanctity of the shrine, killing Polites, one of Priam's youngest sons, before the boy could unsheathe his sword.

Extricating himself from his wife's tearful embrace, Priam rose and took a step or two toward Neoptolemus. "Have mercy for the king of Wilusa," he said gently, entreating the son of Achilles with open arms. "Do not defile the temple and profane the name of Zeus by committing murder in a sacred shrine. Your father and I earned each other's respect. I offer you equal esteem and ask only the same from you."

"I am not my father," sneered the youth, his voice pitched in the crackly chasm twixt boy and man. "He who spares his enemies does not win the war."

And before Priam could say another word, Neoptolemus released his spear. The long shaft split the air with a *whish,* striking the old king in the chest, impaling him all the way through his spine. The stunned Priam tried to speak, but the only thing to issue from his parched lips was a gurgling stream of blood. An ugly stain of lurid purple spread across his chest. The king crumpled to his knees as his beloved wife ran to his side, and cradling his head against her bosom, held him until he breathed his last.

Not content to merely claim his victory, Achilles's son committed the ultimate disgrace to Priam's corpse. Shoving the weeping Hecuba away from her husband's body, Neoptolemus twined his fingers around the king's white locks and with one swift stroke of his sword, beheaded him. Priam's headless body was then flung out of doors, a corpse with no name, the final ignominy.

Neoptolemus ordered his warriors to remove the Troyan women from the temple. The men were butchered mercilessly. A soldier stopped me as I tried to flee. "Don't touch *her*," commanded Achilles's son, realizing who I was. "Menelaus will deal with the whore who married him."

"You disgusting and unnatural child," I spat. "I pray to Zeus that someday your sneer will be wiped from your pimpled face and you will drown in your own arrogance."

I stepped outside what was left of the palace into the center of a most puzzling melee. The Achaeans seemed to be fighting one another. I realized then that the brave Troyans who had managed to kill one of their enemy had donned their rival's armor, the better to blend in among the ravaging Greeks. The citizens were not going quietly into the bloody night: They had climbed up on their roofs and were tearing them apart with axes, hurling the beams on the Achaeans. Arrows rained down on the enemy from the rooftops of the lower city. The night air stank of death and the reeking metallic odor of fresh blood. It flowed like wine along the gutters of the streets and down toward the sea.

And then I heard a terrible groaning, as though the very stones of Ilios were weeping. With a deafening rumble, the blazing south tower of the ramparts toppled to the ground, its weight collapsing the stretch of wall beneath it. Human bodies, engulfed in flames, fell from its observation platform like Icarus tumbling from the sky. Below the crumbling wall, people fled the tidal wave of billowing smoke that pursued them like the Furies, nearly blinded by it. Many of the survivors stumbled on debris or over each other and fell to the ground, only to be trampled by the stampeding hordes seeking safety from the roiling cloud of smoke and ash. The terror that there might be no tomorrow—or perhaps more frightening, that if dawn came, Eos would bring them a worse fate—was evident in the Troyans' frightened faces.

Minutes later, the north tower collapsed, sending a second thunderous wave of devastation rolling through the burning city. The screams of the dying echoed through the night, reverberating off the remaining walls.

Horses, terrified and confused, charged through the streets, their frightened whinnies piercing the night; some people, who had considered themselves fortunate to have escaped the toppling of the towers, were crushed beneath the rampaging hooves.

Dazed survivors injured by falling debris wandered mutely through the city. Coated with ash, they resembled walking statues.

The wells had been drained dry, and no more water was available to douse the burning buildings. Blazing roofs caved in, sending shrieking people running into the streets, their clothes afire, trying to smite the licking tongues of flame that hungrily devoured their garments. Some flung themselves onto the ground, rolling like a cart wheel in a desperate effort to extinguish the flames. The lucky ones rushed out of doors unharmed, only to be run through by an Achaean's blade.

Through the acrid gloom I somehow made my way back to what remained of the home that Paris Alexandros had so lovingly built for us. The courtyard was filled with rubble; my birdbath, fountain, and beautiful statues had all been utterly demolished. My door, carved from a stately rowan tree, had been beaten down and trampled upon, reduced to planks and splinters. The frescoed walls were crumbling. Inside, the furniture had been upended and smashed to bits. I noticed that some of the smaller items, like my inlaid stools, had been stolen.

A foul stench was coming from the second story, and in horror I nearly tripped over the rotting body parts of Deiphobus. His severed head grimaced at me from the floor, the matted black hair caked with dried blood. With one hand pinching my nose and the other covering my mouth, I was not too effective at picking through the wreckage. My dressing table had been overturned; cosmetic pots were everywhere, and perfume alabastrons had shattered, spilling their contents onto the woven rugs. My most beautiful robes and shawls were gone, along with the exotic hangings and textiles that had graced my chambers. All of my jewelry, too, had been looted. One thing alone had remained pristine; it was something of no value to the Achaeans, but it meant the world to me. Resting between the upturned legs of the dressing table was a perfect white swan's feather. I plucked it from where it lay and fled.

Toward first light, the sounds of the dying amid the smoldering ruins of the once-proud and glittering city had diminished from a roar to a whimper. The Achaeans had scarcely left a Troyan male alive. Helenus had survived, as had his kinsman Aeneas, who hobbled toward the beach carrying his invalid father Anchises on his back. Aeneas's beautiful wife Creusa, the eldest of Priam's daughters, had begun to follow her husband out of the burning city, only to be separated in the clamor. Her charred body was found by the vanquished Troyan women as they were herded through the lower city toward the beach-head. From there they would be taken as slaves aboard the Achaean ships, never to return to their homeland and forced forevermore to fetch the water, scrub the floors, light the fires—and in some cases, warm the beds—of their new masters, perhaps the very same men whose weapons had killed their sons and husbands.

A series of beacons had been lit to announce the fall of Troy. The first torch was placed on Mount Ida, the next on the nearby isle of Lemnos, then across the sea to Athos, up precipitous Macistos, from Euripus to Messapion, across Asopus, up Cithaeron, over the marshes of Gorgopis, up Aegiplanctus, and around the gulf to Arachnus, where the flame could be seen from Mycenae and where my sister Clytemnestra would learn that her husband's homecoming was imminent. I wondered how she—and her lover of many years, Agamemnon's first cousin Aegisthus—would receive him.

The gentle beauty of the dawn was made a mockery by the destruction it illuminated with such a rosy glow. In the entire city, only a few buildings had remained completely unharmed. The devastation was even greater in the upper city, where the royal family dwelled, because our riches had been thoroughly plundered. Broken shards of pottery littered the streets. Every item of value had been taken from our homes before they were torched. In the lower city I picked my way over the carcasses of countless horses already attracting clusters of ugly black flies. I gagged from the smell of burnt flesh, textiles, and masonry, and tried not to look at some of the carnage, but there was no avoiding it. Coming across a man whose entrails had been spilled, his eyes gouged out, and his tongue sliced off, I ducked into an alley and vomited. Was that pour soul so tortured in the name of Helen?

Amid the deserted colonnades of Aeneas's abandoned house, the Achaeans counted out their treasure. All the loot from the palace, from the gutted temples and razed homes of the pillaged city—such as robes, jewels, wine bowls of solid gold, artifacts of ivory and amber, and huge feasting tables—had been taken there, with the cunning Odysseus standing guard against dishonesty and theft. I wished that with every stolen Troyan cup that touched their lips, the liquid, no matter how originally sweet, would turn bitter on their lips.

Where had Agamemnon's hubris gotten any of them? The Achaeans had razed Ilios to the ground and were returning home with a few pretty trinkets and a number of demoralized and angry slave women. What of his grand plans to control the trade routes through the tricky waters of the Hellespont? It would take years to rebuild what his men had destroyed in a single night of violence and bloodlust. What a bitter irony that the most valuable prize the Greeks would come away with after a decade of war was the thing they claimed to fight for in the first place: Helen.

The distribution of the slaves was sickening. And the women of Priam's royal family were to be separated, divided among the Achaeans' greatest heroes. Agamemnon seized the beauteous Cassandra; the pimply Neoptolemus claimed Andromache; and to Odysseus's home in rocky Ithaca would go poor weeping Hecuba, snarling invectives at her new master and tearing at her long white hair.

Menelaus took no slaves from among the Troyan women, and he was eager to get under sail. It had taken several hours for the chieftains to agree on the distribution of slaves and to load the ships. Many of the men were completely in their cups, having spent the day celebrating their triumphant defeat of the Trojans. Thus possessed by the spirit of Dionysus the wine god, they were in no condition to reason clearly; nonetheless, at dusk the High King gathered them together in order to sacrifice a hecatomb to Athena. Acknowledging the atrocities his men had committed the night before—against the holy temples and the priestesses, as well as the rampant savagery against the lay population of Ilios—Agamemnon realized it was doubtful that the gods would grant them favorable winds. He believed the hecatomb would suffice to cleanse their hands of butchery.

Menelaus quarreled with his brother; he wished to leave immediately, thinking Agamemnon's sacrifice—so little, so late—would only be scoffed at by the Olympians. The following dawn, Menelaus and the chieftains who had sided with him against Agamemnon pushed their ships off the sand, raised their sails, and dipped their oars in the white-crested waves. We were bound for home. The other chieftains remained onshore with Agamemnon to make their sacrifices.

How strange it felt to be returning to Achaea after so many years! I had not even been on my beloved sea in all that time and found the rise and fall of the hull the only comfort amid my myriad fears. I tried not to show Menelaus how terrified I was. He had scarcely spoken to me, except to tell me to board the ship and where to sit. I had no idea what he was thinking or what he planned to do with me. The only vestige of kindness came when he soundly rebuked his oarsmen for their impertinent snickering. "This lady is your captain's wife—and your queen," he reminded them. "And as such, you will honor her. The first man to disparage Helen again will be whipped." But to treat me rudely was an equal dishonor to Menelaus, and regardless of how he felt about me, he needed to maintain his crew's respect.

As we neared Tenedos, the seas churned up. It was late summer, the setting of the Pleiades, the time of year when the winds began to blow, so the angry waters should have been no surprise to the sailors. Odysseus's ships and those that followed him decided to return to Ilios, fearing that the rough seas were a sign that Agamemnon had been in the right to insist on offering proper sacrifices. We continued our course for Sparta alongside the flotilla of old Nestor of Pylos. And still, Menelaus all but ignored me. Did that bode well or ill? Because he was so enigmatic, I could not tell.

The nearer we got to Sparta, the more anxious I became. How would my subjects treat their errant queen? And my children? Where were they? Were they well? How would they greet me? By now, Nico, the baby I had left behind, was about the same age I had been when I wed his father. I had to ask Menelaus about them. Both of us had been avoiding the subject. Hermione, he told me, still dwelt in the palace in Sparta. She could not wed without a proper *kyrios* to represent her.

"And our sons?" I asked fearfully.

For a few moments, the only sound I heard was the slapping of the waves against the ship's black hull.

Menelaus swallowed hard. Finally, he said, "They died like men."

"In Ilios?"

He nodded, his face a mask of pain and sorrow.

"All of them?"

Menelaus looked at me.

"Even little Nico?"

Silence.

"He was barely more than a boy!" I grimly realized that he was probably the same age as Neoptolemus. Menelaus tentatively placed his hand on my shoulder. I flinched and he removed it. "Leave me be," I said. "I wish to grieve in peace."

I closed my eyes and relived every recollection of my four Spartan boys; from the pains I labored under to bring them into this world to the toys and pets they loved, to the sound of their laughter and of their shrieks and sobs. Pleisthenes and my twins, Aethiolas and Maraphius, would be frozen in time for me as seven-year-old boys, for that was their age when they were taken by the Spartan elders to enter the *agogi* system. And Nico? He would always be a full-cheeked, chubbylimbed whirlwind of energy, who made every moment of his too-brief life into a discovery. Dry-eyed and brave, as they would have wanted their *mitera* to be, I mourned the sons I would never come to know as young men.

Rounding Cape Sounion released another flood of memories. I'd first sailed those dark waters with Theseus, who would remain forever dear to me. It was there that his father, old Aegeus, had so tragically, and needlessly, become a suicide. Menelaus thought it was the sea spray that had misted my cheeks, but this voyage marked a new beginning for us, or so I hoped, and I did not wish to embark by dissembling.

Our frank discussion was interrupted by a frantic shout. Phrontis, the ship's skilled and reliable steersman, had suddenly fallen dead with his hand still gripping the tiller, and we were about to drift off course unless someone took the helm immediately. Poor Phrontis was pried from his post, and two oarsmen swaddled his body in a cloth of white linen and carried him below deck. Menelaus himself took the tiller and steered us toward the nearest port. Phrontis had been a fine man, and my husband wished to give him a proper burial.

It seems so odd to me to write the words *my husband* in reference once again to Menelaus. It was strange then, to think of him that way after so many years, but I forced myself to do so because Menelaus still saw me as his legal wife despite all that had transpired. My beloved Troyan husband was dead, and no amount of convincing myself that I no longer owed a wifely duty to Menelaus would restore Paris Alexandros to my arms. Everything that had mattered to me in Ilios—Paris Alexandros and our four precious children—was irretrievably lost to me. My destiny was once more tied to Menelaus.

After according the steersman full funeral honors, we hoisted the sail and made for Sparta. Soon, we could see the tip of the Peloponnese. Once we had safely navigated the treacherous waters off Cape Malea, we'd not be far from Gythium . . . and home.

Home. That, too, was a strange word in relation to Sparta, for I had been so long in Ilios that my homeland's fertile plains and rolling hills, rich with clover, and the riverbanks where the graceful stalks of galingale grew, would seem like foreign shores.

But the winds changed and the seas kicked up around Malea. Menelaus, lacking a skilled steersman, had trouble negotiating the conditions. His other vessels, too, were floundering. Instead of sailing into Gythium, we were being blown off course to the south and to the east, back toward Crete.

We had been so close. Now, every gust of wind wafted our ship farther and farther away from Laconia.

I would not see the palace of Sparta for another nine years. The storms that we encountered off Cape Malea on the day that Menelaus and I expected to return home, destroyed half his fleet. The remaining five vessels, ours among them, were borne by Poseidon all the way to a most foreign and exotic land.

It was there, in Egypt, that we began to rebuild our lives and our marriage. We had landed on an island at the mouth of the great and powerful Nile River. Called Pharos, it was ruled by Lord Thon and his wife, the Achaean-born Polydamia, who welcomed us with tremendous hospitality.

Our sojourn there was intended to be as brief as possible. At first, we tried once more to sail for home but we met with repeated delays due to unfavorable weather conditions. Then Menelaus grew fascinated by the wealth of commodities available to the Egyptians. Seduced by the notion of replenishing Sparta's empty coffers, the man who had once achieved his wealth by raiding coastal towns and cities turned to trading along the north coast of the Dark Continent, soon amassing a tremendous fortune in precious metals, ivory and amber, textiles and exotic animal hides.

For a long time, I was anxious to return to Sparta, having at last reconciled myself to dwelling once more on Achaean shores, despite my fears that I might be as reviled in my homeland as I was all those years in Ilios. I was well aware that the Spartans no longer bore much love for Helen. Yet I would reclaim my throne and soon recapture their hearts. I was still one of them; I was Leda's daughter. I would meander once more along the reedy banks of the Eurotas and ride into the foothills of Mount Taygetos as I once did in more carefree times. There were days when my heart ached for the familiar scent of eucalyptus. How I longed to revisit the sacred grove.

At first, it was difficult for me to understand why Menelaus did not appear as eager to sail for Laconia as I was. Didn't he wish to regain his kingship? He seemed far more interested in his new role as a skillful merchant. Perhaps the long war had wrought a change in him. I found myself beginning to admire this new Menelaus.

Thus resigning myself to remaining in Egypt indefinitely, I immersed myself in their culture, learning about their system of laws, their medicine—which was far more advanced than the Achaeans', with their abundance of herbs, both healthful and maleficent—and their storytelling. In Achaea, where our tales were sung by bards who passed them down to one another through the generations, the Egyptians told their stories on sheets made from thin strips of the dried, pressed pith of the papyrus plant, through picture writing and illustration. When we finally left Pharos, I insisted that Menelaus bring home a great quantity of the delicate material. As I have availed myself of the papyrus sheets to write this memoir, using my father Zeus's feather as a stylus and a dye distilled from plants, I've found that it is significantly preferable to our method of scratching on clay tablets.

When we first landed at Pharos, I had seen thirty-eight summers and Menelaus had seen forty-seven. While my youthful face and figure showed no signs of aging, my husband had grown thick about the torso. His hair was now more gray than red. And he walked with a pronounced limp from the leg injury he received when the ceasefire was broken by Pandarus. The first time he undressed, I noticed a scar the length of my thumb that ran vertically along his abdomen. The sight of it both moved and deeply troubled me, for it was the result of the wound inflicted by Paris Alexandros. How different things might have been if his thrust had proven fatal. I wept anew for Paris Alexandros, certain that Menelaus's scar would fade long before my memories did.

In many ways, no matter how old any of us had been when the conflict began or when it finally ended, we all came of age during the Trojan War, and very little that was good grew out of its aftermath. Menelaus blossomed late, finally emerging from his brother's ugly shadow; but I had always believed he had it in him, if he could only trust himself.

I remember a conversation we had one day, soon after we'd arrived in Egypt. We were sitting on the Nile riverbank enjoying a pastoral repast, and Menelaus took my hands in his and looked wistfully into my eyes. Even now, with his temperament milder and not prone to outbursts of anger or jealousy, it was rare for me to be able to read his expressions. "Do you know why I couldn't kill you that night in Ilios?" he asked me.

I nodded.

He seemed surprised. "I want to tell you, anyway. It's something that I should have said to you before. Many times. I . . . I couldn't kill you because I still loved you. I know that I was never good at showing it. I realize now that there were . . . years, perhaps . . . when you more than likely had no idea how much I cared for you. Remember on our wedding night, when I was so amazed that you were mine?"

I found myself choking back tears. "Yes," I whispered.

"Helen, I never stopped being amazed. And I had no idea how to live with that. It wasn't manly, as my brother so often reminded me. My love for you made me weak, he said. Well, of course I didn't want to be weak! But I didn't want to be my brother, either. I know how cruel he was to Clytemnestra."

"You should have strived to be unlike him in other ways as well," I said. "Sparta's temples. And her tombs. My family tomb."

"I was a brutal, thoughtless fool then. Wielding my power, asserting my authority as king of Sparta, blindly following my brother instead of heeding the counsel of my wife, whose people I ruled. After all these years have passed, will you forgive me?"

I thought about it as I watched a lily pad float up the river, borne by the swift current. "No," I said. "I can forgive you for sending soldiers to take my cosmetic pots and my mirrors, but not my brothers' armor and not the relics of our sacred sites. Some things are not so simple to forgive."

Menelaus looked away. "If I had that part of my life to live again, I would do things very differently. I would not have despoiled the temples and the tombs." He looked back at me and forced a chuckle. "And you could have kept your mirrors, too. I would have told Agamemnon to go to Hades."

He made me laugh. This, too, was new. Mirth and humor had never been among my husband's qualities. Suddenly I was giggling like a young girl, all out of proportion to his remark. It simply felt so good to laugh after all the ugliness we had endured. "Do you know the real reason why you could not kill me?" I asked Menelaus.

"I just told you," he said earnestly.

I shook my head. By now, the hair I'd lopped off after the death of Paris Alexandros had grown back. It was not as long as it once had been, but still it brushed my shoulders. "No, you silly man," I gently teased. "Although your reason touched me very deeply. You couldn't kill me . . . because you *can't*. I'm half immortal, remember? Only by will of my father Zeus can I depart this world." I reclined on the riverbank, resting my head in his lap. My fingers played in the long grass. "But I *wanted* to die that night. More than anything else in the world, I think—and I have wanted some things very, very much—as we both know!"

Something had happened to us as a married couple. Although we had been apart for more years than we had ever been together, our relationship was beginning to settle into something strangely comfortable. We had shared the most horrifying experience, yet in many ways had lived it separately. Perhaps it provided us with a frame of reference by or through which all human behavior, particularly our own, would henceforth be judged.

A messenger from Lord Thon came running toward us. I recognized him as Proteus, a young man who spent more time swimming in the bay of Pharos than on dry land. He believed himself a reincarnation of the Ancient of the Sea. Apart from a short cloth wrapped about his waist, the youth was nearly nude, although he wore an elaborate collar about his throat that reached partway down his chest.

"News from Mycenae!" Proteus told us. "The High King Agamemnon is dead!"

I gasped in delight as much as in surprise. Menelaus rose and pulled me to my feet. "How did it happen?" he asked anxiously.

In our tongue, the boy spoke haltingly, but we understood this much from what he said: "After making his hecatomb to the gods, Agamemnon and his fleet set sail from Ilios; but, damaged by storms and shipwrecks, only his flagship made it to the shores of Argos. There he and his concubine, the Troyan prophetess Cassandra, princess of the once-great city, were greeted with great pomp by Queen Clytemnestra. Cassandra refused to enter the grand palace of Mycenae, crying that she saw blood on its walls and death inside.

"But Agamemnon, while feigning modesty at first, had walked barefoot on a trail of purple robes that Clytemnestra had spread from his chariot all the way into his Great Hall. Clytemnestra insisted on bathing him herself, and when the High King had settled into the deep tub, the queen ensnared him in a monstrous net, trapping Agamemnon like a fish.

"Cursing him for slaughtering her first husband Tantalus and their infant son before her eyes, for sacrificing Iphigenia, and for his endless whoring, including his intention to replace her with Cassandra in the royal bed, Clytemnestra drew a dagger from within the folds of her garments and stabbed her adulterous husband until his blood rendered the blue-green waters of the bath incarnadine."

My heart rejoiced. I wanted to sing. *O, brave Clytemnestra, you have avenged the death of my beloved daughter, and for this, despite our many quarrels in the past, you will dwell in my heart forever.* I would propitiate the gods for giving her strength and guiding her hand. When next I saw my sister, I would humble myself by kissing her hem. How I longed to embrace her!

I urged young Proteus to continue his story.

"Then Clytemnestra and her consort Aegisthus cornered the frightened Troyan princess, who foresaw that her days were numbered from the moment she had boarded Agamemnon's ship. Cassandra, too, was murdered. Aegisthus is now preventing the people of Mycenae from honoring Agamemnon with the proper funeral rites, to the anger of Clytemnestra's eldest daughter, Electra, who had adored her father."

After the messenger had departed, Menelaus and I sat in silence for several minutes. I think each of us was waiting for the other to speak first.

"I loved my brother, but I cannot say that your sister was not justified." Menelaus was extremely pensive. "And yet I find it difficult to believe that it was she who wielded the knife. It is against a woman's nature."

But I well knew that such savage revenge was most certainly in *Clytemnestra's* nature. "Do you wish to sail for Mycenae?" I asked him. "To confront Aegisthus on your brother's behalf?" Frankly, I cared little for what happened to my sister's treacherous lover as long as Clytemnestra remained unharmed.

After thinking about it, he said no. "You're crying, Helen," he said, enfolding me in his arms. How different his body felt from the way I had remembered it: as hard, passive, and dispassionate. His embrace felt surprisingly comforting. "Don't tell me you weep for Agamemnon?" I looked into his startled gaze.

I shook my head. "I weep for Iphigenia." And then, I finally confided to my husband the secret I had kept for years.

"He thought she was his child. That day in Aulis."

"Does that make it any better? Any worse? That he believed he was slaughtering his own daughter, rather than knowing he was murdering 'the faithless Helen's' child? His crime was unconscionable." I told Menelaus why my sister never felt affection for her other children, that it repulsed her to carry in her loins, then raise, the issue of the monster who had butchered her first husband and their tiny son.

So Menelaus decided not to quit Egypt to avenge his brother's murder; in fact, we remained there for several years after learning of Agamemnon's death. But I sent word to Clytemnestra that her sister rejoiced in her revenge, adding that I hoped this event would provide us with an opportunity to repair our fractured relationship. "We have both suffered much," I told her. "Now that the past has been avenged, can we look with shining eyes toward a better future?" I received no reply.

~~~

All told, we dwelt in Egypt for nearly nine years. And while I stayed in Pharos, learning from Polydamia to speak Egyptian and how to read and write hieroglyphics, Menelaus sailed to Cyprus and Lycia; to Sidon and Arabia; to Libya, where lambs are born horned, and where, with three lambing seasons a year, not a single person ever goes hungry. My husband amassed a fortune on those travels.

For a long time now, I had found myself enjoying his companionship. As I had learned to admire his solidity, he had come to appreciate my sensuality, permitting, even encouraging, me to school him in the arts of Eros so that he might know how to properly pleasure the most desirable woman in the world. He proved himself to be a most apt and ardent pupil.

In many ways, I believe that the intervening years between our leaving Ilios and returning home to Sparta were beneficial to our marriage, for Egypt was a neutral territory on which Menelaus and I could construct a new foundation of love and understanding. Forgiveness does not take place overnight; the scars from the wounds we'd inflicted on each other since we'd first wed needed time to fade in order for us to be able to rebuild our lives.

One morning in our final year in Egypt, Menelaus and I exchanged a glance and mutually acknowledged that it was time to go back to Laconia. Sparta was being ruled by Megapenthes, the bastard son that Menelaus got on the slave girl Pieris after I had left for Troy with Paris Alexandros. It was time for Helen to reclaim her birthright and her throne. Menelaus had permitted the usurper, though of his blood, to reign in Sparta long enough. I insisted that upon our return, he would have to banish Megapenthes and his mother from the kingdom or there would be trouble.

The harbor of Pharos has a sheltered bay, and it was there that my husband's vessel lay. Within a few days, we made our plans to journey home. Menelaus's sailors readied his ship, loading it with provisions and the precious cargo he'd acquired from his many trading ventures. We were only a day's sail from Sparta with a clean hull and a brisk south wind, but no sooner had Menelaus given the order to sail, when the wind died. The doldrums prevailed for twenty days, during which the sailors exhausted their provisions.

Menelaus and I were both disillusioned by the long delay. My husband glumly reasoned that the gods must be against us after all. That night he had a dream that he believed to be prophetic. The sea nymph Eidothea appeared to him in her robes of kelp and informed Menelaus that he had to capture Proteus in order to be able to sail away. She told him how he might achieve this wondrous feat; when he related her directives, I said that I had never heard of anything more disgusting.

Eidothea said that every day, when the chariot of Helios was directly overhead, Proteus, the Ancient of the Sea, waded out of the bay of Pharos to enjoy the sunbright sand, and the seals would emerge from their caverns to bask around him.

"She instructed me to bring three other men and hide ourselves among the seals," said Menelaus. "Then we are to surprise Proteus by seizing him and demanding that he let us know which god it is who is so angry with us that he, or she, will not let us sail for home. We must compel Proteus to tell us what to do to set things right and get home safely."

The following day, I accompanied Menelaus and three of his most trusted sailors to the bay. There, they slew four seals and hid themselves underneath the freshly flayed skins. "If this is what you must do to sail home, you must bathe before you board your ship or I will never join you!" I told him, only half in jest.

And when Proteus emerged from the waters and lay among the sea beasts, my husband and his accomplices wrestled the young man, who fought them furiously, not understanding why he had been assaulted. Menelaus later insisted that the struggle was so fierce because Proteus fought them off with all the strength of a lion, then coiled his limbs about them, trying to strangle them like a serpent, that he clawed their skin with the ferocity of a leopard, and on and on, seeming to impersonate the strongest beasts and elements of nature; but still the Achaeans clung to him.

Finally, Menelaus demanded, "Which god was it who set a trap for me that marooned me here on Pharos?"

"It was none other than the great Zeus," replied Proteus, "for you neglected to make the proper hecatomb before you sailed from Ilios. Now you must remount the Nile in flood to do so."

To my ears, this sounded like a terrifying proposition. Menelaus by now had lived fifty-six summers. There was barely a trace of russet in his beard. His leg pained him more often. Over the past nine years, we had come to rely on each other in ways I had never imagined, and I did not know how I would be able to withstand any more suffering in my life.

Menelaus assured me that all would be well on the river. From King Thon he purchased a hundred bulls and brought them to the mouth of the Nile. At first light the following morning, he slaughtered the beasts and made the hecatomb. Then he returned to the bay of Pharos where I waited onboard his ship.

As soon as Menelaus gave the command to raise the sail, a strong stern wind filled its white belly. Our collective sighs of relief could have blown us all the way back to Sparta.

"I believe I know the real reason Zeus detained us in Egypt for so long," I said to Menelaus as we looked northward, my head resting on his shoulder. His arm encircled my waist.

"And why is that, fair Helen?"

"He wanted you to collect all this," I said, indicating the treasure stored below. "It is my father's dowry for our new beginning!"

ow many of the Spartan people would remember Helen? I wondered anxiously as we neared Gythium. Almost a decade had passed since the fall of Ilios. I had lived through forty-seven summers and had been away from Achaea for nearly twenty-two of them.

When the oarsmen beached the ship, I refused assistance in disembarking. I even removed my sandals, wanting to feel with my bare flesh that first step where sea meets earth. Then I fell to my knees and brought my lips to the damp ground. I had finally come home.

Still, I was uneasy; how would I be welcomed? The road from Gythium was mostly deserted, but as we neared Sparta and the citizens lined the avenue, having learned that their true king—and queen—were finally home, terror closed its icy hand around my heart. I had not anticipated that young girls would strew our path with flowers, but truly, after so much time had passed, I did not expect to be the target of such vociferous derision. Some women even pelted me with olives, though they did not assault the warrior king who rode beside me. Murder is easier to forgive than beauty. By the time we reached the palace, I was distraught and drenched with tears.

"I never promised that our homecoming would be a simple thing," said Menelaus. We entered the palace with six of his men, in search of Pieris and Megapenthes, but no one was able to locate the usurpers. We were told by a serving woman that the two of them had gone to Argos for the summer festival. The few guards who had remained to watch the palace in their absence were quickly imprisoned.

"It will make it easier for us," Menelaus told me. "Megapenthes and Pieris will return only to find themselves displaced. I will send them to Messenia with enough to build a home and recommence their lives there. They will have no choice but to live under your cousin's rule."

A rider reared his horse outside our gates and called loudly for the king of Sparta. Expecting that this represented some sort of formal homecoming greeting, perhaps from the citizens or from the temple priests, Menelaus and I ran outside, calling for a slave to feed and water the horse and to offer the rider a cool drink.

"I bear a message from Argos," the rider said breathlessly.

Menelaus and I exchanged a glance. Perhaps this news pertained somehow to Pieris and Megapenthes.

"The queen of Mycenae and her consort Aegisthus have been slain," he added, without further preamble.

"Cly . . . Clytemnestra . . . ?" I stammered. I clutched my husband's arm to stop myself from collapsing on the paving stones. One thing I had most looked forward to was the chance to greet my elder sister. Each of us had endured much, and I hoped that after a lifetime of sisterly rivalry, now that I had returned to Achaea, we would finally be able to come to terms with each other—perhaps even reconcile. I clutched my breast and screamed hysterically at the messenger, "What demon did this deed?"

"Her son, Orestes," he replied.

Menelaus, shocked and deeply distressed by this news, invited the rider to dismount and step inside the palace. We inquired of a slave if my stepfather Tyndareus still lived and were told that, though ancient and half deaf, Sparta's former king still enjoyed his orchards. We then dispatched the servant to fetch him immediately.

Food and drink were brought forth, in accordance with the proper rules of hospitality, and after partaking of them with us, the messenger from Mycenae told his tale.

"During the war years, when Orestes was just a boy, Clytemnestra's lover Aegisthus had the child exiled so that he would not present an impediment to his rule of great Mycenae. For years Orestes bided his time, waiting to avenge his father Agamemnon's murder, which occurred eight years ago, on the very day that the High King and his concubine, the Troyan royal priestess Cassandra, returned triumphantly from Ilios.

"Yesterday at dawn, Orestes and his childhood friend Pylades, disguised as travelers, returned to Mycenae. Ensnaring Clytemnestra and Aegisthus in a ruse whereby they believed Orestes dead, and with Electra's aid, the two young men slaughtered Aegisthus even as he offered sacrifices upon the altar. Clytemnestra pleaded for her life, reminding her son that it was she who had brought him into this world and who had given him suck, but Orestes remained unmoved. In his father's name, he took his revenge and beheaded his own mother."

I screamed as though the sharpness of the blade had pierced my own fair skin. And then I fainted. Menelaus himself revived me with a cool wet cloth. "By all the gods," I sobbed into his chest, "when does it end? My sister slain by her own son . . ."

"Orestes declared that he and his sister Electra were honor-bound to punish the adulterers who had killed their beloved father," said the messenger.

"Now, hear this!" I railed. "And may the whole world come to understand more than only half the truth. I wonder if my nephew Orestes realizes how much his own life mirrors that of the man he murdered—his father's cousin. Aegisthus, too, was banished as a youth and crept home while his rival was away. But he exacted his revenge upon the House of Atreus by seducing his enemy's wife. Yes, Aegisthus was an adulterer, as was my sister, but Orestes and Electra have an entirely false picture of their father. Agamemnon was no demigod. He was a rapacious monster who enjoyed *myriad* extramarital liaisons, to put it delicately. My sister was far more wronged than wrongdoing. Does anyone dare suggest that Orestes achieved justice with these murders?" I continued, venting the full measure of my wrath on the hapless Mycenaean rider.

"Orestes has much support," he admitted.

"Orestes, and my niece Electra, punished Aegisthus for the same crime their own sanctified father had committed time and time again. They refused to acknowledge Agamemnon's brutality against their mother." I was both disgusted and furious. And with regard to

Clytemnestra . . . how well I knew that the world castigated women for what it was quick to excuse in men, thinking them even mightier and grander for the women whom they bedded and the children who they sired out of wedlock.

My sister's murder offered me perspective. Far greater ills greeted my homecoming than a few indelicate taunts and a handful or two of rotten olives.

Tyndareus wished to make for Mycenae immediately. If he did so with his final breaths, he vowed to see his grandson Orestes brought to justice. My stepfather didn't speak of it, but I was certain that he was overwhelmed with guilt at having allowed his greed to get the better of his judgment so many years ago. He had permitted Agamemnon to wed Clytemnestra, knowing what manner of man he was, deaf to his beloved daughter's tearful protestations.

Menelaus and I counseled Tyndareus to remain in Sparta due to his advanced age and numerous infirmities, but he wished to make Clytemnestra's killer pay dearly for his crime. So, Menelaus summoned a chariot to bring my stepfather to Mycenae. The messenger would stay beside him all the way.

After the messenger had departed, I sat in silence for several minutes. "Clytemnestra worshipped power," I mused aloud. "More like a man than like a woman. And, like a man, she lived—and died—for revenge. I never realized until now how much I learned from her." My tears returned. By her violent deeds and in her own equally horrific death, Clytemnestra had finally achieved the immortality for which she had so envied me. In my mind's eye, I saw her in her bloodred gown. On her wedding day to Tantalus. On mine to Menelaus. On the cliffs at Aulis. On the day she died. She would have seen more than fifty summers. Had her black hair become gray as ash or white as swansdown? "She was fierce, and fearsome, at times, but she was brave. I wish I had my sister's courage."

"You do," said Menelaus softly.

In an effort to settle my raging thoughts, I wandered alone through the cool chambers of the palace. In our absence they had not been well maintained. The paint had faded; the roofs leaked. I returned to our Great Hall and regarded what was left of the fresco that depicted the wedding of Peleus and Thetis, the one I had commissioned for Kronia nearly a lifetime ago. Someone had tried to paint over it, with unsatisfactory and amateurish results, someone perhaps who understood the deeply personal significance of the mural and the story it illustrated.

Hermione! Where was she? I left the Great Hall and ran back through every room, searching for my daughter. Suddenly, I was thunderstruck by the realization that I was not looking for a little freckled girl of nine summers, but a woman of nearly thirty.

The gynaeceum was desolate but for a slave woman washing the floors. Then I thought I heard a snoring sound, and I parted the curtains to the room that had once been mine and my mother's before me. My furniture was gone. The room was empty except for a chair that faced the window . . . and a dusty birthing stool. Someone was dozing in the chair, deep in the arms of Hypnos.

I tiptoed toward the slumbering figure, and with a cry of joy and recognition, I knelt beside her. "Aethra!" I exclaimed.

The old woman awoke with a start. "She's coming home, mark my words," she mumbled, as though she were talking in her sleep to some detractor.

"I feared you might be dead," I murmured, embracing her. My tears flowed hotly over her simple woven robe.

"The Moirai have decided otherwise," she said, tart as ever, referring to the Fates. "Atropos has not yet seen fit to snip my thread. Perhaps she was waiting for your return."

"Don't speak that way," I chided. She was wizened as an apple core, but her eyes were still bright with wisdom and intelligence. "Speak of good things instead. Are you well?" I pressed her hands against my cheek and turned to kiss her gnarled white fingers veined with tributaries of blue.

"I have the infirmities of age," Aethra said succinctly. "No more, no less. Pieris leaves me alone. They all leave me alone. When Ilios fell, I drew my chair here so that through the window I could see you returning home. At first they were amused by my vigilance, the way an old blind dog awaits his master's scent. But then they grew accustomed to my sitting here day after day, and paid me no further heed. I prefer it that way."

I clung to her bony form. "You'll outlive them all," I said, grateful that at least someone I had loved so long ago was still alive. "Come, nurse, tell me where I may find my daughter!"

Aethra shook her head. "Gone."

"When? Where?" I begged to learn.

"Perhaps two moons ago. She left with Orestes."

"Orestes!" I felt my blood turn to ice.

"He used to visit her here. They fell in love, or so Hermione said. She said that he was the only one, except her father, who ever loved her. She was nearly as angry with Menelaus for abandoning her to fight for your honor as she was with you for sullying it and deserting her for the fatuous charms of Paris Alexandros."

"He was anything but fatuous," I said defensively. "But then again, Hermione only saw him through the eyes of a child who thought him a thief, not so much because he stole away with her mother, but because he robbed her beloved father of his finest treasure." My thoughts returned to my daughter's choice of men. "Orestes!" I spat.

Menelaus entered the chamber. "I decided to come looking for you." Time had metamorphosed the possessive aspect of his temperament from bitter jealousy into solicitous protectiveness.

"Hermione eloped with Orestes," I told him, sharing the details of Aethra's tale. "I will not welcome them here, if they dare to return. I never wish to accept my sister's murderer as our son. Not only that, should Hermione, as our only living child, one day rule Sparta, I will not permit the man who butchered Clytemnestra to sit beside her. I cannot conscience it."

Offering no argument, my husband left us alone to continue our conversation.

"You should know," Aethra told me, "many people believe you are dead."

I was shocked. "How is that possible?"

"Your friend Polyxo," she replied. "She lost her husband Tlepolemus in the war and blamed you for making her a widow. The bards sing of how she invited you to her home on the isle of Rhodes for the sake of a reunion, then lured you to a grove of trees and hanged you, just as your mother Leda hanged herself."

I was incredulous. My only childhood friend. "She must have truly hated me beyond all measure."

"People often hate what they cannot understand," Aethra offered wisely.

"And the bards must be foolish old blind men indeed, to think that I can be thus killed—or killed at all."

"Polyxo hanged you in effigy," my old nurse replied. "But in her grief and anger, she needed to believe that it was really you."

~~

Menelaus gave me an exceedingly magnanimous present. Within the year, a hundred craftsmen and laborers had restored, refurbished, and redecorated the palace of Sparta, this time not to rival its Mycenaean counterpart, but as a gift to Helen. All the treasures we'd brought back from Egypt were put to sumptuous use. With the gold that Menelaus had amassed, the rooms glittered as though they had been kissed by the sun god himself. Our living quarters were lavishly renovated, with finely woven bedstuffs, purple rugs, and fleecy coverlets gracing nearly every surface. It amused me that, as he neared the age of sixty, the once-austere Menelaus was finally able to embrace my sybaritic sensibilities. A separate room on the lower floor of the gynaeceum was set aside for Aethra, who, to my delight, continued to enjoy relatively sound health for one so elderly.

New frescoes were painted in the Great Hall. Tall thrones, almost as impressive as the king's, were built to be set beside Menelaus for our honored guests. By day, Menelaus heard petitions and entreaties, now fully content to govern Sparta in a time of peace. Listening to each request, I sat beside him, plying my handiwork; a rolling silver basket rimmed in hammered gold held my yarn and finespun stuff. My golden distaff was swathed in the dusky violet wool with which I was fashioning a cloak for him.

And yet we entertained without pretension, my husband in a woven tunic and mantle, his smooth feet laced into leather sandals; while I often reclined on my light chair with its amber and ivory inlaid footrest, a rug of downy wool across my lap.

In the evenings, water was poured from golden pitchers into silver bowls, and every diner had his own polished table. Minstrels and acrobats enlivened our evenings, although we occasionally needed to correct some of the details when bards sought to pay us tribute by immortalizing our lives in song.

About a year after we had returned to Sparta, I was walking alone at twilight in the sacred grove. Its lyrical beauty and tranquility have always stirred me most deeply, and the power and presence of the Goddess remains remarkably palpable. The poplars whispered to one another, and for a moment or two, I was certain I saw the ghostly image of my mother floating amid their verdant branches.

"Life is a circle, Helen," she murmured, or was it the Goddess who was speaking through her? "It is round, like a woman. Do you know the story of the mother's joy in finding her long-lost daughter? Their reunion completed the circle; and thus the cycle of eternal renewal between mother and daughter is celebrated once again. I deserted you, and you deserted me, but you came back to me," Leda whispered, her voice as thin as the air.

I realized what my mother was telling me. My circle with you, Hermione, was incomplete. I deserted you, and you deserted me. We've spent more years resenting each other than may remain for us to enjoy together.

I opened my arms and began to lift them toward the sky. Two-thirds of the circle was complete. When you stand before me, we'll be whole.

*"Beauty is truth, truth beauty—That is all
Ye know on earth and all ye need to know."*

"ODE ON A GRECIAN URN"
John Keats (1795–1821)

⫷ E P I L O G O S ⫸

Men know so little about the world they live in, and about themselves as well. Most of them do not love wisdom and have little desire to know about their own ignorance. I believe that's why they suffer as they do, and then blame the gods that they have themselves created in their own mortal image. We look to the heavens for answers and for harmony, forgetting that those same gods we have invented spar and spat and behave with dazzling inconsistency like human beings, just the way we made them.

Another thing I have come to understand is that history is a like an undulating crenellation in the Troyan ramparts, rising and falling and repeating itself until something forces it to change. The same is true of families. The House of Atreus—my husband's—is doomed to enact the same tragedy in every generation until someone breaks the curse by choosing to act differently, by selecting life in preference to death.

I have discovered, too, that almost any reconciliation is possible in this world.

A few days ago, while I was at my loom, Menelaus asked if he might briefly interrupt. Naturally, I acquiesced and bade him sit beside me.

"I never shared this with you until now, my love," he began, and reminded me of the dream he'd had during our final days in Egypt in which the sea nymph Eidothea had disclosed what he must do to sail for home and how to capture Proteus. "Proteus, the Ancient of the Sea, had words for me as well. 'You shall not die in the bluegrass land of Argos,' he said, speaking of Mycenae. 'At your world's end you will be met by golden Rhadamanthys, judge of the underworld, whose word shall be inviolate and final. Your shade will not be consigned to dwell in Hades or in darkest Tartarus. The gods intend you for Elysium, Menelaus. It never snows there; there are no frosts, nor are there torrential rains; but the climate is forever temperate. Gentle breezes waft lulling airs from off the ocean, and it is only the mild west wind that blows. For as Helen's lord, the gods hold you a son of Zeus.' "

My husband's eyes were moist. And I decided in that moment how to end my story.

When Atropos eventually sees fit to cut the thread of Menelaus's life and his shade is transported to the Isle of the Blessed, then I will petition Zeus my father to spirit my body from this earth as well, for having finally grown to love and find joy in each other in every way a man and woman do, I have no wish to go on without him. Ever after, we will dwell together in Elysium. Our names and deeds, our passions and our legacies, will live on only in the memory of mankind, in which, I have no doubt, our immortality is guaranteed.

Hermione, it was when I learned of your elopement with Orestes that I sat down to write this memoir. For years you have castigated me for following my passions, heedless of the consequences and collateral damage, and now it appears that you have followed in your mother's footsteps. Examine your heart, my daughter. Are we *fated* to behave as we do, or is it the exercise of free will that compels us to follow our destinies?

Sing in me, Muse, and through me tell the story of the life of Helen of Troy!

AUTHOR'S NOTE

Extensive and exhaustive research went into *The Memoirs of Helen of Troy;* although when all is said and done, it is, of course, a work of fiction. Over the past three millennia, Helen and the heroes and villains of Troy have appeared in many iterations of this tale, each as expressive of its age as it is of its author's imagination. My story of Helen is no exception: It is a tale for our era, that, while based on evergreen legends, has a certain resonance to our own time and place in history. While I tend to be a stickler for historical accuracy, I admit that in a few places, I decided to play fast and loose with ancient history in order to serve the tale I wished to tell. For example, the Spartan *agogi* system, and their nearly single-minded focus on the culture of war, postdates the Bronze Age, but moving it back in time served the story. Additionally, there are often several versions of (or variations on) the myths and legends pertaining to the characters depicted in *The Memoirs of Helen of Troy*. In most instances I chose to accept the most popular version, with a few exceptions, where a lesser-known variation better served my story—such as the parentage of Iphigenia and the method by which Achilles achieved his near-immortality. Any errors of fact are my own. For the ones that are *not* deliberately reimagined, I beg my readers' indulgence.

ACKNOWLEDGMENTS

Thanks to den farrier and M. Z. Ribalow who believed in this book when others thought it was a pipe dream and who encouraged me every comma of the way; to my brilliant agent Irene Goodman and my terrifically insightful editor Rachel Beard Kahan; to Professor Getzel Cohen at the University of Cincinnati for taking the time to discuss with me the ongoing excavations at Troia; and to Susanne Ritt-Nichol for a "crash course" on the effects of pregnancy. Thanks, too, to my late maternal grandmother Norma Carroll, who instilled in me a passion for ancient Greece and the story of Helen when I was a little girl. This is as much her book as it is my mother Leda's.